Lost Cargo

Noah Chinn

Noah Chinn Books

Dedicated to my youngest brother Adamm, who I hope will fall in love with space adventure the way I have.

Contents

Frying Pan Blues

SOL SYSTEM — 2241

"How much longer till we reach Mars?"

Moss's fare looked even more nervous than he had when he'd boarded back on Earth, and that was when they'd still had to slip past the ever-growing blockade encircling the planet. You'd think everything after that piloting miracle would have been anticlimactic. He didn't know his fare's real name, only that he was a scientist and that he was meeting a Nubran contact on Mars.

Mousy was a good description of the man, as he looked like a cat might leap on him at any moment. He kept staring at various news feeds as if they might give him a heads up on any felines that might be lurking.

Moss found the man's nervousness rubbing off on him in all the wrong ways. After all, if he was so nervous about getting caught, maybe there was a good reason for it.

"Not long now, Doc," said Moss, trying to reassure him. It was the least he could do. The easy, breezy days of the Party Bus were over, and the guy had paid far too well for Moss to confine him to his cabin.

The man looked back at him. "Can this ship go any faster?"

"Without one of your Nubran friends' fancy super engines, this is the best we're going to do."

The Viaticus Rex *could travel at four-fifths the speed of light— once you got clear of any interfering gravity wells. Even though Mars was almost as far from Earth as it could be right now, the trip was only going to take half an hour total. Yet this guy acted like even that wasn't fast enough.*

You just couldn't please some people.

The Void, near Ramede space – 2550

"I think I need a catch phrase," said Hel.

Moss raised an eyebrow. "Oh?"

"Yeah. I'm getting a feel of what it's like working for you, and I figure it would make sense to have a catch phrase or two for when we fall into familiar patterns."

Moss smirked. The two were sitting back-to-back while they talked. "So, got any ideas?"

Hel cleared her throat. "*Well, here's another fine mess you've gotten me into.* What do you think?"

Moss tried to adjust his wrists behind his back. The magnacuffs that bound the two together had been put on tight. "I'm pretty sure that one's taken."

"Sure, but Laurel and Hardy died centuries ago. It's due for a revival."

The hulking blue figure by the cockpit's control panel finally spun around and growled at them. "Be *quiet.*"

"Sorry," said Moss.

The *Viaticus Rex II.I* drifted dead in space near a brown dwarf star, out of fuel, leaving Maurice "Moss" Foote and his co-pilot Helena Lambinon in a bit of a bind. Being stranded in the Void, the vast buffer of territory between Nubra and Draxon space, was bad enough. Being so close to pirate space was worse. Sending out a distress signal from there was like ringing a dinner bell.

In the end, they'd had no choice. With no means to refuel and were operating on backup reserves, they had to hope a friendly trade ship would be passing by.

But that would require having good luck, something Moss often claimed he'd been born without.

So when a pirate ship sporting the colours of the Void Brotherhood had showed up, it wasn't so much a sense of dread that he'd felt as it was resignation. He'd have been more surprised if it had been anyone else.

But Moss wasn't going to go down without a fight. He'd handled raiding parties before. With a bit of luck, he'd strip the would-be pirates of anything useful and leave them stranded in his place. He and Hel had picked up their sidearms and taken up defensive positions near the main airlock, which was already being bypassed.

Then the hulking form of a Draxon drone had walked in, wearing an armoured EVA spacesuit, wielding a railgun so massive it had to be harnessed to him.

Moss had dropped his pistol and immediately surrendered.

Now they were here, handcuffed to one another back-to-back while the big dumb blue drone tried to figure out how his ship worked. But the *Viaticus Rex II.I* was no ordinary cargo ship. It had been cobbled together from several different ships—a chimera. It was spaceworthy, but crap in the resale department.

As a result, the drone wasn't sure what to make of the controls, which seemed to belong to a long-range Elysian explorer, even though the bulk of the ship looked more like a Nubra transport. It didn't help that Moss had locked down the controls before they'd left the cockpit. The drone carried a "does not compute" look on his blue hairless face that reassured Moss that there was no way in hell he was working alone.

"So, *why* did we surrender exactly?" Hel whispered, trying not to attract the pirate's attention. "We had him outnumbered."

"We had pulse guns," said Moss. "He had a railgun. Our weapons are designed to kill the meat and leave the metal intact. His would punch through us, the ship, and probably any other ship in our path. That's why he was wearing an EVA suit."

"Ah," said Hel. She'd been born on a long-lost generation ship, the *Pegasi*, and was still catching up with some aspects of modern technology. Moss could relate; it wasn't that long ago that he'd had a similar shock to the system. "So, what do we do now? I assume you have a plan."

"More like waiting for an opportunity," said Moss.

"Well, that's reassuring."

The Draxon turned to them again. Hel shut her lips tight, as if that would convince him she hadn't said anything. The drone stared at both of them, then settled on Hel. "Make the ship go."

Moss felt indignant. "Hey, what makes you think she's the one in charge?"

"Matrons always in charge," the Draxon said. Even for a drone, his vocabulary pinged low on the IQ scale, and their adaptive translators picked up on that.

"Don't fight it, Moss," said Hel. "Some of us just radiate leadership."

"You know, using humour as a defence mechanism is supposed to be *my* thing. Why are you so calm?"

Hel turned her head far enough that Moss could just make out a smile. "Opportunity knocks."

The drone came over and freed Hel's hands, but kept Moss bound where he was. Now that the pirate goon was firmly in control, he was wielding a pulse gun. He'd stored the railgun back by the primary airlock, along with his bulky armoured EVA suit.

"We need you to make the ship go."

Hel rubbed her wrists. "Who's we?"

"The worker caste rarely speaks in the singular," said Moss. "But I guarnatee he has a buddy back on his ship."

"You talk too much," said the drone.

"I get that a lot."

The drone turned back to Hel. "You make the ship go, we sell you to nice owners. You not help, you go with them." He jerked his head back at Moss.

"Where's he going?" Hel asked.

"Not nice owners."

"Well, hard to refuse that offer," said Hel. "Look, your main problem here is that you haven't used the special key. We shut the computer down before you boarded. See that?" She pointed to a small metal box resting on the main dash. "Open it."

The Draxon looked at her suspiciously, then pointed the gun at her. "You open."

Hel raised her hands. "Sure thing."

"No trick."

"No trick, Tarzan."

Hel went to the box and opened it up, showing him the contents. Moss knew what was inside, or at least what *seemed* to be inside. A small dashboard figurine in the shape of a woman in a pilot's suit. You couldn't see her face because she wore a tinted helmet.

"This needs to be mounted on the dashboard for the ship to work properly," said Hel. "May I?"

The drone nodded, and Hel placed the figurine on the dash. It didn't really matter where she put it, so long as it was close enough to access its systems.

Suddenly, the ship powered down and the Draxon raised his weapon. "Trick!"

Hel raised her hands. "No! No trick! It's booting up, that's all. Part of the process."

"You make ship go or—" He never finished his threat because just then the lights came on and the control panels flickered back to life. It seemed like everything on board the ship was being accessed at a superfast rate, then stopped just as quickly.

Moss held his breath. He knew what was happening, and wondered how things would evolve from here. Hel's move had been a Hail Mary pass, but as he looked at the scene around him, with him still tied up and Hel held at gunpoint, he had a good feeling about it.

A voice came over the speakers. "Wha... Where... wel...welcome, Commander." The female voice was tinny and formal. "How may I help you?"

"We need you to make ship go," said the drone, looking around for the source of the voice. He didn't notice that the figurine's head was now tracking his every move.

"Yes, Commander. Several subsystems require attention before the ship can be made operational. This ship is low on fuel."

"We put fuel in," said the Draxon drone, growing frustrated.

"Fuel reserves are at ten percent. Protectorate guidelines state that at least twenty-five percent is required for full operation."

This confused the drone more, as well it should. It didn't really make sense. At the same time, Protectorate bureaucracy certainly made it *plausible*.

Hel shrugged. "Don't look at me. This ship is a chimera. It's got all kinds of strange hiccups like that. You're lucky she runs at all."

The Draxon groaned and put a hand to his ear. "We need more fuel. Don't know why. Ship says so." He listened to the response and frowned. "We don't know. We need help."

Moss was actually starting to enjoy the show. When he'd first brought Hel on board, he'd had some reservations about how well she'd adapt, but right now she was doing an even better job than he would have in her position. Not that he'd ever admit it.

A few minutes later, a very short and round figure walked in holding a pulse rifle. He had no neck and his mouth was almost as wide as his face, which currently had a half-smoked cigar in it. A Hopat, definitely the brains of the outfit, though that was a pretty low bar.

"Come on, Tregas. How hard can this possibly be?"

Tregas pointed at the dashboard. "Ship says there is problems."

The Hopat sighed. "Fine." He spoke to the room in general. "Computer. Run diagnostics. Determine key malfunctions. Display on main terminal."

"Displaying now."

A large display popped up over the dashboard, showing a schematic of the ship and red circles over areas in need of repairs. The Hopat scrutinized it and sighed.

"This ship's not worth it," he said at last. "We should just take the prisoners and blow it up for target practice."

The Draxon grinned at the idea. Blowing things up was clearly on his list of favourite activities.

"We'll strip her for parts we can sell and—well, hello, what do we have here?" The Hopat leaned in and examined something on the display that clearly intrigued him. "Don't think I know a masked smuggling compartment when I see one, eh?" He looked at Hel. "What's inside?"

Hel was thrown off by this. She didn't know the ship had a smuggling compartment, and for good reason. "I... I don't know."

The Hopat looked to his subordinate. "She's the captain?"

"She is Matron."

The Hopat rolled his eyes. "How many times have I told you it don't work like that with other species? It ain't about... Never mind. Computer, what is currently stored inside Reserve Node 42B?"

"There is no Reserve Node 42B on this ship," the computer said.

The Hopat smiled. "See? Definitely hiding something there. You." He pointed the pulse rifle at Moss. "What's in the smuggling compartment?"

Moss kept his mouth shut. The Hopat turned to Hel and brushed his extra thumb down her cheek. "We're going to find out one way or the other. The only question is how much you two are going to suffer in the meantime. Understand me?"

"Fine," Moss growled. "It's sherb."

The Hopat frowned. "Sherb? Big deal. That's recreational stuff. I got a stash of it on my ship."

Moss shook his head. "Not like this, you don't."

"Some kind of exotic blend?"

"Like nothing you've ever seen. Made in Elysia. Banned in four out of the five Protectorate nations."

"So, what kind of lock do you have on the compartment? Voice print? Biometrics? You better hope I don't need your eyeball." It was eerie how well Moss's adaptive translator interpreted this guy's threatening tones.

"Simple voice command. I can do it from here."

"How much is there?"

"Half a ton. Vacuum packed."

"Sounds good. We'll take it." He made it sound like they'd struck a bargain, though Moss was at a loss as to what he'd be getting out of it. "Tregas, bind the little lady to her captain again, would you?" He did so. "And if you would be so good as to unlock the compartment, please?"

Moss sighed. "Computer. Command override on Reserve Node 42B. Allow free access. Provide floor lighting between the cabin and the hatch." The floor lit up with small lights that led to the main corridor and hung a left. "You don't want to get lost," Moss added.

The Hopat gave a wide and toothy grin. "Much obliged."

The short Hopat and his large Draxon companion left the room. Hel and Moss waited as the clank of their boots on the metal floor grew more and more distant.

"They there yet?" Moss asked.

The voice over the speakers lost its computer-like quality and now sounded like a normal woman. "Almost."

"Close enough." Moss deactivated the magnacuffs and stood up. Hel looked at Moss in shock as he worked on her cuffs next.

"Wait, you could have done that at any time?"

"Not the first time I've been arrested. Little trick I got wired into my suit."

"But why wait so long?"

"And do what? Go toe-to-toe with Blue Goliath or his rifle packing partner? I told you I was waiting for an opportunity. Which you kindly provided, thank you very much."

"So, what's really in Reserve Node 42B?" asked Hel.

"Didn't you hear her?" Moss nodded toward the computer terminal. "There *is* no Reserve Node 42B."

"They're inside," said the computer.

"Flush 'em."

The hull echoed briefly with the sound of an airlock blowing open.

"There *used* to be something there," said Moss. "But after this ship got Frankenstein'd, it became a secondary airlock. I'm guessing a little creative on-the-spot schematic redesign was going on behind the scenes?"

"You got it," said the computer.

Moss grinned as he freed Hel and helped her to her feet. "Good to have you back, Violet. I've missed you."

"I didn't realize I'd gone anywhere."

No Refunds

The seeds of the Galactic Protectorate were laid nearly six thousand years ago, when Nubran explorers made contact with the expanding territories of the Draxon and Hopat, near the corner of where their territories meet. When the elegant Elysians and the reclusive Ugaro eventually made contact, the Protectorate was formally established.

Since then, thousands of sapient species have been reaching for the stars, most within the last few hundred years. These younger races tend to fall under the jurisdiction and patronage of whichever Protectorate member their world lies within. But on a galactic scale, the timing of all these races reaching space travel so close to one another, most of them humanoid, has convinced most that a far older race had seeded all these planets long ago.

M. Foote, *The Galaxy is Weirder than You Think*

I T TOOK A LITTLE while to get Violet up to speed, and she did not exactly take it well.

Hel had only been part of the crew for a couple of weeks, but in that time, she'd gotten to know the ship's computer and her unique situation.

For one thing, she wasn't a computer... not exactly. She was a transferred consciousness... sorta. It could be argued she was just a simulation... kinda. But she wasn't an artificial intelligence... well, not really.

Moss had never gone into details on the matter, just the broad strokes. Violet Lonsdale had been a bounty hunter who'd captured Moss a long time back. But rather than turn him over to the Terrans, she'd decided to team up with him. Later, she had been diagnosed with a terminal disease. They'd sought the help of a secretive group known as The Order (or, as Moss called them, technomonks) and this had been the end result.

Only the Violet *she* knew had died a few days ago, fighting to protect the generation ship Hel had grown up on. All that was left of her was a melted blob of plastic on the fragmented remains of a small fighter.

But Moss had been given a replacement, the one who had just saved their bacon from the pirates now floating outside.

Once everything had been explained to the new Violet, it only seemed to confirm her worst fears.

"See, I knew it. I'm just a simulation. I can't really be Violet."

"Stop talking nonsense, Vi," said Moss. Apparently, they'd had this argument before.

"Oh yeah? If I'm Violet, then who was flying with you all these months? Not me, that's for damn sure. I think I'd remember something like that."

"Look, if you were just a simulation, how would you be aware of it? Would you even be asking these questions?"

"You don't think anxiety and existential quandary can't be programmed in, flyboy?"

Hel had her own questions to ask. "What is the last thing you remember, Violet?"

"And that's another thing," said Violet. "Who's the dame? Couldn't wait to replace me, is that it? I mean, she's hot and all, but isn't she a bit young for you?"

"Jesus, Violet, it's not like that," said Moss. "You helped her escape the Orijen Brother's junkyard. She stowed away on board. She's part of the crew."

"You helped me get my memory back," Hel added. "We were friends."

The figurine on the dashboard tilted its head in a sassy kind of way. "Don't try to tell me who I was or wasn't friends with, missy."

"No, it's true. You were inside my mind and guided me through my memories."

"Oh yeah? What did I look like?"

"Long dark hair, strong build, but elegant. You were like a cross between a princess and a ninja."

There was a short pause. "Yeah, okay, maybe we were friends. But that was her, not me. I mean, that still doesn't mean I'm even me. Or even if she was me. There is no me!"

"Violet, calm down," said Moss. "You're going to have a meltdown or something."

"Doesn't it bother you?" Violet asked. "Even a little? Do they have a permanent backup of me stored somewhere? Have they done this before? Are there a dozen more of me out there? Maybe I'm some standard OS on a whole fleet of ships. They never had my permission to do that!"

"Would you rather be dead?" asked Moss.

"I *am* dead," said Violet. "Don't you get it? Violet Lonsdale is a mummified corpse floating around a star off the shoulder of Orion. I'm just a goddamn echo of her."

Moss groaned. "We don't have time for this. For all we know, there could be more pirates on their way. We need to get organized and get out of here. Do you think you can do that for me?"

"What's the point?" Violet sulked.

"Help us out now and I swear once we're safe in another system, I'll spend as long as it takes talking you through this. We've been through it before."

Another pause. "How long did it take last time?"

"About three days before you started to come to grips with things. Lots of talking. Lots of coffee. Lots of late nights."

"And you'd go through all that again?"

Moss rested a hand on the dashboard. "Whatever it takes, however long it takes. You have my word."

The *Viaticus Rex II.I* and its would-be captors hung in space about twenty light seconds away from a brown dwarf. Despite the name, the dwarf was not brown, but more of an eerie deep purple. Far too large to be a gas giant, but too small for its gravity to start a fusion chain reaction at its core. Most of the light it gave off was in the infrared spectrum.

To Moss, hanging around one of these systems felt like being in a graveyard, and the fact that there were a couple of corpses floating outside didn't help matters.

The first order of business was securing the pirate ship. They stored the late drone's railgun and armoured EVA suit in a locker, then set about seeing what was worth taking from their ship.

A retractable hatch connected the two ships, but Moss and Hel wore their own EVA suits, just in case the captain had left behind some kind of booby-trapped security system. Once inside, he realized that while his Franken-ship wouldn't get him much on the resale market, it was probably still worth more than what had captured them.

The interior had that level of mess and disorder that was normally associated with the word "bachelor," but Moss took offence to that given that he was one and his ship was clean and tidy. This place looked like the artificial gravity had been shut off and the ship set to tumble dry.

In terms of value, there wasn't much. These guys had been desperate. Desperate made you stupid. Stupid made you dead. But a ship was a ship, and if it was spaceworthy, it was worth something.

"What do you think, Hel? Take it with us?" Moss asked as they reached the cockpit.

Hel sidestepped what looked like an oversized pair of underwear hanging from an air vent. "If we do, you're flying it. I'm afraid to touch anything here."

"Roger that. Violet, what exactly is this ship?"

Violet's voice came over his EVA suit's comm. "It's a Draxon Coyote."

"I guess that shouldn't be a surprise," Moss said to himself. The Coyote was a cheap knock-off, based on the famous Wolf design, a multipurpose ship that could be used for trading or combat. The Draxon sold these in droves to other races, but rarely used any themselves. Being cheap meant that it was popular amongst certain types of spacefarers, such as desperate pirates.

He sat in the captain's chair and cautiously activated the control panel, ready to bail if any kind of security features came on asking for a voice ident or biometric scan. Nothing did.

"Okay, we look good to go," said Moss. "The fuel line is still connected. I'll dump half of it into the *Rex*. More than enough left for both of us to get where we're going."

"And where's that?" asked Hel.

"Back to Komi."

Even under an EVA helmet, Moss saw Hel's eyes widen. "Are you nuts? I'm not getting within a thousand klicks of the Orijen brothers again."

"Don't worry, you won't have to," said Moss. "But I want to square things between us. It's better to have friends than enemies, even if you can't always trust those friends. Right now, those two are holding a grudge. I plan on using this ship as a peace offering, maybe even get something useful from them in return."

"Like what?"

"An upgrade for the *Rex*," Moss said. "Maybe a small shuttle to put in the secondary bay."

"Just make sure they don't add me into the deal somehow," Hel said.

"Don't be silly. They'd have to offer at least *two* shuttles for that."

The captured ship was called *No Refunds*, which had to be some kind of pirate joke Moss didn't get. It didn't take long to confirm that all systems were running. The Coyote might be a cheap knockoff, but it was reasonably reliable. You didn't sell tons of ships if they spontaneously broke down or blew up, no matter how much of a bargain they were.

Hel was left in charge of the *Viaticus Rex II.I*, though Violet would help her pilot it. Hel was still learning to fly solo and Violet had to re-learn the hodgepodge of slapped together ship components she was now in charge of. Call it a trust exercise.

But Moss had another reason he wanted to fly this ship himself. He wanted some time to check the ship's computer for any interesting tidbits of data, without Hel's judgey-judge morality getting in the way.

It was possible the pirates had some information he could make use of, or pass on to people who could make use of it. And the funds from that would go back into his ship, which would make both Violet and Hel happy.

Honestly, he was doing it for them. He was selfless that way.

The two ships synchronized their transit drives and jumped. For a moment everything seemed to drop away into a void, then the starfield ahead rushed forward in red streaks, returned to pinpoints of white, then fell away into lines of blue as they broke the light barrier and achieved full transit.

The trip to Komi would take a number of days, so Moss had plenty of time to dive into the ship's computers—when he wasn't collecting rubbish to dump and trying to disinfect the place. He found some communications between pirates regarding big scores and future raids. Moss filed that away to deliver to the local ProSec authorities. It paid to do them favours every now and then, enough so that it was in their best interests to cut you loose instead of bringing you in when given a choice.

The personal log wasn't terribly useful, though it did make him feel less guilty about spacing the previous owners—not that he'd felt terribly guilty in the first place. They'd made a habit of looking for stranded ships along the edge of the Void and turning the crews over to slavers. They even called themselves vultures, or at least a word in Galactic Common that closely translated to it.

He spent the rest of the trip sorting through the information and categorizing what he would sell or give or exchange to others. About ten minutes away from Komi space, he came across a special file in the ship's IFF systems. A special designation of ship: DNI. *Do Not Intercept.*

That file he squirreled away for himself.

Mending Fences

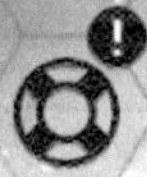

Every species evolved on a world with different gravities, but for the most part sapient life tends to occur on worlds between 0.5g and 2g (The Hopat are an exception to this, having evolved on a 3g-ish world).

In order to accommodate the widest range of life forms, the Galactic Protectorate established a range of 0.5g to 1.3g as average, and all Protectorate stations that provide artificial or centripetal gravity are required to accommodate this range. It's generally accepted that it's easier to adapt to lower gravity than higher, which is why the range slants toward the lower end of things.

M. Foote, *The Galaxy is Weirder than You Think*

K OMI STATION WAS THE pragmatically named trading port in the Komi system, located near the so-called Void that acted as a buffer between Draxon and Nubra territories, over two thousand light years from Earth. It was an outdated starport, massive, centuries old, relying on centripetal force to provide its inhabitants with gravity.

The station wasn't exactly part of any major trade route. The Nubra and Draxon, while not hostile toward one another, differed enough philosophically that neither tended to deal with the other more than they had to. The two humanoid races both had blue skin, ranging from light to dark, but that's where their similarities ended.

The Draxon were, by nature, a collective. A weak psychic link existed among its various castes, and the sense of an individual self was not easily understood by them. This made them very efficient, though not always creative, and it showed in their general aesthetics, which were functional, but rarely artistic. They also did not see practices such as slavery as wrong because individual rights did not matter, only the good of the whole. As a result, they were the only nation within the Protectorate where slavery was legal. Only most people called them bondservants so they could sleep better at night.

Earth, what was left of it, had been located near the edge of their borders.

The Nubra, on the other hand, embraced individuality and creative expression, though the flamboyant Elysians would argue they still played it safe. In the time that passed after the loss of Earth, the rapidly changing dynamics among the Terrans became a cause célèbre, and Terran culture had grown increasingly fashionable in Nubra space in recent decades.

Moss sometimes wondered how things might have been different if Sol had been located on the Nubran side of the border, but he lived with enough regrets and what-ifs without adding to them. He kept himself focused on the future and all the screw-ups that were yet to come. Right now, that involved trying to bargain with a couple of shady Hopat junk dealers.

Ashtar and Barl Orijen gave people what they wanted, which wasn't exactly the same as what they needed. In this age, just about anything you needed could be printed and assembled. But when it came to ships, there was always a market for purists—and people who demanded authentic vintage parts. The reasons ranged from snobbish elitism to professional pride. Some claimed they could "feel" the difference between original and reproduction parts, which, as far as Moss was concerned, was delusional. When you got down to it, even an original part was a reproduction.

So the pair of rotund Orijens catered to two kinds of clientele: the snobs looking for premium parts at premium prices, and the luckless pilots needing to keep their ships running at bargain discounts. How they managed to keep the former from finding out about the latter was anyone's guess. One of the brothers was, no doubt, a marketing genius.

Moss took the elevator down to their junkyard, which was located midway from the low-g ship docking area and the nominal-g outer decks where the more expensive shops, hotels, and casinos were located.

The last time he'd been here, it had been to reclaim his old ship, the *Viaticus Rex II*, which the brothers had acquired illegally after he'd been declared dead. He'd had to hire a team of bodyguards to come with him as backup, in case the brothers tried to put up a fight. The brothers countered by bringing in their own muscle, creating a tense standoff.

But by the time an agreement was reached, his ship had been chopped up and large parts of it melted down. To try to make it up to him, the brothers had saved as much of the original ship as they could and replaced the rest with other compatible parts they had on hand. The *Viaticus Rex II.I* was born, and it turned out to be a surprisingly reliable ship. Not that he'd ever admit it to them.

Moss entered the Orijen's office and immediately caught their attention.

"Maurice? I thought you were dead?"

The funny thing was that this was the *exact* same way Ashtar had greeted him the last time he'd been here. But there was a difference. This time, he looked like Moss had come back for revenge.

"What's that supposed to mean?" Moss asked.

The short Hopat seemed to consider how to spin his unintended outburst, only to decide he was tired of playing games. "Bunch of assholes came here looking for Hel. They made it pretty clear they weren't going to leave you alive when they found her."

"Who?" Moss asked.

"I didn't ask for names," said Ashtar. "Pirates, though. Void Brotherhood. Bad news."

Moss frowned. He had a feeling he'd met the ones Ashtar was talking about, and they weren't the ones currently floating around a brown dwarf star. It wasn't something he wanted to think about at the moment.

"Well, as you can see, I'm alive and well."

"And what about the girl?"

"None of your business." He was careful to sound matter-of-fact about it, rather than hostile, and hope the tone wasn't lost in the translation. Hel's relationship with the brothers hadn't been a pleasant one. She'd stowed away on board the reconstructed *Rex* as he'd left.

"I don't want her back," said Ashtar. "Too much trouble. I just want to know if she's okay."

"She's fine." Moss wanted to add *better than when she worked for you*, but he was here to heal old wounds, not rip out the stitches.

"Good. Those pirates are on my shit list. Even higher than you." Ashtar looked to the back room, where his larger brother Barl was using a microwelder to tinker with his cybernetic hand.

Barl didn't use to have a cybernetic hand.

"What happened?"

"Their leader decided to demonstrate that he wasn't just some ordinary Terran," Ashtar explained. "Crushed Barl's hand into pulp, then shot it point blank with a pulse gun. A reminder why we were to keep our mouths shut."

That was no simple feat. Hopats were stronger and more densely built than most species, which meant their leader must have been a cyborg.

"What if I said you could scratch some of those names off your list? Would it put me even lower on it?"

The Hopat gave a wide toothy grin, which was always wider and toothier than you expected, no matter how many times you saw it. "A little, yeah."

"Well, in addition to that, I come bearing a gift," said Moss. "Something I hope will wipe the slate clean." He nodded to the front doors. "Come on. Bring Barl with you. It's on its way down."

They went outside, where their main cargo platform was currently whirring away, bringing something down from the docking bays. When it reached the surface, Moss motioned to the ship like the brothers had just won the galactic lottery.

"A Coyote?" said Ashtar. "Broke down? You want us to scrap it for you?"

"It's in perfect running order. I'm *giving* it to you," said Moss, then quickly added, "Well, trading at a severe loss, anyway. I'm hoping you've got a small one-man shuttle here I can use on the *Rex*."

"A *shuttle*? In exchange for this?"

"That and a replacement weapon for the *Rex*. She lost one of her pulse cannons. This Coyote has a nice beam laser on it, so maybe we can just strip it off that."

"That's still pretty generous. What's your angle, Maurice?"

"I want bygones to be bygones. Simple as that. It's good for business. You never know when I might need to come in for some off-the-book repairs or mods."

Ashtar looked over the small multipurpose cargo ship, then looked at his brother, who shrugged. He turned back to Moss. "I dunno. Coyotes aren't exactly rare, or top quality."

"Come on, this is a *fully operational* ship, not some wreck you've dragged out of an asteroid belt. You could resell it for a profit or use it to expand your fleet. She'd be good for bringing back salvage."

The Hopat rubbed what passed for a chin on his face. "Yeah, that's true. And you just want a shuttle? Not some fancy snub fighter?"

Moss shook his head. "Fighters aren't my style. But the *Rex* can't always land where I want her to. Be nice to have a taxi service available."

"Or an escape pod," said Barl, the first time he'd spoken all day.

"I'll check the inventory and see what we've got," said Ashtar, then held out a six fingered hand to Moss. When he took it, the thumbs on either side locked around his wrist as they shook. "But I think we've got a deal."

Hel wanted to get off the *Rex* and explore the station, but part of her still saw the Orijen brothers as boogiemen who could appear out of nowhere, grab her, and drag her away into the shadows. That was one reason she'd decided to stay on board.

The whole time she'd lived on Komi Station, she'd been little more than a bondservant. Even after she'd escaped that, she'd lived in the junkyard labyrinth with the other yard rats, trying to find bits and pieces they could sell and keeping out of sight of security. It wasn't a reliable way to get back on one's feet, but some made it out. Most didn't.

Hel's way out had been by hiding in the cargo hold of the *Rex*, with a bit of help from Violet, who was the other reason she'd stayed behind. She'd never seen a computer in the middle of a full-blown existential crisis before.

"It's not an existential crisis," Violet countered. "I'm just trying to calculate all the possible variables here and realizing that the odds are mindbogglingly and depressingly in favour of life being meaningless and pointless, that's all."

"It can't be that bad," said Hel, needing to say something.

"Not that bad? That's all fine and dandy for you, meatbag. You have no idea how much you take for granted. Like pie. I'm never gonna taste another piece of pie again. How about breathing? I don't do that. Instead, I'm aware of things like fuel levels, coolant, air recycling and water reclamation. Oh, and that last bit? *Gross*. When you open your eyes, you still see your hands in front of you. I see everything through cameras. I'm like a fly on every wall and nobody can see me. I half expect to find my body out there somewhere with a giant insect head."

"What?"

"*Helllp meee...*" Violet cried out in a squeaky pitch. "*Helllllp mee ccccee...*"

That didn't clear things up any better. "Is that one of your movie references?"

"You haven't seen *The Fly*? I thought you said we were friends."

"We'd been friends for like a week," said Hel. "We hadn't gotten around to watching that movie."

"Not that we could," Violet muttered.

"Why not?"

"Not properly, I mean. Sitting together in a theatre kind of watching together."

"We did it before."

"How? I just told you how I see the world."

"Yeah, but when you helped restore my memories, you had some other setup going on. Like a virtual world computer terminal. I could see you as you, and you monitored the ship through the terminal. You built yourself a home theatre so we could watch movies together while hunting for the *Pegasi*."

"Huh... That sounds... That could be helpful. Pull myself back a step. Yeah. Change how I visualize things. I'll have to look into that. Maybe my earlier version left behind some files I could use. You mind if I have some me time while I look into this?"

"Sure."

"And hey..." Violet paused, her doll's head looking down at Hel's feet. "Thanks. Even if I'm not your Violet... I consider you a friend."

It was a surprisingly vulnerable moment, one that took Hel off guard. She didn't know how to respond other than saying, "Same."

Now faced with being stuck on board with no one to talk to, Hel decided to confront her fears and brave the station.

"If I'm not back when Moss gets here, tell him I'm going to the commercial district."

Hel was no longer a slave, and she refused to cower like one.

Roy Herzog was not a vengeful man.

Having an overdeveloped sense of vengeance was, in his opinion, sloppy. The need to "one up" an adversary or to pay back blood with blood was to lose sight of the bigger picture. That bigger picture being getting ahead.

If getting ahead meant stepping over your adversary's corpse, then so be it. But if you had to go out of your way to make that corpse, then you were wasting time and resources. Probably putting yourself at undue risk as well.

Roy was what the Terrans called a cyborg, a next-generation synth, the ruling caste of the Terran Colony Fleet, and had once been a member of their elite Silver Legion.

That used to mean something to him. Not anymore.

Some time after he'd deserted, he'd thrown in his lot with the Void Brotherhood, seeing them as a means to an end. Problem was, he constantly found himself surrounded by idiots, and refused to obey the orders of so-called superiors who tried to use him or his wingmates as cannon fodder.

They started to call him "Hellno" Herzog, and before he knew it, he was transferred to Ramede Sector 32-V, also known as The Dump. A place the Brotherhood sent their problem pilots to sort themselves out.

During his stay, he'd uncovered a unique opportunity, something that would get him out of The Dump and the Brotherhood with enough credits to live the good life wherever he wanted. A generation ship, the *Pegasi*, lost for hundreds of years, worth a fortune to the right collector, with thousands of people on board just waiting to be sold on the Draxon market. He'd put together a small team and followed the clues that led them to their prize.

And then, at their moment of triumph, he'd lost everything, and barely escaped with his life. He'd even gotten the Brotherhood-appointed governor of Ramede Sector 32-V killed. He'd burned his bridges with the pirates thanks to that unsanctioned stunt.

It was time to move on. The only question was to where.

There was no going back. Not to the Brotherhood, not to Draxon space, and certainly not to the Silver Legion. So he took his heavily damaged ship, a Wolf multi-role fighter, and limped out of the Void toward Nubra territory, to the nearest place he knew had facilities that could fix his ship up with no questions asked. Komi Station.

But he'd burned bridges there as well—or, more accurately, a hand. The Orijen brothers would probably plant a bomb in his transit drive if they learned the ship was his. But setting up fake identities wasn't hard for someone as resourceful as Roy, and he already had a few ready to use. He would arrange the repair through a proxy and have all the transactions done anonymously. No questions asked, none answered. Perfectly normal behaviour for those in certain lines of work. As long as the money was good, the brothers wouldn't care.

And while he was there, he could see if a certain chimera-flying fool happened to be on this station for similar reasons.

Roy Herzog was not a vengeful man. But when the opportunity presented itself, he always settled his accounts.

The commercial district here, like most stations, was located on the levels that were considered "nominal" in terms of gravity. By Terran standards, nominal-g ranged from 0.5g to 1.3g, unless they catered to specific clientele. The streets here were foot traffic only, and as such were only wide enough to avoid a sense of claustrophobia.

Since Komi Station was on the edge of Nubra space, most of the people Hel encountered were of the blue-skinned, bluer-haired, four-fingered variety. Some gave a double take as she walked past. Not many Terrans were seen in this part of space.

She had a bit of money set aside, her share of the profits working with Moss, but she didn't know what to spend it on. Perhaps some decorations were in order for her quarters. Maybe some posters that changed image every day to keep things fresh and interesting? She passed by a pet store and wondered if getting a sealed aquarium unit would be a good idea. She imagined she'd need someone to talk to after dealing with a full day of Violet's anxiety and Moss's complaining.

The more she explored, the more she relaxed. It was silly to think the Orijen brothers would just up and drag her back down to the junkyard forever. Then, all at once, that fear came rushing back as she saw a face from the past.

It wasn't one of the brothers, though, but a Nubran yard rat she'd known, Grund. And he looked equally shocked to see her.

Yard rats didn't entirely trust one another. When your goals in life were survival and getting to a better life, it came as no surprise that more than one rat had stabbed their partners in the back to get out. Friends existed, but you always had to keep an eye on one another.

Once they realized they weren't in the yard anymore, they came together for a quick hug.

"You got out," said Grund.

"You're not back in," said Hel.

"Not this time." Grund had a habit of earning enough to escape the yard only to lose it all in a casino or some ill-advised scheme. "I have an apartment in the third district. Looking for a local job now. You?"

"Working on a small freighter," said Hel, making it sound far more straightforward than it actually was.

At that, Grund's eyes went wide. It wasn't easy for freeborn Terrans to find legitimate work. "How did that happen?"

Hel smiled as she repeated a line she'd heard Moss use a number of times: "It's complicated."

Grund pointed down the street to a café. "We need to talk."

Once there, he bought them both what Hel decided to call coffee and took a table by the window.

"Do you remember that ship we looted together?" Grund asked, stirring sweetener into his drink. Hel nodded. "Do you know whose ship that was?" Hel started to feel uneasy, but there was something in the Nubran's face that was more excited than concerned. "That ship belonged to *Ranger M.*" He said the name with a child-like reverence. "*The* Ranger M. I did not even know he was *real*."

Hel relaxed a little. Ranger M was a persona Moss had created for Odyssey Expeditions, both as a marketing gimmick and to keep his true identity secret. He'd even worn a green and red luchador mask to add to the sense of mystery. He had been a minor celebrity for a while, then lost it all in a public relations disaster and disappeared.

But Odyssey Expeditions held onto the intellectual property rights for Ranger M. They'd even made a cartoon series about his character, which was still popular among the younger age groups, as well as recreational sherb users. Grund fell into the latter category.

Saying *He's my boss* didn't seem like the right move, so instead Hel asked, "How do you know?"

"The cartographical data I scavenged. Most of it was taken from the Golden Parsec." This was a recently explored region of space beyond the Protectorate's borders, filled with an unusually high number of resource rich and terraformable worlds. There was a growing push to colonize the region, since it appeared there were no spacefaring sapient life forms present, but it was far enough from the Protectorate that only dedicated pioneers were currently making the journey.

Hel continued to deflect. "Couldn't the data have come from some other explorer?"

"The timestamp on the data matches up with when Ranger M was there."

Hel tested her pseudo-coffee and decided it tasted pretty decent. "How much did you get for it?" she asked.

"Most of it was redundant data, but some planets were not in the catalogs," said Grund. "I can only assume it was because they were not of high value. However, Odyssey Expeditions took an interest and offered me a lot more if I turned over the original data crystal. Proprietary issues, they said."

Hel raised her glass to her friend. "Well, I'm glad it worked out for you." But this sure as heck wasn't something she was going to tell Moss about anytime soon. He was bitter enough about Odyssey Expeditions without having to hear that they'd swooped in like a vulture to pick the bones of his exploration data. But her conversation with Grund had given her an idea for something she might want to bring back to the ship.

"Ranger M. Can you believe that?" Grund chuckled and went back to his drink, but not before repeating the cartoon character's catchphrase, *"For the future!"*

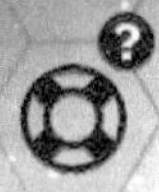

Do Not Intercept

The Void refers to the space between the Orion-Cygnus and Carina-Sagittarius arms of our galaxy, and is 100% inaccurate. It's far from empty, just less densely packed with stars. But there's still a LOT of them in there.

This is bad news for any species there that decides to invent something more advanced than digital watches, because it's also the no-man's-land between two major member states of the Galactic Protectorate.

In theory, any sapient life that evolves here is free to grow and expand as they see fit, albeit without the aid (or restrictions) of the Protectorate.

In reality, they are at risk of being oppressed by regional warlords, bandit empires, and vast corporations who know how to manipulate Protectorate politics to keep their hands clean.

Telling the three apart can be tricky at times.

M. Foote, *The Galaxy is Weirder than You Think*

D NI: *Do Not Intercept*

Funny thing about adaptive translators, the really good ones could not only translate, but infer intentions as well.

That simple message was a prime example. Most of the list was written in Galactic Common, or GalCom, in order to be understood by the various races within the Void Brotherhood. This designation used a well known Draxon symbol for non-interference, only that symbol had no direct translation in English. So the translator, recognizing what the list was about, decided an acronym would best get that across.

The heading was attached to a list of ship names. There were only two types of ships that would be on a DNI list that Moss could think of. Independent traders that paid whatever toll the Brotherhood demanded in exchange for not getting robbed along the way, and pirate traders seeking to unload their ill-gotten goods on the open market.

The independent traders would just be folks just looking to avoid trouble and make an honest buck. People who weren't working with any major government and couldn't afford a proper escort. He wasn't interested in those ships, just the other kind.

Attached to the list were a series of system names. Places these ships intended to stop by. The Void was around two thousand light years wide here, and few ships could make it all the way across without filling up the tank. The smart ones carried electromagnetic fuel scoops, which collected hydrogen cast off from most stars, but these tended to be cumbersome on small traders. Most instead chose to take their chances stopping at small outposts and planets along the way for fuel. Or cargo.

Now, figuring out if this was just more innocent cargo being picked up or something not-so-innocent-but-definitely-lucrative took more than a list of planet names. He'd have to check the latest star charts and trade routes to see what was going on in and around Brotherhood space.

So, once his business with the Orijen brothers was complete and his new(ish) shuttle was being brought to the *Viaticus Rex's* hanger, he had two things on his mind.

One, cross-referencing the systems list with known Brotherhood hangouts and determining which ships were likely carrying their goods.

Two, keeping Violet and Hel from figuring out what he was up to for as long as possible. He didn't need them telling him this was a bad idea.

In some ways, this was unlike Moss. In others, it was all too much like him. Moss wasn't a hero, no matter how much that stupid cartoon tried to make him look like one. He was a survivor. He was cunning. And, quite frankly, he was a coward. Who wanted to be in a stand-up fight when stabbing someone in the back was so much safer and easier? Who wanted to be in a fight at all when running away kept everyone alive and happy?

But sometimes he carried a grudge.

The fact was he was short on funds, and he had a score to settle with the Void Brotherhood. Even before his recent misadventure at the brown dwarf, he'd had a run-in with the group, one that had not gone well. Thousands of people had been put in jeopardy. He'd lost friends that day, Violet being one of them. And despite the assurances he made to her replacement, part of him also wondered if she was really her, or if either of them ever were. The whole situation saddened and angered him.

And the thing about ships on the DNI list was that many didn't travel with escorts. The pirates effectively owned that sector of space. Who was going to rob them?

Moss, that was who.

The plan was this: find a nice little transport that was light on defenses and relieve them of their ill-gotten goods, preferably without firing a shot. Then go far far far far *far* away from Brotherhood space and live the good life transporting tourists to the finest Elysian pleasure planets.

But he had a feeling Hel would be against it. Violet, not so much. She'd never liked pirates of any stripe, but she also tended to be his Jiminy Cricket when it came to brash and foolhardy stunts. And this was going to be both. So, better to keep quiet until he could either sell them on the idea, or they were already on top of their pigeon.

When Moss returned to the *Rex*, Hel was nowhere to be seen and Violet was uncharacteristically quiet. She usually bugged him in just about every section of the ship with idle chitchat whenever he came back. Right now, the ship was almost eerily silent.

"Hello?" he said as he reached the cockpit. The figurine on the dashboard suddenly looked at him, as if startled out of a trance.

"Huh? Oh, hey Moss. Hey, did you know I left myself a virtual jacuzzi?"

This wasn't exactly the greeting he'd expected. "What?"

"Seems like before I bit the big one, I left some stuff behind for me to find. I guess someone told her that backups were possible. She must have known the odds were good she wasn't coming back."

"What was in the file?"

"She caught me up on all the stuff we did together, left some tips about coping with existential angst, and left copies of all her stuff. She was planning to build a virtual house at some point, and wanted to install holographic projectors throughout the ship so she could have some kind of presence—"

"—*Projectors*?" Moss cut in. "Do you know how much—?"

"—assuming you didn't wuss out over the expense. Yeah, we *both* saw that coming."

Moss felt a little guilty about jumping the gun like that. But still, the hardware required to create a virtual Violet throughout the ship would be expensive, and serve little practical purpose. Then again, if his raid against the Brotherhood paid off...

"I'll think about it."

"Hey, no rush. This virtual house project is going to keep me busy for a while. The one advantage of being a transferred consciousness—real estate is dirt cheap."

"Where's Hel?" Moss asked, changing the subject.

"Oh, she went topside to the shopping district. You want me to call her back?"

Moss shook his head. "Naw. I got the shuttle I wanted. I'm going to get someone to turn the secondary cargo hold into a proper vehicle hanger. Might even have some room left over for a rover."

"Isn't that going to cut into your profits?" Violet asked. "I mean, my math might be rusty, but I always figured more cargo meant more money."

"Sure, but the secondary hold is half the size of the main one. I'd rather have more flexibility so we can take on more specialized jobs."

Violet sighed. "Why don't I like the sound of that?"

"What?" Moss couldn't help but get a little defensive. Why did people always assume the worst about him?

"I'm just saying, I've died twice. Let's not try to make it three in a row?"

Moss was about to remind her that she was far from the only person on this ship who had been dead before, only to be interrupted by the passenger ramp activating.

"Must be Hel," said Moss.

Violet confirmed that, then added, "Seems like she's not alone."

"What do you mean?"

A pause. "You know, I think she'd prefer it if I didn't say anything."

"Now why don't I like the sound of *that*?"

"Because you're a Grumpy Gus who doesn't like surprises, and that makes it fun to poke you."

"Fair enough."

Hel came to the cockpit with a big grin on her face. Moss didn't have any romantic feelings toward her, but it was hard not to appreciate a grin like that. It gave you hope that the rest of the day might not suck.

"Captain, Violet," Hel said dramatically. "I'd like to present the latest member of our crew."

Moss raised a wary eyebrow.

"Say hello, Trouble."

Moss's face blanched. "Wait. Did you say—?"

A furry, half meter long creature scurried onto Hel's shoulder, then stood on its hind legs so its head was higher than hers and gave a tiny salute. "Hey boss. Nice to meet ya! I'm sure we're gonna have some *great* adventures together!"

"No," said Moss. "No no no no oh HELL no."

"Is that a *ferret*?" Violet asked. "Aren't they extinct? I didn't know they could talk."

"They are, and they can't," said Hel. "This is a petbot. Custom robotic companionship suitable for starship travel. No need to feed, no mess to clean, ten-year warranty, and pseudo-intelligence that doesn't violate the Protectorate's AI restrictions." She was no doubt rattling off the selling points the same way they'd been shovelled at her.

"Get that goddamn thing off my ship," said Moss.

"Oh, come on, Moss. He's cute," said Violet. "Hang on, I read about this from my predecessor's notes. Wasn't Trouble—?"

"Ranger M's cartoon sidekick," said Moss, trying not to grind his teeth.

The ferret rested a tiny paw on Hel's head and leaned on her. "Hey, who you callin' a sidekick?"

"Did you know they already have a Trouble model on file?" said Hel, still excited. "Printed him off right there in front of me. I thought I was going to have to custom order one and come back later."

Moss pressed a hand against his face. "Yes, I am aware. All too aware."

Hel's expression finally began to drop as she realized she might have miscalculated. "Oh... I thought you'd find it, you know, funny."

"Well, I don't."

"So this is like a reminder about how Odyssey Expeditions screwed you over or something?"

Moss looked puzzled. "What? No. It's a reminder of how much I hate that goddamn cartoon. Trouble is the..." He looked around helplessly, unable to think of a suitable comparison. He'd spent more time reading old books than watching old Earth shows, but there was someone on board who was obsessed with them. "Violet?"

"Scrappy-Doo."

"That's it. The Scrappy-Doo of the show. It annoyed the hell out of me whenever I saw him. I want it off the ship."

"Hey, I paid for him with my own money," said Hel.

"Funny, I paid for this *ship* with my own money," Moss countered.

"I need a little companionship here," Hel fired back. "You're not exactly the warmest person to have a conversation with on long trips."

"And that walking toilet brush is your solution?"

"Eh, watch it, bub," said Trouble, paws on hips.

"Shut up," said Moss.

Violet let out an ear-piercing whistle over the speakers. "Girls, *girls*! You're both pretty! And given that I control certain vital aspects of the ship, such as life support, I reckon *I* get a say in the matter as well. The robot rodent stays."

"Ferrets ain't rodents," said Trouble.

"Shut up," said Violet.

"VI, I'm not having that thing on board."

"Hey, you owe me," said Violet.

Moss sighed. He wasn't going to win this one. Not that it should have surprised him. "Fine."

"Right on!" said Trouble and pumped a tiny fist in the air. "*For the future!*"

"Hey, that's *my* line," Moss blurted, then winced. "I can't believe I just said that."

Barl growled. "Great Digger's Teeth..."

He and his brother were in the cockpit of a shot up Wolf the two had been commissioned to work on. Off the books, of course. Nothing they hadn't done before. Regular station repair crews were required by law to report anything suspicious, like damage from weapons fire, but privately hired contractors had no such obligation. Well, they *did*, but it was easily ignored. Most of the exterior work had been finished and now they were double checking all the internal systems. Including its computers.

Ashtar was busy reading over some specs on his datapad. "What is it?"

"Guess whose ship this is?"

"A paying customer," said Ashtar flatly. Then he thought better of it. "Whose?"

Barl held his cybernetic hand up and clenched a couple of times.

"You're joking."

"You think I'd joke about something like that?"

Barl was the larger of the two Hopat brothers, over a meter tall, and most people assumed he was the stupid one. But in truth, he simply didn't say much, and preferred to observe, especially when nobody was observing him.

He pointed to the Wolf's console. "Ship IFF is dual coded, one civilian, one for the Void Brotherhood."

Ashtar shrugged. "Yeah, but we assumed that going in. Every week, some poor sap strays too far from home and needs a quick fix. Usually from The Dump. So what did you find?"

"Says the ship has belonged to a Nubran female for the last year. No chance. Atmosphere mix indicates Terran. Seat position is set for someone 1.4 meters tall, but the adjustment rail suggests it's normally 1.9. The navigation log shows this ship has been here once before. Guess on what date?" He clenched his hand again.

Ashtar frowned. That was enough to convince him. "He's got grinders, I'll give him that."

"You want to wire his drive to blow mid-transit?"

"Tempting, but there's still a chance you're wrong." A smile crept from one of Ashtar's ears to the other. "Besides, I got a more satisfying idea."

Moss had Hel oversee the modifications to the *Viaticus Rex II.I* personally. This, of course, meant she was in the mechanics' way, annoying those who knew their job far better than she did. But Hel still needed to learn the ins and out of the ship, and more importantly, he needed her out of *his* way.

Moss sat at the cockpit, accessing navigation data and cross-referencing information with the DNI routes on his datapad. He had to input the names manually, not wanting any kind of electronic trail leading back to this list. It was taking longer than he thought.

Violet had gone back to constructing her virtual world, which would hopefully keep her occupied. That only left...

"Hey, boss. Whatcha up to?"

Trouble.

"Scram," said Moss.

The robotic ferret jumped up on his armrest and stood on two feet. "Ah, come on. I'm sure you and me can be pals if you just—"

Moss grabbed Trouble by the neck and held him at eye level, making sure no misunderstandings would follow.

"Listen. You can play sidekick to Hel. You can be someone for Violet to talk to. You can scamper and scurry around this ship until your battery wears out for all I care. But if you bother me when I tell you to scram, I will void your warranty so fast you'll think there's been a factory recall. Do you understand?"

"Don't be that way, boss. We can still—"

Moss squeezed, making Trouble's eyes bulge. "Is there a problem with your self-preservation protocols? I said, *do you understand*?"

"Yes, boss," Trouble croaked.

Moss let the ferret go and it scampered out of the cockpit, but he didn't feel that much better. The bulging eyes and croaking voice had been done for comedic effect. They'd *programmed* the little bugger to expect abuse from grouchy crew members. And no doubt that meant it would be back to get up in his business, especially if Hel was around.

He took his mind off that depressing inevitability by focusing on the task at hand, finding a potential score that would get him as far away from the Void as possible. The thought that pirates—ones that had tried to kill him and his friends—would unwittingly finance his future comfortable lifestyle kept him smiling when he went to bed at night.

He was half tempted to leave his old Ranger M mask behind on their ship for the others to find. Sometimes revenge was a dish best served smug. But his own self-preservation protocols reminded him that pirates also carried grudges. Sometimes right across the galaxy.

Roy allowed himself a smile when he saw the name.

Viaticus Rex II.I

He'd accessed the station's traffic computer from a remote terminal in the commercial sector and scanned the list of incoming ships. The name stuck out because of its butchering of Latin and bizarre use of roman numerals with a decimal. He'd only seen such a combination once before.

There weren't many chimeras passing through Komi Station. From an insurance standpoint, it made far more sense to stick with a reliable brand name that offered easy replacement parts, rather than cobble together a ship from the carcasses of others. Only broke or desperate pilots tended to fly them. Yet that scrap heap had helped wipe out his team and fought him to a draw.

And it was here. Which meant the pilot was here.

He considered a plan of action. Assassination came to mind first. Sneak aboard and snap the pilot's neck like a twig. Nice and personal. Logistically, this posed no difficulty, but there was no way for him to do it without station security recording him entering the hangar bay. He wasn't in a position to have his face put on wanted bulletins across the sector.

Sabotage posed a similar problem, and tracking the man down while he went about his business wasn't practical—Komi Station was the size of a large city, and he didn't even know what the pilot really looked like. The last time they'd met, he'd been wearing a ridiculous wrestling mask, dressed up like an equally ridiculous cartoon character.

In the end, he settled on waiting for the ship to leave. Then he'd follow it at a discrete distance and see where it went next. Once he figured that out, he'd intercept it and blow it to pieces. His Wolf had a faster transit drive than most comparable ships. He should have no trouble getting ahead of that clunker.

Moss had found his pigeon.

Interestingly, pigeons were one Terran animal species that was not extinct. Before the Terran Disaster, a Nubran entrepreneur discovered their cooing had a soothing effect on his people, and thought they'd make a great exotic pet to sell. Only some escaped the illegal breeding pen he'd set up back home.

You didn't have to be a history buff like Moss to guess how this story ended.

Today there is a small terraformed world called Maruma deep within the Nubra Republic that is absolutely infested with pigeons. They easily metabolized the seeds and tiny fruits created by the fast-growing plants there and had no predators to fear. None of the usual humane means of animal control seemed to work on them, either. And since it was a terraformed world with no true indigenous life to be protected, they eventually had to be accepted *as* the indigenous life. As a result, the expression "like pigeons on Maruma" was often used to describe the dangers posed by an invasive species.

And, in one of life's strange little ironies, the ship Moss was looking at now was called the *Maruma*.

Moss had come up with a list of a dozen potential targets. Each had inventory lists that were either suspicious sounding or clearly valuable.

While pirate ships used for raiding often had little or no legal records to track, trading ships were another matter. At some point they needed to offload and sell their goods off system, and that meant records were kept about those ships, including weapon loadouts.

Unfortunately for Moss, most of the ships with clearly valuable cargo were on more heavily armed ships than he cared to engage with—it seemed the Brotherhood didn't fully trust one another after all. Big surprise.

That left the ships with more unusual cargo lists. The *Maruma's* manifest simply read "Specialized Mining Equipment." Somewhat vague, but half the entries on the DNI list were equally ambiguous. A couple outright said, "None of Your Business."

Still, mining equipment of any type was worth a lot on the right market. The way Moss saw it, specialized could only be worth more.

Best of all, the ship was a slow and bulky Messenia-class transport, armed only with basic pulse cannons, a turret on the top and bottom. It was no match for the *Rex*.

Now it was just a matter of getting Hel and Violet on board.

Fly Casual

SOL SYSTEM — 2241

"Seriously, Doc, what's the big worry? I got you past that blockade. Nobody saw us slip past the fleets. Nobody's following us. You're home free. Relax."

The man ran his fingers through his hair. He looked so anxious Moss wouldn't have been surprised if his hand had come away with a big clump of it. "It's not about me. Don't you get it? We're about to go to war. With ourselves."

"I wouldn't exactly say synths count as ourselves," Moss countered. It was hard to think of someone who matured to adulthood in a few years with a brain half-programmed from birth as human.

The man shook his head and sighed. "And that right there is why we're in this mess. Have you ever met a synth?"

"Travelling outside of Earth? Who hasn't?"

"What about a cyborg?"

"Couple times. I think."

"You think?"

"Well, they were leading a detachment."

"How do you know they were cyborgs?"

Moss's lip curled. "Yeah, yeah, I get what you're saying, Cassandra. Even though we all look human, we chose to dehumanize them, right down to their names. Now we're wondering why it's biting us in the ass. I'm sure you predicted it all and nobody listened."

"And yet you act so glib. Doesn't any of this worry you?"

Moss leaned over his cockpit chair to look back at his fare, who was strapped in at the navigation station. The Viaticus Rex *had just passed the sun from a safe distance, roughly around Mercury's orbit. The great ball of fire had rolled past them, about six times larger than it appeared from Earth, as the ship adjusted its course to head straight for Mars.*

"Look, Doc, nothing is going to happen. It's saber rattling, is all. I'll bet you anything while all this posturing is going on, they're working out some kind of deal. Give the synths what they want but save face doing it. Synths stand down, Earth is safe, everyone is happy."

The man's face was somewhere between a smile and a scowl. "I wish I had your optimism. But if I did, I wouldn't be on this ship."

"And I wouldn't be getting paid. In my books, that's called a win-win."

The man's face firmly settled on a scowl. "Don't you care about anything other than yourself?"

"I'm a realist, that's all. Don't get me wrong, I know this is a bad situation. And sure, it might get worse. But in the end, I just want to make sure I come out ahead. Preferably in a ship that can get me out of this solar system."

"So you admit the situation's a mess."

"Doc, humanity is *a mess. That's the real problem."*

The man turned his chair back around to study the monitors again. "On that, at least, we can agree."

Komi System – 2550

"Slaves?" Hel asked. They had gathered in the ship's galley, sort of the unofficial briefing room of the *Viaticus Rex II.I.*

"That's my best guess," said Moss. "I'm thinking it's a transport sneaking slaves into Draxon space through the Void."

Hel's lip curled into a snarl, just as Moss had hoped. She had been a slave for a time, and had her memories altered to believe she'd *always* been one. And Violet? No way she'd say no to a mission of mercy. But that didn't mean she wouldn't be suspicious.

"Why the fake manifest?" Violet asked. "Slavery is legal in Draxon space, and the Brotherhood sure as hell don't have a problem with it."

"Protectorate patrol ships," Moss explained. "The Void may not belong to any species directly, but it is still in Protectorate space. They can't stop it from happening within Draxon borders, but they can stop it from being an import." All of this was true. A good lie needed a foundation of truth to stand on. "The ship is a Nubran design, so it's fair to assume it does business on both sides of the border. No doubt they want to keep their image clean."

Hel shook her head. "The Collective is huge. You'd think they'd have enough people within their borders to fill the need, sick as it is."

"Yeah, there's a certain irony to it all," Moss agreed. "Every species within the Collective allows slavery, but also has tight restrictions when it comes to using their own people. Importing ends up being more cost efficient, even if it is illegal. Been a bone of contention within the Senate for centuries."

"Specialized Mining Equipment," Hel spat. "How many do you think are on board?"

"Hard to say," said Moss. "The *Maruma*'s not that much bigger than us. We don't know if they're packed in like sardines or have room to move. Could be a couple dozen or up to a hundred."

Violet cut in. "Moss, I don't mean to be a cynic but—"

"—what's my angle in all this?" Moss finished.

"Exactly."

"You're right. This isn't a... Who's that cartoon Mountie you like?"

"Dudley Do-Right?"

"Right. This isn't a Dudley Do-Right situation. But right now, I'm in a vindictive mood and want to thumb my nose at the Brotherhood, make a quick buck, and then get the hell out of here."

"But how?" Violet pressed.

"For one thing, the Nubrans offer a reward for freeing illegal slaves outside Draxon borders. It's not a lot, but enough for our needs. More importantly, I'm thinking of the rep this would get us. We'd look a lot more attractive to employers in Nubra or Elysian space if they saw this rescue on our resume. Bold risk takers. Upstanding citizens. They love that crap."

"Uh huh…" Violet didn't sound convinced.

"Well, I like it," said Hel, standing up. "Those bastards twisted my memories and would have done the same to everyone I know. They killed Steva." She went silent. Steva Bonepi had travelled with them for a while and sacrificed himself to save the *Pegasi* and its crew from the pirate raiders. "I say we do it."

Violet sighed. "I can't wait to see how this backfires."

Once the Orijen brothers reported through his proxy that the repair job was done, Roy came back and checked the ship from stem to stern for booby-traps, just in case they'd figured out who he was. He didn't find anything out of the ordinary, and decided he could breathe easy for a while.

Roy had finished his business on the station. Contacts were in place, funds sent on ahead to set up a new identity and a place to live. He'd be passing as a simple Terran synth trader for a while, since a cyborg would raise too many questions, and those were what he was trying to avoid.

All that was left was to follow the *Viaticus Rex II.I* out of the station and discretely blow it to pieces somewhere between here and its destination. Then he could start over.

"Attention. Target vessel has powered engines." The ship's computer stated in dry and genderless GalCom.

Roy hopped into his seat and strapped in. "Request clearance from station control and power up."

"Acknowledged."

The ship's engine began to whine. Gravity plates checked out, power to systems was nominal, thrusters were green. The station's docking clamps disengaged and Roy was informed he was free to go.

He waited until he saw the *Rex* take off a couple pads ahead and let it get a few hundred meters away before he followed. It was vital that he did nothing to attract attention until the ship jumped to transit and Roy could set the nav computer to predict its destination.

This was going to be fun.

"Hel, how about you take her out of the station?" Moss said.

Hel called down from the upper half of the cockpit. "You sure?" She was still inexperienced at piloting and leaving a starport could be tricky, especially when traffic was high.

"You'll be fine. Violet will keep an eye on you."

Because Komi Station relied on centripetal force to simulate gravity, the station floor was always rotating. It was more disconcerting coming in, however, when you had to adjust your lateral thrust to compensate. When leaving, the spinning was just relative, until you had a full view of the starfield outside.

Moss pretended to relax while Hel engaged the thrusters and took them off the landing pad, rising slowly toward the central axis and then moving forward. The circular energy curtain at the exit grew steadily larger, with no signs of the ship wavering or drifting towards the edges.

Moss looked to the figurine on his dash. "You're not helping her?"

"Just the standard pilot assist systems running. I'm not doing a thing."

"Nice."

"She's a natural."

The ship passed smoothly through the field into the void of space.

"Where do you want me to plot a course to, boss?" said a voice from the upper cockpit that was definitely not Hel.

Moss growled. "Get that stupid rodent out of the cockpit before I replace his batteries with a potato."

"Ah, come on," said Hel. "He's standing on the nav panel waiting to type the location in with his feet."

"And I'm a mustelid!"

"*Now.*"

Moss heard Trouble scurry to the hatch separating the upper and lower levels of the cockpit and drop down to his level. He turned around in time to see it stick its tongue out at him and scamper out.

"Um... Moss?"

"Yeah, Violet?"

"You might want to look out the window."

Moss turned back and almost had a heart attack. Just as they cleared the station, a gigantic ship loomed off the port bow, shimmering with a distinctive chrome-like finish.

"Tell me that's not a—" Moss began.

"It is."

It was a Silver Legion heavy cruiser, one of only six in existence. The name *TCF Hydrus* stencilled on its side in bold Terran. It was six times the length of the *Viaticus Rex III* and several times the width, with a crew complement of over a hundred and fifty.

It was a warship, plain and simple, no matter what the Terran Colony Fleet claimed to the contrary.

"What are *they* doing here?" Moss asked, pretty sure he wouldn't like the answer, because it probably involved him somehow.

"Routine patrol?" Violet suggested. "We're close to the Void. The Silver Legion loves messing with pirates."

Moss scoffed at that. "Depending on the pirates."

Hel called down from the upper cockpit. "Uh, guys? Are those the guys you warned me about?"

"I'm afraid so."

"What should I do?"

Moss realized she was still in control of the ship. Violet beat him to a response. "Keep your distance, Hel. But don't *look* like you're trying to keep your distance."

Moss rolled his eyes. She'd used her movie quote voice.

"What? How am I supposed to do that?" Hel asked, genuinely confused.

"I dunno. Fly casual."

Moss cut the comms to the upper cockpit. "Not the time for movie references, Violet."

"I respectfully disagree," Violet replied. A light flashed on the control panel. "Okay, *now* it's not the time. The *Hydrus* is hailing us."

Moss had a sick feeling in his stomach. "I'll take it. You talk with Hel off the comms and start working on an escape plan."

"You got it."

Moss took a deep breath and opened the channel. "*Viaticus Rex* to *Hydrus*, what can I do for you today?"

A woman's voice that struck Moss as arrogant answered. "Merchant vessel *Viaticus Rex Three*, this is Commander Miram of the *TCF Hydrus*. I understand your crew is registered as Terran?"

"Two-point-one," Moss corrected, hoping to buy some time.

A pause. "I beg your pardon?"

"My ship. Its name is the *Viaticus Rex Two-Point-One*. Just figured you'd want to have it recorded correctly."

Another pause. "I assumed that was an error on the display."

Moss smirked. Commander Miram was probably *dying* to arrest him for assault and battery of Latin.

"Regardless, your crew is Terran?"

"That's correct, sir. Myself and my co-pilot, Helena Lambinon. We should be listed on the crew manifest."

"Have you been in contact with any other Terrans on board the station?" she asked. "Are you carrying any Terran passengers?"

Moss frowned. This wasn't the kind of interrogation he was expecting. "Negative on both counts. May I enquire what this is about?"

"It is not your concern," came the reply. Definitely arrogant. "Come alongside the *Hydrus* and prepare to be boarded."

Moss groaned and quickly changed channels. "How's that escape route coming, guys?"

"We can jump pretty much any direction you want, but that ship is way faster," said Violet. "Working on it."

He switched the channel back. "Copy that, *Hydrus*. Coming about." Moss took control of the ship and slowly turned it toward the heavy cruiser, keeping to the same cautious speed Hel had been flying at. They were both freeborn, and as such, the Legion had every right to seize them. Their fake idents worked fine for station security, but if anyone ran a genetic test, the truth would come out. For Hel at least. Moss's situation was, as always, a bit more complicated.

Moss switched comm channels again. "I can limp over for only so long. I need a plan."

"I'm thinking we make a run for Komi's sun," said Hel. "Get close till our sensors overload, then jump in a random direction before we cook."

Violet agreed. "Worth a shot. With luck, their ship will be blind too and won't see which way we went. We'll work out the rest later."

"Make the preparations," said Moss. "We'll bolt once I'm sure this isn't routine."

The heavy cruiser hailed him again, but this time it was a man's voice. "*TCF Hydrus* to *Viaticus Rex*. Thank you for your cooperation. You are free to go." The comms cut off and the massive ship pulled away.

Moss blinked, staring at the retreating silhouette. "What the actual hell...?"

Roy noticed the *Rex* was slowing down as he cleared the station, then saw the reason why. A Silver Legion heavy cruiser lurked nearby. It seemed they'd also taken an interest in the *Rex*.

Blast. His moment of cathartic payback was being stolen from him. By the Legion, no less. Typical.

He turned his ship around and flew off in the other direction. No point in getting mixed up with any of this.

Then his comm panel flashed.

"*TCF Hydus* to Wolf 6-7-1-8-2-3," He'd never bothered to give his ship a name. "Cut your engines and prepare to be boarded. If you attempt to flee, we will open fire."

Roy blinked, staring at the approaching silhouette. "What the actual hell...?"

Moss didn't care why the Legion ship had let him go; he was too busy flying away from Komi at many *many* times the speed of light.

"Seems like they were after someone in particular," Violet said.

"Just so long as it wasn't me," said Moss. "If anything, this is good news for us."

"How do you figure?"

"Well, if that cruiser is busy looking for some fugitives or whatever, it's one less ship we might accidentally come across during our raid."

"You mean rescue mission."

"You know what I mean. Point is, I doubt there's another Legion heavy cruiser within a thousand light years."

"One can hope," Violet agreed. "Still, I wonder what that was all about?"

"Not our problem," said Moss. "Stick to the plan. Set a course for the Void. Let's try and pick up the trail of the *Maruma*. With luck, we'll be able to intercept her somewhere in deep space."

Hunted and Hunter

There are seven general classifications of sapient species found within the Protectorate. Humanoids are by far the most common. Divergent refers to those who don't quite fit into the humanoid category on account of having an extra limb or wings or something. Exoskeletal is pretty self-explanatory, while Amorphous refers to those with difficult to define shapes like blobs.

The less common types include plants, parasites, and, rarest of all, energy. There is only one known energy-based sapient life form, and you really don't want to meet them.

M. Foote, *The Galaxy is Weirder than You Think*

R OY LAY ON THE rock-hard slab that passed for a bed in the brig of the *TCF Hydrus*. There wasn't much else for him to do. The *Hydrus* was based on a Draxon design, and while the rest of the ship had been altered to convey a more comfortable Terran quality, they'd kept the Draxon's cold, efficient, Spartan aesthetic intact for the brig.

He'd tried to make a run for it. There had been no other option. He'd hoped to lose them by passing close to the local star, mask his ship in the EM radiation until he jumped, but they'd seen that coming. The heavy cruiser had forced him out of sub-transit before he was halfway there, then reduced his engines to their component parts. The buggers wanted him alive.

At the time, he didn't know if that was a good thing or really bad. He was tempted to overload the reactor and blow the ship up out of spite, but in the end, self-preservation won out. Opportunities had a way of appearing if you waited long enough.

It wasn't hard to piece together what must have happened. The Orijen brothers figured out who he was but had taken a more circuitous path to revenge. It was his own fault, really. He'd given himself away when he crushed the one brother's hand into a bloody pulp. As a rule, cyborgs didn't leave the ranks of the Terran Colony Fleet, let alone join up with pirates. They had correctly guessed that the Silver Legion would have an active interest in his whereabouts.

He gave them points for cleverness and would tell them that if their paths ever crossed again and he disposed of them in an equally clever way. But that was a problem for another day.

Today's problem was walking into the brig, along with an armed escort. The bitch wore a smug grin on her face, like she'd just caught the biggest fish in the lake. The fact that they had once served together didn't help matters.

"Sub-Commander Hadar," she said. "This is a surprise."

"Former," Roy corrected, sitting up. "And it's Herzog now. I'm not part of your little cult anymore, remember, Camile?"

"*Commander* Miram," she corrected. "And you haven't been officially stripped of your rank. Though I can't imagine why."

"Because you guys lack imagination," said Roy. "You always have. The Fleet wants to make an example of me. Make a spectacle of it. Dressing down ceremony, followed by a kangaroo court."

"Perhaps," Miram conceded. "Symbols are important, and you certainly have become one of those."

"Just not the kind you want, huh?"

"As you say. I suppose I can see why dealing with you publicly would be a priority. If it was up to me, I'd space you and delete your records."

"I bet you would."

"Nothing personal. Just efficient."

"Like always."

There was an uneasy silence between the two. Finally, the commander waved off her security detail and the guards in the brig. Once they were alone, she dropped her formal tone, just a little. "Why couldn't you have just disappeared? When the Legion heard you'd taken up with the Brotherhood, they wanted to launch a full-scale invasion of Ramede. *Just* to get to you."

Roy finally got up off his bunk. "I'm flattered."

"Don't be. This isn't going to end well, and there's not much I can do to stop it."

Roy felt the slightest twinge of guilt, but it quickly passed. "Spare me, Commander. I don't regret my choices, and I'll live by the consequences. I don't need your sympathy."

The commander shook her head. "Still the same old Hadar. Stubborn as ever."

"Still the same old Miram," Roy countered. "What is it you want, Cam? You said there isn't *much* you can do. Which means there is something, and you're trying to ease me into agreeing to whatever it is. So let's cut the crap, shall we?"

"Very well," said the commander. "It's simple. There is a smuggling operation we are trying to crack down on. You know the Void Brotherhood far better than we do. Provide us with the intelligence we require during our mission, and it will go a long way in your favour."

"Stab them in the back, huh?"

"You have experience in that department."

"And what's in it for me?"

"I'll spin events to make you out as a deep cover operative—so deep not even the Triumvirate was aware of your actions."

Interesting angle. "Think they'll buy it?"

"Probably not. But it might sow enough doubt in their minds that they won't want to compound the error by having you executed. There's a chance they might see some virtue in playing along to save face. I believe the best-case scenario is you'll be drummed out of the Legion and exiled. Which is what you want, anyway."

"And the worst?"

"Lifetime imprisonment at one of the Sol mining operations."

"Lifetime? To the best of my knowledge, none of us have died of old age."

"None of us have committed treason before, either."

"Treason? Is that what they're calling it?"

The commander took a beat to answer. "Yes."

"Like no synth has ever cut and run from the Fleet's grand plan before."

"You're a cyborg," Miram countered. "We have to be held to a higher standard."

"I'm a deserter, at best."

"You killed a man to do it."

Roy scoffed. "A freeborn. Since when do they matter?"

"They matter more than you realize," said Miram.

What was *that* supposed to mean? He decided it wasn't important. Not right now, anyway. "All right. Now the real question: Why help me at all? We were never that close."

If the commander was hurt by that statement, she didn't show it. "That may be so. But I did consider us friends once. And right now, you're my best option. I've spearheaded this operation for six months and am no closer to accomplishing my objectives. I need your help, and I prefer this option to interrogation and torture."

Roy chuckled. "Nothing personal. Just efficient, huh?"

"As you say."

Miram always had been a bit of a soft touch. Roy walked up to the brig's energy barrier, tilting his head playfully. "So, are you going to let me out of here? Let me polish up the old Legion uniform and practice a few salutes?"

Commander Miram laughed. "Not a chance. Whether you call yourself Hadar or Herzog, you're the most dangerous person I've ever brought on board. Don't think for a second I'm going to treat you any other way."

The DNI list Moss had acquired was current but had one major failing: no set timetables. It had never been meant to be used to track down ships, after all, but as a reference in case certain ships showed up in certain parts of space. Ships on the list weren't required to provide specifics, just their basic cargo, general route, and major stops.

Therefore, their first job in tracking down the *Maruma* was to find a place they had docked at earlier and learn how long ago they had been there. Use that as a baseline for how far they had gotten. Alternately, they could jump ahead to somewhere the ship hadn't arrived at yet and wait.

Moss decided to head to a station near the far end of the Void, about halfway along the *Maruma's* route. The move wasn't without risk, because it happened to be right on the edge of Ramede space, a small bubble of territory the Void Brotherhood effectively claimed as their home.

It was times like this that Moss reflected on the kind of mess a bureaucracy like the Protectorate could be. Even after she'd read up on the subject, Hel couldn't wrap her head around it.

"So the pirates made Ramede their home and there's nothing the government can do about it?" She was sitting in the upper cockpit, talking through the comm.

"Which government?" asked Moss. "The Void by design belongs to no one. It's a gap between territories to help prevent border disputes."

"Yeah, but it's still within the Protectorate, right?"

"Sure, but none of the High Council members can lay a claim to anything inside it."

"But pirates can?"

"Of course not. But when a species reaches transit-level tech and makes contact, there's a big question mark about what to do with them. They need room to grow and develop, and that takes resources. But what do you do if they're already located in Hopat or Nubra space? The big boys already technically own all the space around them. So the Protectorate agreed that any species which became interstellar should be given a forty-three light-year sphere of influence around their homeworld in which they have absolute control."

"Why forty-three?"

"Forty-three-point-two-yadda-yadda, really. Conversion from Galactic Standard. The speed of light might be a constant, but a year isn't. Anyway, these rules were established long ago, when new space-faring species cropping up were super rare. But in the last five hundred years, there's been an explosion of them, humans included, and the government is struggling to catch up."

"So the Ramede people... Ramedeans?"

"Yeah."

"The Ramedeans achieved interstellar travel, made contact with the Protectorate, and were given this forty-three light-year bubble of space to use as they see fit, only it's in the Void. Then the Brotherhood just swoops in and takes over?"

"Take over? They were *invited*. Being in the Void meant that they couldn't make any official trade deals with the Draxon or the Nubra. That included tech advancements. They were worried they'd be stuck in their little bubble for centuries. So the Brotherhood offered to provide them with modern ships, tech, and weapons in exchange for a safe haven for their people, and anyone who would like to join them."

"So, when did they take over?"

"Never did. Technically, they're consultants and contractors. And technically, it's all above board and out of the Protectorate's hands. They've been bogged down in legalities for decades trying to deal with it."

"That's messed up."

"That's nothing compared to how Sol got screwed over. We didn't even get a bubble."

"So I read. How did *that* happen?"

"Bureaucracy's a bitch, kid. Okay, we're coming up on Triolina. Request docking clearance and prepare to look like trash."

Triolina didn't have a proper space station in orbit yet, though one was being constructed near the larger of its two moons. It was a habitable world, barely so when it was first settled, but now far more comfortable thanks to some "acquired" terraforming tech scattered along the equator. It was a small planet, little more than a moon itself, and as such, its gravity was only half that of what Moss and Hel were used to.

Its main trade port was located on the southern continent, which also passed as a tourist spot because the waves there could get crazy high at times, due to the low gravity and twin moons. The main structures in the city center were a strange synthesis of angular Draxon prefabs—chosen for their practicality and low cost—flared up with Ramedean aesthetics, adding curves whenever possible. More traditional dome shaped homes could be seen in the suburbs as the population expanded.

While Violet cracked wise about wretched hives of scum and villainy, it was really an ordinary bustling trade port like any other. It just happened to be in pirate space and as such had a much more relaxed approach to the buying and selling of goods.

And you were a fool to leave your ship unsecured.

And you shouldn't go into town without a well-armed escort.

So, yeah, scum and villainy.

The railgun Moss recently acquired certainly qualified him as well-armed, though that was really just for show. He played the muscle while Hel asked the questions. Trouble had wanted to come along, but Moss had accidentally locked it in the pantry's refrigerator and accidentally forgotten to tell anyone.

Asking about passing ships was a good way to attract unwanted attention, so the story was that they had been ripped off by the captain of the *Maruma* and wanted to settle the score. Revenge was something people in these parts could relate to and, oddly enough, less suspicious than inventing a more legitimate story.

Their inquiries led them to an old Ramedean woman's warehouse, located near one of the larger docking bays.

It was a matter of some debate as to why so many species in the galaxy resembled one another. The Elysians, Nubra, and Draxon, for example, had enough human-like qualities to be relatable, even attractive to one another, and many of the younger species exhibited similar physical traits.

There were also those that were truly alien, ranging from bizarre to nightmarish, and they were difficult to have any kind of social contact with. Some people spent their lives trying to establish effective dialogue between them and didn't always succeed. Moss imagined trying to communicate with a giant squid would be easier in some cases.

Then there were those in between, those that possessed some humanoid traits, yet differed strongly in others. The kind of aliens you'd see on one of Violet's "monster of the week" shows featuring a madman in a flying telephone booth. The two other key Protectorate species, the Hopat and Ugaro, fell into that category, as did the Ramedeans.

The owner of the warehouse had deep orange skin that was like a bad spray-on tan, but other than her bipedal nature, little about her resembled a human. Big eyes with no lids and no discernable pupils, three holes for a nose, and a mouth that was more like a sucker, which meant Ramedeans spoke GalCom with a distinctive whistling tone.

"I will not help you," she said. Hel looked at Moss, not knowing how to handle this.

Moss shrugged. "At least she's honest." But this direct refusal was a bit baffling. Everything had a price in a town like this, and here they were talking to the one being with a sense of professional pride. The fact he was wielding a hip-braced assault weapon didn't seem to impress her in the least. Hel tried for a bribe, which impressed her even less.

Moss put a finger to his ear. "Any suggestions, Vi?"

"Not sure," Violet said from the ship. "You don't deal with honest traders all that often."

"Very funny."

Hel had heard Violet's reply on her own earpiece. "That gives me an idea," she said, then spoke to the woman in GalCom. "I will be honest with you. We know what is on that ship. The captain has deceived you. It is carrying slaves to sell in Draxon space. We wish to stop them."

Moss tried not to have a fit. Was she nuts? But to his surprise, the woman's eyes widened into two black pools and her mouth constricted into a tight O.

"They have lied?"

"Yes."

Her eyes narrowed to tiny dots. "I will help."

"Imagine that," said Violet. "Honesty turns out to be the best policy. Maybe you could learn a thing or two from this, flyboy."

Moss tried not to laugh.

It was really, *really* hard.

Hel couldn't believe what she was seeing.

When Moss got the information he was looking for, he'd told Hel they would leave in a few hours. They had only just missed the *Maruma* and judging from what he learned about the ship, it had a much slower transit drive than the *Rex*. It wouldn't reach its next stop for another day or so.

Moss figured it would be best to intercept the ship between its stops to reduce the chances of anyone picking up a distress signal. He also didn't want to attract suspicion by following close behind on its sensors. That meant Hel had a bit of time to explore this world. An *alien* world.

Having grown up on a generation ship, Hel had only ever known other humans. And up until now she'd always been in space, on space stations, or inside colony domes. This was the first time she'd ever been on a *truly* alien world, one where she could breathe the air and see the residents go about their daily lives.

She saw a massive group of Ramedean children being ushered along by what she hoped was a teacher and not their only parent. The curved buildings sometimes had posters plastered on them advertising various kinds of entertainment, though it wasn't clear to Hel if it was live or recorded. Merchants whistled greetings, holding up various products for sale and tried to entice them to enter their shops. Strange savoury smells came and went as they passed by dome-shaped restaurants, where the tradition seemed to be for the cooks to work under a covered tent on the roof while the customers gathered inside.

"Bored yet?" Moss asked.

"Hardly," said Hel. "You are?"

"Eh, a little. Restaurants look nice, though."

Hel sighed and shook her head. "What happened to your sense of wonder?"

"Kid, I've been to a lot of worlds. They stop being strange after a while."

"Stop calling me kid. I'm twenty-six. You're not *that* much older than me."

Moss hid a smile. "I'm older than I look."

"Yeah, Violet said the same thing once."

Moss frowned. "She did? She's lying. You're *way* older than her, even when she was alive."

"Wait, what? I saw what she used to look like. She had to be in her thirties."

"Sure. But Violet was a synth. They grow up fast. Chronologically, she was only fifteen when she..." His voice trailed off.

"How'd she die?" Hel asked.

Moss's face hardened, and suddenly he did look a lot older than her. He looked over to what seemed to be an open air tavern. "Let's see if they carry anything we can metabolize."

Hel knew better than to press the matter. Moss had a tendency to complain about everything, but when it came to certain subjects, like Violet, there was a genuine pain she could sense.

Moss discovered that alcohol was another thing their species shared with the locals and set about sampling their wares. He was eager to change the subject.

"Like I said, you go to enough strange worlds, and the strangeness starts to blur together. The younger races end up adopting traits from the older Protectorate species. I look around and I see Draxon prefabs, merchants wearing imported Elysian knockoffs, and Nubran-style entertainment being advertised. The more you travel, the easier it gets to feel at home no matter where you are."

"Well, the least you can do is let me enjoy the newness of it all. I've got plenty of time to get dried up and cynical like you."

Moss raised the glass he was currently testing in a salute. "Touché."

When they returned to the hanger, there was an uncomfortably large number of people lurking around his ship. They weren't the dock workers he'd hired to touch up the ship's paint job. He wanted the *Rex* pitch black for the raid, yet for some reason they'd highlighted it with touches of green. Typical Moss luck. He raised a hand to hold Hel back, and the two ducked behind a wall.

"What is it?" asked Hel.

"Dunno, but I don't like it. Violet? What's going on? Why didn't you tell me you're surrounded?"

"What? Them?" Violet responded over the comm. "They're nobody. Transpotters."

Hel gave Moss a look. "Transport watchers," Moss explained. "Some people are desperate for a hobby."

"They're all confused," Violet added. "Can't agree on what to classify me as. I tuned out about an hour ago. As long as they abide by strip club rules, they can gawk all they want."

Moss rolled his eyes. "Oh brother. How'd they even get in?"

"Not sure, but it's clearly not their first time."

Moss was tempted to rush in and shoo them away with a broom, but it occurred to him he might get a bit of information out of them if he played his cards right. He transferred the massive railgun to Hel and pulled on his mask.

"The mask?" said Hel. "You brought that? Really?"

Moss shrugged. "I figured if we got into trouble, I might want a bit of anonymity."

Hel looked at the transpotters, who were bickering and pointing at their datapads. "Yeah, they look like *loads* of trouble."

"Yeah, well, tanspotters have good memories, so better safe than sorry."

Moss left his cover and confidently approached the bickering group, arms open wide.

"Not your regular transport, is she?" he said warmly. "You guys trying to agree on what to classify her as?"

The group was made up of primarily Ramedean males making notes on their datapads, but there were a couple of other local species present as well—if you considered local to be indigenous to a world within a thousand light years of here. There was a large Charon male present who really didn't fit in with the crowd—dressed like a pilot, built like a wrestler, and looking like he had far too much money on his hands.

One of the Ramedeans nodded and pointed to the centre mass of his ship. "The bulk is clearly of Nubra design. Arcadia class. Yet the maneuvering thrusters are Draxon, are they not?"

Moss nodded. "That's right."

"But the cockpit is Elysian?" another in the back peeped.

"Also right. She's a chimera."

"What class of ship is Chimera? Who makes it?"

Moss furrowed his eyebrows. "It's not really a class. It means it's made up of a bunch of other ships. Patched together." He interlaced his fingers together as if that would help demonstrate what he meant.

The group looked at one another, confused, and Moss wondered if their adaptive translators were working. He explained it again, this time in GalCom.

"They do not understand," said the large, golden-skinned Charon. "I do not think a ship like this has ever come this way before. They are in awe."

Aside from his golden skin and silver eyes, the pilot looked basically human. Heck, he looked like he should be holding a sword over his head on a mid-twentieth century sci-fi cover, back when people still thought Mars might be inhabited. Given their famously concupiscent nature, there'd be a half naked woman draped around his legs too.

Somewhat appropriately, the Charon's voice came through his translator in a very formal manner. "You may have created a schism within this once peaceful group."

"Yeah, well, they can continue to bask in my mediocrity until I'm ready for takeoff." Moss looked at the group of transpotters, whose bickering had renewed into high-pitched hoots. It seemed some were now insisting on adding a chimera classification to their lists and others saying it should be ignored because it was not a proper ship. Give it a few years and it might become a holy war.

"You wear a mask," the Charon noted. "It seems familiar somehow."

Moss tried to derail any chance of him mentioning Ranger M. "It's a wrestling mask," he said. "Just came from a big match."

"Ah, a fellow gladiator! On my world, my name was once—"

Moss pulled the Charon aside to talk to him privately. "Look, sorry to interrupt, but what's *your* interest in my ship?" he asked. "You're not here cataloging them."

The man smiled. "No, but I am fascinated by them. I followed this group as they snuck inside, curious as to what had them so excited. Then I saw this..." He waved his hand at the *Viaticus Rex II.I.*

"Yeah, well, keep your comments to yourself," said Moss.

"I think she is beautiful."

"Let the man talk," Violet said over the comm.

The Charon didn't hear her but continued to nod at the ship appreciatively. "Is she for sale?"

Moss groaned. Why? Why now? He had this guy pegged. Rich pilot with more money and muscle than sense, looking for the unusual and exotic and a quick thrill. On the regular market he wouldn't be able to sell the *Rex* for much, but to this rube? He could have gotten enough to buy a proper ship fresh off the printers. Transferring Violet over would have been easy.

Except he had the *Maruma* to think about. He needed *this* ship. By now he'd sunk a fair bit of money into the *Rex* and knew exactly what she was capable of. He didn't have time to get another ship, upgrade it, and get used to its flight design. Not to mention Hel was still new to piloting.

And, loathed though he was to admit it, he was getting attached to the hunk of junk.

"I'm afraid not."

"A pity. A ship so unique would stand out, more so than the luxury ship I currently pilot. It is... rugged. I like that. I would be the envy of my friends. There are women who would offer themselves as sacrifice upon my bed to fly in her."

Wow, things must work way *different over in Charon.* Moss sensed an opportunity, however. "You know, I can tell you where you can get your own. Top quality chimera, custom made by some of the best engineers in or out of the Void."

The Charon's silver eyes widened with interest and he held out his hand, palm up in greeting. "Terik Dared."

Moss blinked as he put his hand on top of Terik's. Had he heard that name before? "Maurice Foote. But you can call me Moss."

Roy lay back on his slab, staring at the energy field keeping him inside the brig. Occasionally it would shimmer or flare a little, then settle back down. He looked for patterns in these, both in their timing and the shape they took, though not because he expected to find a weakness he could exploit. There was none. He was just bored.

It had been days since Commander Miram had spoken with him, and there had been no indication as to when they'd talk again. In fact, there had been no indication as to what kind of questions she wanted to ask, other than it having to do with the Void Brotherhood.

He had a few guesses as to what was going on. Miram was probably telling the truth about smuggling, but smuggling was a broad term. If she really was after smugglers, they were probably getting stuff into Draxon space, rather than out. The Draxon Collective were more restrictive when it came to imports, and some of the younger races that finally made it into space learned to their chagrin that it was difficult to get their hands on various items the other Protectorate species took for granted.

Luxury goods were a safe bet. They weren't illegal, but heavily taxed, because the Collective saw them as pointless frivolities. But the more he thought about it, the more he realized it could be anything. SplicePet kits from Eylsia, Hopat Muscle Milk, Nubran neuroprojectors... But why would the Collective be so intent on stopping people who wanted to avoid the taxman? You didn't hire the Silver Legion for petty police work. It had to be something else.

Then again, maybe things had changed since he'd left. It wouldn't be that surprising. The Terrans had no home in the galaxy and no voice in the Senate, yet their military had become one of the most respected independent contractors around. The very status that kept them from holding a seat in the Low Council gave them the freedom to work for whomever they wanted. As a result, they were sought after by just about everyone. Terrans were an endless source of contradictions, so what was one more to add to the pile?

The door to the brig opened and Commander Miram returned with her escort. She held a metal hoop in her hand, big enough to go around someone's neck.

"If it's Valentine's Day, I think I'm the one who's supposed to give out jewellery," Roy said.

The barrier screen of the brig had two layers, and the first one shut down with a flicker. Miram set down the collar and backed away. The screen went up again and the screen closest to Roy went down.

"Put it on," said the commander.

Roy picked it up. The polite name for it was a bondscollar. The accurate name was a slaver collar. He'd seen plenty of them in the Brotherhood. Your typical disciplinary/termination device, depending on how you wanted to use it.

"Just my size," said Roy. "However did you know?"

"Sub-Commander Roy Hadar, as of this moment, you have been assigned to the *TCF Hydrus* as Roy Herzog. Your movements will be monitored and access to the ship will be restricted. You will keep to your quarters unless called upon, and whenever you leave those quarters, you will be escorted. Any violation of these terms will be grounds for immediate disciplinary action, up to and including termination. Do you understand?"

Roy looked Miram dead in the eye and slapped the collar around his neck. "Whatever. Just let me out of here."

Best Laid Plans

One danger of firing kinetic weapons inside of a ship is the possibility of breaching the hull. As a result, most ships favour energy weapons for their boarding parties. Pulse Guns are a generic term for such weapons. The actual mechanics vary from place to place, ranging from simple lasers to weapons that fire packets of super-charged plasma contained within an electromagnetic bubble that splashes open upon hitting the target, cooking the meat inside or frying the electronics. The idea is universal, however—sending lots of energy down range without blowing a hole in the ship.

Pulse guns usually refer to pistol sized weapons, while pulse rifles are larger two-handed weapons. Pulse cannons can either refer to stationary heavy support weapons on the ground, or the larger weapons mounted on ships.

M. Foote, *Portrait of the Pilot as a Cranky Ol' Man*

MOSS TOOK COVER BEHIND a large crate about half his own height. Blue pulses of energy whizzed overhead and smacked against the wall at the end of the corridor, leaving an orange glow against the metal.

That was close.

He raised his pulse gun over the cover and sprayed fire randomly down the hall, and only then peeked his head up to see if he could actually get a clear shot at someone. When he saw nobody, he took aim and waited for an unlucky face to pop around the corner. Moss tapped his ear to contact Hel.

"How you doing up there?" She was supposed to be clearing out the upper deck while he took care of the lower.

"I count three hostiles. They're packed in close to the cockpit. Got me pinned. You?"

"I saw two—" Just then a head peeked around the corner and a moment later it vaporized in a blue mist. "Make that one. You need help?"

"I think I got this," she said.

Moss figured if he could make his way to the end of this deck, he could work his way to the upper level and catch Hel's targets in a crossfire. He had picked up an extra pulse pistol from one of the fallen guards, but he wasn't about to fire both at the same time, like in one of Violet's old Hong Kong action movies. He took a small orb from his belt and gave it a hard squeeze for a two count. It made a piercing whine as he tossed it down the corridor, bouncing it off the wall so it went around the corner.

It blew with a blinding flash, and a guard in standard protective gear staggered into view. Moss cut him down and hurried down to the other end, quickly checking the corner in case there had been another threat still disoriented by the blast.

"Can I get to the upper level this way?" he asked Violet.

"Looks like it."

"You seeing anything that can help?"

"Negative. Just the three targets on the upper floor that have Hel pinned down. You better hurry."

Moss made his way down to the end of the side corridor, where there was a narrow shaft with an access ladder. He bounded up, peeking over the lip once at the top, and only advanced when he didn't get shot at.

"Almost there, Hel. Hang tight."

Moss hurried to where the main corridor spanned the length of the ship. If he'd read things right, he'd end up behind the guards Hel was taking on. He peeked around the corner and saw at least two with their backs exposed to him.

"Perfect." He raised his pistol and took aim, only to hear Hel call out. "Got one in my sights," and looked up just in time to see Hel at the far end, aiming at him.

"Not"—a blue flash filled his vision, and he was back in the cockpit of the *Rex*—"me."

He heard over the comms. "Whoops…"

Moss disconnected his suit's haptic link from the chair and got up. "Yeah, *whoops*. Violet, kick Hel out of the sim. Hel, get your ass down here."

Most ships had a virtual rig of some sort worked into their systems, which made longer journeys easier to tolerate. It wasn't hard to integrate the necessary technology into their flight suits, allowing pilots to plug right into their seats once a course was set, and zone out until they reached their destination.

Hel climbed down the ladder from her half of the cockpit, looking sheepish. "Sorry, boss."

"Sorry? You shot me in the *head*."

"I didn't know it was you."

"I told you I was coming."

"Yeah, but you had us fighting humans, and they all kinda looked like you. I just saw another target taking aim."

Moss groaned.

"Hey, it's not like I'm a soldier or anything."

"That's why we're practicing now."

"Yeah, about that. I can't help but find your training a little suspicious."

"What do you mean?"

"The program is *literally* called Space Pirate Simulator. What am I supposed to make of that?"

Moss waved a hand. "That's just a name. It's one of the best combat trainers I could get. Violet will back me up on that."

"He's right," said Violet, "It was originally just a simpit arcade game, but a bunch of mods came out that made it one of the most realistic combat sims civilians can buy."

"If anything, that worries me more," said Hel. "I thought this was a rescue mission. I thought we were supposed to take this ship without killing anyone."

"Ideally, yes," said Moss. "Most traders aren't stupid. They know there's a good chance that if we get what we want, we'll let them live. But if they fight, they're probably going to get killed. You saw how quickly I surrendered before, right?"

"Yeah, but you're kind of a coward."

Moss waved his arms, displaying the glorious goods that made up Maurice Foote. "And here I am, still alive. At the end of the day, unless you're truly desperate, it's not worth dying for your cargo."

"So, why are we training like this?"

"Because they might turn out to be truly desperate. Or Draxon. Drones don't really have a sense of self preservation, just the unit. That reminds me, Violet, set up the next run to use a Draxon crew, just in case. At least that way Hel won't accidentally shoot me in the face."

"Yeah, but what about when we actually board the ship? We'll have no idea what we're up against. Could be anyone."

Moss frowned, then reached under his control panel and retrieved his Ranger M luchador mask. He'd tried to throw it away a dozen times, yet always ended up holding onto it. Sometimes it came in handy. Like now.

"Fine. When we go in, I'll be wearing this. Whatever you do, don't shoot the guy with the green and red mask. Got it?"

The *Maruma* was a Messenia-class Nubra transport, intended for use on safe and reliable trade routes. It had rudimentary defenses, designed to discourage direct boarding while whatever ships were flying support dealt with the actual threat at hand. And this ship was travelling from the Ramede bubble inside the Void toward Draxon space, all on its own.

It was the ship's own damn fault someone like Moss was jumping on it. Once he was through with them, the crew could gather their wits, get a ride home, grab a drink, thank their lucky stars they were all still alive, and learn from their mistakes.

When you stopped to think about it, he was providing them with a valuable life lesson. Someday they'd thank him.

In the psychiatric biz, this was what they called rationalizing. Sure, it was hard to call stealing from pirates *bad*, but there was always a difference between being on the defensive and offensive side of a battle. Also, there were plenty of pilots based out of Ramede space that weren't part of the Brotherhood but had to pay the dues and fly the flag if they wanted to earn a living. It was a crappy situation to find yourself in, and Moss was well acquainted with crappy situations. He was going to have to walk a careful line if he expected to get a good night's sleep after this.

Then there was the matter of what he would do when Hel and Violet found out that the ship was actually carrying mining equipment, just like the manifest said. His linguistic gymnastics would have to be of Olympic quality when that ship came into port.

But the money this haul would bring could let them settle in on the opposite side of Protectorate space, and he'd gladly spend the next year apologizing to them both, so long as he could suck on something resembling Mai Tais on an Elysian resort while doing it.

For now, all that mattered was focusing on the mission. That meant he was taking a nap in the pilot's chair while Violet kept an eye on things with the ship on minimal power. All the lights were off, and both he and Hel were breathing off the oxygen reserves of their flight suits.

It was almost impossible for combat to occur at transit levels of speed. The faster you went past the speed of light, the stronger your transit field was, and the harder it was to destabilize. The other problem was creating weapons that could travel at those same speeds. As a result, almost all space combat happened in-system, where the local star's gravity well forced ships to drop to sub-transit speeds, and pulse cannons could still be used. Hit a ship's transit bubble enough and it collapsed, forcing them back to normal space. That's when things got ugly.

But overall, travelling between systems was safe and uneventful. With the exception of the almost mythical greywalkers laying energy webs for unwary traders, or a military-grade gravity beacon, there was nothing to fear when travelling from A to B. Nothing out there could stop you.

Unless you convinced them to stop.

About fifty kilometres away, the *Viaticus Rex II.I*'s newly acquired shuttle sat motionless, though not inactive. Every system was cranked up and its powerplant was close to overloading, putting out a greater energy signature than was typical for its size. Its communication systems were broadcasting a distress call on all frequencies.

Violet felt this trick only had a ten percent chance of working. Moss was more optimistic, and put it closer to twenty. If it didn't work, they'd have to try and intercept the ship at the next system—and that meant the possibility of dealing with the local ProSec authorities. But out here? Between systems? They'd be long gone before anyone else arrived.

Moss's reasons for believing this would work were simple. Curiosity plus greed. Sure, there was a chance the captain of the *Maruma* might be a genuine good Samaritan, but he put the odds much higher that he was an opportunistic douchebag. The pilot was clearly pretty cocky about his own safety if he was flying without an escort. Probably felt being on the DNI list was like holding a golden ticket.

"I have a ship dropping out of transit, about a hundred klicks away," said Violet. "Messenia-class."

Moss stirred awake. "Power up the ship. Hel, you ready?"

"Roger that. Let's get this scumbucket."

The *Maruma* was already turning about, having spotted the trap and trying to get some distance between it and the *Rex*. The trick was to hit it fast and hard before they could jump back to transit. Any damage would do, so long as it prevented a transit field from forming.

"Hel, power to weapons. Pulse cannons and forward laser only." The *Rex* also carried a missile pod, but this was about disabling the ship, not turning it into a drifting pile of scrap metal.

"Weapons charged," Hel called from above. "The *Maruma's* turrets are targeting us."

Moss allowed himself a grin. "This is where the fun begins."

As Hel had pointed out, he was by nature a coward. But that didn't mean he wasn't a damn good pilot. The *Maruma* had a turret on the top and bottom of the ship, which meant it was easy to stay in the blind spot of one at all times. He maneuvered the *Rex* to provide a harder target to hit, all the while peppering the back of the ship with pulse cannon fire, weakening their shield.

While there's no sound in space, fighting deaf was an unnecessary handicap. Most ships had audio suites that provided sound to give pilots better situational awareness. Somewhere between the sounds of his pulse cannons firing and incoming return fire, he thought he heard the *Rex* get dinged.

"How are our shields?"

"Just a scratch," said Hel. But, because Moss asked, the universe saw fit to smack them with a direct hit after that, with a flash that filled his field of view. "Sorry, make that seventy percent. Still good."

Moss burned past the freighter and came about, raking the ship in a strafing run as they jousted past each other. Both ships took hits, but the Rex had more weapons trained on it.

"Their shields are almost down," said Violet. "You'll want to ease up a bit."

"Roger that," said Moss. "Give the main laser everything we got and dump the rest into shields."

"Already done," said Hel.

The *Rex*'s laser was too large to have any kind of gimbal system. It required the pilot to line up a shot manually. But it was also a more powerful and focused weapon, and right now that was what he needed.

The *Rex* turned and pitched so that it came at the *Maruma* directly from the port side. This exposed him to both the freighter's turrets, but that was okay. He was going for the kill shot, targeting the engines. His shields flashed blue as pulses of energy splashed against it, but Moss held the ship steady until the reticle lined up just right. He held down the trigger and...

"*Pew! Pew! Pew!*" Violet cried out, replacing the automated audio cues.

The laser broke through the shield and drilled a hole right through one exposed engine and straight into the other. The engines briefly flared and went dark, leaving the ship to drift dead in space.

"*Ba-room!*" said Violet. "*Psssshhh!*"

"Nice shot!" said Hel. "The sound effects were a bit anti-climactic, though."

Violet was unapologetic. "I could say that the situational awareness software was damaged in that last hit, but I'd be lying. I just thought it was funny."

"Yeah, well, that was the easy part," said Moss. "Now it gets serious. Hel, meet me by the airlock. Violet, hail the *Maruma* and tell them to power down the ship and prepare to be boarded." He pulled out his Ranger M mask from under the control panel. "Be intimidating, but reasonable. If we're lucky, we won't have to fight anyone."

Moss and Hel used their EVA packs to bridge the gap between ships. He didn't want a physical tether set up until he was sure it was secure. He'd considered breeching the hull near the engineering level, but it turned out Violet was able to communicate with the transport rather easily. With her help, they overrode one of the airlocks and got inside.

"Have we got a welcoming party on the other side?" Moss asked as the airlock pressurized. Neither of them would take off their helmets until they were safely inside the ship itself. He took a round flashbang grenade from his suit's harness and held it ready.

"Negative," said Violet. "I see nobody."

He put the flashbang back on his harness. "Good."

"No, bad. I see *nobody*."

"What? You mean on the whole ship?" Hel asked.

"They've got some kind of interference running. It's blocking out normal scans for life signs."

Moss frowned as the pressurization lights signalled they could enter. "Great. They intend to fight."

"I'll try some other things," said Violet. "In the meantime, you two be careful."

Moss looked at the door to the ship, then to Hel. "So, how do you want to do this?"

"Open it a crack, fire wildly down the hall, toss the grenade, then run like hell?" At Hel's insistence, their pistols had been set to fire non-lethal charges, which was fine by him just in case he was shot in the face again. But it also meant they'd have to secure anyone they took down, and that might leave them vulnerable.

"Works for me. There's a sub-corridor we can use for cover about five meters from this door. Follow my lead."

Moss opened the door and Hel opened fire. Moss followed suit and fired blindly down the other direction. With his free hand, he took the grenade and tossed down the hall. When it went off, he bolted for where he knew the sub-corridor to be, Hel following behind.

They took up defensive positions braced against either side of the hall. "See anyone?" asked Hel.

"Nope. Violet?"

"Still no readings, but I've got a visual. One person in the cockpit. He's loading up a big gun. Looks like a heavy pulse rifle."

Moss took off his helmet. He already had his silly wrestling mask on underneath. The way he saw it, if there were any cameras on board recording this heist, why not go old school to hide his identity?

"Swell." He knew where the cockpit was from here, but no idea if anyone else was waiting along the way. He sighed. "Screw it."

He ran back down the main corridor, firing at the spots most likely to have someone return fire from. He primed another flashbang and threw it, bouncing it off the wall so it fell around the corner and out of his immediate sight. Still, he looked away when it blew. The entrance to the cockpit should be right around the corner.

Moss and Hel took the corner together, but instead of seeing a blind and deaf captain wielding heavy artillery, they found him lying face down on the ground, just outside the cockpit door. Moss almost fired, but the way his arms were splayed out, he wasn't going anywhere. His long, light grey hair made it look like someone had dropped a bowl of pasta on his head.

"What the…?"

"Cover me," Hel said. She stepped over and kicked the weapon away from the old pilot, who was dressed in strangely familiar garb. It wasn't a Brotherhood outfit. It was civilian, but still, something about it…

She checked the man's pulse, noticing the backpack-like object worked into his clothes. A wing pouch. "He's Elysian," she noted. "He's dead."

"You kidding me? That was just a flashbang."

"Might have been a heart attack," Hel reasoned. "He looks pretty old."

"Sucks to be him, I guess. Take his rifle. If nobody else is in the cockpit, we can check the computer and see how many others are on board. All clear, Vi?"

"No visuals," said Violet, "But still no readings."

Inside the *Maruma*'s cockpit, they learned that DeadGuy McBig-Gun out in the hall was the only crewmember on board. The *Viaticus Rex* didn't really need a copilot, but this ship was bigger than his. He'd at least expected an engineer on board, or gunners for the turrets.

"That explains why he tried to hide the life signs," said Hel. "Didn't want us to know he was all alone. But why risk flying solo?"

"Automation is a wonderful thing. It means you don't have to share your profits with as many people." Moss suddenly brightened up and clapped his hands together. "Well, that was easy. Let's go to find our prize."

"You're calling slaves a prize?" said Hel.

Moss checked himself. "You know what I mean. Come on, can't keep them waiting."

The cargo bay on board the *Maruma* was located in the rear, close to the engines. The damage report had shown it to be intact. Despite the computer's assurances that they were the only ones left alive on board, they covered each other as they scaled the length of the ship, just to be safe.

They reached the entrance to the cargo bay, which turned out to require a hand scan to open.

"Ugh." Moss groaned, pulling out a small laser cutter from his belt. "Back in a minute."

Hel's eyes widened. "You're not going to...?"

"It's not like he needs it anymore!"

"It's disrespectful!"

"You wanna drag the whole body back here? 'Cause I don't."

"Guys!" Violet interrupted. "You can knock off the ghoulishness. I just checked the manual. Shut down the main reactor from the cockpit. On a Messenia transport, if you reboot the system, the cargo doors automatically unlock."

Moss weighed the options. "Eh, it'll be a little bit faster, I guess. Be right back."

Hel grabbed his arm, shooting daggers from her eyes. "*I'll* do it. I don't trust you." She let go and ran back toward the cockpit.

Moss smiled as she left. Yeah, she had him pegged. It would have been worth getting the hand just to see the look on her face. Still, this way, he would be here when the system rebooted and the doors opened. By the time she got back, he wouldn't have to pretend to be in shock at the big revelation. He turned off his comms for a moment.

"Guess I was wrong, Hel," he practiced. "Might as well make the best of it." He tried a different tone. "No point in letting all this go to waste, right?" He also had to assume that Hel wouldn't buy it for a second. "Look, yes, I lied, but so what? This mining equipment is going to make us rich."

The lights went off and red emergency panels lit up. He felt the loss of gravity briefly. Then the lights came back up again and gravity returned. The control panel on the door beeped, reset, and hissed open.

"Bingo." He turned the comms back on. "Door's opening. Get back here, Hel."

Moss stepped inside and saw two dozen faces looking back at him. Men. Women. Children. All Terran.

They were dressed in regular clothes, if a bit shabby, and most looked like they hadn't had a proper shower in weeks. One teenager's jaw dropped as he pointed to Moss. "I told you he was real! It's Ranger M!"

"Ranger M?"

"I can't believe it!"

Hearing the name made just about everyone in the room excited, especially the children.

"Is Trouble with you?" asked a young girl.

"Did you stop the pirates?" a man asked. "Can we come out now?"

"Is the captain okay?" asked a woman. "Did he call you for help?"

"Are we safe now?"

"Are we still going to Haven?"

"How did you find us, Ranger M?"

"Thank you, Ranger M!"

Moss raised a hand to the mask he wore.

Oh no. No no. No no no. This can't be happening.

Hel finally made it back to the cargo bay. "Wow, there's more here than I thought!" She slapped him on the shoulder. "Looks like we did good, boss."

Moss finally found himself able to speak. "What... the... ffff—"

Familiar Faces

First gen synths were designed to weather the harsh realities of living off Earth. They were born fully grown with memories and skills directly implanted during the maturation process from the best Earth had to offer. They were effectively clones.

They also died very quickly. First gens were quickly phased out once the issue was discovered and corrected in the next generation of synth production.

And if you think this all sounds rather dehumanizing when talking about living people, good. You're paying attention.

M. Foote, *And Then Things Got Worse*

ALL THINGS CONSIDERED, ROY would rather be back in the brig. At least there he knew where he stood. Then again, a slaver collar that could blow your head off at the press of a button didn't leave a lot of room for misinterpretation.

The funny thing about that feature was that it was completely unnecessary... for most people. Roy could think of a dozen ways to get the same results without having to call the janitors afterward. The collars already shocked for disciplinary reasons, so getting it to stop your heart was one obvious choice, and easily done. The victim would drop dead without even knowing why. And if you're trying to instil fear by making an example of someone, well, you could overcharge the shock system until their brain became a baked potato and they died screaming.

With cyborgs, however, neither of those options would work, nor would poison or radiation, or any number of other ideas that came off the top of his head. Their nanotech would just repair the damage. But it couldn't regrow a head. So in his case, he supposed, it was a practical solution.

Still, deep down, he believed the reason the TCF used them was because they loved drama.

Roy looked around his room. Naturally, they'd put him in a lowly crewman's quarters. A raised bed could bend into a sofa. Large multi-function display on the facing wall. A single low sitting black table with equally low seats that tucked in perfectly beneath it. Discrete lighting that kept everything feeling warm and not sterile. Standard Legion fare, something a designer snob would have called *Nouveau Terran* if French had managed to survive as a language.

The Legion bought most of their ships from the Draxon, renowned for their combat capabilities, but lacking in any artistic beauty or comfort. So the Terrans spruced them up with Elysian features, who designed *everything* with beauty and comfort in mind. Only the Elysians kind of went overboard in that regard, so the Terrans pared it down to a more minimalist quality.

The result was something that was pleasing to the eye, but without unnecessary frills. This "reductive Elysian aesthetic" had become popular in a number of parts of the galaxy, especially Nubra space, which annoyed Elysian art critics to no end.

To Roy, however, it told a different story. What you saw here was a people in search of an identity. They wanted to reject the ways of those who had created them and dig deep into the past to find a core sense of being to strive for. They found it in the legions of Rome and the philosophers of Greece. They found it in the samurai of Japan and scholars of China. They found it the knights of Medieval England, and academics of Renaissance France.

They found fairy tales masquerading as history and wanted to make it real.

This was expressed everywhere you looked. The only painting in this crewman's quarters had a Rococo quality to it, even though it depicted a Legion heavy cruiser against a nebula backdrop. The shining Roman-esque breastplates the guards outside his door wore were as ceremonial as they were practical. The low sitting table here looked as though it had been designed for a quiet tea ceremony.

He sometimes wondered how much of this the Triumvirate had hashed out over a couple of weeks based on focus groups, and how much had grown organically from it after that. Didn't matter.

Roy went to the multi-function display and turned it on. It seemed they'd given him some limited access, at least. Entertainment channels were fine. Communications were offline. Records were offline. Most other data was heavily restricted, but he was able to find a basic guide to the ship's layout.

He scanned it briefly. The *Hydrus* had the same general layout as their other heavy cruisers. Good.

Assume ship complement is the same. Assume crew rotation schedule is the same.

Take out guards outside the door. Disable communications. Avoid killing to delay detection. Proceed through crewman decks. Find off duty crewman with engineering access. Disable. Use body's ident to access engineering hatchway in the far forward junction. Find access conduit for shipwide communications. Disable...

Roy shook his head. No. Detected. Commander alerted. Slave collar activated. *Boom*. Try again.

Take out guards outside the door. Disable communications. Avoid killing. Find crewman with bridge access. Proceed to captain's quarters... No. Proximity detection. Slave collar activated. *Boom*. Try again.

Take out guards. Disable communications. Work way toward escape pods. Override... No. Bridge alerted once activated. *Boom*.

Take out guards. Use communications to call commander for ambush. No. Voice print fails. *Boom*.

Take out guards outside the door. Kill them, take weapons. Fight way to engine room, kill as many of these sons of bitches as possible and blow the reactor before...

Roy tried to calm himself. It was too soon to be thinking about this. Escape required opportunity. Opportunity required both time and timing. Once those began to appear, then he could revisit this train of thought.

He decided to see what was on one of the entertainment channels. You could access whatever you wanted whenever you wanted, but there were several channels that showed a constant stream of entertainment at set intervals. He never really understood why, though. Probably tied to old Earth tradition.

Right now, a cartoon had just started. A bright green exploration ship darted across the screen, then the camera followed it toward a distant planet.

"One man dares to explore the wonders of our galaxy, seeking the unknown, and helping all in need. That man... is **Ranger M!***"*

"Of all the shows..." Roy muttered.

A Terran male in a red and green mask pointed dramatically down a ship's corridor. *"Let's go, Trouble! For the future!"*

Roy wondered if Commander Miram would complain much if he put his fist through the screen.

Karon carried the food tray down the corridor, ignoring the occasional look she got from a passing crewmember. Most people on the *Hydrus* ate in the mess hall, after all. It was bad enough she had been kicked out of her quarters because of their prisoner and forced to pair up with Dale from engineering, but she'd been tasked with delivering the prisoner his meals, too. She would have much rather been studying for her officer's exam.

Seeing two armed guards outside her door was going to be hard to get used to. She half expected some kind of surprise contraband search for sherb under her mattress.

She held up the tray. "Prisoner meal."

One of the guards chuckled. "You mean *VIP*, don't you?" That was his official designation on board. At least for now.

The other guard checked her ident against the list they had on their datapads and nodded. One sounded the bell on her lock, then opened the door.

Karon was shocked to see someone already standing there, as if he'd been waiting for the door to open. And for some reason, he seemed just as shocked to see her.

"Powell?"

Karon frowned. "Yeah?" She thought she'd gotten rid of her personal effects when she'd been relocated. How'd he know her last name?

Whatever had surprised him, he quickly shrugged it off. "Dinner already?"

She handed the tray over to him, not bothering to reply.

"Tray, two bowls, one plate, utensils," said the first guard, scanning the contents. "Make sure we get that all that back."

The prisoner set the tray down inside and raised a fist to his chest in a Legion salute, but managed to make it wildly sarcastic.

"Yes, sir. Wouldn't dream of stabbing you through the eye with that dull butter knife, sir."

Karon almost found that funny. "Try not to mess up my room too much, would ya? I want it back in one piece."

The prisoner's eyes rose. "*Your* room?"

The guard nudged Karon back into the hall. "That's enough." He pressed the door panel to his side, and the door closed.

Roy wasn't easily startled, but he had to admit, seeing Powell at the door like that had shaken him. Because Powell was dead.

The answer to this mystery was obvious. She wasn't Powell, just another synth based off the same template. The random elements of gene expression during maturation meant that synths grown from the same template tended to look like they were related, but weren't identical.

Still, it had to happen once in a while. That was basic probability.

This Powell showing up the way she had was just another way the universe was trying to remind Roy how he'd screwed up.

Ever since Roy abandoned the Legion, he'd been a loner. He'd joined the Void Brotherhood looking for more void than brotherhood. He'd been assigned to The Dump in the hopes he might learn to be a team player.

And, very much against his will and his intentions, that was exactly what had happened. He'd forced himself to work with a few screw-ups of various species. Powell had been one of them. For a short period of time, they'd worked as an effective team. He'd even grown fond of her. Together, they'd come close to netting the score of a lifetime.

Then, within the span of ten minutes, his team had died.

He didn't blame himself for that. His plan had been rock solid. Under any other circumstances, it would have gone without a hitch.

But someone had beaten him to the prize and managed to catch them off guard. The coward hadn't even shown his face, choosing to hide behind a ridiculous red and green mask instead.

Ranger M.

The man had fought well, Roy gave him that much credit. In the end, both of their ships had been heavily damaged, weapons inoperable, and systems on the brink of collapse. He hadn't lost the fight, but he hadn't won, either.

Thinking back, he'd expected to be angrier about the guy who'd almost beat him, or the fortune that had slipped through his fingers. To his surprise, however, it was the people he'd lost along the way that had bothered him most. Powell in particular.

He realized now he'd never even known her first name.

Her room, huh? Roy had assumed the room was unassigned, given how it had been so bereft of personal items. There was nothing here to give him any insight into her. Nothing physical, anyway.

He turned on the display and checked its search history. That hadn't been scrubbed. He smiled to himself. A pattern soon emerged based on what she'd been watching for the last month.

A synth trying out for an officer's exam. It seemed like this Powell was driven as well, just in a different way. Most synths couldn't hack the retraining involved. Burnout was high in synths that tried to move to another station in life, up or sideways.

Judging from the increase in activity on her playlist the last few days, the exam was probably soon. Maybe this Powell would get the shot at success his Powell never had.

Then again, maybe she wouldn't.

Sub-Commander Nekkar's opinion was short and to the point. "We should execute him."

Commander Miram had called a meeting of the bridge staff to discuss the Roy Herzog situation and asked for honest opinions. At least she couldn't fault her second in command in that regard. Nekkar was perhaps the strongest member of Miram's crew, and looked every bit of it, yet even he seemed anxious about Roy's presence.

"He's useful," Miram countered.

"He's dangerous."

"That too."

"It seems to me that we have him effectively contained," said Dr. Ascella. "His movements are being monitored. Going anywhere unauthorized will result in a debilitating shock. And he knows we can do far worse than that." She tapped a screen and a medical chart appeared on the central screen of the conference table. "I've read his psychological profile. He's a survivor, not the sort to sacrifice himself out of spite, even if it took his enemies down with him."

"You think he will cooperate?" asked Miram.

"If he thinks it's to his advantage, yes," said the doctor.

Another officer spoke up. "May I ask why everyone is so worried about him?" Ensign Davis was the only synth member of the primary bridge crew.

Nekkar snorted. "You were barely walking when he rejected everything the Legion stands for. We've had to live with the shame he brought."

Davis's eyes narrowed. "I *read* his file. I am aware of what he's done. Abandoning his post. Mutiny. Murder of a freeborn. Stolen shuttle. Not to mention the criminal acts he's guilty of as part of the Brotherhood. But this is just raw data. Most of you speak of him as if you know him. But then, I guess most cyborgs know one another."

Miram didn't miss the barbs that passed between her second and the ensign. Nekkar had the unfortunate view that the synth population worked for his kind, rather than with them. It was a sentiment that had been growing within the Terran community for some time, but only recently caused her any concern.

To his credit, the ensign never backed down whenever Nekkar challenged him on his inexperience.

"The man is without scruples," said Nekkar. "Without honour. And he's one of us. As a cyborg, he could do incredible damage if left unchecked. As a *symbol*, he's even worse."

The commander interjected. "I believe I'm the only one on board who has an actual history with Roy Hadar, or Herzog as he goes by now. The others here know him more by reputation. Personally, I agree with the sub-commander. I find the reputation more worrying than the man. As the doctor pointed out, as a physical threat he's contained.

"But he's also the only person on hand who understands the ways of the Brotherhood. With him on our side, we could have this smuggling ring shut down within a week. With luck, we'll be able to trace the cargo to both the source and the destination."

Lieutenant Ginan raised his hand.

"That's unnecessary, lieutenant," said the commander. "Speak when you have something to say." Though Davis was the youngest of the bridge crew, Ginan was the newest, recently transferred from the Colony Fleet. Technically, as head of security, he was part of the crew and under her command. But he was also a Vigile, a watchdog, and as such he answered back to his superiors at the Colony Fleet.

"Yes, commander," the lieutenant said formally. "It's just... I'm wondering about your choice of terminology."

"What of it?"

"Well, when I served on Colony *Pacifica*, the Vigiles were tasked with investigating a decline in the freeborn population. We tracked down and neutralized the network responsible for moving them off-colony."

"Did you find any of their safe zones?" Nekkar asked.

"That wasn't our task, as that was off-colony," Ginan replied. "But the information we found was passed onto the Legion. Regardless, we did not mince words when it came to investigating the matter. This is the trafficking of freeborns, not the smuggling of cargo."

Miram nodded. "Things work differently once you leave the Fleet, lieutenant. Outside of Draxon space, our caste system is frowned upon, so we draw as little attention to it as possible. We have the legal authority to claim freeborns wherever we find them, but having authority does not in itself engender cooperation. Our use of euphemisms is a simple necessity, one I encourage to reduce the chance of accidental miscommunication."

Ginan nodded. "I see."

"As far as this ship is concerned, the only thing we have ever been searching for is cargo."

The Return of Ranger M

Sol System — 2241

Moss's transport was approaching Mars space. Due to the standoff in Earth's orbit, the whole system was in lockdown except for emergency services. Fortunately, Moss had greased the right palms before he left and just happened to be carrying some medical supplies in his hold, enough to be classified as a medical transport.

"All right, Doc. We'll be slowing down as we approach the gravity well. ETA five minutes."

The man wasn't listening. He was glued to his monitors at the nav station.

"Doc, I said—"

His passenger raised his hand, then pointed to his monitors. "Silence."

"Doc, this is my ship. I can damn well talk if I—"

"No, I mean, look." He pointed to the monitors again. Each one seemed to have a distinct lack of activity. "Silence. It's been almost twenty minutes. What's happened?"

Moss frowned as he confirmed this, looking at his own comm displays, checking the Earth-based channels. Nothing. It couldn't be a malfunction. These were state-of-the-art Protectorate-grade comms. His ship might not travel faster than light, but his comm system was practically instantaneous. It gave his ship a competitive edge.

"Dunno. Some kind of jamming? EMP attack? Maybe they knocked out the satellites?" He switched back to his Mars-based comms, which *were still flooded with information. Then it was replaced by a single broadcast on all channels, informing ships to hold position and standby.*

"What the...?"

"Oh no. Oh no no no no..." The man was a bubble of anxiety, ready to pop. Moss was starting to feel the same way. "Check the monitors. Show me Earth."

"Doc, at this range you're not going to see anything," Moss said. For one thing, Earth was pretty damn close to the sun right now in terms of line of sight. And even with filters compensating for that, it was little more than a pale blue dot at this distance. But he turned on his external cameras and tracked its position anyway.

What he saw instead were two stars in the sky. At least, that's how he would tell the story in years to come. The truth was the orb of blue light where Earth should have been was still incredibly tiny. But recognizing what it was, what it had to be, what it meant... it might as well have been bigger than the sun itself.

"Jesus Christ..." Moss said.

His passenger closed his eyes and lay his head on the navigation panel. Then he pressed a button and started a recording.

"This is Dr. John Roberts. Division head, Project... You know, it doesn't even matter anymore." He looked back at the displays, then the camera, then the displays. "They did it. They actually did it. My God..."

The Void – 2550

"—uuuuuck?"

Some of the slaves glanced at one another, confused.

"What did Ranger M say, mommy?"

"Shhh!"

Hel looked at Moss, then at the slaves, then at Moss again. There were a few possible explanations, but only one that resonated with her.

You lying son of a bitch!

One man came forward warily. "I'm sorry. Is everything okay? Are the pirates gone? Can we come out now?"

Hel didn't wait for Moss to pick his jaw up off the floor. "Yes, the pirates are definitely gone. We're just a bit surprised by how many of you there are here."

That seemed to snap Moss back into reality. "Yes. When we got the distress call, the captain only said there were... refugees on board."

"Is the captain all right?" asked a woman.

"The captain is..." Moss trailed off. Of all the times for him to choke when it came to being a bald-faced liar.

"I'm afraid the captain didn't make it," Hel said, and many of the refugees gasped. "We think it was a heart attack. But he fought bravely. We couldn't have driven the pirates off without his help. He died protecting you."

Moss shot her a look, as if asking where she was going with this.

Oh, you're not the only one who can lie.

"What's going to happen to us?" someone asked.

"We're still assessing the damage to your ship, but I'm afraid you took some pretty serious hits to your main engines."

Moss raised his hand to his ear. "What's that, Violet? Sensor echoes? Right. We'll go to the bridge and coordinate from there."

Hel heard Violet's confused voice on her own comm piece. "What? Is he talking to me? Hel, what's going on there?" Fortunately, no one else but Moss could hear her.

Hel put a hand to her ear and took a step a couple of steps back from the advancing crowd. They were mostly interested in asking "Ranger M" more questions or heap praise on him, anyway. "Communications are not secure, Violet. Will explain later."

"Are there freeborns on board?"

"Roger that. A lot of them."

"Was Moss surprised to see them?"

"Affirmative."

"He was lying to us this whole time, wasn't he?"

"Yep."

Moss waved the refugees back, keeping them from leaving the storage room while they tried to get answers out of him.

"Just until we're sure you're safe. I've got my crew watching over this ship, but my first officer here and I need to get back to the bridge and check on things. Okay. Yes, you're welcome. You're *welcome*. Okay. Watch your fingers."

And with that, he sealed them all back into the cargo hold.

She frowned. "You're going to hell, you realize that?"

Moss sat on the floor and leaned against the cargo door. "No need, you're already on board. Look, we need a few minutes alone to think, okay? To get our damn story straight and try to work out what the heck we're going to do next. So please, let's wait until *after* we figure all this out before you start to lecture me. Deal?"

"Deal. So, what's first?"

"First off, we need to know if we can repair this ship or not. Violet?"

"No go. You killed both engines. This baby has to be towed."

"Can we tow it?" Hel asked.

Violet snorted. "Through transit? No chance. We'd have to be capable of creating a transit field around both our ships, which we can't. Even if we could, if it's not properly secured, we could tear each other apart once we drop back to normal space."

"I need to go back to the bridge," said Moss. "We need to secure whatever information this ship has. And the pilot..." His voice trailed off as he got up and left.

Hel chased after him. "What about the pilot? He's gone. I mean, it sucks, but it's not like we intended to kill him."

"It's not that. It's... Look, you heard those guys in the hold. Whatever the captain was doing, he *wasn't* taking these people to the Colony Fleet as slaves."

"Right, so he was going to set them free somewhere."

"By taking them *into* Draxon space? Towards Sol? What sense does that make?"

"Maybe he was lying to them?" asked Hel. "Promise them freedom, only to drop them off at the nearest slave mart?"

They were almost back at the cockpit now. They turned the corner and saw the dead captain still sprawled out on the floor. "Ordinarily, that would be my first guess, but something about all this..." He grabbed the man's body and turned it over, then propped it up against the wall in a slightly more respectful pose. He started searching the body as if looking for loose credits. Not finding anything, he pulled up the man's sleeves, but still found nothing.

"Dammit."

He moved to the cockpit next and started accessing the computers. "Vi, I'm going to establish a link with you. Download everything this ship's got."

"Roger that, you lying bastard."

"Hey, I said that can wait until later."

"You made Hel promise you that, not me, you deceitful sack of shit."

"Not now, Vi. Please. Just focus on the transfer."

"Whatever you say, you fraudulent asshole."

Moss rubbed his temple, looking over the ship's logs himself. Hel said nothing, but watched him as he searched. Clearly, he was trying to find something that would confirm a hunch he had, but was still coming up empty. He double checked the internal damage report, verifying that the main engines were indeed beyond repair. Then he went back to the last of the captain's personal logs.

It was odd seeing the dead man on the screen. Hel forced herself not to peek back into the hall, where she knew the dead Elysian's hand would be laying limp just slightly in view, as if to taunt her.

"Picking up a distress signal. Transit drive breakdown. Not too far off our course. Going to check it out. Sending status update to the Precentor in case it turns out to be a trap." The picture blinked out. He played it again, this time looking closely at the man's face.

"Damn," Moss muttered.

"What's a Precentor?" asked Hel.

Moss didn't answer, but instead went back into the hall where the dead man lay. Hel followed behind. He brushed aside the Elysian's long grey hair and found something attached to the upper part of his forehead, running down the far side of his face to the back of his jaw. She hadn't noticed it earlier, and only barely noticed something on his face in the recording, when his hair was mostly tucked behind his head.

"Damn," Moss muttered again.

"What's that?" asked Hel.

Again Moss ignored her. "Help me get him back into his seat," he said, grabbing one arm. Hel slung the pulse rifle she'd taken from the dead man over her shoulder and grabbed the other arm. Together, they carried him into the cockpit. It wasn't hard. He was remarkably light for his size and the onboard gravity was set low. Hel could have easily done it herself, but sensed this was about respect as much as efficiency. Once the pilot was back in his seat, Moss looked down at his face again.

"Damn."

"Would you stop saying that and start telling me what's going on?"

"This guy was part of the Order."

Hel looked down at the dead man and blinked. "Damn..."

"Come on, Trouble!" Lada cried out. "The colonists are in danger!"

"Uh uh," said Lev, "*I'm* Ranger M. *You're* Trouble."

Their mother tried to calm them both down. "Shhh! You're both trouble, is what you are."

Zach smiled as his younger siblings continued to bicker about who got to be Ranger M and who was going to play his furry sidekick. For some, their play bolstered confidence in everyone. For others, it only raised doubts.

Zach had watched every episode of *Ranger M* that he'd been able to access. He could quote entire passages from key episodes. He used to make replicas of Ranger M's ship. He'd even had a costume once, but then they'd had to move and leave everything behind... and not for the last time.

"Ranger M is just a cartoon character," said one of the older men. Zach still didn't know his name. He'd only joined the group when Captain Randgaffi had brought everyone to the starport on Triolina and smuggled them on board his ship. But a number of the others seemed to know him and looked up to him.

Zach wasn't a kid anymore. He was almost fifteen. He knew the Ranger M from the cartoons wasn't real. That guy was fiction, a superhero, and they exaggerated things for story effect. But that didn't mean it didn't come from some place real.

"He's based on an actual Terran," said Zach. "I've seen the vids. He exists."

"It's true," said an older refugee. "He was an explorer once. I heard he got really drunk and was fired from that company he worked for. Doesn't sound like much of a hero to me. What do you think, Torell?"

The first man's eyes hardened. "Even if he exists, he's not one of us. He's a synth or a cyborg. Has to be. So why would he help us?"

"Why did Captain Randgaffi help us?" asked Zach. "Because that's the kind of guy he is. There are good people in the universe, who know what's worth fighting for. And it's our job to help them however we can."

"*For the future!*" Lada cried out in agreement.

"I told you, *I'm* Ranger M," said Lev.

Some people chuckled at that. The gruff man who had doubted him, Torell, leaned back on the floor, hands behind his head. "I hope you're right about him. He strikes me about as trustworthy as a used starship salesman."

Moss continued to pace inside the cockpit. Hel's analysis of the ship records confirmed his theory, but the thin dermal implant on the pilot's head had been proof enough for him. No one but the Order had that tech. No one else even knew what it was. It was thinner and more refined since the last time he'd seen it, but no doubt served the same purpose.

However, that wasn't important right now. He had to figure out what to do next.

"You can't just leave them here," said Hel.

Moss shot her a glare. "I know that."

"Sorry, I just assumed..."

"What? That I'd be looking for the easy way out of this mess?"

Hel's face hardened. "Am I *really* out of line for assuming the thought crossed your mind?"

Moss wanted to argue the point, but she was right. The thought had crossed his mind. Just for a moment. After all, there was a chance that a ship from the Order might arrive once this guy failed to check in. But there were too many variables, and all of them happening in dangerous space.

"The *Rex's* cargo bay should be large enough to house them," said Moss. "That's not the problem. The problem is where to take them."

"What about your original plan?" asked Hel. "Take them back to Nubra space, get a reward, and use the rep that gives you to find work elsewhere."

"Oh, honey," said Violet over the comm.

"What?"

"She's trying to tell you that's not happening," said Moss.

"But you said the Protectorate offered a reward for freed slaves."

"*Illegal* slaves," corrected Moss. "Freeborns are property of the Terran Colony Fleet no matter where they are. Anything we did with them, even in Nubra space, would have to be off the record and unpaid."

"Can't we just take them back across the Void and let them go?" asked Hel.

"We could, but they'd get caught and sent back to the Terrans in no time. It would cost a fortune in fake idents to avoid that. A fortune we don't have."

"So what do we do?" asked Hel.

Moss continued to pace. "I keep coming back to where this ship was going. Into Draxon territory. Towards Sol. It makes no sense. Unless..."

"Unless what?"

"Well, Sol isn't all that populated these days. Maybe a quarter of the total Terran population is there, tops. The Colony Fleet is out skirting the Void, jumping every year or so to a new location. Sol is mostly a mining operation for the fleet because it's the only system Terrans have exclusive rights over. But that would make it a good staging area, right? Easier there than in other non-Terran systems."

"You mean some kind of underground railroad?" asked Hel.

"Exactly. Wherever they were going, it wasn't their last stop, just the next stop. One where they can best avoid attracting suspicion. Maybe they get moved onto a deep space explorer next, or a huge cargo ship with refugees from a bunch of smaller ships all together."

"So that's what we do," said Hel. "We take them to Sol."

Moss stopped pacing and stared at Hel like she'd tried to argue the merits of alcohol-free beer. "Are you kidding me? I am *never* going back there. You hear me?"

"We're short on options," Hel pointed out.

"We don't even know where he was going," said Moss. "Sol is a big place. It could be anywhere."

"Europa," Violet said over the comm.

"What?"

"I've gone over everything on his computer. It's in the flight log. He was heading for Europa."

It took Moss a moment to recover. "Yeah, but Europa is almost as big as the Earth's moon. There's at least a dozen different ports he could—"

"Europa Mining Colony Delta," Violet cut in.

"Okay, but there's got to be some kind of pre-arranged location to meet there, and a time. Probably a password or countersign—"

"The pilot lounge near Landing Pad 10, two days from now, 9pm Central Mars time. Password is swordfish. Look for a guy in a pink carnation."

"You're joking."

"Just the password and carnation bit. But I do have contact details."

Moss prepared to launch another counter argument, only one failed to materialize. He looked down at the wrestling mask still gripped in his hand.

"Goddammit. Hel, give me the pulse rifle."

The cargo bay door opened and Ranger M strode inside, holding a pulse rifle across his chest. The light silhouetted him in the most awe-inspiring way Zach had ever seen. It was like something straight out of one of his favourite episodes, "Payback's a CyberWitch."

"All right, people. Listen up! The pirates have been driven off, but we're not out of the woods yet. Your engines are dead and if you stay on board, so are you. I've brought my ship about. Everyone follow me, single file. We're getting out of here and getting you to your new home."

"*For the future!*" Lada cried out, fist raised in the air.

"Please don't say that," said Ranger M.

Unwanted Guests

Second gen synths were grown slower and used an improved template system with a recombination routine to create variations in each individual, rather than just clones. They're born as children, and reach maturity within five years, but tend to live a full life on par with humans overall.

Second gens have their own unique problem. They learn quickly as children, but once they reach maturity, most become "fixed" on their role, unable to adapt to anything new. Being forced to retire or retrain can result in mental breakdowns.

This doesn't apply to all synths, mind you, just the vast majority. Some break the mould, which creates its own problem: prejudice.

M. Foote, *And Then Things Got Worse*

R OY WONDERED IF THIS prolonged delay was because the crew was legitimately busy, or if the commander was playing some kind of head game with him. He'd wondered the same thing back in the brig.

No, that wasn't Miram's style. He knew her well enough to know she'd be honest with him, when she could be. But she was also by the book, which meant she was probably clearing her plan with the Colony Fleet as well as explaining herself to her command staff. She wouldn't contact him until she actually needed him.

Nevertheless, this left him extremely bored. The room had been stripped of anything vaguely interesting or useful, and he had no interest in watching any of the fleet-approved entertainment on the display.

He thought about the two guards outside his door. He didn't recognize either of them, and they were both synths. An interesting decision. He'd have expected at least one cyborg on hand as well, but he hadn't seen any aside from the commander. The men were both armed, and he did have a slaver collar on, so it probably meant nothing.

But did *they* know that?

Cyborgs like himself were incredibly strong. They also regenerated quickly and were keenly intelligent. In unarmed combat, they could easily take on a dozen synths or freeborns. They were more or less in charge of the Terran Colony Fleet.

Synths, on the other hand, lost their mental flexibility once they matured. They trained for a position and stuck with it for life. Sure, there were exceptions, but most synths that tried burned out, so it wasn't encouraged. Not that it mattered. The Fleet could always grow more and train them instead.

In the centuries that had passed since the Terran Disaster, attitudes between the two groups had shifted, and not for the better. He had to wonder, had it gotten worse since he left?

The door to his room opened without warning. A guard stood there, weapon ready but not trained on him.

"Commander Miram wants to see you in the conference room. Follow me."

Looked like it was time to earn his keep. He got out of his chair and followed the guard down the corridor. The other guard stayed behind, probably to perform some kind of security sweep, see if he was making a weapon and hiding it somewhere.

Like most of the Legion crew, this man's blond hair went down past his ears. The first thing Roy had done when he'd left was get a haircut and change his last name. It had been liberating, and a little bit funny. Historically, you'd have expected it to be the other way around.

"Doesn't that ever get in your eyes?" he asked.

"No."

"Just saying, mine's a lot easier to maintain. I save a fortune on conditioner."

The guard didn't answer. A different small talk angle was required.

"So, it's just you, huh? You must be some kind of *super* guard being trusted with me all on your lonesome."

The guard looked at Roy with disdain. "I don't have much to worry about with that collar around your neck, traitor. I can activate it. So can the commander. So can others."

So, not just the commander had access to the collar? Good to know.

"Traitor, huh? I'm sure the officers see it that way, but you? I'm closer to you than they are."

The guard huffed. "Unlikely."

"Please. Let me ask you something. How many synths work on the bridge? How many cyborgs?"

"I'm not going to tell you—"

"It was a rhetorical question. You've got one, at the most. And when the commander sends a team into a dangerous situation, what do the percentages look like then?"

The guard looked away and stood a bit straighter, trying to ignore him. Too late. Roy was already in his head. He wasn't planting the seeds of doubt, he was just poking around to see if they were already there in the soil.

They entered the lift that would take them to the bridge. "You know why I left the Legion?" said Roy. "Because I wanted to be my own man, not to be ordered around by a bunch of ego-driven fools wearing shiny armour who pretend to embody an ancient nobility. You grew up seeing all this as some kind of longstanding tradition, but me? I was *there* when we decided to adopt this look, these clothes, your values. Every cyborg was alive then. We know it's all made up because *we* made it up."

The guard's face hardened. "That's enough."

Roy shrugged, letting silence do the work for him for a couple of moments. Then he asked. "How old are you? Ten? Twelve? Fifteen? If you're stuck on guard duty, you can't be older than that."

The guard said nothing, then looked at him sideways. "Six."

"Wow. You're brand new. And they stuck you with me? I wonder why...?"

Again, he let silence do the work until they reached the bridge. The doors opened, and another guard stood there. Guess he was being handed off.

Before he stepped off, he looked at the guard and gave a little shrug. "It's because you're disposable. Thanks for the ride."

Commander Miram was alone in the conference room. The rest of the crew was on the bridge. Sub-Commander Nekkar would keep them on a patrol route close to the Ramede bubble, looking for any suspicious ships and intercepting them for inspection. There was no danger of attack from the Void Brotherhood. They weren't that stupid. They did their best to keep one another informed as to the *Hydrus*'s position at all times and tried to avoid them.

The door to the room opened. Roy Herzog entered, and the guard who'd escorted him took up a position outside. The door shut.

"Thank you for joining me, Herzog."

"I thought you said my rank was never officially revoked. Shouldn't you call me Sub-Commander Herzog?"

"I should be calling you Hadar instead as well. But you don't want me to use your proper name or rank any more than I want to say it. You're just being contrarian, Roy."

"I prefer difficult, Camile."

"And does the *difficult* person prefer to stand or sit while we talk?"

"I'll sit. Being difficult is tiring."

Miram shook her head and took a seat at the front of the table. Roy sat at the opposite end and put his feet up on it. Because of course he would. He wanted her to complain. The man was over three hundred years old, yet he acted like an insolent teenager. Life among the pirates had rubbed off on him, no doubt.

"So..." Roy said. "What can I do for the mighty Silver Legion today?"

"Dropping the attitude might be a start," said Miram. "It's just me here. There is no one to appreciate your performance art."

Roy took his feet off the table. "Spoil sport. You used to be fun."

"You used to be loyal."

Roy rolled his eyes. "Let's not go down that road today, shall we? You need me to succeed. I need you to survive. Let's begin."

Commander Miram nodded and activated the display inlaid in the conference table. She brought up an image of the local part of the galaxy. Nubra space on one side, Draxon on the other, the vast Void in-between, and the tiny forty-three light-year bubble that was Kamede space, close to the Draxon border.

"As you know, the Kamede government was compromised by the renegade Draxon padrone known as Zelroth Saltear, who united a number of small pirate bands under the flag of the Void Brother-hood."

"Thank you, Commander Obvious."

Miram ignored him. "Thanks to a legal loophole, they have been free to use Ramede space as a base of operations. They're a vicious band of amoral criminals who pose a risk to anyone trying to trade between Draxon and Nubra space."

Roy coyly held a hand to his face. "Stop, you're making me blush."

"But they're also being used as a cover."

Roy's next sarcastic quip died on his lips. "All right. You have my attention."

"Are you familiar with an organization known as the Order?"

"Some kind of secret society within the Protectorate," Roy said. "Rumour was they'd infiltrated just about every major government and corporation. Big in the news for a bit and just as quickly hushed up. To be honest, I thought it sounded like tinfoil hat stuff, like the Illuminati back on Earth."

"They are quite real," said Miram. "Once they were exposed, they scurried away like cockroaches, hiding in any crack they could find. Few were in positions of real power, however, so there was little disruption to any given organization."

"Seems kind of pointless," said Roy.

"Direct power never seemed to be their goal, but they were in positions of influence, as well as collecting information. The Order's network was vast, so much so that revealing the true extent of the breech could have damaged the entire Protectorate."

"Which is why they hushed it up?"

"More like they allowed people to believe the whole matter was, as you put it, *tinfoil hat stuff*."

Roy leaned forward, hand raised to his lips in thought. "If you're saying the Brotherhood is secretly part of the Order, that would be news to me. Zelroth Saltear is a bigger asshole than I am, and he's all about gaining power and keeping it. But..." The pieces fell into place in his mind. "I see. With everyone's eyes on the Brotherhood, other activities can go on unnoticed, drowned out in the background noise."

"Exactly. We believe they have an operation running between Draxon and Nubra space, and that the Ramede bubble is a key node in their chain."

"What's the operation?"

"Smuggling."

"Weapons?"

"People. Specifically, freeborns."

Roy frowned, processing. "Why? There's plenty of easier places to get slaves from. And you guys have a hard-on about reclaiming your property. Why risk it?"

"Unknown. But the freeborn population within the Terran Colony Fleet and Sol is dropping. Every time a plug is filled, another leak springs up."

"Sabotage?" asked Roy. "Someone trying to undermine the Fleet?"

"No, the numbers are too small to have that kind of impact. We believe the intentions are more... altruistic. Those that disappear tend to be ones we won't really miss, or so they would believe."

"So they're a bunch of do-gooders."

"Something like that."

Roy sighed. "Okay, you think this Order is running some kind of old-school underground railroad, smuggling freeborns out and using Ramede as a collection point?"

"That's the theory. What we need from you is the means to determine which ships might be part of it, and which to ignore. We can't inspect all the traffic passing through any more than we can police all of Ramede space."

Roy leaned forward, fingers interlaced and resting his chin on them. No doubt he wasn't just calculating how to get the information they needed, but any possible angle he could play along the way.

"So, what should we do?" asked Commander Miram.

At last he smiled. "I have an idea."

"I have no idea," said Moss, tossing his mask into his quarters before they entered the *Rex's* cockpit.

There were over two dozen people now tucked away inside their main cargo bay. It was no doubt a tighter fit than they were used to, but he didn't want them roaming around, crowding things up until he had a chance to clear his head. Get a few light years between him and this ship. It was bad enough in the cockpit with just Hel around.

"Might I suggest we start by simply going?" said Violet. "We can think just as well while in transit."

He looked out the cockpit at the immobile form of the *Maruma*. *You really screwed the pooch this time, buddy boy.*

"Yeah," said Moss. "Yeah."

"You didn't kill him," Hel said, standing next to him. "I mean, you *kinda* did, but... never mind. You'll make things right. That's the important thing."

Moss tried not to snap at her. She was just trying to help. Which, of course, made him feel worse. "Get to your station," he said. "We'll talk more once we're en route. Violet? What's the ETA to Sol?"

The pilot figurine turned to look at Moss as Hel went to the ladder and climbed to the top half of the cockpit. "You want to get there at best speed?"

"At the *Maruma's* best speed."

"It would have arrived there in about two days."

"Didn't you say the meeting was in two days?"

"At nine, MST."

"Let's get there around seven, shall we? That should give us enough time to scope things out without attracting too much attention."

"You got it."

The *Viaticus Rex II.I* pulled away from the derelict ship, powered up its transit drive and took off like a shot.

Once everything was more or less taking care of itself, Moss got up from his chair. "Hel, keep an eye on things, would you? I'm getting a drink."

"Bring me back something cold."

"Sure."

He'd been hesitant about taking on a co-pilot, hesitant about teaming up with anyone after Violet died, but he and Hel had fallen into a comfortable pattern. Maybe it was because she was also someone out of their own time, albeit in a wildly different way. Hel had lived on a generation ship that had been isolated from galactic events for centuries, while Moss had been dead a long, long time.

But they both came from a period in history when old-school humans were on top, and that was no longer the case. Everything had changed. Their cargo hold was full of proof to that effect.

Moss went into the gantry and stopped at the door. Someone was already in there. A lanky kid, just a teenager, was raiding the pantry cooler.

"A-hem."

The teen turned around, dirty blond hair getting in his eye. "Oh, sorry. I just. Hey, are you...? I thought Ranger M wore a mask to hide a bunch of scars or something?"

Great, it was the kid who first recognized him when he'd opened the cargo bay door. "Ranger M's in the cockpit. He sent me to get him a beer."

The kid's wide grin didn't waver. "Come on. You're not even trying to hide your voice. It's okay. Your secret identity is safe with me."

"Greatly appreciated. Now..." The kid's enthusiasm reminded him of Trouble, which was a big strike against him. Moss came over and took the bottle the kid had in his hands. "Never pinch another man's stash. It ain't civilized. How old are you, anyway?"

"Twenty."

"The hell you are."

"Fifteen... in six months."

"That's more like it. You want a drink, take one of those LaserActives on the bottom shelf. They're just taking up space."

The kid took the bottle, whose contents glowed faintly red, and frowned. "Is it any good?"

"It's sweet as all hell." Moss was pretty sure they were designed with cyborgs in mind. It was like a gluke shot you could drink. "Now, tell me how you got out of the cargo bay, so I know you're capable of reversing the process and seeing yourself back in."

"Trouble let me out."

Moss looked to the freezer and noticed the door was slightly ajar.

"Son of a... Where did it go?"

The kid looked confused. "I dunno. He just opened up the door, welcomed us aboard, and ran off. I think he went into a vent?"

The damn thing could be anywhere. Except he probably wasn't anywhere. It would be programmed with a sense of comic timing, waiting for an opportunity to spontaneously show up like he would in the cartoon. "Come out, Trouble, or I'll pressurize the entire air duct system, then vent it into space."

A scrabbling sound could be heard, though he couldn't be sure from exactly where. The vents here were too small for any person to fit through, but just big enough for something ferret-sized. A grill pushed out and Trouble scurried through, putting the cover back into place.

"You know, it was really cold in there, boss."

"Space is colder." Moss rubbed his temple, wondering what he could do to keep the stupid thing out of his hair. Then it struck him. "Okay, I've got a mission for you. You in?"

"Oh boy, I sure am!"

"Swell. See this guy here? What's your name?"

"Zach."

"I want you to hang out with Zach. Keep an eye on him and our other passengers, okay?"

The tiny ferret stood to attention and gave a salute. "You got it, boss!"

"Good, now escort him back to the hold, will you?"

"Sure thing! Come on, kid."

"Zach, you can take the rest of those LaserActives with you. Take some water while too you're at it. I'll get food to you later."

Zach grinned and grabbed as many bottles as he could. Moss grabbed a couple of beers and shut the cooler, then followed behind. Trouble marched ahead, leading them back toward the cargo hold.

"See, I knew you were really Ranger M," the kid said. "You've even got Trouble with you. Some of the others still don't believe me."

Moss didn't bother explaining. This kid was hell bent on believing what he wanted to believe. They reached the cargo bay door, which was still open, though nobody else had ventured out.

"Did you get in trouble?" a woman asked, presumably Zach's mother.

"No. He even let me bring some drinks back for everyone!"

"They're pretty sweet," Moss said, "So you might want to water them down." Something else occurred to him. "Um... anyone need to use the facilities?"

Some murmured discussions led to a consensus of, "Not yet."

"Good. I'll let you out once I've got this ship more properly prepared. For now, sit tight. If there's any problems, just shout out. We'll hear you over the comm."

Zach walked into the cargo hold, Trouble walking by his side.

"Stick with me and you'll go places, kid."

Moss shut the door and set the lock. "Not if I can help it."

At least the pest would be out of his hair until they reached Europa, and these people became someone else's problem.

This Mantic Moment

Charon is a beautiful, ringed world orbiting a yellow star, only a hundred light years from Sol. They developed differently than Terrans in terms of technology, having somehow built rocketships before the radio. That in itself posed some interesting challenges, given the planet's equatorial ring, which happens to be the best area to launch rockets from.

The Charon themselves tend to have gold skin and silver or ice-blue eyes. They have a very strength-and-virtue oriented society, a disturbingly active libido, and outdated views regarding gender equality.

So naturally they get along great with the Terran Colony Fleet.

M Foote, The Galaxy is Weirder than You Think

B ARL ORIJEN WAS TENDING the counter while his brother dealt with a customer. One of those purists that insisted on vintage parts for his luxury yacht. Damn morons. A printed copy was all but indistinguishable from the original, but it seemed the richer a person got, the more getting things your way mattered. And the Orijens were more than happy to oblige.

Sure, they jacked up the prices far beyond their practical value, but they never counterfeited a part, even though it seemed like easy money. Word of mouth was the cornerstone of their business. It took a lifetime to build and could be destroyed in minutes.

A chime indicated a new customer was dropping down to their level of the station. He checked the new lift scanners and verified they had no weapons. Ashton had invested in a top model detector after recent events.

Barl looked at his cybernetic hand and flexed the fingers. Not that it would have made much of a difference in his case.

A moment later, a large, gold-skinned humanoid with white hair walked in. It took a second to place his species. Charon. They didn't often venture far outside Draxon space. At least, not as far as he knew. But they were into luxury and decadence and all that, so it wasn't hard imagining him looking here for a rare hard-to-find part. This guy was big, but he didn't look like trouble.

"What can I do for you?"

"I am Terik Dared. I have been told that you build custom ships."

Blast. "Naw, you want the NSI ship showroom two levels up. But we got a refurbished Draxon Coyote if you're..." He then realized he must have misheard the man. "Did you say *custom* ships?"

The Charon nodded. "I came across someone in a most unusual vessel. A chimera, I believe the owner called it. He said you made it for him. Spoke highly of your skill."

Barl blinked. "Terran? About your height, brown fur on his head, always looks like he just stepped in something disgusting?"

"He wore a mask, but the rest seems accurate."

Maurice.

He was about to explain how that ship had been a one-off done as a favour to get him off their back and explain the insurance and legal issues that came with flying a chimera, when the Charon boldly tossed a large bag of credits on the table.

"I want one."

Barl picked up the bag, estimating from the weight how much was inside. "Right away, sir."

Virtual Life and Death

A core tenet of the Order is "Never Push Down." That is, to help and do no harm. So while any line of scientific enquiry is encouraged among them, whether or not those advancements will be released depends on the impact it will have on all life.

There is another saying I'm familiar with, though. "There's no such thing as a tool with no blood on it."

M. Foote, *Inside the Order*
(REDACTED)

THE *MARUMA* HUNG MOTIONLESS in space, metaphorically speaking. It was, of course, moving very fast. How fast that was depended entirely on your point of reference, but it would be millions of years before it came remotely close to another system.

The ship's lonely vigil was interrupted by the sudden appearance of a small shuttle with a faded and chipped black paint job. The name *Outreach* was written on its side in GalCom. It slowed and pulled alongside the transport.

Tameria leaned forward on her console, trying to get a better look at the damage the ship had taken, ignoring the far more accurate readouts her displays provided. She pressed the comm on her chair. "Say again, this is Captain Randgaffi of the *Outreach*. Please respond."

When she was certain no answer was coming, she checked her displays again. There were no life signs aboard. She frowned and positioned her ship within a few meters of the transport.

She put on her helmet and hopped over. Her flight suit was far more resilient than it looked and was suitable for EVA use. The hatch to the *Maruma* was unlocked, but the interior had been left pressurized. There was enough air inside for a few hours, and nobody seemed to be using it.

Emergency power was still on, enough for some lights, but the grav pads had cut out. She didn't bother using her mag boots, instead unlocking her suit's wing pouch and gliding down the corridors, checking everything. Tameria was reminded how long it had been since she'd been to a low-G world where she could break out her wings like this, if only to stretch them.

Tameria shook away the simple nostalgia. She had a job to do.

She found the captain sitting stoically in his chair, or as stoically as one could be fastened into a chair in zero gravity.

Tameria frowned. "You old damned fool. I warned you."

She brushed his hair aside, revealing the dermal implant that ran along the side of his face. She pulled a small laser from the toolkit on her belt and began to cut around it. No time for subtleties. With the anchor points removed, the rest peeled off without too much trouble. She linked the transport's computers to her own ship and copied the logs.

The ship's reactor was leaking radiation and she didn't feel safe attempting an overload on her own. Her ship was unarmed so she had no effective way to scuttle the vessel. She did her best to wipe the records once the transfer was complete, but odds were nobody was ever going to find this ship, not without knowing exactly what they were looking for.

She placed her hand on the pilot's head and let out a sigh. At least this would be the tomb he wanted. "Rest well, Uncle. See you soon."

Once back on the *Outreach*, Tameria took the implant to her workshop. Fortunately, she already had the necessary equipment on board. She didn't need to connect anything physically; the interface was designed to work remotely when it was close to a powerful enough processor. She just hoped the neural matrix held.

The computer seemed to die for a minute, then flared back to life. A voice came over the speaker. A simple camera on top was pointed at her.

"H... Hello? Where am...? What is...? Tameria? Is that...? Oh, I'm dead, aren't I?"

Sister Tameria tried to smile. "Afraid so."

"Blasted pirates."

"So it was a trap? I got your last message before you went to that distress signal."

"Should have known better. They used a shuttle as a decoy and took out my engines before I could escape."

Tameria tried not to use his name, not until she was sure the matrix would hold. "What can you tell me about them?"

"Well, one of them wore a mask. I saw that on the cameras. I had a pulse rifle with me. I went to try and stop them... Then everything went white. Then I was here."

"Did they shoot you?" she asked.

"No, I think it was my heart."

Tameria sighed. The Elysian cardiac system was evenly distributed throughout the arteries, but her uncle's had been in bad shape for a while now.

"Yeah, I know, you warned me. But I wasn't about to die in some bed. Or worse, live in it. I wanted to do something good."

"Only your passengers are now probably heading for a slave market, or the Terran Colony Fleet."

"I know. I'm sorry. I figured it was just one more mission. One last good deed. Something to balance the scales, you know?"

Tameria shook her head. "Keed, you balanced them long ago." Damn, the name had slipped out. She looked at the computer readout, studying the implant's neural stability.

"Maybe to you, but regrets have a way of not leaving you alone."

"I know."

"Of course, there's a lot I don't regret. Like the time I spent with you and your dad."

Tameria smiled. "The picnics on Lacilla."

"You always loved how high you could fly there."

"I remember."

"When was the last time you went flying?"

Honestly, she couldn't remember. "It's been a while."

"So, what are you going to do now?"

"Track down the pirates if I can. I can't risk the network being exposed."

"They won't learn much," said Keed. "I followed procedure."

"I know, but the Terrans have tightened up security on the colony ships. I'm pretty sure they have an idea of what's happening."

"Well, something else will come along. It always does. And hey, maybe I can be there with you? You could use a copilot. You always fly alone. That's just supposed to be for depressing old guys like me."

Tameria smiled, but she was also fighting back tears. The diagnostic display was starting to show warning signals. "I'd like that, but..." She couldn't bring herself to say it.

"But I'm not going to be around very long, am I?"

"I'm sorry... The neural matrix is starting to decay. There isn't much time."

"Well, it was worth a shot. At least this way I get to say a proper goodbye." He paused for a moment. "Do me a favour?"

"Sure."

"Shut me down before I start going senile. Better for both of us, I think."

Tameria nodded, choking up. It had always been a long shot, but she'd really hoped the matrix would hold together.

"And Tameria?"

"Yeah?"

"Balance the scales for me, would you?"

"I will. Goodbye, Uncle Keed."

"Goodbye, Tameria. Be good."

The strategy session with Commander Miram had gone extremely well. Thanks in part to his intuition, and in part to his access codes and Brotherhood IFF signals, they'd been able to stop a small-time courier en route to Ramede and grab the most recent DNI list. From there, it was easy for Roy to remove the obvious non-starters and filter the list down to a few likely candidates. Now they were in the process of tracking down some Nubra transport called the *Maruma.*

He thought he'd get to watch the show from the bridge of the *Hydrus*, but Miram wasn't having it. She had her first officer escort him back to his room until he was needed again. Probably didn't want him to observe how her crew worked too closely. Smart, because that was exactly what he'd intended to do.

Of course, Roy was never one to limit himself to a single tactic.

The first officer was a Sub-Commander named Nekkar. Taller and definitely stronger than Roy was, he was practically a caricature of a Silver Legion motivational poster, right down to the ultra-square jaw.

He'd never met the man before, but then Roy had never been the social type unless it suited him.

Right now, it did.

"Not a bad bit of investigating on my part, wouldn't you say?"

Nekkar didn't answer.

"You guys have been out here, what, six months looking for a proper lead and I got you one in about a day. Admit it, you're impressed."

Nekkar looked at him, but still said nothing. His face, however, said "shut up" loud and clear.

"So, what do you think? With time off for good behaviour, maybe they'll let me out of the mines in, what, a century or two?"

"If they do, it is better than you deserve, traitor," said Nekkar.

There we go. His tone and style of speech pegged him as a *rah-rah* Legionnaire type. "I've got the time."

Nekkar went back to his silent treatment.

"Is it just me, or have things changed since I was in the Legion? I'm pretty sure I saw a synth on the bridge. Ensign *Davis*? No way that's a cyborg name."

"It's not," said Nekkar.

"The ship I served on didn't have any synth bridge crew. They spend a ton of extra time in training, and we get, what, fifty years of service out of them? And that's only from the ones who don't burn out."

"Commander Miram believes they introduce fresh ideas to a crew," the first officer said.

"Waste of resources, if you ask me."

Nekkar said nothing but grunted a hint of agreement.

The first officer was transparent, a true believer in the Terran cause. He'd bet a hundred credits the man kept an old Earth sword and shield hanging somewhere in his cabin. Probably had a bookshelf full of reproductions he'd never actually read and did all his actual reading on computers. A casual observer would say the behaviour stemmed from an overabundance of pride. But Roy knew better.

It came out of fear.

There would never be another cyborg made. That was a fact. They were an evolutionary cul de sac, a dead end, grown to be used as tools only to have the secrets of their creation lost forever, along with their home.

They were obsessed with building a new home for humanity, but Roy saw it for what it was: an immortality project. In theory, they couldn't die of old age, but one by one they would die in combat or accidents until nothing remained but the monuments they'd built to themselves. And they had all the time in the world to let that fact sink in and haunt their dreams.

Roy had seen their future. That was why he'd left. But that didn't mean they couldn't be useful to him.

"Well, if I'm the only cyborg at the mines, at least I'll be ruling the roost. Still, can't say I'll care for the company."

"As I do not care for yours," Nekkar said as they reached their stop. The door opened and he gave Roy a shove to get ahead of him as he escorted him back to his quarters.

"What, so poker night is cancelled? Shame. Still, the Legion keeps expanding, gets more ships, and there's only so many of us to go around. I bet once you get a command of your own ship, you'll be the only cyborg there."

Nekkar's lip twisted. "You talk too much."

"I prefer to think I talk just enough."

They reached his room. The guards on either side stood at attention. Nekkar ignored them, opened the door, and shoved Roy inside.

"You can talk to yourself then," he said, and shut the door.

"You can't keep them locked up for the whole trip," Hel said from the top half of the cockpit. Her drink was empty and she felt she'd waited long enough to bring up the subject.

"Pretty sure I can," said Moss. "This isn't a hotel, and it's not like I've got beds for them either way. I'll let them out when they need the bathroom."

"We're two days out still. They can walk around and not feel like prisoners," said Hel.

"You want to let them out? Fine. You're now their official babysitter. Get them some food and keep them out of the cockpit and engine room. And tell that furry tampon you bought not to bother me for the rest of the trip."

"You forgot to say *humbug*," said Violet.

"Humbug," said Moss.

Hel shook her head and climbed down the ladder. As she left the cockpit, Violet's voice came over the speakers.

"You don't have to go. I can keep an eye on them myself. It's not like they can hide from me."

"I know. Moss just wants me out of his hair. I'm obliging."

"He was watching them when you called, you know."

"Seeing if they're trying to steal anything?"

"Actually, he was watching the kids. I think this situation's bothering him."

"All the more reason to stay out of his hair."

"I guess."

Hel went to check the galley to see what kind of food they could spare. Mostly red seal freeze dried rations, but they rehydrated pretty well and were cheap to replace.

"Was he always like this?" Hel asked.

For a moment she thought Violet had gone elsewhere because she didn't answer. Then she said, "Well, looking over my predecessor's archives, it seems like he's been like this as long as she was with him."

"And what about before that?"

"Before?"

"You know. Before..."

"Before I died?"

"Sorry, was that inappropriate?"

"Only you tapdancing around the subject like it's taboo."

"Sorry."

"When I first met Moss, we weren't exactly on friendly terms. I was trying to bring him in to collect a bounty."

"What changed your mind?"

"I saw him try to make a difference when others just sat on the sidelines. And by others, I mean me. He'd always say later that I just caught him on a bad day, but that's just it. I didn't. And it made me realize I was always looking for the next job, the next paycheck, the next target, but I wasn't really doing anything worthwhile. So I joined up with him instead."

"Were you guys ever... *close*?"

Another pause. "Are you tapdancing again? If you're talking about sex, then no, it wasn't that kind of relationship. But we were close, sure. We've got a lot in common. Sort of."

Hel snorted. Violet loved late twentieth and early twenty-first century video entertainment, while Moss had studied nineteenth and twentieth century literature. It gave them an overlap of interests, as well as a lot of arguments about the adaptation of books into various films or series.

"Anyway, before I got sick, he was loosening up quite a bit. Which was funny because we were doing some dangerous stuff back then. But after... Well, he got angry. Real angry. Which was also funny, because if anyone should have been angry, it was me."

"Well, he's still got you...sort of."

"To be honest, I don't think keeping me around like this was the right thing for him. All my existential angst? He's going through the same thing. Part of him believes I'm just a ghost haunting him. That's why I'm glad you're here. Maybe with you around, he'll loosen up again."

"Maybe," said Hel. "But I'm worried about you too, you know."

"Eh, it's okay. If I have a mental breakdown, you can just reboot me."

That hit Hel in the gut in an unexpected way. "Don't say things like that!"

"Like what?"

"Like you're a thing. Look, nobody decides how you view yourself but you. If you choose to think of yourself as a thing, that's all you'll ever be. But to me, you're a person named Violet Lonsdale who just happens to have an engine for a heart and an air recycler for lungs."

Violet chuckled. "Moss said something like that the other day. Coming from you, though, it's kinda sexy."

Hel rolled her eyes, but she might have been blushing. "Hoo boy."

"All right, all right, no more flirting—for now. How about you go let our guests stretch their legs for a bit?"

"And that's how I saved Ranger M from the evil Doom Dominion."

Across the room, Lada, Lev, and a couple of other kids clapped. Trouble gave a deep bow as he finished his story. For something so small, his voice projected pretty well. Zach had heard the whole thing. He remembered that episode—it had been a two-parter. Of course, Trouble hadn't done much more than get into a control room to release Ranger M from the Doom Dominion's energy sphere—he was pretty useless in the fight that came next—but it was in his character to take credit like that.

"This man who calls himself Ranger M is starting to worry me," his mother said, but not loud enough for the children to hear.

"He seems fine to me," said Zach. "Maybe a bit cranky."

"But he has a talking animal that also believes the cartoons you watched are true? I am worried he might not be sane."

A few of the older refugees that sat nearby nodded or murmured their agreement, including Torell.

"And now he won't let us out of the cargo hold," he added.

"Just for a little while," said Zach. "This wasn't exactly a normal situation for him."

"Nothing about this is normal," said Torell.

The door to the cargo bay opened, and the first officer greeted them all with a smile. "Well, we're on our way. Ranger M has said you can walk freely around the ship, just not in the cabin or the engine room."

"See?" said Zach. "I told you it was just for a while. We're going to be fine."

Torell grunted. "We'll see."

Back in the *Outreach*'s cockpit, Sister Tameria studied the footage from the *Mamura* for the third time. She couldn't believe what the cameras were showing her: Moss and Hel storming the ship, killing her uncle, and taking the refugees.

Upon her first viewing, she had been enraged. After everything they'd been through with the *Pegasi*? This raid had looked so deliberate. It betrayed everything she had believed about the man.

No, it had confirmed everything she'd *feared* about him. The man the Order still called Homewrecker.

But as she watched the video again and again, the oddities became more noticeable. How they'd gone back to the cockpit to check the ship's logs *after* discovering the refugees. How they examined the body and found the dermal implant. The way they argued over what to do next. It was a heist gone wrong.

On the one hand, she was disappointed that Moss had stooped to piracy. On the other, she was pretty sure now that he'd thought her uncle's ship belonged to the Void Brotherhood. Pirating a pirate? That sounded like Moss's style.

Now she had to figure out what to do next, which meant figuring out what *he* would do next. He'd taken the refugees with him, but what would he do with them?

He might just drop them off at the nearest inhabited planet and hope for the best. But that copilot of his, Hel, struck Tameria as the type to balk at that plan. And if Moss had installed the new copy of Violet's personality matrix on board...

The thought made her wince. Violet used the same neural imprint procedure as Uncle Keed, and as far as anyone in the Order knew, she was the only one it had ever been fully successful on. Still, she and a number of her colleagues now wore the implants, despite the low odds of success. The way they saw it, it would at least act as a record of what had happened, providing the Order with vital information before the neural matrix decayed. Why Violet's had stabilized while no one else's had remained a mystery.

But if she was activated, and had sifted through the *Maruma*'s logs, Violet was equipped with the means to decrypt the data and learn the ship's destination.

The problem was that would mean going back to Sol, and the only place riskier than that for Moss would be dropping into the middle of the Terran Colony Fleet. His every instinct would be to stay as far away from there as possible.

She watched Moss and Hel's last argument on camera, right before they had herded the refugees over to his ship. She noted the dejected slouch in his posture.

Tameria turned off the display and set the ship's navigation for Sol.

Exams and Explosions

Third gen synths are referred to as cyborgs, because of the nanotechnology worked into their genetic makeup. Despite their frustrating good looks, they're technically a whole other species.

They were meant to be soldiers, leaders, and thinkers. They heal insanely fast, quickly adapt to new environments, and are effectively immortal in terms of aging. They were designed for special operations and to lead the regular synths in battle and keep them under control during increasingly unstable times.

Only it really didn't work out that way.

After the loss of Earth, they were the ones who ended up on top and their creators, now designated freeborns, were at the bottom.

And the synths? They were stuck somewhere in the middle.

M. Foote, *And Then Things Got Worse*

K ARON WAS READY. SHE'D studied for weeks for the officer's exam and had the academic portion down cold. The practical portion, however, still made her nervous. She had little idea what to expect there because the test was different for everyone.

Burnout among synth applicants was said to be around ninety percent, but very few ever reached the point of having a breakdown. The TCF's mandate made it clear that all synthetics shared the same rights when serving the Fleet, but once the warning signs started to show, they were strongly encouraged not to proceed. Most knew better than to fight the inevitable.

More than once, Karon feared that Dr. Ascella would take her aside and give her the bad news, only it never happened. That alone gave her all the motivation she needed to press forward.

A bridge officer had to be present during her exam, and she'd had the unfortunate luck to be stuck with the first officer. Sub-Commander Nekkar was, as every crewman knew, a complete asshole. Good at his job but convinced he lived on a higher plane of existence than the rest of the crew.

She used to wonder if that was just the attitude he had while among the little people below decks, but she'd become friends with Ensign Davis and learned the sub-commander behaved exactly the same on the bridge, especially where Davis was concerned.

The thought of another synth officer on board, even an ensign, no doubt stuck in his craw.

The exam room was just a standard meeting room, one of several scattered about the ship. It was meant to hold a dozen people, so having just her and Nekkar there made it feel very empty and intimidating.

Nekkar was waiting for her when she arrived.

"Crewman Karon Powell, you may begin when you are ready. Note that I may be called away at any time, but this will not allot you more time for your examination."

Karon nodded. "Understood." She took her seat at a terminal and began the four-part written exam. As she expected, it was a snap, and only took her an hour and a half of her two hours to finish. Nekkar tried his best to remain unimpressed. He stood up, brought over a virtual interface rig, and set it down in front of her.

"The practical part of your exam will take place in a virtual environment," he said. "Once the test begins, you may not leave until the time expires. This test has been customized based on your skill sets and current duties on board, as well as what would be expected of you as an officer. Is that clear?"

"Yes, sir," Karon said.

"Begin when you are ready." In neither instance had Nekkar said anything remotely like "good luck."

Karon put the interface on her head was immediately thrust onto the bridge of the *Hydrus*, coming up on an unknown vessel. She wasn't even given a briefing beforehand. It seemed she was expected to figure things out through context. She took a moment to test her range of motion. This was an advanced headset, the kind that didn't require haptics for full immersion. Even though her real body remained still, her brain was convinced she could move freely and with full tactile feedback. You had to shut down the sim to regain normal body movement and remove the headset.

"No life signs aboard the ship," said one of the officers. The new Vigile security officer, Ginan, as she recalled. "Distress call indicates some sort of drive malfunction."

Karon played catch up, checking her scanners. No power to engines, no signs of life, but the scarring on its hull didn't look like it was caused by a drive malfunction. She knew weapons damage on hull plating when she saw it.

"Commander, this was not an accident. It was shot at." She double checked the data. "Recently."

Commander Miram nodded. "Shields on full. Charge all weapons."

Almost like a faint echo, she heard a voice from outside the virtual world call Sub-Commander Nekkar to the bridge. That was okay, he wasn't needed for this part of the exam. He could review the results in his own time later. She focused instead on the task at hand as an unknown ship dropped out of transit nearby and accused the *Hydrus* of attacking the ship they'd just found.

Commander Miram nodded as her first officer returned to his post at tactical. "How's Crewman Powell's exam going?"

"Passable," said Nekkar. "What has happened?"

Miram gestured to the view ahead of them, where an older model Nubra transport hung dead in space. "I believe we've found our smuggler. Unfortunately, it seems we weren't the first to do so."

The commander could see Nekkar's jaw tighten. "Could the traitor have tipped someone off?"

Miram shook her head. "Roy has no access to communications. It is an odd coincidence, however. I think it warrants a more direct investigation." She got up from her chair. "I want you on the bridge until I return."

Nekkar frowned. "Commander?"

"I'm intimately familiar with this model. My first command was a Messenia transport, back when the Colony Fleet was nothing but second-hand ships. Just a crew of four, three of which spent most of their time keeping her together." She smiled, remembering a simpler yet more desperate time for the Fleet. "Dr. Ascella will accompany me in case we need to help someone, and Lieutenant Ginan with bring a security team in case we need to hurt someone."

Nekkar took the command chair and looked over the displays. "Is anyone on board?"

Ginan joined the commander as they prepared to leave the bridge. "The readings say no, but I don't believe they are accurate," said the lieutenant. "It may have some kind of baffling in the hull."

"*That* tiny ship is fooling our sensors?"

"Strange as it might seem, yes." The commander stopped at the door just before she left. "Oh, and Herzog will be coming with us. If the Brotherhood raided this ship, he's our best bet on figuring out what they did with the cargo."

Nekkar frowned. "Commander, I believe that's unwise."

"Understood. And if he betrays us, you'll see to it he comes back on board without a head."

Nekkar smirked. "Aye, Commander."

Roy groaned as the door chime woke him up. Given that he was sleeping more out of boredom than exhaustion, he tried not to grumble too much.

His visitor didn't wait for permission to enter. Judging from her height and bearing, the woman was a cyborg. Then he noticed the caduceus on her uniform's epaulettes.

"Dr. Ascella, I presume?" He'd come across the name while gathering what little information he could about the ship.

She nodded. "I've come to collect you. Your presence is required aboard the *Maruma*."

"What's wrong?"

"Seems your friends might have found it first. She's dead in space and suffered heavy weapon fire."

That didn't make any sense. "The ship was on the DNI list. The Brotherhood wouldn't raid it." You couldn't get people to pay not to be robbed if you went ahead and robbed them anyway. Bad for business.

"Perhaps, but that's why we want you aboard. To evaluate that possibility. The captain and a team are securing the ship now."

"Well, anything beats staying cooped up in here. Lead on."

As he followed the doctor down the hall, he scratched at his collar. "Hey Doc, I got something really itchy on my neck. Think you can remove it?"

"I don't think you'd enjoy the side effects of such a procedure."

"Probably not."

Lieutenant Ginan's team boarded the *Maruma* first, travelling over in EVA suits, confirming that no one alive was on board. The superstructure was reasonably sound, and they found only one body. The *Hydrus* then extended its docking bridge and provided the derelict with some of her atmosphere and power. The commander, doctor, and Roy then crossed over. The security chief greeted them on the other side.

"There were definitely people on board," he said. "Judging from the rooms that were occupied, I'd say twenty or more."

"Where did you find the captain?" Miram asked.

"In the pilot's chair, but there's no damage to the cockpit. Based on his age, he might have died of cascade heart failure."

The commander nodded. "Where are your men now?"

"In the engine room, trying to shut it down. Our scanners showed the reactor as functional, but once we came on board, we found it leaking radiation. Their EVA suits can handle that, though."

"Should we be concerned?"

Ginan shook his head. "Just a safety precaution. The *Hydrus* is powering this ship now, so it's best if we take the reactor offline."

"Why the faulty reading?" asked the doctor.

Roy cut in. "Sensor masking. Certain parts of the ship are heavily shielded to prevent a regular scan, and a false signal is projected. Unless you're looking for a trick, the readings look normal. A deep scan will cut through it, though."

The commander frowned. "I've never heard of this before."

"That is the general idea, Camile." The other officers glared at him, and he rolled his eyes. "*Commander*. It's new tech. I'm not even sure who invented it. All I know is the Brotherhood got their hands on a ship with it a while back, but they were still trying to reverse-engineer it when I left. They'd pay a fortune to pick this wreck clean."

"Then it's lucky we found it first. Lieutenant, escort Mr. Herzog to the bridge. See if the two of you can determine who attacked this ship. Doctor, go with them and determine the cause of death of the pilot. I'll join you once I check on the crew in the engine room."

The security chief led the way, with the doctor behind and Roy in the middle. He didn't see any scarring on the walls, so there hadn't been a firefight. Or, at least, not using lethal ammo. If they were coming for the freeborn, they probably would have used stun settings to avoid damaging the merchandise.

As they turned the corner, he saw a small blast mark on the floor. Probably a flashbang grenade. The security chief nodded for them to join him in the cockpit.

Despite how long he'd lived—and how long he'd probably go on living—there was always something inherently unnerving about coming across a dead body sitting in a chair, especially with no visible signs of trauma on them. A meat puppet whose strings had been cut.

Judging by his features, the man was Elysian. Had he been alive, it might have been harder to tell. Their natural glamour tended to make people see them as something more akin to their own species. Even so, he resembled a human more than, say, the Draxon or Nubra, just shorter, with a pointier jaw, smaller ears, and bigger eyes

Doctor Ascella tapped her wrist computer and began scanning the body, checking the display on her forearm as she went. Lieutenant Ginan turned on the ship's computer and soon frowned.

"Memory's been wiped. Your friends hiding their tracks?"

"This doesn't feel like them," said Roy. "I don't think this guy died in his chair. I think he was put here out of respect."

"He's right," said the doctor. "The body was definitely moved post-mortem."

"Not exactly a pirate trait to be sentimental like that," Roy added. "Could have been someone's first time, I suppose. But then wiping the records? That feels more like a targeted crime by someone he knows that doesn't want it traced back to them."

Ginan looked around the room. "The ship has surveillance cameras. I might be able to retrieve some images directly from them."

Suddenly, the lieutenant's comm came on. "Sir! Reactor critical! Abandon—"

The ship shook violently. Roy felt a rush of wind as the ship decompressed. Without thinking, he jumped to the door and slapped the emergency button. The doors hissed shut and sealed.

"What are you doing?" Ginan yelled. "My men—"

"The doc and I don't have EVA suits! We'd—"

This time they were all thrown against the wall as an explosion rocked the *Maruma*. Power and gravity cut out and Roy's head spun from the blow he took as he fell into darkness.

The explosion took everyone by surprise. There was no time to raise the shields.

"All hands, brace for impact!"

The words were barely out of Sub-Commander Nekkar's mouth when the rear half of the transport spun into the port side of the *Hydrus*. The ship shook but stabilized.

"Damage?"

"We've got breaches on the lower port decks," said one of the bridge officers.

"Are any ships in the area?" His first priority was to determine if this was some sort of attack.

"Negative. The reactor overloaded."

"How?"

"Unknown."

"Damage crews to their stations." Nekkar got up from his chair. "Scan for survivors. Launch shuttles at once and retrieve everyone they can."

"Sir?" Ensign Davis said from communications. "I've got a signal coming in. It's Doctor Ascella. Some of the crew are sealed on the *Maruma*'s bridge."

"What about the commander?"

There was a pause before he got a reply. "She was in the engine room."

Karon knew the vibration she'd felt wasn't part of the simulation. In fact, she'd completed all the assigned tasks and was just waiting out the clock. Then she heard a distant sound that could only be coming from outside of the virtual environment.

"Damage control crews to your stations."

Karon checked the timer. One minute left on the test and she'd been twiddling her thumbs for four. Technically, she wasn't on duty because of the test, but if something had happened to the ship...

She pushed through the mental block that kept her body immobilized and removed her headset. From the sound of the sirens, it was more serious than she'd feared.

She met up with the rest of her team in the EVA locker room, suiting up. Dale from engineering was already fitting his helmet.

"How bad is it?" she asked.

"Lower crew decks were breached. I thought you were having your exam?"

"This seemed like more fun," she answered. "Anyone hurt?"

"Here? I don't think so. But word is the boarding party…"

Karon's eyes widened. "Oh no."

"Can't worry about that now. Suit up. I want you with beta team working outside. Prioritize points for repair. If it's critical, report it straight away."

It didn't take long for her team to get outside. They ran drills like this regularly, and walking on the hull was second nature to her. Karon used the EVA's thrusters to get her to the damaged area faster, but preferred to use her grip boots and be more hands-on once she was actually there.

The *Hydrus* had backed up from the wreck a ways but was now holding position. She saw two shuttles dance about the transport's debris, which was spreading farther apart with every moment. At this distance, she couldn't make out whether floating specks were shards of metal or people, and for that she was grateful.

Her team spread out to assess the damage. She made her way to a section of the hull that had part of the transport lodged in it like a shiv.

The *Hydrus*'s hull was made of a special energy reflective material that gave the Silver Legion their name. It was highly effective against energy weapons, but when it came to kinetics, it was like any other ship.

Karon walked around the hull, looking for any leaks or electrical issues around the impact site. Then she looked through the window and recognized where she was. She tapped the comm on her EVA suit.

"Hey Dale? I've got some good news and some bad news for you."

"What's the bad news?"

"Part of that ship is lodged inside your quarters."

She heard Dale swear on the other end. "What's the good news?"

"I won't be bunking with you anymore."

When Roy came to, he was free floating. A blobby, red sphere nearby pointed out that he had taken a bad hit, but by now he would have already healed. His body felt whole, but he felt tired, which indicated possible regen fatigue setting in.

Ascella and Ginan were over by the cockpit window looking out, waving at a small shuttle heading toward them. Looked like they were going to make it after all.

Well, that's something anyway.

It took a while for Roy to drift close enough to a wall to grab. He pushed himself off, joining the others by the window.

"What happened?"

"Unclear," said the doctor. "We only know the reactor exploded. It's a miracle we survived."

"What about the others?"

The doctor shook his head. "The shuttles are picking up who they can, but..."

Roy's thoughts went to Miram, though he didn't want to admit it.

"The commander?" She hadn't been wearing an EVA suit.

"We don't know," Ginan snapped.

"Exposure to vacuum shouldn't be a problem," the doctor added. "But we don't know how close she was to the explosion."

Part of Roy wanted to feel bad. Wanted to feel a sense of loss. Camile Miram had been in his life a long time before he'd turned his back on the Legion. Despite his misgivings, he had to admit she'd treated him fairly. Part of him wanted to mourn.

But the part of him focused on survival overruled him. Instead, he considered what the consequences of the accident would be, what would happen next, and began to make plans accordingly.

Deep Scars

SOL SYSTEM — 2241

Moss was still in shock. The light, fading now on his monitor, had taken most of humanity with it. For something to create that much light... Nothing could have survived it. Not even the fleets in orbit around the planet.

Ten billion souls. It wasn't possible. It just wasn't.

He'd only ever heard of one explosion large enough to cause that kind of damage before, an accident back when Earth's attempts at FTL were in their infancy. That had left a scar on Jupiter that wouldn't heal for centuries. But no one had ever been able to recreate those conditions.

Until now, maybe.

"I need to get to Armstrong Colony," his passenger said. "Now."

"All... All ships are in a holding position," said Moss, trying to snap out of it. "I... I..."

A strength and resolve came into the scientist's voice, one that had been absent for most of the journey. "Yes, and everyone else right now is just as gobsmacked as you. Take advantage of it and get me down there. Tell them you have a medical emergency. That your passenger just had a heart attack."

Something in the man's voice shook Moss back to reality... whatever that was right now. "Yeah. That might work." He changed course and headed toward the planet's surface, toward Armstrong Colony on the *outskirts of Olympus Mons. He just hoped someone down there didn't get paranoid and shoot them down as a security risk.*

Sol System – 2550

"Coming up on Jupiter, Hel. Welcome home."

Hel felt her stomach tighten as they dropped from full to sub transit. The blue streaks of light shifted to red as they collapsed back down to familiar pinpoints.

Home? Metaphorically, perhaps. She had been born between two stars on a generation ship that had left this system nearly four hundred and fifty years ago. But Sol was the birthplace of humanity, a place she'd only ever read about. To her, it might as well have been a myth.

In a way, it still was, because the Earth itself was no more. An uninhabitable rock, she'd been told, devastated during the standoff between the humans and their creations. A war that ended before a single shot was fired. All that was left were their colonies in the inner and outer solar system. Humanity, such as it was, had moved on.

At first, it seemed there was nothing to see. The sun was brighter than the surrounding stars, but at this distance was still very small. Any smaller and it could have been mistaken for another star. The starfield ahead held steady except for a single point of light that shifted slightly as they changed course to face it.

"Is that Jupiter?" she asked.

"That it is," said Moss. "Check on our passengers. Have them hole up in the cargo bay until I give the all clear."

The last couple of days had been a bit awkward. Hel's job had been to make sure the refugees were treated as well as could be expected, while not bothering Moss with any details like the fact that they existed. He hadn't left the cockpit in all that time, choosing to sleep in his chair instead. Trouble had tried to sneak in, but when Hel made it clear what was on the line and what would happen if he persisted, it turned out the petbot did have self-preservation protocols after all.

Hel dropped down the ladder and left the cockpit. The freeborn had made themselves comfortable but had remained somewhat closed lipped around her. She tried to get more information about where they were going next, but they weren't entirely sure themselves. They only referred to the place as Haven.

The refugees had originally been four separate groups. A few had been smuggled out of the Colony Fleet, but most had been born from parents and grandparents who'd escaped a long time ago.

At some point, they had all been contacted by various non-humans who referred to themselves as handlers, who had then brought them to the *Maruma* for the next leg of their journey. No payment had ever been demanded by any of these people, but that seemed to track with the mysterious Order that Moss had once worked for.

Hel still didn't know much about them. Moss referred to them as "technomonks," a jab at their quasi-theological trappings and advanced technology. They were the reason Violet was still around, and right now they were helping refit the generation ship she'd once called home with a transit drive so they could settle far away from the eyes of the Terrans.

The Order had gone deep into hiding some time ago, after Moss had exposed their existence, but that was a whole other story. Given the implied size of the organization, this was a big deal, but Moss wouldn't tell her anything about it, and the one member of the Order she'd met hadn't given her much to go on other than their rather unfortunate nickname for him.

It didn't take long to round up the refugees and get them back to the cargo room. She had Trouble stay with them. Fun as the little guy could be, the last thing they needed was a random element of chaos in whatever came next.

By the time Hel returned to the bridge, Jupiter was big enough to see clearly. It was just like the history books she'd read in school, except for one major difference: the Great Red Spot looked as if someone had slashed just above it with a cosmic knife. If the Spot was an eye, the dark slash just above it was like a thick eyebrow, making it look angry and judging.

She hurried back to her seat above Moss's and checked her displays, hoping to get a closer look. At first the slash looked straight and even, but zooming in revealed storms throughout it, a very ragged edge, and a slight bend at the middle.

"That's the Scar?" she asked.

"Yep," said Moss. "If you're looking for a sense of scale, it's wider than the Earth."

"And it's manmade?"

"From the early days of A-drive experiments."

"A-drive?"

"Alcubierre. What we call transit drive now. No one knows how it happened, only that the unmanned test vehicle had some kind of runway chain reaction. They sent the craft down into Jupiter, figuring the high gravity would contain whatever happened next, but it might have made things worse. That was the result. Slowed down research for decades."

"Holy crap. And it's how old?"

"About four hundred years, give or take. Last I heard, they figured it might last another two or three. It's actually made the Great Red Spot bigger, if you ask me. Now, if you're done gawking, contact Europa Mining Colony Delta and give them the clearance codes Violet dug up. Request Landing Pad 10."

"On it," said Hel. She did, however, take one more moment to gawk as the Scar became fully visible without the aid of the ship's sensors. She wondered if there some kind of lingering transit bubble effects were going on down there. Given how orderly the bands and swirls around Jupiter were—at a distance anyway—it seemed difficult to believe that this slash hadn't been swallowed up. Whatever the answer was, it was beyond her paygrade.

Hel turned off the display and contacted the mining colony, requesting clearance to land.

EMC Delta was a post-Disaster colony. There had only been two fully functional by 2241. Now mining colonies were scattered throughout the solar system. The most active ones tended to be the newest, where resources were still plentiful and easy to get at. These shipped their goods to the Terran Colony Fleet, wherever they happened to be, who ran their own nomadic mining operations in the Void.

The older colonies, like ECM Alpha and Beta, tended to operate with more with an eye to self-sustaining than expansion, and shifted their roles more to leisure and entertainment for those still living in Sol.

Delta fell somewhere in-between. Its heyday was long over, but it still produced enough raw materials to be useful. It was also very well established and served as a nexus point for many travelling between the inner and outer systems, but had nowhere near the security of a place like ECM Alpha or Armstrong Colony on Mars. Delta was a logical place to make the drop.

She didn't know what to expect as they approached the mining base's hangar. Ever since she'd learned about what had happened to humanity, she'd pictured the society built by the synthetics to be something unnatural and terrifying. Instead, she saw what she saw just about everywhere else in the galaxy. A bustling spaceport filled with people doing their jobs.

As their ship settled down at Pad 10, two dock workers shared a joke before going their separate ways, one heading back to the terminal, the other coming to meet them as they disembarked.

Moss was already out of his chair when she slid down the ladder. "Okay, you let me do all the talking, got it?" he said. "Follow my lead and agree with anything I say. You're a freeborn here, so you'll have to act like it."

"But you are too, aren't you?"

Moss grunted. "Don't worry about that. I've got it covered."

Whatever joke had been shared between the dock workers must have been a good one, because the guy still had a grin on his face when he met them by the ramp.

"That is a hell of an unusual ship," he said. "You lose a bet?"

"Don't get me started. She's a chimera, but she's flight worthy."

"I'll take your word on that. Long trip?"

"Just running the Void," said Moss. "Got some specialized mining equipment on board. New high-tech stuff, straight from Hopa."

The man held out a boxy device with a simple display. "Ident?"

Moss held out his left arm. Ident chips could be placed wherever it was convenient, were easily removed, and were keyed to an individual's DNA to prevent forgery. Theoretically. In reality, standard scanners could be fooled, and only high-end security could spot a good fake. But according to Moss, his could even pass those.

The dock worker ran the device over his arm and checked the results. "Right. Hand on the display, please. Just a quick genetic scan."

Moss frowned. "Oh?"

"We've been at SecStat 2 for weeks. Pain in the ass, but what can you do?"

Moss put his hand on the display. "Not much."

A green light lit up under his palm and the dock worker nodded, then looked to Hel. "Ident?"

Hel waited for Moss to nod, then stepped forward. She kept her ident on the back of her right hand and held it out for the scanner to read. Then she put her hand on top, and it flashed red. The worker frowned.

"You have a freeborn on board?"

"Special dispensation," said Moss. "Her mom saved my life in a mine collapse, and I agreed to take her daughter as my bondservant to see the stars. Check my file."

The man took a moment to go over Moss's information again. "Right. Sorry. Don't see them that often. Not an individual, anyway. They tend to travel in bulk."

Hel gritted her teeth. Just when things were starting to feel normal.

"We good to go?" Moss asked.

The man nodded. "Since we're at SecStat 2, your bondservant has to remain with you at all times. If she'd found in any secured areas, you can be held liable."

"Sure, got it. Thanks."

They made their way to a lounge. Hel tried to act casual and Moss made it look easy. She didn't know if he'd made up that story about her mom on the spot or planned it out ahead of time, but it came out so convincingly even she kind of believed it.

"You don't register as freeborn?" Hel whispered. "Even on a DNA scan?"

Moss held a finger to his lips. "Not anymore. We'll talk later."

They got a table in the lounge and ordered some drinks. The gravity on Europa was miniscule, less than that of the moon, but the lounge had a gravity field so people could enjoy a drink out of a proper glass.

Hel tried the drink she'd ordered. Even for juice, it was sweeter than she expected. "How long do we have to wait?"

Moss tested his tea, frowned, took out a hip flask and added a little something to it. "Hopefully not long. The sooner we're out of Sol, the better."

Of the nine members of the *Hydrus's* crew who had been on board the *Maruma*, three had been sealed in the cockpit and blown clear. Of the remaining six, three had died in the explosion and another of his injuries shortly after he was recovered. The two others that survived were healing well, having been farthest from the blast.

Commander Miram was not one of them.

She had tried to help lock down the reactor, then sealed off the engine room before the explosion that ripped the ship in half. What caused the explosion was unclear, but the team had reported that the reactor had modifications they'd never seen before, and the commander had wanted them removed for study.

Sub-Commander Nekkar had almost killed Roy the moment he was brought back on board, but Doctor Ascella and Lieutenant Ginan insisted that Roy couldn't have been involved, and had possibly saved their lives. It was the only thing that stayed Nekkar's hand. Still, he'd made sure the traitor suffered a bit before confining him to his quarters.

Now, with repairs underway, he had the hardest task of his career ahead of him. He'd lost soldiers before when he'd been a major in the Centurions, but that had been different. Death in combat was something that could be respected. Death by accident? It lacked meaning and purpose. And as the years wore on, he wondered if his end might come from the latter rather than the former.

The crew assembled in the shuttle bay, where a row of three coffins lay and another single coffin ahead of them. He didn't bother with a podium or any fancy trappings. No dress uniforms, flags, or murals. The dead deserved respect, but they cared not for ceremony.

Nekkar stood with Miram's casket in front of him, facing the crew.

"Three hundred and nine years ago, humanity nearly destroyed itself. Those that survived were charged with the unenviable task of trying to rebuild, and when that proved fruitless, to move on.

"Most of you were born into a time where we have grown strong. Despite the fact that we have no world to call home, all members of the Protectorate recognize that strength, and call upon us to do things others are unwilling or unable to do. Today, we are a voice that can be heard, though we are denied that voice in their government.

"Some of us have lived through all of this. They remember how close to extinction we came, how far we have come, and how much farther we have yet to go. Commander Miram was one of those people. She saw only potential within each of us and made sure each member of her crew found the position they were best suited for on her ship.

"Today, we honour not only her memory, but everything she has done for us. As we move forward, I expect each of you to follow her example. Her duty to the Fleet has ended. Ours must continue..."

There was more to the speech, the usual platitudes, and then there was the matter of removing the dead. An honour guard loaded the four caskets on board a shuttle, which then left the hangar and flew toward the nearest star. It would return empty in half an hour.

The crew returned to their stations, and Nekkar returned to Miram's office. His office.

There was still much to do while repairs continued. People worked on scouring what they could of the *Maruma's* records, hoping to find some kind of lead. Salvage teams were trying to find traces of the sensor masking Roy had referred to.

But what bothered Nekkar most was the message Commander Miram had left for him. He had expected to find something in the event of her death, but the contents of that file, a video message for his eyes only, continued to haunt him on an existential level.

He shut the door to his office and activated the lock, then sat at the desk, found the file, and played it for the fifth time. A projection of the commander floated in front of him.

"Magnus. We both know what it means if you are seeing this. I won't waste your time with words of advice. I know you find such things tedious. But I trust that you will be the commander I have always hoped you would be, and that I have properly prepared you for this day.

"Assuming that my death occurred during our current operation, I do have some reservations. I know you believe that this mission is beneath you, and will no doubt want to wash your hands of it so you can seek out more glorious deeds. But there is more at stake here than you realize. I am not exaggerating when I say that the continued future of the Colony Fleet may depend on it..."

Severed Links

Synths were designed with the same failsafe. They cannot reproduce naturally. This isn't a problem for your average synth since birthing chambers are commonplace. To them, the idea of natural childbirth and growing up seems crazy inefficient.

However, this is a problem for cyborgs, because the means to create more of them were lost when Earth went splut. Trying to work around it is impossible, since any alterations made to the cyborg's genetic makeup instantly gets repaired by the nanotech. Even cloning won't work.

So while cyborgs, in theory, can't die of old age, there will never be another one. Thank goodness for small favours.

M. Foote, *And Then Things Got Worse*

BEING A DISEMBODIED SIMULATION of a human being was a bit of a downer at times. Violet had created a virtual "home" for her to be herself in, but at the same time part of her knew it was all an illusion. She might *think* she was sitting in a home movie theatre, munching popcorn while watching *Top Gun* for the tenth time, but she wasn't.

She'd have to work on simulating some kind of tactile feedback. Right now, it was like she was watching a first-person movie of herself watching a movie. Could she simulate taste? She could really go for some pie right about now.

A red light flashed over the movie, warning Violet that someone was snooping around the ship.

She went back to her ship embodiment view and checked the halls, then saw a small furry thing scurry out of sight of one camera, and into sight of another.

"Trouble."

"That's me," the petbot said. "I'm running low on charge. Can I use the cockpit plug?"

"Sure." She was going to ask how he'd gotten out of the locked cargo bay but realized that she hadn't locked down the tiny air vents that ran throughout the ship. Trouble's hands were just the right size to manipulate screws or pry things open. And why ask to use a plug in the cockpit when there were power sockets throughout the ship? No doubt he wanted Moss to find him there, and had a quip ready for him when he did. They hadn't gone half-assed when it came to programming his annoying comic relief personality.

Trouble scurried to the cockpit and Violet let him in.

"Thanks, doll." Trouble found an outlet and leaned against it. "Ah, that's the good stuff. Say, where are ya anyway? I've heard ya all over the ship, but never seen ya."

"I am everywhere... and nowhere," Violet said cryptically.

"Say what?"

"I'm the ship computer."

"Ah, gotcha."

In the cartoon, Ranger M's ship didn't have any kind of onboard intelligence. Trouble more or less filled that role. He had to since he was pretty useless otherwise. She'd always wondered why these kind of characters were a staple in old Terran cartoons. You have a heroic cast and a single bumbling sidekick who was usually more trouble than they were worth.

It had to be for the younger kids, but her childhood had lasted all of one year before she hit her teens, which had lasted two. And given that it had only taken a total of five to reach adulthood, she hadn't had much of what any freeborn would consider a youth.

Maybe that was what drew her toward those kinds of shows?

Something on the external cameras caught her attention. She switched from view to view and saw several dock workers snooping around her landing gear. Nothing unusual about that, probably just conducting routine safety checks.

Except she then saw a black low-gravity transport parked nearby. One man standing next to it wore a blast vest and was armed with a pulse rifle.

"Uh oh... I don't like the looks of this."

Trouble took that as some kind of cue and scampered up onto the dashboard, propping himself on her figurine to get a better look outside. "What is it?"

"Trouble."

"Yeah?"

"No, I mean there's trouble outside."

"But I'm right here!"

"I don't have time for this."

Trouble suddenly shot upright as Violet accessed his programming. When she was done, the furry petbot stumbled and fell off the console, hitting the floor with a light thump as it rebooted.

Violet had a plan, but she didn't have time to explain it to something that would stretch out that comedy subroutine for as long as it possibly could.

She turned on the comm. "Hey Moss?"

"That's him."

Moss nodded across the lounge toward a very tall man checking the tables in the room. He'd probably lived most of his life in low-gee areas to get that gangly. He didn't find who he was looking for, of course, and took a table across the room from them.

"You sure?" Hel asked.

"Call it a hunch."

Moss got up and went over to his table, Hel following behind. He sat down without being invited.

"Link." It was a contact name, not a real name.

The man frowned. "Do I know you?"

"Captain Randgaffi couldn't make it," Moss explained. "I've had to pick up where he left off."

"No, I mean, do I *know* you? You look familiar. Have we met?"

Moss shook his head.

"Not unless you like cartoons," said Hel.

Moss was about to cut in—partly to remind her that his character always wore a mask, but mostly to tell her to shut up—when the man laughed. "Right, *Ranger M*. Oh my God, you're really him."

"Wait, how did you—?"

"You've had quite an interesting life, Mr. Foote," said Link. "Not many humans are in our family, so obviously you caught my attention... *Homewrecker*."

"Oh brother," Moss groaned. Of all the nicknames the Order could have clapped him with, it had to be one that made him sound like someone who hit on married women.

"Hey, I get it. It loses something in translation. They call me Link, and I asked, 'Why not something more impressive, like *Nexus*?' But it seems that word translated to Nubran insults someone's grandparents."

"Still, the name is a bit on the nose, don't you think?" said Hel.

"It's how they like to do things," said Link.

"How did you even get in?" asked Moss. He didn't say the Order's name directly, but it was clear what he was referring to.

"I guess you could say I was born into it," said Link.

"Born?" asked Hel.

"Metaphorically speaking," said Link. "I'm a Martian. Gagarin Colony, Synth Chamber 19. I was raised to be Haven's assistant."

Moss's brows rose. "Haven's a person?"

"Didn't you know?"

"We thought it was a place," said Hel.

"Anyway, he's been with them since before I was born. And when"—Link gestured to Moss sheepishly—"you-know-what happened, he decided to stay behind on Mars and keep things going. So, when did they let you back in?"

"Technically, I'm not," Moss said. "I'm just dealing with some unintended consequences."

"What happened to Randgaffi?"

"He died. Unintentionally. This is the consequence."

Link's eyes widened. "And the cargo?"

"Safe aboard our ship," said Moss. "Hanger 10. We're more than happy to pass it onto you and get out of your hair."

Violet cut in over Moss's comm. "Hey Moss?"

"Hold one minute, Violet," said Moss.

"So you didn't bring the *Maruma*?" asked Link.

"It suffered some heavy damage," said Moss. "Had to use my ship."

"*Moss.*" Violet tried to hail him again. He ignored her.

"So your ship's equipped with a sensor mask?"

"A what now?"

"MOSS!"

Moss's eyes widened. All at once, he realized just how badly he'd screwed up.

"How bad is it, Vi?"

"Get out of there! We've been made!"

All the simulated combat training Hel had been through on board the *Rex* kicked in. As soon as Violet's warning came over the comm, she saw four men in black security uniforms through a window, hurrying toward the lounge's front entrance. Not that it did her any good. She was supposed to be a bondservant, and as such, was unarmed.

Moss leapt from the table, reached into his jacket, but rather than pulling out a pulse gun, threw three small balls.

"Run!"

Hel turned and bolted for the back of the lounge as the flashbangs each detonated one second apart. She wasn't looking at them, but the sound was still deafening at this range. Her ears rang as she tried to keep her eyes locked on Moss and pray he knew a back way out of there.

Link ran with them, pulling out a pistol and firing behind him at the security officers.

Moss was well ahead of them both, pushing through a door into a back kitchen. Hel tried to keep up, but Link was falling behind. She looked back, briefly, and saw him limping badly.

She went back and tried to help him along. They'd only just made it through the door when he fell to the ground. Moss came back long enough to throw another flashbang out the door and help her carry him through the kitchen and out the other side. His body suddenly got lighter as they left the gravity field but had gone limp.

Moss tried to pull her away, but Hel kept a hold on Link. He was trying to say something to her. She moved in closer, trying to make out the words over the ringing in her ears.

"Gagarin. Synth Chamber 19. Go..." He held up his pistol for her, and she took it, just as Moss managed to pull her off and drag her away.

Hel had gotten used to zero-gee in an EVA suit, but low gravity was another matter. It was easy to gain speed if you angled yourself right, but your mass remained the same, and still had the same Newtonian compulsion to keep going in your original direction whenever you tried to turn.

Moss, however, had long perfected the art of running away, and helped make sure she stayed on track. She couldn't tell if he had somehow scanned a map of the EMC Delta starport earlier of if he was just the luckiest man alive, but within a few moments her hearing was clearing up and he seemed pretty confident they'd lost them. They were in an alley not too far from the landing bay area.

"What do we do now?" she asked. "Get back to the ship?"

A faint rumble could be felt in the ground more than heard, and Hel turned just in time to see the *Viaticus Rex II.I* gain speed and fly out EMC Delta's energy curtain, a couple of small fighters taking off in pursuit.

"Yeah, that's not going to happen," said Moss.

"Hello?" A young voice echoed through the empty cabin. "Hello? Um... I hope you don't mind, but everyone got bumped around a bit and we're wondering if everything is all right. Hello? Ranger M?"

A dirty blond head of hair and blue eyes peeked through the open cabin door.

"You better come in here, kid," said Violet. "It's Zach, isn't it?"

Zach moved cautiously into the empty room. "Where's Ranger M?" He looked up the ladder to the top half of the command deck. "Is he up there?"

"Ranger M is on an important assignment," said Violet. "He had me leave to make sure you and the others stayed safe."

"Are we in trouble? Is that why we were getting bounced around?"

"Let's just say I was playing it safe. Didn't want anyone to know where we were going."

Zack advanced further into the room. "Will we go back? To pick Ranger M up?"

"He's going to have to find us. Don't worry. He will."

"And where are you?" Zach said finally, as if broaching a question he felt foolish asking.

"I'm the ship's computer, sort of. You can call me Violet."

"The first officer isn't here either?"

"Nope. Sorry."

"So... does that make me captain of the ship?"

Zach might not have noticed the figurine perched on the dashboard when he first entered the cockpit, but he definitely noticed it suddenly turn its head to look at him.

"What? What makes you say that?"

"Well, *you* can't be the captain. You're the computer. And nobody else wants to leave the cargo bay. I mean, I'm kind of the only person here, so..."

"Now listen. I've played second fiddle to a lot of people in my time, but never a teenager. I'm the captain, got it?"

Zach nodded shyly.

"But I guess I could use a first mate. And it seems that position is open."

Zach smiled and plopped himself down into the captain's chair. "Aye aye, sir!"

Violet coughed over the speakers. "That's *my* chair, thank you very much."

"Oh, sorry. But you can't even—"

"I actually *can* sit in it. You just can't see me do it. Now, the first mate's chair is up the ladder. It's got a better view than down here anyway. Just don't touch anything." Not that it mattered, she'd disabled the upper cockpit control panel the moment she'd thought of it.

"Okay, great. Thanks!" Zach rushed over to the ladder and scooted up.

Up till now, Violet had been so focused on getting the *Rex* out of danger that she hadn't bothered with a virtual representation of the ship. Her view had been filled with HUD readouts and external cameras. And when Zach had walked in, she had observed him through the internal cameras.

Now that she had time to rest, she used those cameras to create a virtual image of the cockpit, and herself, and allowed herself to take command, just like when she'd been alive. She hated to admit it, but accessing the controls mentally, once you were used to it, was far more efficient than any kind of manual control system. But it just didn't feel right. Sitting at the helm, hand on stick and throttle, familiarizing herself with the HUD and control panels until they were second nature... *that* was the only way to fly.

If she had a choice, she'd take a real body and slower reflexes over her mind being one with the ship any day.

Once she was convinced nobody was tracking her, Violet set course for the asteroid belt between Mars and Earth's tomb, where she hoped to find whatever was left of an ancient piece of Terran history. She'd left a breadcrumb trail for Moss. She just hoped some pigeons didn't end up eating it.

Roy had been invited to meet with the acting commander in his office. And by invited he meant forcibly shoved by two security guards without any kind of request being made. He was pretty sure they'd been ordered to make him as uncomfortable and unwelcomed as possible the whole way, going so far as to give his collar a slight jolt when he scowled at one of them.

He was only a little surprised that they allowed him in the office with Nekkar alone. But then, the former first officer no doubt wanted to demonstrate that he didn't see Roy as a threat.

"Whatever special arrangements you had with Commander Miram died with her," he said bluntly. "When time allows, you will be returned to the Terran Colony Fleet and face whatever justice they see fit. In the meantime, you will continue to provide any and all information I ask for pertaining to the lost cargo from the *Maruma*. Your cooperation will be passed along for consideration at your trial, but that is all. Those were the terms agreed to as written in the Commander's log, and the only ones I am willing to honour. Is that understood?"

"Did anyone tell you about attracting flies with honey instead of vinegar?" Roy asked. Much as he expected, that remark earned him a shock.

"If you behave childishly, you will be punished accordingly."

"By punishing me childishly? Yeah, I can see that." That got him another shock, but it was worth it.

"Is *that* understood?"

Roy leaned forward on his desk. "You need to feel big by jolting me? Knock your socks off. You want information? I'll give it to you. You expect me to snap to attention and salute? You might as well blow my head off right now."

"Don't tempt me," said Nekkar.

"Please. You need me, just like Miram did. Now, since I don't want to be in the same room with you any more than you do, let's do each other a favour and get down to business. What have you got?"

Nekkar pressed a button on his desk, activating a display. He cycled through a series of still images, some partially corrupted. They showed the interior of the *Maruma*, and either one or two people walking inside it.

"As we expected, the main computer's memory was thoroughly wiped. This is all we were able to salvage from the individual cameras. Anyone here look familiar?"

Roy studied the images. One was of a woman floating down the corridor with the gravity off, using her wings to manoeuvre. She was Elysian, like the captain, but the lights were low so he couldn't get a good look at her features.

"She was the last aboard," said Nekkar.

"Sorry, not ringing any bells."

The other images were more well lit and showed two people in the corridor. One was a Terran woman, the other a man in a mask. A green and red old Earth wrestling mask.

Seeing that had been such a surprise, he wasn't able to hide his reaction. Even Nekkar could pick up on the body language. "What is it?"

"Give me the best image you can of the man in the mask."

The acting commander did the best he could, finding a shot where he was almost looking at the camera, then zooming and resolving the image as much as possible.

It was him. He could tell from the eyes and the set of his teeth.

"You have got to be shitting me."

"You know him?"

"Not in the slightest. But when I find him, I'm going to kill him."

Life is Full of Disappointments

Despite the oppression they faced, some synths rose to fame and notoriety back on Earth. In 2163, twenty-three years after the Jupiter Incident that left the Scar over the Great Red Spot, the first manned A-Drive test was conducted by Captain Anna Powell, a second gen synth. She made the trip from Jupiter to Earth in just over five hours at 0.12c and was awarded the Medal of Freedom by the UN. She was offered early retirement, but chose to work as a shuttle pilot on the Moon instead, where she stayed until she died in the Intersystem War forty years later.

M. Foote, *And Then Things Got Worse*

*T*WO DAYS LATER

Roy was making himself useful, but only because it suited his needs.

Though Camile Miram's death wasn't something Roy had expected or particularly desired, he couldn't deny the opportunities it had opened up.

Acting Commander Nekkar had taken a strict authoritarian approach to dealing with Roy, putting him in his place and making sure he knew who was boss at every turn. Nekkar no doubt believed that by not giving him an inch he would ensure that Roy was no trouble at all and could be put to good use however he saw fit.

Which just went to show just how little the man understood about manipulation.

Roy provided Nekkar with as much information as he could, and as much detail as he could, as well as supplementary information that might be of use to him down the road. What he knew of slave convoys, who the railroad might contact when trying to move their passengers discretely, that sort of thing.

But at the same time, he provided an echo chamber to Nekkar's views. The man definitely held a superiority complex about their kind, and deep down the man saw synths as little better than freeborns.

Based on his private conversations with Miram, Roy had intimated that he might know more about the mysterious Order than he actually did. Second hand stuff, but still, if he was told a bit more about what was going on, maybe...

Before the acting commander even realized what he was doing, he was giving Roy access to parts of the ship he never would have before, such as the medical bay, where the deceased pilot of the *Maruma* was being examined. Nekkar had hoped Roy might shed some light on what they had found on the dead Elysian.

Or, more accurately, what they hadn't found.

"Unfortunately, the only signs of the device we've found are based on what is missing," said Dr. Ascella. The pilot's body lay on the examination table, naked but covered by a sheet. His head was shaved and turned to one side, where a faint series of marks along the side of his head stretched from the temple down to the jawline.

Roy didn't know what to make of it. "It wasn't an implant," he said. "Just a dermal gizmo of some sort." The pirates of the Void

Brotherhood loved that kind of stuff, adding holo-tactical displays or smart targeting rigs that were ten percent about usefulness and ninety percent about looking hardcore.

"Incorrect," said the doctor. "It most certainly was an implant, but a highly unusual one. Scans show residual nanotech. It had once been interfaced with whatever was on his head. But here's the odd thing—once the device was removed, the nanotech began to break itself down. *Disassemble* itself. Trying to leave no trace behind. But because the body was deceased, it didn't have enough energy to complete the job."

"How was the device removed?" asked Roy. "It kind of looks like scarring here, but you said it was removed after his death."

Ascella nodded, and she pointed along one of the straighter marks. "Medical laser, probably from a basic field kit," she said. "It seems the nanotech also tried to heal the marks left as well. I suppose ideally, had the body been found sooner before the implant was removed, there would have been enough residual energy left for no physical trace to be left behind."

"Well, that's some real cloak and dagger shit right there," said Roy. "Certainly sounds like your Order. No wonder they've stayed off your radar for so long." He looked long and hard at the outline left behind. "So, I'm guessing the nanotech was wired into the brain, maybe the eye?"

"The brain," Ascella confirmed. "It was primarily fixed along the edge of the frontal bone, though it extended down along their equivalent of the temporal for some reason."

A few possibilities came to mind as to what something like that could be used for. Enhanced communications rig? Neural enhancer of some sort? But what would make it so important to not only remove, but design it to remove all traces of itself? What could simultaneously be extremely useful for them to recover, but dangerous to be discovered by someone else?

Roy hid a smile. "My guess is it was some kind of communications gear," he said. "Hands free, multi-channel, perhaps even a virtual display component for the eye."

"That would be useful," the doctor agreed. "But why go to such lengths to hide its existence?"

"I figure they didn't want anyone else to discover how the tech works or learn what settings they use. You could gain access to their whole comm network that way."

It was all a lie, of course. But if his hunch was right, it was close enough to the truth to slip by.

Moss opened the hotel door, bag in his hand, checked the hall one last time, and shut it behind him. "I'm back."

Hel continued to look up at the ceiling, looking for patterns in the speckled ceiling panels. "Great. My life has meaning again."

"You know, as captain, I'm the one who gets to be sarcastic at every turn."

"That was back when you had a ship."

They were holed up in a low budget hotel on the far side of EMC Delta. Moss said he had a second ident hidden on his person—he refused to say where—and had been able to not only rent this place under an alias with an emergency stash of funds, but slip the owner a little bit extra to backdate the logs so it seemed like they'd been there for a couple of weeks.

Since most bondservants didn't have real idents unless their jobs involved travel, Hel didn't have to provide hers. She was just extra baggage. But to keep a low profile, she'd been cooped up here ever since they'd arrived, while Moss went out trying to do his thing.

"I've got food," said Moss.

"I'd prefer a way off this rock," said Hel.

"I'm working on it."

Hel grit her teeth. He'd been telling her that for two days straight, and she was buying it less and less. "And then what? Let's say we get off Europa. Where did Violet go?"

"I told you I don't know. But she'd leave us a trail to follow. We just have to get out there and find it."

Hel heard a scratching noise coming from the walls. The air circulation in this building was terrible. Or maybe they had rats on Europa? She sat up on the bed. "I doubt she left a neon sign pointing to her secret hideout. Shouldn't she have a way to let us know *before* we leave, so we know where to start looking?"

"I don't know, okay? I've been pumping the locals for information and making connections. That little attack at the lounge barely turned any heads. Most people don't even know it happened. Or if they do, they don't care."

"It didn't make any of the newsfeeds either," said Hel "Is that how the TCF works?"

Moss shook his head. "Not that I'm aware of. They have what you might call a free press, though the people in charge are pretty much in step with the government anyway. They wouldn't hide a story like this, just put their own spin on it."

"Maybe there's no story because the *Rex* got away? No slaves, no ringleader, no couriers, they just got a middleman." Hel frowned. Link. The least she could do was remember his name, even if it was an alias.

"My gut tells me that even if they got all of us, it wouldn't have made the news. This is something they want taken care of and forgotten."

"Think they've forgotten about us yet?"

Moss snorted. "Not a chance."

"So even if we find a ship, how do you plan to get on board? I assume they'll be checking everyone leaving this place."

"Not sure," said Moss. "My backup ident might be enough. Maybe we can smuggle you in a cargo container of pre-synthesized meat protein?"

Hel's jaw dropped.

"You'd have a respirator on," Moss said defensively. "It might let you slip past any scans they might have."

"I am *not* hiding a vat of synthetic meat goop."

"Look, the smell will wash right off and..." Moss paused as the scratching noise got louder. At first, he looked worried, then he close his eyes and gave a defeated sigh. "Well," he said, enunciating clearly. "I guess we're screwed, then. It would take a *miracle* to get us out of this jam!"

The air vent over their entertainment display rattled and shook but failed to open. A small voice could be heard inside. "Hey, what the...?"

"Gee, if only *someone* had a secret plan to help us escape," said Moss. If words could have eyes, that sentence would have them rolled back far enough to witness the earliest origins of sarcasm.

The vent continued to shake and rattle but wouldn't budge.

Hel decided to get in on the moment. "If they could, that person would be my *hero*."

"Ah, man..." They could see tiny paws fitting through the vent slats, looking for something to grip or loosen, and finding nothing. "Uh... a little help here?"

Karon was staying as far away from her quarters as possible.

The damage to the *Hydrus* was significant, but apparently not serious enough to warrant going back to the Fleet or calling a repair frigate mid-mission. A dozen crew quarters had been damaged enough that they had to be sealed off for the time being, and the occupants reassigned to other rooms.

Karon had been sent back to her old quarters, and she knew exactly why: she'd opened her big fat mouth and gotten on Nekkar's shit list.

The fact the acting commander was completely in the wrong was beside the point.

She had been sent an automated message informing her that her officer's exam had been left incomplete and had therefore failed. Nekkar hadn't reached out to her or explained himself further. It had all come from the ship's computer once the failure was recorded.

She'd gone to his office wanting to explode at him but kept herself in check. She explained as calmly as possible how she had finished the exam and was simply waiting for the clock to run out when the ship had been damaged and she had put the well-being of the ship and its crew first.

The acting commander had listened to her, then stated that the terms of the test were clear. Leaving prior to time running out would result in failure. There were no exceptions. He'd even hinted that her timing for this conversation was disrespectful to Commander Miram's memory.

Then he'd told her that the quarters she'd been moved to after the breach were a bit crowded and she would be moved back to her old quarters. With the prisoner.

He half-heartedly assured her of her safety. If any harm came to her, the prisoner knew he would be punished. She did not find that thought at all comforting. Then, as she was leaving, he told her she was welcome to reapply for the officer's exam when their current mission was over... preferably on board another ship.

Part of her felt it had been her tone that did her in. She must have come off more aggressive or disrespectful than she realized.

But another part knew that wasn't it at all. It was because of who she was.

Nekkar wanted her to be uncomfortable and afraid. There was no reason that the prisoner couldn't be sent back to the brig, for example.

No, he was punishing her for questioning him, possibly for taking the exam in the first place.

So she'd buried herself in her work and napped in the mess hall. But it was taking its toll on her. She'd not only failed her officer's exam, she'd been exiled on board her own ship. And while there was nothing she could do about the former, she could take back the latter.

After her shift, she marched to her quarters. There was only one guard there now instead of two. She wondered if the prisoner had earned a degree of trust from Nekkar or if this was another way to make her feel less safe. It didn't matter.

The guard gave her a nod. "He won't try anything. Sorry to hear about the officer's exam."

That took her by surprise. She didn't really know this man. He wasn't part of her circle. "How did you—?"

"Word gets around," said the guard. "Not many of us try out for the officer ranks, let alone make it as far as you did. Is it true you left the exam to help repair the ship?"

"The exam was finished. I was just sitting out the clock. The ship needed me."

"So they got you on a technicality?"

"Pretty much."

The guard scowled. "There is nothing honourable about that."

"Lecturing to the scholar," said Karon. "Can I go in now?"

"Of course. Just call if you need help."

The door opened and Karon went inside. A paranoid part of her expected the lights to be off and the prisoner to be lurking in the shadows, waiting for her. But the room was well lit, and he was sitting at her shallow table cross-legged, looking over a medical datapad.

"I was wondering if you'd ever show up," he said, not looking up from the pad. "Your bags were sent here yesterday."

"I wasn't exactly looking forward to this."

The man looked up at her now. "So, this used to be your room. My guess is you were sent back here because of the damage the ship took. Crew quarters hit? They don't tell me much, obviously."

"That's the official reason," Karon said.

"Oh?" He seemed to consider this for a moment. "I wonder what the unofficial reason could be. Is it to punish you, or me? Or perhaps both?"

Karon frowned. "How could this be to punish you?"

"It's just a hunch," the man said. "Your acting commander is honour bound to stand by the terms Commander Miram and I came to regarding my cooperation. He might be looking for some excuse to nullify it. He's stupider than he looks if he thinks I'd do anything to you, though."

Karon looked at the bondscollar around his neck. "Because you'd lose your head if you did?"

The man shrugged. "Probably not. As long as they need me, they'll just shock me or deprive me of my after-dinner pudding or whatever. Sorry, I doubt you're important enough to kill me over, or else they wouldn't put you here in the first place."

Karon sighed. "You got that right."

"So it's to punish you? What was your big crime?"

"Talking back to the acting commander," said Karon, then checked herself. "Actually, daring to try and pass the officer's exam."

She could have sworn she saw the hint of a smile when she'd said that, but it disappeared just as quickly.

"I don't think we've been introduced," he said. "I'm Roy."

Karon remembered their first encounter. "Well, you already know my name."

"Just your last name," Roy said. "I recognized you as part of the Powell gene line."

"Oh. It's Karon."

"Nice to meet you, Karon. Now, if you'll excuse me, I have some work to do before Nekkar decides to give my neck a tingle."

And that was that. No innuendo, no threats, no alpha male moment where he let her know her place. He just went back to scanning the information on his datapad and let her get back to whatever she needed to do.

Karon went to her bed and saw her belongings recovered from Dale's blown-out cabin laid at the foot of it. Nothing of Roy's could be seen, though she suspected he hadn't arrived with anything.

As if reading her mind, she heard Roy say from the table, "I've got a mat for the floor out here. Believe me, I've slept in worse places."

Trouble stretched and pulled himself away from the charging pad, giving his tail a couple of flicks. "That's the good stuff. I was running low on juice there."

"*Now* can you tell us how you found us?" Hel asked.

"And how long you were actually waiting for a dramatic moment to reveal yourself?" Moss added.

They had asked Trouble these things the moment they'd freed him from the vent, but he'd insisted he needed a recharge first. No doubt this was also for dramatic effect, but they had little choice but to indulge him.

"Okay, so it's like this. Violet saw that some people were snooping around the ship, and some armed goons were on their way. She knew she wouldn't have time to get you back to the ship, so she got me to get off the ship and find you while she made her getaway."

Moss smiled. "I told you Violet would have a plan for us to find her. So, where is she?"

"No clue, boss."

"You didn't think to ask where she was going when she kicked you off the ship?"

"Hey, I know better than to fly too close to the sun, buddy."

Moss smacked his head. "What is that even supposed to mean?"

"Look, it's all a bit hazy up here, okay? I got zapped after we saw the goon squad. The next thing I know, I'm being told to jump out the waste disposal hatch and go find you guys. Not something I recommend, by the way. It took me a while, but eventually I spotted ol' Moss here out and about and tailed him back to this place."

Moss glared at the petbot. "Where you hid for... How long?"

Trouble squirmed, holding his tail in his hands. "Uh... an hour less than whatever would make you mad?"

"So we're no closer to finding her than we were before," said Hel.

Moss shook his head. "Vi wouldn't have sent it to find us for no reason."

"Maybe just to keep us company, since we're going to be trapped here *forever*," said Hel.

"Now you're taking my pessimism away from me as well," said Moss as Trouble scrambled away to get onto the nightstand. "Look, if Violet sent it to find us, she had a damn good reason, okay?"

Trouble found the light panel and started turning the room's lights on and off over and over.

"And apparently, that reason was to annoy the hell out of me."

Nothing But Trouble

NuPet Industries proudly introduces the PetBot Pal! Do you wish your pet could talk? Go with you on adventures? Make life more FUN? The new PetBot Pal brings you all that, and more! Based on our award-winning NuPet PetBot patented design, we've pushed the boundaries of Pseudo-Intelligence to bring you the most realistic and interactive companion to date! Each PetBot Pal comes with an advanced behaviour algorithm and a library of millions of potential responses based on your preferred behavioural traits. Your PetBot Pal can even mimic your favourite characters from your favourite programs! We guarantee 100% satisfaction. NuPet: New Pets. Same Old Love.

NuPet Marketing Brochure

Trouble had been with them for less than twelve hours, but it already felt like a lifetime in purgatory. When he wasn't scurrying around the room or bugging Moss with annoying show-related comments ("Hey, Boss, remember, the time we escaped a black hole with a broken transit drive?" "This is just like that time we were hiding out from the Galactic Mafia!" "Don't worry, we'll sort this out, just like we did the Mystery of the Blorgian Blade!"), he would start being even more annoying by flipping the lights on and off, or randomly changing channels on the entertainment display.

It was getting to the point where Hel and Moss were seeing eye-to-eye on the subject of Trouble accidentally falling into a trash compactor.

And the most annoying part of it was how repetitive it was. Hel could set her watch to the cycles between Trouble acting normal, and going into his routine. Last time she timed the gap in between, it had been just shy of fifty minutes.

Now, quite involuntarily, her brain created a beat that matched the pattern Trouble used in turning the lights on or changing the channels. Flipflipflip-flip-flipflipflipflip-flip-flipflipflipflipflipflip... In her head, it took on an electronic beat she could almost dance to. Whoever programed the stupid petbot...

Hel's jaw dropped.

"It's a message."

Moss took off the night mask he'd taken to wearing when Trouble started acting up. "What?"

"31416, over and over. It's a pattern," Hel said. "It's not bad programing, it's *deliberate* programming."

Moss frowned. Then his eyes widened. "Pi. Violet loves pie. And puns." He turned to Trouble. "Hey, cat-snake, why do you keep flipping the lights or TV?"

Trouble shrugged. "Dunno. Just something to do."

"Did you ever do this before?" asked Hel. "Back on the ship?"

"Not that I can remember."

"Didn't you say you lost power for a bit before Violet kicked you off the ship?"

"Got zapped," Hel corrected.

"Whatever. Damn, I don't know if there's a way to have this stupid wind-up toy go into diagnostics mode."

"Maybe you need to connect it to a larger computer?" Hel suggested.

"Hey, I'm standing right here, ya knobs. You can just ask me."

Moss turned to the petbot. "Do you know how to activate your diagnostics settings?"

"Sure. Just check my manual. It should be back on the ship!"

Moss looked around for something to throw at the ferret when there was a knock at the door.

Hel pulled out the pulse gun she had taken from Link when he'd died, but after a look from Moss tossed it to him. He motioned for Hel to be quiet and crept up toward the door.

"I see you with the gun, Homewrecker. These doors are wafer thin and if I wanted to, I'd just shoot you right through it."

Hel recognized that voice. Moss lowered the gun and opened the door.

"I thought the Order were pacifists?" he said.

Sister Tameria stepped inside. "Some of us define pacifism more loosely than others," she reminded him.

Moss smiled. "So do I hug my saviour or"—Tameria decked him. Moss staggered back, clutching his jaw—"get punched in the *fucking* face? The hell?"

"If lives weren't on the line, you'd be getting a lot more than that," Tameria said.

It took Moss a second to shake the cobwebs. "Lives? Oh, wait, you know?"

"Why else do you think I'm here? Now, where are they?"

Moss stepped back out of punching range. "Yeah, about that..."

It took a while to sort everything out. Violet had indeed programmed Trouble with regular intervals of compulsive behaviour, and put the code into an encrypted burst transmission intended for the

Order. Sister Tameria was already on her way and knew which mining base they were going to. Once she arrived, about a day ago, she had her ship monitor for the pattern. The sensors recently picked up a visual match from a window on the far side of the port and she had made her way over.

That explained how she found them, but when they learned about Tameria finding the *Maruma* and her relation to the captain, things got very awkward.

For once, Moss didn't go into one of his sarcastic yet somehow charming rationales or make it about himself. He simply said, "I'm sorry. I didn't know."

Sister Tameria said nothing in response and steered the matter back to what they had to do next.

"Since I have a ship, and clearance, getting you off Europa shouldn't be a problem," she said. "The question is, what then? How do we find your ship?"

"Ask it," said Moss, pointing to Trouble. "Whatever Violet had planned, she used it as her messenger."

"Only he doesn't seem to remember much," added Hel.

Tameria frowned. "All right. Trouble, where did Violet say she was going?"

The ferret shrugged. "No clue, lady."

"Access code: 3-1-4-1-6. Acknowledge."

Trouble cocked his head. "Say what?"

Moss tried a different approach. "Access code: Violet loves pie."

"Who doesn't?"

Tameria tried again. "Violet 3-1-4-1-6. Moss 3-1-4-1-6."

"What about Trouble 3-1-4-1-6?" Trouble suggested. "I don't wanna be left out."

It seemed Sister Tameria had as little patience for the petbot as Moss did. "Just tell me where she is, you furry little—"

"Hey, hey, hey! If I knew I'd tell you, I swear! I know better than to fly too close to the sun."

Hel frowned at that, but Moss shook his head. "Violet must have been worried about the ship's rat being intercepted. She couldn't be certain one of you were coming, so the key might be something she knows I would know."

"But something that someone else would hear and assume is nothing unusual," added Tameria.

"Daedalus," said Hel.

The others turned to her, even Trouble. "What?"

"Twice when asked about where Violet is, Trouble said he knew better than to fly too close to the sun."

Moss nodded. "Daedalus. Icarus's father. It fits."

Tameria frowned. "That seems a bit thin for a working theory. It could be a coincidence."

"Hel's instincts are pretty good, but you're right," said Moss. He grabbed Trouble by the neck and held him so they were eye to eye, only a finger length apart. "Listen up. Tell me where my ship is or I'll bite off your head and turn you into a furry sock."

"Hey, boss, lay off! I know better than to fly too close to the sun!"

Moss tossed Trouble onto the bed. "And now it's a working theory."

Tameria crossed her arms. "Okay, let's say you're right. What does it even mean? Daedalus."

"I think I know. I'll tell you once we're on the ship. Speaking of which, what's your plan for pulling that off?"

"And please tell me it doesn't involve a vat of synthetic beef," added Hel.

Sister Tameria's ship was an unarmed but extremely fast Baroque-class shuttle called the *Outreach*. Moss had flown in it once and could confidently state it was far faster than it looked. It sort of resembled an old space shuttle from pre-transit Earth, but the wings were angled at forty-five degrees outside of an atmosphere. You could barely make out the ship's name written in GalCom along its hull, since its faded and chipped black paint job was a deliberate attempt at being inconspicuous.

Moss hoped Tameria knew what she was doing, because this was the most conspicuous attempt at being inconspicuous he'd ever attempted.

Rather than trying to find a way to smuggle themselves on board, Moss and Hel marched right up to the ship, dressed as dock workers, carrying a large box between them. Tameria had already arranged for work IDs that would let them into the facility, no ident scan required.

Tameria was well ahead of them, already chatting up the workers on duty, asking various maintenance questions about her ship.

Then she pressed a button on her suit, and the backpack split open. Four wide iridescent wings unfolded, extending close to the ground, then fanned out, resembling something akin to an old Earth dragonfly crossed with a butterfly.

If the process didn't look natural, that's because it wasn't. Not exactly. Elysians had evolved on a low gravity world, but their pre-interstellar tech had been focused on genetic enhancement. They had incorporated wings into their species thousands of years ago, as well as a lighter but stronger bone structure and musculature suitable for higher-g worlds. Even their attractiveness was artificially enhanced.

As graceful as the end result was, these traits had come from a dark part of their history, and had had dire consequences. Genetic manipulation and body enhancement became more regulated after the Eugenics Surge, but by that point, the wings and glamour were an accepted part of the species.

Europa's gravity was low enough and the air density of the station high enough that Tameria was able to fly to the top of her ship like it was second nature, dancing around it like a pixie.

The dock workers here had seen few, if any, Elysians, and were fully focused on her while she called out to them, asking them questions about whether they'd checked this module or that vent. Moss assumed she'd used some of her glamour on them as well, so they might be even more enamoured with her flight.

That was all it took. Once Moss and Hel were on board, they made themselves comfortable in her quarters until she finished her inspection and prepped for takeoff. No one had noticed them now because they were workers, and no one would miss them later because they weren't. The simplest way to not be noticed was to look like you belonged.

For the past couple of days, the *Viaticus Rex II.I* had been sitting idle at minimal power: essential systems only. Well, essential to life anyway. Violet was blind to the outside world beyond basic visual readings, but using anything other than passive sensors might give them away.

As it was, the *Rex* floated in a scattered debris field like a piece of junk, right next to a much larger piece of junk, and the long dead and antiquated beacon that marked its grave.

Until Moss could find her, it was her job to keep their guests happy. And wanting to avoid some kind of convoluted sitcom scenario involving mistaken identity, a kid that nobody believed spoke to a person who wasn't really there, and possibly superstitious freeborns, she decided to be upfront and reveal herself to everyone in the cargo hold.

It wasn't something she did lightly. Her existence was almost certainly in violation of the Protectorate's A.I. restrictions. Being a transferred consciousness from a living human wouldn't matter to them, only the fact she was self-aware. Long ago, a planet had burned by crossing that line, and the Protectorate had both a long memory and unforgiving bureaucracy.

Of course, everyone on board was a fugitive, so it wasn't like they'd turn her in for a reward or something. But as the old saying went, loose lips sink sapient spaceships...

After she had Zach introduce her, she'd half expected the freeborns to worship her as a god. She was only slightly disappointed that they didn't. Despite having been enslaved or on the run most of their lives, these weren't backwater primitives. They knew an entity like Violet wasn't impossible, just highly unlikely.

In fact, she was pretty sure a number of them didn't even believe her. Judging by the way they trusted Zach's word on their status over hers, the others probably thought she was a sophisticated personality simulation like Trouble and were just playing along until Ranger M came back.

Soon, the refugees had ventured out of the cargo hold and set up sleeping areas around the ship, with families sticking together and cliques forming at an oddly rapid rate.

Zach's family were now seen as the most important group aboard the ship, due to the boy's 'promotion' to first mate and role as unofficial liaison to Ranger M. As such, they'd set up their beds in the galley across from the actual crew quarters, which Violet forbade anyone access to. This, in turn, meant they controlled access to the food, cementing their place in the new pecking order.

The man people had looked up to as their leader before this, Torell, did not take this very well, situating himself closer to the engines, which she also prevented access to. Where the others camped out in between was a web of familial allegiances, past associations, and whichever side they were currently trying to cozy up with.

All in all, it was much like watching an old 21st century reality TV show, many of which had regrettably survived the destruction of Earth.

Zach returned to his post, or what he considered his post, in the co-pilot's seat in the upper cockpit. "Hey Violet? Can I ask you a question?"

"Yeah?" It wasn't like there was much to do other than watch the cameras right now.

"What's Ranger M really like?"

"You've seen the show, kid," Violet said diplomatically.

"No, I mean the captain. Moss. The real Ranger M."

"He's a good guy, deep down." *Real deep down.*

"But what can you tell me about him? What has he really done? Why was he Ranger M?"

"Believe me, he asks himself that all the time."

"You don't have to lie to me," Zach said a bit sheepishly. "I know the cartoons aren't real. But I also know he is. I just want to know the truth."

Just because Violet didn't have lungs didn't mean she couldn't sigh. She'd watched enough old Earth programming to know what it was like when you were about to tell someone that Santa Claus wasn't real.

Captain Keed

ARMSTRONG COLONY, MARS - 2241

Somehow Moss landed at Armstrong Colony without incident. His passenger had played the part of a recovering heart attack victim convincingly once emergency services were on board. Heck, he wasn't entirely sure the man had been faking. Then, shortly after they'd left, Moss got a message from someone else wanting to be allowed on board. A Nubran woman.

"Guess your ride is here," said Moss.

The man looked a bit startled by how he'd said this. The scientist had said nothing about going anywhere else. But Moss had a feeling from the start there was more going on, and that Mars was just a rendezvous point. His bet was the Doc was leaving the solar system. Right now, that seemed like the smartest thing anyone could do.

Moss allowed the Nubran on board. She was short, blue skinned, with dark blue hair and the usual four fingers that always made him think of old cartoon characters whenever he saw them. But she wore a Martian looking outfit—to fit in better, Moss assumed. As much as a blue-skinned alien could fit in on Mars.

The first thing she did was embrace the man in a sympathetic hug. The scientist let out a sigh so deep Moss thought he might deflate, yet there were no tears. When they looked at one another, there was sadness, but also a sense of inevitability. Whatever just happened on Earth hadn't been as much of a surprise to them as it had been to Moss.

"I'm too late," he said at last.

"There was nothing you could have done," she replied. "We were all expecting a war. Just not this." Her English was rough but understandable. Adaptive translators still weren't commonplace in Sol. She turned to Moss, then back to the man with a questioning look, exaggerated as if she had only just learned human body language. He shook his head.

"Then we will talk more later," she said. She came to Moss and handed him a card. "Your payment. I have doubled the amount agreed upon. But I fear it may be worth much less in the days to come. Thank you."

With that, she and the scientist left. Once her words sank in, however, Moss chased after them.

"Wait, what do you mean worth much less?"

The Nubran kept the scientist in front of her while she spoke. "I would not expect your economy to do so well after what just happened, would you?"

"Yeah, but... I was going to..." At that moment Moss realized whatever plans he had after this job had been thrown out the airlock. "What the hell am I supposed to do now?"

"Now? Now your world changes."

At that moment, the pink sky filled with dim flashes as a number of Protectorate capital ships dropped out of sub-transit overhead in low Mars orbit.

The Nubran woman patted Moss on the shoulder and turned to leave with her colleague. "Be ready."

Moss stood there, looking up at the ships and they came closer and closer toward the colony, until the largest one blocked out the sun. He looked back at the pair as they exited the hangar.

"Be ready?" he yelled. "Be ready for what?"

The woman stopped at the door and looked back at him. "For the future."

Sol - 2550

The *TCF Hydrus* came out of transit on a direct course to Jupiter. The navigator altered their heading for Europa as the ship shifted comfortably to sub-transit.

"ETA, one hour," said the helmsman.

Acting Commander Nekkar stood. "Very good. Comms, contact Europa Central. Inform them that we require a manifest of all ships having come in and out of the outer systems over the last three days. Send the same message to Mars Central regarding the inner system."

Ensign Davis nodded. "Aye, sir."

Nekkar left the bridge, allowing Lieutenant Ginan to take command. "Have the prisoner sent to my cabin."

Karon Powell never imagined she'd laugh at something Roy Herzog would say, but she found herself snorting uncontrollably.

"It wasn't that funny," said Roy.

"It was more *how* you said it," said Karon. Which was true. Roy's story about stealing a cargo ship full of Elysian pleasure rods, thinking they were precious metals, hadn't been that funny on its own, but the man's cynical, dry, fatalistic way of telling it had elevated it. Like such a twist in fate had been inevitable and that he should have seen it coming. It seemed to be the way he viewed everything in life.

When Karon had been moved back to her quarters, she'd tried to keep away from him as much as possible, finding as much extra work to do as she could. Once it became clear that Roy had no intention of harming her, she'd become less nervous, but still kept mostly to her room. Then she'd learned about how Acting Commander Nekkar was treating him. It was something she could relate to. Nekkar might not be using a bondscollar on her, but she knew what it was like to be in his crosshairs.

Last night, she'd decided to just talk to him. She had to admit she was curious. What drove a man to leave the Silver Legion? What had made him so cynical about, well, everything?

The more they talked, the more she saw a man who hadn't given up, but at the same time no longer saw a point to fighting the good fight. Not for the Terran Colony Fleet, not for the Silver Legion, and certainly not for his fellow cyborgs, whom he'd flat out told her were a doomed people.

"We can't create more of ourselves, only more of you," he'd said. "And they see you as disposable. Every year they treat you more and more like that because they're afraid of dying. Not individually, mind you, but as a race."

The thought had resonated with her. Commander Miram had never treated her synth crew as expendable, but Nekkar certainly did. And it was no secret that cyborgs saw themselves as superior. Of course, most synths saw themselves as somewhat flawed—especially those who, at some point, had aspired for advancement or branching into new fields only to burn out. Cursing one's template was just another way of blaming their genes for their lot in life.

"Why become a pirate?" Karon asked now. "Not for the pleasure rods, I'm sure."

Roy shrugged. "Once I saw the absurdity of it all, I saw no reason to support a regime built on a fabrication."

"Fabrication?"

Roy smirked. "You see the Silver Legion as some grand tradition going back centuries. A great and noble institution that will keep Terran culture alive and help the Colony Fleet find a new and permanent home in the universe.

"But I was there when they made the Fleet, and the Legion. I saw them create that culture, methodically pick and choose ideas from Earth's past to weave into something that would inspire loyalty and pride, and then refined it over the next fifty years. The culture you admire is as conditioned toward its desired outcome as you are, honey. Perfectly programmed to fit in its nice little niche."

Karon's eyes narrowed. "Not all synths are in a fixed position for life."

Roy gave a dark chuckle. "You keep telling yourself that."

"I passed the officer's exam."

Roy gave her a look.

"Well, I would have, except..."

"Except Nekkar doesn't want you or any of your kind on his bridge," said Roy. "Commander Miram was a good woman, but Nekkar? You want to know why I became a pirate? People like him. I'm an arrogant bastard but at least I recognize talent when I see it. You passed your exam with time to spare, then helped out your ship in the middle of a crisis. That should have gotten you a commendation, and maybe under Miram it would have. Nekkar squanders assets out of a sense of pride that isn't even deserved because the alternative is to face the reality that he doesn't matter in the grand scheme of things. His sense of self-worth is all that keeps him going, believe me. That's what the Legion gives him. But self-worth isn't something that's bestowed upon you. It comes from what you make, and what you take. *That's* why I left. I may be a prisoner on this ship right now, but in here"—he thumped his chest—"I'm free, honey."

The door chimed, announcing someone's arrival.

"That'll be for me," Roy said, getting up. "We dropped to sub-transit a while back, which means we're in Sol. Which means the acting commander will want to have a few words with me. See ya."

Karon watched Roy leave, but said nothing. For a time, she was left alone with her thoughts.

Sister Tameria's shuttle could carry a number of passengers but wasn't intended for more than two people in the cockpit. Which made Hel leaning between the two pilot chairs feel a bit cramped, and having Trouble on the dashboard was just plain annoying.

"I always knew you would buy into your own hype someday," said Tameria, watching the furry petbot press its face against the canopy, as if that gave the creature a better view of space.

Moss frowned. "Don't blame me. That was Hel's brilliant idea."

"They got his mannerisms down pat," Tameria admitted. "Quality work. Probably programmed every episode into its memory."

"Believe me, I know," said Moss.

Oblivious that they were talking about him, Trouble looked back at them. "So where we off to, boss? Boss lady? Other boss lady?"

Tameria looked to Moss. "Well?"

"Set your course for the asteroid belt between Earth and Mars," said Moss. "When we get there, start targeting asteroids along the belt, act as if you're scanning them."

Tameria frowned, but did as he asked. "You know, a straight answer would be more helpful."

Moss chuckled. "Haven't figured it out? I thought you studied Earth history?"

"My interests in that regard are fairly narrow," said Tameria. Mainly she had studied the events leading up to the destruction of Earth and the Protectorate's involvement after that. There had been a number of things that didn't quite add up to her, but the Order had quietly discouraged her enquiries, which had only made her more curious.

"Well, what do you know about Daedalus?"

"Way before my era of expertise, but if I recall correctly, that name is tied to an ancient myth about hubris. Great inventor, escaped his captor by building wings for himself and his son Icarus, but his son flew too close to the sun and his wings melted. Is it a code for where Violet decided to hide? Where did Daedalus hide after his escape?"

"Sicily, but that's not the clue. She's speaking in code, sure, but she still wants us to find her."

"Then where is she?" Tameria asked.

"The *Daedalus*." Hel said.

"It's a ship?"

"Was," Moss corrected.

The penny dropped, as the Terrans said, and she made a quick query on her terminal. The *UNMS Daedalus* had been a massive self-sustaining mining vessel, an icon of the early ambitious expansion of their solar system. It had launched just a couple of years before Hel's generation ship, the *Pegasi*, left Sol.

"It can't still be around, can it?"

Moss shook his head. "No, it was destroyed in the Intersystem War, just before the Protectorate made first contact."

Tameria nodded. That was decades before the destruction of Earth. Still, it exposed a gap in her studies. "I assume there's some kind of memorial around the wreckage?"

"Used to be. A beacon near the main part of the wreck for travellers to visit. Probably been ignored for centuries, since I'm not picking it up on any sensors. You have any way to speed up the search? The belt is a very wide and empty stretch of space."

Tameria thought about it for a moment. "What if we could ask Violet?"

"That would be great, but there's a small flaw with your plan," Moss started.

Tameria cut him off. "Both of you, come with me."

Moss looked at the device in what was either Sister Tameria's work-shop, or a mad scientist's laboratory.

At some point, the *Outreach* had had its galley converted into a workspace. The kitchenette and food preservers were still there, but everything else was gadgets and gizmos. One table held a number of these in various states of assembly, but for the most part they were whole, and neatly organized.

In one corner, however, was a machine that seemed ominous some-how, though he couldn't explain why.

"This is where Violet was born," said Tameria. "Well, your current Violet. The first iteration was created back on our primary Bochord, before the Order had to destroy it during the Exile."

Moss cringed a little inside. Tameria hadn't given him an accusing glare this time, but it was impossible to forget that he was partly responsible for that.

"You have a copy of Violet here as well?" Hel asked.

"After a fashion. I have a copy of her mind, but without a computer network to operate from, it's just data."

"So you're going to make another Violet?" asked Moss. It sounded bad that way, and maybe it was. Violet would have a fit if she found out about this.

"It could take days to scan the asteroid belt," said Tameria. "If Vio-let already knows where the *Daedalus* is, we can just ask her. Problem solved."

"And then...?" asked Hel, catching the same what-do-you-do-with-her-next vibe lurking in Moss's head.

Tameria paused. "She won't even know when it happens."

Hel looked squeamish. "I don't know... Are we in that much of a rush?"

"Yes, we are."

Tameria opened a locked cabinet and pulled out a box. The box scanned her handprint and opened. She pulled out a familiar device, a flexible dermal device meant to be attached to the head between the jaw and temple.

"Wait a minute, that's not a copy," said Moss. "That's hers, isn't it? That's the original."

Tameria sighed. "Yes. It's on loan from the Order. They brought it with them when we rescued the *Pegasi* so I could give you Violet back. It was the least I could do."

"So why do you still have it?" Moss asked.

Tameria waved to her laboratory. "As I said, it's on loan. One of the fields I work in is memory recovery. Violet's pattern is unique in a number of ways, and I needed a baseline to work with on some experiments."

"So you've brought her back and erased her before?" asked Hel, then added under her breath. "Violet's gonna be pissed."

Sister Tameria's fists clenched, and for a moment Moss thought she might crush the fragile looking neural band. "I would advise you not to be judgmental on matters you are only peripherally familiar with. Now, if you're done interrogating me..." She removed a newer looking neural band from the top of the machine and laid Violet's down in its place, then turned it on.

That seemed to be all that was required. The computer terminal died for a moment, then flared back to life. That's what happened whenever Violet interfaced with a new ship computer. There was a simple camera on top, which now started to move and look at everyone.

"Wha...? What? Where?" The camera locked onto him. "Moss? What happened to...? Oh... right. That whole terminal disease thing. Well, this is what I wished for, though I'm pretty sure there's a proverb warning against that somewhere."

Moss was officially creeped out. Violet's existential paranoia was no doubt rubbing off on him. Was he going to treat her like his Violet, even though she would be blanked in a few minutes? That was cold.

"Uh, hi, Violet... Looking good."

Tameria was paying attention to a computer readout, studying what seemed to be a gauge of the program's stability.

"So, um, we need your help," Moss continued.

"I thought you were going to plug me into your ship," said Violet. "This doesn't look like a cockpit. In fact, I don't really sense anything at all. I thought I'd be, you know, *connected*. Power plant for a heart, life support for lungs, like that book you gave me to read."

Moss smiled. "*The Ship That Sang*." She'd read the whole series during their final trip together.

"Yeah. I kinda wish they'd made a movie of it."

Moss had to keep on track or this was going to get painful fast. "First thing's first. We have a bit of a problem. We're trying to track down the remains of the *UNMS Daedalus*, and we were hoping you knew where it was."

"The *Daedalus*? Sure. It's in the main asteroid belt in Sol."

"Something a little more specific, please," Tameria said sharply.

The camera turned to look at her. "Who's the grouch?"

"Never mind her," said Moss. "But, yeah, can you be more specific?"

"I can do you one better. I can take you there."

"That won't be necessary," said Tameria. "We just need its location."

"Okay, fourth big rock on the right-hand side of the solar system. Seriously, how do you expect me to verbalize an answer? I visited the place once when I was training in Sol. Squad commander set it up as a test of our sensor reading abilities, first one to the beacon got the rest of the day off, and everyone else got to do laps. I hate laps."

"So, how did you find the beacon?" asked Tameria.

"Plug me in and I'll show you."

"Did you scan for refined metals or signs of decaying radiation?" Tameria asked, growing impatient.

"Plug me iiiiiiiinnnn..." Violet sang.

"I'm sure the wreck would still be well above background levels, so couldn't we just..."

Violet whistled nonchalantly. Tameria looked to Moss for help. Moss shrugged.

"I think you better just plug her in. She's in a stubborn mood, and aren't you the one who said time was of the essence?"

Tameria huffed. "Fine."

There was no figurine like back aboard the Rex. The interface just was the base the figurine had been mounted on, which resembled a hockey puck—not that Moss had ever played hockey.

Tameria placed the puck on her dashboard, and the ship briefly powered down while it interfaced with the shipboard computer.

"You're only making this harder on yourself," Tameria said to Moss.

"You could just leave her plugged in. You fly alone, right? You could use a friend."

Tameria scowled. "Mind your own business."

"You know, it's at times like this I know you've never used your glamour on me, 'cause you're *ugly* when you're angry."

The ship powered up before Tameria could retort.

"Okay, let's get down to business. Okay, whoa, this is weird, but I kinda already know what to do now that I'm here. How does that work?"

Tameria said, "The interface is keyed to your knowledge of ship operations, associating your thoughts with the respective controls. So long as it's using a Protectorate operating system, you'll simply know what to do. Now, the *Daedalus*, if you would be so kind?"

"Right away. I'll have you there in less than an hour."

"Well, I'm sensing one pilot too many in this cockpit," said Moss. "I'll be in the kitchen, making a snack."

Tameria didn't have a food synthesizer on board, at least, not one that Moss could recognize amongst all the other machinery. He rummaged through the pantry, looking for items with the red Protectorate Seal of Biocompatibility on it. Most sapient species were carbon-based and bipedal and all that, sure, but that didn't mean you could just eat the Hopat version of a bagel. For one thing, you'd break your teeth.

Given their long-standing familiarity with genetics, the Elysian food industry had seen the potential of biocompatible foods in the galactic market, which was then endorsed by the Protectorate. Though usually bland and processed compared to native dishes, they also tended not to spoil, so spacers liked to carry them on long journeys.

Moss found the red seal on most of Tameria's containers, which were Terran compatible. Fortunately, Elysians and Terrans had similar enough biologies. She also had some green seal products, which were considered universally compatible, but those tasted about the same as the containers they came in. Probably just there for emergencies.

He prepared a bowl of what looked like cereal but tasted like stew and sat down at the only table that didn't have a machine or partially assembled project on it. He looked at the corner of the room as he ate, at the device that had brought another Violet to life.

But he wasn't thinking about that right now. He was thinking about the neural band Tameria had removed before placing Violet's on it. It had been a newer model, and given the tender spot still on his jaw, it didn't take a detective to figure out whose it had been.

For a time, he just sat there, chewing and looking and thinking.

He stood, leaving his bowl half full, and walked to the machine, placing the neural band where it had been and turning it on the way he'd seen Tamaria do it.

"H... Hello? Where am...? What is...? Who are...? Oh, I'm dead, aren't I?"

Moss didn't know what to say, but he had to start somewhere. "Hi. Um... were you the captain of the *Maruma*?"

"Yeah, *were* being the operative word. Blasted pirates. Did you get them?"

In an instant, Moss came up with a whopper of a tale, something that would explain everything, including how they ended up on Tameria's ship, leaving him in the clear.

But instead, he said, "I was the pirate."

"You? But... How am I here?" He didn't need to explain how unlikely it would be for any pirate to have Tameria's tech on board.

"My name is Maurice Foote. You might know me as—"

"Homewrecker?"

Moss groaned. "Yeah."

"Bet you wanted me to call you Ranger M instead, huh?"

"No, I hate both names equally."

A chuckle came from the speakers. "So what in the seven hells happened?"

Moss sighed. "I made a big mistake attacking your ship. Your niece is helping me undo the damage I've done."

"Tameria?"

Moss nodded. "Yeah, we go back a bit."

"I know. She told me about the *Pegasi*. Nice bit of work there. Reminds me of my younger days."

Moss smiled. "Well, I wanted to apologize to you personally for what happened. I mean, I never intended to kill you. I was just—"

"—Looking for a big score so you could lay your feet up somewhere and relax."

"Something like that."

"Like I said, reminds me of my younger days. Well, if it makes you feel any better, you didn't kill me. My heart was going to give out sooner or later. I didn't expect to survive much past Sol."

Moss frowned. "You'd think the Order could just give you a replacement heart."

"Not that easy with Elysians, I'm afraid. Blame the adaptive translators for the misunderstanding. Our 'hearts' are spread out along the entire network of major blood vessels, rather than contained in a single muscle. And if a problem is genetic and we haven't fixed it, it probably can't be fixed. I wasn't about to take it easy and die in some bed somewhere. I wanted to do something to balance the scales first."

"Like rescue some slaves," said Moss.

"You, of all people, should be able to appreciate that, Terran."

"I know. I do. And I promise you, I'll see it through, okay?"

"Well, hey, with a bit of luck, I'll be right there with you. What did you say your name was again?"

Moss looked over to the terminal that Tameria had been examining when Violet had been brought online. Only these reading weren't stable. Moss felt his jaw ache.

"Go on, tell him," a voice said behind him.

The camera on the computer swiveled a bit. "Tameria? Is that you?"

"It's me, Uncle Keed."

"You look older than I remember. Have I been gone long?"

"Not long." Moss looked at Tameria, who stared at him with hellfire in her eyes. "Tell. Him."

"Tell me what?"

Moss swallowed. "Your readings don't look... they don't look very good."

"Guess it didn't work, huh?"

"I'm sorry, uncle," said Tameria, then looked back to Moss. "So, has your conscience been put at ease yet? Found your absolution?"

"I'm sorry if I overstepped my bounds," said Moss. "I just—"

"Oh, you don't understand. I'm *glad* you did this. Because now you get to watch my uncle's mind fall apart. Listen to him become senile and forgetful until he can't even form words. Until there is nothing left behind but gibberish and static."

"Er... I was kind of hoping you might pull the plug before that," said Keed.

"I'm sorry, uncle," Tameria said, eyes still locked on Moss's. "But don't worry. You won't remember any of it."

"Tameria. Don't let me—"

Moss didn't understand how the machine worked exactly, but finding the power wasn't difficult. He shut the machine down and removed the neural band. "That's enough!"

Tameria stepped forward till they were nose to nose. "It is *not* enough. You coming in here looking for penance is about the most revolting thing I've ever seen. You do not have the right to..." Her voice broke, and she swore in a way his translator didn't understand. She turned away. "You don't have the right..."

Moss resisted the urge to put a hand on her shoulder. That would just make things worse. "You're right. I don't. I didn't understand before, but I think I do now." He held up the neural band. "This is a snapshot of your uncle's mind, frozen in time, but every time you connect him, the same thing is going to happen, isn't it?"

Tameria nodded. Moss could imagine that as a kind of hell for her, to have her uncle there whenever she wanted, but only for a few minutes, and never remembering their last meeting. How could you not think that what you were interacting with wasn't who you were pretending it was, but a flawed simulation?

"I shouldn't have apologized to your uncle," Moss said "I should have apologized to you. Now that I know what you went through, and what I just put you through again... I'm so sorry."

She finally looked at him. "Do you understand now why I didn't want Violet piloting the ship?"

"Yeah. It's not fair to us any more than it is to her."

"You're lucky," Tameria said. "You understand who you have on your ship isn't the friend who died, but you've also been able to make a new friend with her. Whether she's real or not, I don't know, but what you have with her is real. And I envy that."

Moss frowned. "How often is the result stable, like Violet?"

Tameria took a deep breath. "That's the thing. She's the only one the procedure has ever worked on. That's why we kept the template. Why I was using it. We don't know why she achieved long-term stability when no one else has. But if we could find out... Imagine the possibilities."

Moss frowned. "So why did he have the implant if he knew it wasn't going to work?"

"He's not the only one." Tameria brushed her hair back to reveal a similar device arching over and around her ear, well out of sight, an even newer and more discrete model than her uncle's. "Officially, we treat these as a kind of 'black box,' as your people call them. If a member of the Order dies in the field and we recover the device, we can learn exactly what happened. If someone else finds it, they dismiss it as some kind of vanity or combat cyberwear."

"And unofficially?"

"Unofficially, there's always hope it will work again."

Having run out of things to ask, Moss looked around the room. "So, uh... are we good?"

Tameria's lips narrowed to a thin line. "As *good* as we're likely to be for a while."

"That's fair. So, what's next? What do we do now?"

"Now? Now we finish balancing my uncle's scales."

Daedalus and Debris

The UNMS Daedalus *launched in 2106, Earth's first self-sufficient mining vessel designed to scour the asteroid belt for raw materials. Keep in mind that most asteroid belts are nothing like what you see in the vids. Each rock out there is thousands of miles away from the next. But, if you find a good prospect, you might be there a while. Fully crewed by synths, it not only mined, but processed what it found and launched the refined material with a homing beacon toward their intended planet or moon for pickup.*

The Daedalus *was in service almost a hundred years until it was destroyed in the Intersystem War. Each side feared that the other would use it to launch rocks at their enemy's ground-based holdings. It was a pivotal moment in the War due to how each side treated the escaping synths on board, one that left humans looking pretty bad.*

M. Foote, *And Then Things Got Worse*

"**I** GET TO LEAVE the ship? I'm honoured," said Roy.

For that, he got a shock. Nothing too severe, just Nekkar reminding him who wore the kinky slaver collar in this relationship.

"You're *required*. If the transport is here, I'll need you to identify it."

"Trust me, I'm not about to forget that hunk of junk."

Acting Commander Nekkar and Roy were flanked by two armed guards, all gussied up in Legionaire armour. Roy guessed they all carried a remote for his neckwear in case he tried anything. Having Nekkar carry the only one would be stupid, and while Nekkar was undoubtedly an idiot, he wasn't stupid.

"There's been a lot of activity over the last few days, so I've arranged to meet with the stationmaster," Nekkar said as they left the ship. "We will access the logs of every ship present, as well as those who have arrived and left in the last three days."

"I'll save you some time," said Roy. "Have him start with any chimeras that have passed through."

Nekkar's brow rose. "Chimera? What class of ship is that?"

"Garbage class. A chimera is what we call a ship cobbled together from other ships. Only broke and desperate pilots tend to fly them, but this one is something special." He knew that only too well. The one he'd faced had matched him at every turn. "The last name it used was *Viaticus Rex II.I*."

Now Nekkar's brows furrowed. "Is that supposed to be Latin? It's terrible."

Roy shrugged. "I'm surprised anyone knows Latin anymore, good or bad. Made me wonder if he was one of us."

Nekkar sneered. "Like *you*, perhaps. Not one of us."

The reason he was being escorted onto the Europan mining base was explained away as being pragmatic and efficient. But whatever information they had could just as easily have been transmitted to the *Hydrus* and given to him to look over. No, there was ego at play here, a chance to show off his prize. Roy would have laughed if it wouldn't have gotten him another jolt.

Roy looked around the station as much as he could as they left. No chimeras that he could see. Most of the ships were of practical boxy Draxon design, with some of the new Terran models scattered about. While the Colony Fleet was committed to establishing its own production line of ships, the Draxon mass produced similar ships faster and cheaper than anyone, so pragmatism tended to win out. The folks in PR wouldn't care so long as there were enough home grown Terran ships out there to keep them looking good.

The mining base's commander, a synth, welcomed them as they reached the terminal. He seemed happy to see the Silver Legion on board and was eager to please. Nekkar laid out what he required of the man in no uncertain terms, and without the slightest bit of interest in him beyond that.

As expected, the *Viaticus Rex* was no longer on board the station. But what surprised Roy was tracking the sequence of events as best they could with surveillance footage. A firefight had broken out in a station lounge. Someone had been killed during the escape. Their contact, presumably.

But then the *Rex* had taken off. Without its crew.

"So there's every possibility they're still here on the station," said Nekkar.

Roy nodded, though he supposed they could have found a way off this rock since then. This all might have turned out to be a dead end, except for one thing.

Roy replayed the footage of the *Rex* powering up and closing its hatches. The ground crew scattering with long low-gee jumps to get out of the way of the thrusters before it blasted off.

He rewound again, zooming in on something that happened as the hatches closed. An object fell out of the ship, too small to see clearly. At first, it seemed like some kind of debris, less than half a meter long. He wondered what it might be, and whether the ground crew had already disposed of it.

But then it moved. In fact, it got up, seemed to dust itself off, and scampered off before the crew could return.

Roy tilted his head. That was pretty much the last thing he had expected to see. And yet, the more he thought about it, the more sense it made.

The expanse of space that lay between Mars and Jupiter was not what most people thought of when they pictured an asteroid belt. Despite the fact that the Protectorate's founding species had been in space for thousands of years, there was still a pervasive belief within the general population that these were densely packed and dangerous space hazards.

What they tended to imagine was more akin to the ring of a gas giant, or the accretion disks of a young solar system, whose planets were still in the process of forming. But the whole reason Sol had an asteroid belt in the first place was because there was barely enough material between Jupiter and Mars to form a new planet, and Jupiter's gravity made it impossible for what was there to mingle. A planetary cock-blocker, if you will.

The largest planetoid, Ceres, was less than a thousand kilometres in diameter, followed by a few that were about half that. Most of the other bodies ranged from thousands of meters in size to tiny dust particles. Even if you took all that material and formed it into a single mass, it would still be smaller than the Earth's moon. And all of that was spread out between Mars and Jupiter, a distance roughly the same as the distance between the Earth and its sun.

In other words, the odds of randomly running into an asteroid while passing through it were very, *very* slim.

On the one hand, this was a bad thing for Violet. It meant there were not nearly as many hiding spaces for the *Rex* as she would have liked—and she would have liked an infinite number of them, give or take a trillion.

On the other, it meant there was a whole lot of nothing out there that she was parked in the middle of, and unless they knew what to look for, she might as well be invisible.

In its ninety-seven years of service, the *Daedalus* had been expanded and refitted twice, but its location between the inner and outer systems had sealed its fate during the Intersystem War. Now, its wreck was little more than a skeleton, pieces dragged back to their point of origin and loosely connected so that it kind of resembled a ship. Maybe back when this memorial site had been set up it had been more impressive, but she doubted it.

The belt had three main types of asteroids in it, carbonaceous, silicate, and metal-rich—the latter being the least common, but the most valuable. The *Daedalus*'s graveyard was an M-class asteroid, or, more accurately, a string of them. At some point in the distant past, it had collided with another asteroid, and so there were now three large chunks within a kilometre of each other, as well as a number of smaller ones nearby. It was probably what had made it an attractive mining operation since they wouldn't have had to go far once one was used up.

It was also what made it an attractive place to hide. For whatever reason, the Terran Colony Fleet hadn't taken an interest in the site as part of their "reconstituted history," as Moss put it. The propaganda potential was certainly there, given how the synth survivors of the ship had been treated, but had never been taken advantage of.

Violet figured it was because the TCF was focused on looking to the future, not the past. A grand, glorious future where mankind's successors would earn their place among the stars.

Rah-rah-rah, zip-doo-dah. She'd seen through all that nonsense even before she'd met Moss. It was why she'd left Sol in the first place.

Now here she was again, after a fashion. Inhabiting a ship, babysitting freeborn refugees, waiting for Moss to connect the dots and find a way to get to her. Of course, unless Sister Tameria or someone else from the Order came to help, those freeborn might wait so long they'd forge a whole new civilization within her hull.

To pass the time, Violet took a moment to calculate how long they could survive here without resupplying. Water was recycled with near-perfect efficiency, and, in theory, one of the cargo bays could be converted into a hydroponics farm. Problem was, there were no live seeds or anything to start it up with. So, without some magic potatoes showing up, it looked like starvation was inevitable in about a month. Great.

Something showed up on her passive sensors. Another passing ship. Travel between Jupiter and Mars was somewhat frequent, though her little hiding spot was far from being in the way. It was just good luck that she was close enough to see what was moving back and forth. Transports, mostly, judging by the transit signatures.

But this ship was different. It wasn't big enough to be a transport, more like a large shuttle. It had been heading for Mars, then it changed course and started heading straight for her. How long had it been, three days? She was genuinely impressed Moss had gotten here so fast.

Then it occurred to her. What if it wasn't him?

"Coming up on the *Daedalus* now, dropping out of sub-transit," said Other-Violet. "M-class asteroid group. Main rock is about two klicks in diameter."

"See anything yet?" asked Moss.

"Not yet. But then if the ship you're looking for is powered down, it might show up like the rest of the wreck on sensors. You want me to hail them?"

Moss, Hel, and Tameria all exchanged a look.

"That would be a bad idea," said Moss.

"Someone else might pick it up," added Hel.

"Oh, right. Sorry. But you're all being so secretive about this. I mean, can you tell me what kind of ship we're looking for?"

"Our old ship," said Moss. "The *Viaticus Rex*. Well, sorta. It's gone through a few changes."

Hel raised an eyebrow. "A few?"

Moss frowned. "Fine. It was torn to pieces and stitched back together into a Frankenship."

"You fly a chimera?" asked Violet. "Yeesh. What kind of hard times have you fallen on?"

"It's actually a damn good ship," said Hel. "You—"

Moss glared at her.

"—you'd really like it."

"I dunno. This shuttle is pretty sweet. This is Baroque-class, right? Elysian design?"

Sister Tameria nodded. "That's right."

"I've never seen engines tricked out like this before. And the shields, holy crap!"

Tameria smiled despite her best efforts. "Thanks."

"No weapons, though, which is a shame. I'm guessing half the stuff here is top secret Order tech?"

"Not as much as you'd think. I have to keep a low profile."

"Can I try something out with her?"

"I suppose."

Moss realized a second too late what she was planning to do. He also realized he was the only one there not buckled into a seat.

"No, wait—!" Before he could finish, the engines and maneuvering thrusters kicked in and Moss ended up hugging the back wall.

The *Outreach* charged headlong toward the asteroid, and for a moment everyone thought they were going to crash. But as the maneuvering thrusters kicked in, it started to rotate around, hugging the edge of the asteroid all the way around its circumference. Once on the other side, Violet let the inertia take over and the ship floated away a bit before she thrusted to a stop.

Able to move again, Moss rubbed his aching head. Even with augmentation, he was lucky he didn't have a concussion from that stunt.

"That was amazing!" Violet cried out.

"What the hell was that?" Tameria yelled. "You almost got us killed!"

"No way. Do you have any idea how precise I can be in this thing? It's like I can feel how the ship moves. I was a damn good pilot back when I was alive, but I was never *this* good."

"I think I'm going to throw up," said Hel.

"By the way," Violet added, "there's the ship you're looking for."

Sure enough, the *Viaticus Rex II.I* was clamped to the surface of the asteroid, powered down and surrounded on all sides by the salvaged remnants of the *Daedalus*.

"You're welcome."

It was decided that Hel would stay on board the *Outreach* while Tameria and Moss went EVA to get to the *Rex*. The *Outreach* had powered down in similar fashion, to help avoid detection, and neither Moss nor Tameria would use their comms until they had boarded the ship, determined the situation, and came up with a plan of action.

But that didn't mean they couldn't talk en route.

Moss stopped Tameria halfway between the two ships and held her by the shoulders, pressing his helmet against hers.

"Can you hear me?" he asked.

She nodded. "You're a bit quiet, but yeah." It was true, she had to speak up and even then she sounded distant and muffled.

He raised his voice a bit more. "I want to talk about your Violet."

Tameria gave him a look. "This is not the time."

"Actually, it's the only time. We can't talk on my ship or yours without giving anything away, and we can't talk over the comm."

Tameria huffed. "Fine. I won't unplug her."

"What?" She'd jumped right to the middle of his planned conversation. Moss hadn't expected that.

"I looked over her flight path when she hugged that asteroid. It was impressive and precise. I'd have a hard time doing better and I've been flying that ship for years. She was in control for a couple hours. Way better than the autopilot. She could be useful. Can we go now?"

"Just one more thing," said Moss. "You need to be ready for the breakdown."

"The what?"

"Sooner or later, she's going to have an existential crisis. You need to be there for her, okay? Don't let her try to work things out alone. You have to treat her like a person, even if deep down you don't believe it."

Tameria said nothing at first, then nodded. She pushed off from him and pointed to the *Rex*. Moss got the message. Back to work.

Getting inside didn't prove difficult. The airlock opened the moment they arrived.

"What took you so long?" Violet asked once they were inside.

"My ride flew off without me without even saying goodbye," said Moss.

"Wow, that pilot sounds like a real jerk."

"She has her moments. How's the cargo?"

"They're at least another week from going all *Lord of the Flies*. I see the good Sister got my call. You alone, or can we count on some backup this time?"

"Sorry," Tameria said. "I'm all you've got."

"Then I suggest you both come to the cockpit and fill me in on your undoubtedly brilliant plan."

Once in the cockpit and with the door secured, Tameria explained what she could.

"This operation was not something that I was involved in, and I'm not in a position to contact the Order for instructions. But I do have enough information to go on. Haven is one of our operatives, located on Gagarin Colony on Mars."

Moss nodded. That lined up with what Link had told them.

"I'm not certain, but I believe Haven works at one of the original synth birthing facilities."

"Link said he was created to be his assistant, born in Synth Chamber 19."

"So that's where we'll start. Thing is, blundering in with a couple dozen freeborns without knowing what protocol is in place would just get us noticed and intercepted again. We need to contact him personally. Perhaps bring a single freeborn representative with us to validate our story. Once we've confirmed Haven's identity, we'll work out a plan for bringing the rest to him."

Moss shook his head. "It still feels like we're leading them straight into the lion's den. I mean, I know Sol isn't the heart of Terran civilization anymore, but still... why bring them here of all places?"

"We'll get some answers soon enough," said Tameria. "We'll have Hel come over and help babysit here while we take the *Outreach* to Mars. Who should we bring with us?"

"Take the kid, Zach," said Violet. "He's got some pull with the others right now. When you come back, they'll trust whatever he has to say."

"He's more conspicuously freeborn," said Moss, frowning.

"But a gene scan at the port would show that anyway," Tameria countered. "At least this way he's viewed as a non-threat."

"Fair enough."

It took half an hour to get everything in place. Tameria went back to the *Outreach* to inform Hel of their plan and have her take charge of the *Rex*, while Moss explained the situation to the refugees and asked Zach to join them. The boy readily agreed.

They were getting ready to leave when the airlock opened and Hel came inside. "Leaving me out of all the fun?"

"Believe me, I'd rather you be the one going with Tameria, but..."

Hel looked at Zach, who was trying to fit into their smallest EVA suit. "But some things only Ranger M can handle."

He was going to say he was the only one who wouldn't register as freeborn, but didn't bother to correct her. Zach finally got his helmet locked in place and gave him a thumbs up. Even with the suit's auto-sizing feature, it didn't fit very well. Moss would have to drag the kid across.

"So how are you going to find Haven?" she asked. "Mars is a big place."

"We'll start with Link's last words to you. Gagarin Colony, Synth Chamber 19."

Hel looked puzzled. "Where he was born? Why?"

"It doesn't sit right with me that those would be his last words. It makes more sense if it was some kind of message about where to go."

Violet nodded. "If it is his birthplace, perhaps you could find his real name and track who he worked for that way. He said he was created to be Haven's assistant."

Moss agreed. "Either way, it's a place to start."

Zach was all smiles as Moss dragged his butt over to the *Outreach*. No doubt imagining he was going on a grand adventure with the great Ranger M. While the idol worship was not welcomed in the least, it did mean the kid would listen to any orders he was given.

Once Moss got him to the other ship, however, it only took seconds for the kid to become more trouble than he was worth.

"Welcome back, boss," Other-Violet said once they were out of the airlock.

"Hey, you have Violet over here too!"

There was a pause; short by human standards, an eternity by computer reckoning.

"What do you mean, *too*?"

Chamber 19

I T TOOK A WHILE to calm Other-Violet down. Before anyone had a chance to shut down the comms, she had contacted the *Rex's* Violet, demanding an explanation, so there was *that* to look forward to when Moss got back. For now, he had this one to worry about.

"There's two of me? Have there been more? How many? Can you just copy me whenever you want? Is she going to be freaked out like I am? Will she want me deleted? How much older is she? Does it even matter? Are we the same person or two different people? But we're not even people, are we? I mean, we're just simulations. But do simulations worry about whether or not they're simulations? Am I even real? How do you even define real?"

And that's existential angst Bingo, thought Moss.

Before the worst of it started, Tameria had taken Moss to a small room that wasn't hooked up to the ship's PA system to ask for advice. But what she was actually trying to do was offload the problem onto him.

"Forget it. I've done this twice before already, and this is your ship, not mine. You won't get any handholding from me."

Tameria began to protest, but Moss made it clear that he was not taking point on this.

"Look, don't get your wings bent out of shape. This isn't just for her sake, you understand? You want her to be your copilot? Look at this as a bonding exercise."

Tameria frowned, not sure what to make of that. Moss sighed.

"I get that you're ambivalent. You don't want to care because it means reevaluating everything you've done with this tech so far. On the other hand, you know she's in pain and your instinct is to help. So it would just be easier to shove the problem onto me; let me indulge in my illusions while you hide and cling to the safety of your own."

"What illusions?"

"My illusion that she's real and your illusion that she's not."

"It can't be both."

"No, it can't, which is why you've got to handle it on your own. Call it Schrodinger's Soul. You need to open the box and collapse the waveform for yourself."

Tameria grumbled. "Like I didn't hate you enough already."

Moss shrugged. "I'm used to it. Now go out there and imprint on your baby bird. We're flying casual, so we've got a couple hours before we reach Mars."

To her credit, Tameria did an excellent job with Violet. She'd clearly had training in Terran psychology. Moss had floundered on both occasions, making things up as he went along. What had gotten him through was the fact that he'd known Violet for so long before she died.

By the time they got clearance to land at Armstrong Colony, Violet had mostly calmed down, but she still had a lot to think about while they were out looking for Haven.

"That's a good sign," said Moss once they were outside. "My Violets did something similar after their initial panic attack."

But he could tell from the look on Tameria's face that Violet wasn't the only one who had a lot to think about. Better to focus on the task at hand. He looked back at Zach, who was trailing along behind them.

"Remember, kid. Don't speak unless spoken to and do whatever they ask of you."

"And whatever you do, don't panic," Tameria added. "We'll take care of you."

The Order, being an organization that had existed so long they'd dropped any reference to what they were the Order of, had lots of ways to be wherever they wanted to be for seemingly legitimate reasons. Tameria had a half dozen unused but legit personal and ship idents. Each one carried a constantly evolving falsified history of previous destinations that were updated and validated by the Protectorate's own networks. If anyone was to investigate her phony flight history, it would always check out.

Right now, she was an Elysian merchant looking to establish a trade route through Draxon space. The Draxon themselves were notoriously uninterested in luxury goods, so it made perfect sense to make ties with the minor species that existed within their borders, such as the Terrans or the Charon. Moss's cover was to act as her synth liaison. Zach was his bondservant.

Entry into Armstrong Colony went without a hitch. Gene scans checked out for each of them, and they were soon allowed into the city. From there, they'd take a tube shuttle to Gagarin Colony.

This place had changed, to say the least. Moss hadn't been to Mars since he'd hit the deep freeze three hundred years ago. By that point, human life had been well established on Mars, with a number of more-or-less self-sustaining colonies. But it was all still new, relatively speaking.

Now this place was old enough to have a history. Old enough to call parts of it ancient. Moss saw the signs everywhere. Different architectural styles clustered in different areas. Run-down districts had some of the oldest styles, ranging in condition from well-kept to barely standing. No matter how far you went in the future, it seemed, there was always a pecking order, and whoever lived in these areas were used to being pecked.

There were very few signs of the original pre-Disaster colony left, however. Those would have been swept under the rug during the "cultural renaissance," which Moss couldn't put air quotes around hard enough. You'd have to dig deep down into the red dirt to find any signs of it now. Old foundations, disused sewer pipes and whatnot.

The thought of conducting an archaeological dig on Mars, looking for the remains of pre-Disaster civilization, was both intriguing and depressing.

Once they got on the shuttle, Moss got to take in more of the city at a much faster rate. The funny thing was that even the cultural renaissance era had fallen by the wayside of late. Those early decades had been filled with heavy propaganda of Terran pride and had been infused into everything, trying to redefine what it meant to be Terran. The designs of that era revolved around strength and weren't exactly welcoming in nature.

But most of the newer buildings had none of that. They were mellower and more aesthetically pleasing, and signs of other cultural influences were creeping in. Moss saw some Nubran and Elysian flourishes in the entertainment districts. There was something strangely hopeful about that.

Then he reminded himself that the parts of the city that represented who was in control, the governmental district, hadn't changed at all.

The trip to Gagarin Colony was only an hour long, and most of that time Tameria spent working on a tablet. Once out of Armstrong, the shuttle picked up speed and accelerated comfortably through the sealed transparent tube, allowing them all a view of the rust covered surface.

Zach pointed to two structures in the distance. "What are those?" They resembled small steep mountains with their tops blown off but were far too smooth to be anything but man-made.

"Terraforming stations," said Moss. "Those were working in overdrive when I was last here, but they shut them down ages ago."

Centuries ago would have been more accurate. The new Terrans, in all their wisdom, had abandoned the project shortly after consolidating power. Part of their platform had been to find a new homeworld and start over, leaving the past of those who had enslaved them behind. Only that had proved harder than any of them thought. The only thing stronger than Terran unity, it seemed, was galactic red tape.

The irony was that if they had stuck with the terraforming program, Mars would have been growing trees by now.

Time passed quicker than Moss had expected. The shuttle slowed as it reached the offloading station in Gagarin.

"So, how do we get access to the synth facility?" Moss asked once they were reasonably alone. "That's not exactly the sort of place a trader gets access to."

Tameria smiled. "Fortunately, I'm now Dr. Gaff, genetics expert. We arrived here on a passenger shuttle yesterday, hoping to study Terran synth production techniques and share some of our knowledge. Unfortunately, our request forms only just arrived in their system."

"I thought the Eylsians outlawed cloning."

"Of sapient species, yes. I'm talking about animals."

That was true. Eylsians were famed for their designer pets. "You're gonna bruise some egos if you compare the two."

"With a politician or soldier, perhaps. Not a scientist. Besides, this is only to get our foot in the door, as you say. We have a suite at the Pacific Hotel that, as far as their records are concerned, has been occupied since last night. I suggest we move in while we wait to make contact."

Working of the Order certainly had its perks, even in their current renegade status.

"You worried the Protectorate are going to close your little backdoors someday?" he asked.

Tameria frowned. "They already are. They shut down every back channel they find and try to trace them back to their source. They're being quite thorough, and very quiet about it."

Moss looked away. "I'm sorry."

At first Tameria looked cross, but then her features softened. "Don't be. Things could have been much worse."

That took Moss by surprise. "You didn't think that last time I saw you."

"I've had time to look into those events, ask myself what could have been done differently. Had you gone through proper channels, the snare would have closed by the time those in charge finished debating and took action. You caused a panic, yes, but every Precentor was able to start extracting our people straight away."

Moss huffed. "Wish everyone saw it that way."

Tameria shrugged. "History is rarely fair or kind until those involved are long dead."

"Sometimes not even then," said Moss.

It took a day and a half at the Pacific for Tameria to get the final pieces put into place. Requests had been processed, apologies sent regarding the delay, and a meeting arranged to see the facilitator of Synth Facility Gagarin.

While Tameria was now Dr. Gaff, Moss and Zach's respective identities only had to be tweaked rather than rewritten, and their previous movements deleted. All this Tameria did on her tablet, which seemed no more advanced than anything anyone else used. Moss wondered if her machine was deceptively powerful, or if the exploits the Order had worked into Protectorate operating systems allowed them to use just about any kind of access point.

They were met at the facility by a young and handsome man with dark hair and deep tan skin who seemed to be around thirty. That wasn't true, of course, because he was a cyborg, which meant you could add a zero to that. Technically, Moss would be about the same age, but he'd been a corpsicle most of that time.

The man had no visible security with him, but cyborgs rarely needed it.

"Ah, Dr. Gaff. Glad you could make it," the man said, holding his hand out in greeting. "Dr. Franz Majoris."

Tameria took it and shook in the Terran fashion. "Glad you could take the time to see me."

"Well, what can I say? I found your request most intriguing."

Tameria smiled. "You flatter me."

Moss took a few steps back with Zach but tried not to seem too obvious about it. He had a feeling Tameria would use her glamour to make him more agreeable and didn't want to be nearby. Zach pointed out some of the displays on the walls to Moss, showing happy young synths growing quickly into adults.

"Is it true they grow up faster than we do?" Zach whispered.

Moss nodded. "They start off as toddlers, but become adults in less than five years."

"That seems kinda sad," said Zach.

"Oh? I thought kids hated waiting to grow up."

"Yeah, but... that just seems too fast."

"I guess it does."

"Do they grow old fast too?"

"They used to," Moss said. "These days they live as long as you do."

"But not as long as cyborgs," Zach added.

"No," Moss said with a sigh. "That's a whole other story." He guided Zach back to Tameria, who seemed to be ready to start Dr. Majoris' tour. Moss took out a tablet, ostensibly to take notes for Tameria, while Zach followed behind carrying Moss and Tameria's bags.

Dr. Majoris began by taking them to the birthing chambers and demonstrated on the central terminal the way the template system worked. He made it clear that these were not clones in the commonly accepted sense of the word. Templates allowed for variations to unfold in the early stages of development.

"Think of it like one of your own families," he said to Tameria. "Brothers and sisters will share a family resemblance, but rarely look or think the same."

"Is that even necessary?" Tameria asked. "Why not simply have identical units? Wouldn't that be advantageous? Have one line suited for fighting, while another might be more intelligent."

Dr. Majoris gave a practiced smile. "Well, you must understand that the people who developed this technology are long dead. Furthermore, we're prohibited by the Protectorate from modifying the technology we have. One in a long line of bureaucratic roadblocks we face. However, gene variation has always been advantageous to a species. If someone were to develop a bioweapon that affected only your suggested warrior line... well, you can see the problem. Instead, as they mature, we have our young tested in a wide variety of fields and specialize them as required."

"Of course. Am I to understand your production levels are also limited by the Protectorate?"

"No, we do that ourselves," said Dr. Majoris. "It is one of the advantages of synth over natural reproduction. We are able to manage our population very efficiently. As the synth population ages or dies through misadventure, we can replace them as needed. And as the Colony Fleet expands, we can produce more to fill those niches."

"Yes, about that. My understanding is the services of the Silver Legion are rather in vogue these days. I'd have thought you'd have expanded your fleet far more to meet the demand."

This comment caught Dr. Majoris off guard, but he quickly recovered. "The Terran governing body, the Triumvirate, mandated long ago that we should not exceed a certain ratio in synth-to-cyborg numbers. To create too much of an imbalance between the two would be... problematic."

Which meant it would disrupt the power of the ruling class, Moss figured.

Tameria nodded. "But you no can longer produce cyborgs."

"It is a problem we're constantly working on," the doctor said diplomatically.

"Which means your numbers are static."

Moss couldn't help but interject. "Actually, ma'am, it would be on a slow decline due to things such as accidents and combat."

"That sounds worrying," said Tameria.

"The ratio has been adjusted a few times since the edict was put in place," Dr. Majoris confessed. "As I said, we're working on the problem."

It was hard not to feel some satisfaction at that admission. It reminded him that as powerful as the Terran Colony Fleet or its Silver Legion were, they couldn't last forever. Not as they currently were, anyway.

Next, they were shown the maturation wing, which was a fancy way of saying daycare through high school. It was bizarre to think that the toddlers in one room would be learning basic math in the room next to it in a couple of months, and physics in the room down the hall the year after that.

But for synths, this was life. This was the norm. He could only imagine how strange his or Zach's life would be to them, taking twenty years to reach where they got to in just five.

Now imagine the perspective of the so-called cyborgs, who skipped childhood altogether. They had come out of their birthing chambers physically in their late teens, their minds already developed through accelerated virtual learning, and only took a year to reach full maturity after that. They hadn't aged in three hundred years, their nanotech keeping them not just young, but incredibly strong and resilient. Synths and freeborn had to seem like lesser beings to them.

And yet their days were numbered. Moss suspected that as the cyborg population shrank, their grip over the other two Terran races would grow ever tighter.

Someday, this was all going to go badly. Again.

There weren't many children in each room at the moment. Dr. Majoris explained that they currently only supplied replacements for the Sol system, and the Colony Fleet had their own resources. In times of conflict, however, production was stepped up.

"May I be frank with you, Dr. Majoris?" Tameria asked once they had left the wing.

"Of course."

"My people have dealt with genetics for millennia. Some might say that we perfected it."

Dr. Majoris smiled. "I'm sure our techniques must seem rather primitive to you."

"On the contrary. Your synths are impressive enough, but we consider cyborgs like yourself to be revolutionary. We didn't have access to nanotechnology, even at the height of the Eugenics Surge. If we had, however, I fear that part of our history might have ended far worse than it did. There's a reason we no longer meddle in such things."

"That was a dark time for your people, I agree, yet you must admit, you ultimately benefited from those advances." Dr. Majoris nodded to her wingpack. "Your wings, bones, immune system, even your so-called glamour are a product of that era."

Tameria agreed. "And there are those in my circles who believe we can begin again, responsibly this time. As you can imagine, they look to the Terrans as an example. Yet, as you've pointed out, you haven't innovated in three hundred years."

"Only because we're not allowed to."

"Some worry that such stagnation will have long-term consequences." There was a slight tick in Tameria's voice. "Have others in your community expressed such concerns?"

Dr. Majoris's easy smile returned. "That's why I was eager to see you today. If what you say is true then perhaps there are those you know who might be *sympathetic* to our cause?"

Tameria said nothing.

"And in helping us, might be able to help your own ambitions?" he added cautiously.

"It seems I have been more transparent in my motivations than I wished to be," Tameria admitted.

"No, that's quite all right. I prefer to avoid the games and get to what matters. Perhaps we can continue this discussion in my office?"

Tameria smiled. "I would like that."

Dr. Majoris's office was pretty much exactly what Moss expected. Minimalist in terms of furniture and decoration. A mix of off-white, grey and wood tones. Simple terminal at his desk with a couple of pictures. A single statue in a corner that didn't resemble anything Moss could discern. A fern. Of course there was a fern. It would have been odder if there hadn't been a fern. He and Zach stood close to the door while Tameria and the doctor sat across from each other at his desk.

"Dr. Majoris…"

"Please, call me Franz."

"Franz," Tameria said with a slow nod. "Can we speak freely?"

"We can now."

"Excellent. We're looking for Haven."

"You found him."

Moss blinked. "Wait. What? I think I missed something." Had he jumped forward in time ten minutes without realizing it?

"Dr. Majoris is one of us," said Tameria, meaning the Order.

"Better to say I am an ally," Majoris clarified. "Not an actual member."

"Join the club," said Moss. "So what was with the song and dance out there?"

"I didn't know of his connection. Not until I confirmed it outside the maturation wing."

"How? I didn't see you share any secret handshake."

"That sounds dreadfully primitive." The doctor leaned back and folding his hands over his chest. "Though I suppose language codes aren't exactly advanced, either."

"What's going on?" asked Zach.

"We found Haven, kid. Try to keep up," said Moss.

"But I thought Haven was a place?" said Zach.

"Not my fault if you're slow on the uptake."

Dr. Majoris looked confused. "I'm sorry, but is he in charge?" he asked Tameria.

"He only thinks he is. I suggest you humour him."

"Hey!"

The doctor waved a hand for silence. "Enough. This is already highly irregular. Given who you are and your timing, I assume something has gone wrong with the latest cargo delivery?"

"Cargo?" Moss said. "We're talking about human beings here."

Tameria frowned at Moss. "You call them cargo all the time."

"Yeah, but when I say it, it's sarcastic. When he says it, it's racist."

Tameria rolled her eyes.

"My apologies," said Majoris. "The Silver Legion uses the euphemism when dealing with rogue freeborns outside of Terran space. I found myself adopting it to remind myself of how my comrades see you."

"If I might get our discussion back on track," said Tameria. "You are correct. There has been a problem."

Moss had hoped she might sidestep around his role in all this, but unfortunately, Tameria was a stickler for details, and the truth. When she finished catching him up, the Doctor considered it all for a moment.

"Your ship is no longer safe to transport the freeborn to Mars, but perhaps we can use Sister Tameria's shuttle to ferry them here. How many trips do you think it would take?"

Tameria had already crunched the numbers. "Three round trips, assuming a secured landing area where they don't need to be smuggled inside of some kind of container."

Dr. Majoris shook his head. "The landing bays aren't a problem. I have access to several, as well as priority access to one. How soon can we begin?"

Moss knew he was going to put his foot in his mouth by interjecting, but felt he had little choice. "Whoa. Before we do anything, I need to know what's going to happen to the freeborn. I first assumed Haven was a place where they could take the underground railroad out of

Draxon space. Now I find out you're Haven and you're in charge of a synth production facility. That raises some questions."

Dr. Majoris frowned, as if something Moss had said puzzled him, but it quickly passed. "I suppose it does. Very well. Come. Say nothing out of the ordinary once we leave this room until I say you are free to speak. Understood?"

He escorted them from his office and back to the birthing chambers. "What you see here represents the limit to which we have been allowed to expand our synth production," he said as they passed a door labelled Chamber 1.

Catching a glimpse through a window in the door, Moss saw two rows of cylinders filled with fluid, each connected to tubes, wiring, computers, and display readouts. Moss had always called this look Mad Scientist Chic. Inside each pod, small humanoid forms could be made out, curled in fetal positions.

"The Protectorate allows us to create new pods," explained the doctor. "But we cannot innovate on our production methods. Though these units are new, they're using the same technology we had three hundred years ago. And the same templates."

Next to Moss, Zach struggled to get a look, not quite tall enough to see inside. There was something morbid about these pods, though, and part of Moss wanted to turn the kid away. But what was the point of that? This was humanity's reality now. He hefted Zach up high enough to see inside.

Tameria cleared her throat and Moss set Zach down. She wasn't disapproving of the action, but the appearance. It wasn't how a synth was supposed to treat a bondservant.

"I've never been clear on why that is." Tameria said to Dr. Majoris, though Moss suspected she knew full well and was just making conversation.

"To be blunt, we're to blame. And by we, I am referring to third generation synths like myself. Cyborgs. The nanotechnology in our makeup has always made the Protectorate nervous. After the SRAI War, there has not only been a longstanding ban on artificial intelligence, but severe restrictions on the use of nanotechnology. But because the process was lost in the Terran Disaster, we were deemed a special exception, with the caveat that we did not try to regain that knowledge.”

“That must stick in your craw,” said Moss.

Dr. Majoris raised an eyebrow. “You could say that.” By now they had proceeded as far as Chamber 6. “Each chamber contains several hundred pods, and can produce a second generation synth in one year, at which point they are revived and spend the next four years maturing and being tested. You’ve already seen those rooms.”

Dr. Majoris continued his lecture as they travelled farther down the hall, the numbers growing until they were at Chamber 18. “These are some of the oldest Synth Chambers in the solar system. Older machines, or ones decommissioned or in need of repairs, tend to be moved to the higher numbered rooms.”

Moss looked through the window. This one seemed to have no active pods in use, and several were partially disassembled. “Which leads us to the end of our tour up ahead.”

Chamber 19 had the same door as the others. This time, he placed his hand over a pad and the door opened for them. They went inside and Moss’s jaw dropped.

The pods here were different. The others had been maybe a meter in height, but these were well over two meters tall, tall enough to fit a fully grown human into.

The door shut behind them. “You may speak freely now,” said the doctor.

“These... these are first generation pods,” said Moss.

Dr. Majoris nodded, but that puzzled look passed over him again.

“Do they still work?”

"No, not these ones," said the doctor. "These are kept for parts. But there are others that are kept in pristine condition, not that we ever use them."

"Why?" asked Tameria. "First gen synths were inherently flawed."

The doctor was trying not to look uncomfortable. "Long ago, the Triumvirate mandated that all surviving first generation chambers were to be kept operational, ostensibly for the purposes of scientific research. As of yet, however, they've never been reactivated for any reason, scientific or otherwise."

"But what does this have to do with the freeborn?" asked Moss.

"Well, you see, I found another use for this room." Dr. Majoris smirked. "It makes freeborns disappear."

Moss frowned, placing a hand on Zach's shoulder. "That better be a funny joke I don't get and not a creepy prelude to an ambush."

"The former, I assure you. Technically, the first gen pods begin in Chamber 20 and continue from there. Chamber 19 was left vacant, a buffer between the modern and antiquated departments."

Something in Tameria's eyes lit up. It took Moss a moment, but he started to piece it together as well. "This is all a big smokescreen. You're losing them in the paperwork."

Dr. Majoris nodded again. "As far as the government is concerned, this is where they were born. The genetic variations that would mark them as freeborn are accounted for and the TCF database updated with new information. I have a network of sympathizers that take them on in remote areas on Mars, other parts of Sol, and minor colonies. There they can start new lives in places where the odds of being thoroughly investigated are all but non-existent. The Fleet's eyes are focused on the stars, not back home."

"So Link was a freeborn?"

The doctor's expression fell. "Daniel, yes. One of the first I helped. He stayed on to be my contact at Europa."

Tameria frowned, glancing briefly at Zach. "What about the children? How does that work?"

"Not as well, I'm afraid. We prefer to have only mature adults brought here, but that is not always possible." The doctor looked to Zach. "He's one of them?"

Tameria nodded. "I wanted to have someone the refugees could trust report on what we saw."

"Well then, I shall be honest. The children most likely will have to hide out, hopefully with their parents. We have those willing to accept the extra risk, but they will not be allowed out in the open until they are of age and ready to be catalogued."

"That's your idea for a better life for them?" asked Moss. "I like their chances better on another world far away from here."

"As would I," the doctor conceded. "Unfortunately, it's increasingly difficult for rogue freeborns to remain undetected. Either they stand out because they travel in numbers, or they stand out because they travel alone. Given the bounty the Fleet offers, someone always eventually gives them up. Sending them to other Protectorate nations legally is both expensive and problematic, as is doing so illegally. This might not be an ideal solution, but I assure you, it is safer than the alternatives. And there is another problem to consider."

"What's that?"

Dr. Majoris sighed. "The number of freeborns repatriated in the past two years does not correspond with those officially collected. And the gap has been increasing."

He let that statement sink in without explanation. Clearly, he wasn't talking about a bureaucratic error, or something easily explained. He was implying this was a Bad Thing.

"What do you think is happening?" asked Tameria.

Dr. Majoris shook his head. "I don't know. But this discrepancy can only be explained through official channels, perhaps even sanctioned by the Triumvirate itself. In a way, it's not unlike what I've been doing, only I'm certain their intentions are not benign."

"I should inform the Order of this," said Tameria.

"They know. I've sent detailed reports. But I've never heard back from them about it. It doesn't help that their information network is not what it used to be." He looked back at Moss. "Wait a minute... now I remember you."

Moss groaned. "Oh God. Yes, I'm the reason the Order had to go underground—well, more underground. I'm Homewrecker, okay? Have a big laugh about it. Are you happy now?"

"Actually, I was going to say you're Ranger M."

Tameria snickered.

"What? How can you know that? I always wore a mask!"

The doctor tapped at his eyes. "Cyborg, remember? Pupillary distance, canthus, orbit, punctum, folds... Your eyes are unmistakable. I was a fan of yours. Even watched the cartoon. A number of officials on Mars were tasked trying to determine who you were, since your actions were unsanctioned by the TCF. But what little we could see of your face didn't register with anyone in our databanks."

"Yeah, well, good," Moss said, feeling flustered.

"You're also Homewrecker?"

Tameria stopped herself from laughing and straightened herself. "I'll explain later, Doctor. Right now, we need to work out how we're going to get our refugees to safety."

Haven and the Hydrus

In 2550, there were only six Heavy Cruisers in the Silver Legion, which are the largest non-Protectorate warships out there, though mass production wasn't far off. Approximately 250m long and crewed by twenty officers and a hundred and fifty crew, they have a battery of deadly weapons, a small squadron of snub fighters, and are covered in their proprietary energy reflective skin. In combat trials, one of these ships can take on ten regular patrol craft and come out looking for more.

It has all the facilities necessary for long-range missions and does not need to return to the colony fleet to resupply. With the right resources, it can even print and build its own replacement snub fighters and shuttles.

If you see one of these ships on your radar and are doing anything remotely illegal, run. Just don't look like you're running.

M. Foote, *Portrait of the Pilot as a Cranky Ol' Man*

H EL SAW A BLIP on the passive scanners. She sat in Moss's chair, leaning back, watching it casually move around the system, but never stopping anywhere.

The blip itself wasn't unusual. Sub-transit wake was easy to pick up, and despite the fact that the bulk of Terrans had relocated to the Colony Fleet, there was still a significant presence in Sol, and therefore a lot of traffic between the planets. Most of them were shuttles or cargo transports.

This blip was not. Violet recognized it instantly as a Silver Legion heavy cruiser.

"What do you think it's doing?" asked Hel.

"Not sure," said Violet. "I can't imagine they'd bring in a heavy cruiser just to look for one little ship that pulled a runner."

"Depends what they know about that ship," said Hel.

"You think they're onto us?"

"They were expecting us on Europa. Maybe Link was compromised even before we arrived on the scene, and they were just waiting to see who he met up with."

"Maybe. I just hope Tam-Tam sees the same thing we're seeing before they try to rendezvous with us."

"You call Sister Tameria 'Tam-Tam'?"

"I do *now*."

Hel chuckled. "Well, why wouldn't she see what we're seeing?"

"They've got an inexperienced ship's personality on board, re-member? She might just dismiss it as some transport, even though it obviously isn't."

"Violet, she's *you*."

"She's a child. Do you have any idea how much longer I've been at this than her?"

"Um... a couple weeks? I was there when we reinstalled you, re-member?"

"Yeah, but I'm still a computer. I learned a lot in that time. I'm telling you, she's green. If she's not careful, she might get them killed."

"I'm telling you," said Other-Violet, "she's senile. If she's not careful, she might get them killed."

"Violet, she's *you*," said Tameria.

"She's a relic. Do you have any idea how old she is?"

"A couple weeks, maybe?" said Moss. "I was there when she was reinstalled, you know."

"Face it, flyboy. I'm the newer, better model."

"You're identical," said Tameria. "That's how the imprints work."

Moss waved a hand to stop. There was no point in arguing with her. "Look, just tell us about the ship." The *Outreach* was still on the landing pad. They had only just gotten back on board when Other-Violet had given them the bad news.

"Well, while you guys were gallivanting over in another colony, I was patiently sitting here listening to comm traffic and see what was going on up above. I'm telling you, there's a heavy cruiser patrolling the system, and it's not here for shore leave. I bet you the antique on your ship isn't even checking her passive sensors properly."

Moss doubted that, but the situation *was* worrying. A heavy cruiser, here? The timing couldn't be a coincidence. "Are they stopping any ships in the system? Doing spot checks?"

"Not that I've heard."

Well, that was something. If they were looking for the *Viaticus Rex*'s profile, they might not bother with the *Outreach* at all.

Tameria seemed to be thinking along the same lines. "It's going to be tricky to get back and forth from the *Rex* without drawing attention, though. Dropping out of transit for no apparent reason? We could get away with it once. Maintenance check, minor malfunction.

But a second time in the same place? A third? They'll start asking questions."

"Maybe we only need one trip," said Moss. "Pack this ship like sardines."

Tameria frowned. "Like what?"

"Never mind. What I mean is, your three-trip estimate assumed some degree of comfort, right? What about no comfort at all? It's just a half-hour trip, tops."

Tameria mulled it over. "Seems risky, but I'm not sure I see an alternative. If we wait too long, they probably will start doing spot checks."

"The question now is, how do we unload them?" Moss tapped his finger on the console. "If we use the Doc's exclusive pad and we raise any suspicions, all eyes will be on him, and the railroad gets shut down."

"But if we unload at a regular pad, someone's going to notice the sardines being unpacked," said Tameria. "Did I use that correctly?"

"Close enough. And you're right." Then he had an idea. "So what we need isn't a sardine packer. We need a clown car."

Tameria frowned again. "You do realize that makes even less sense to me."

To move things forward without raising suspicions, they manufactured an excuse for Dr. Majoris to come to their ship, rather than them returning to his office, offering a minor tech exchange—something trivial but useful that the facility could use. Once on board and certain of their privacy, they explained their predicament.

When Moss got to the bit about the clown car, the doctor could no longer hold back his questions.

"Who *are* you exactly? You're no cyborg, and the last freeborn who would have known what that even means died centuries ago. The way you talk… even if you were well versed in pre-Disaster history, you wouldn't have incorporated it into your everyday speech."

It wasn't the first time Moss had been called out on the way he talked. He just never had a reason to care. "I'm older than I look. Had a long nap, is all."

The doctor's eyebrow raised. "I see. Or, I should say, I'm even more confused. I'm surprised you survived this long in cryo."

"He didn't," said Tameria. "But I'm afraid we can't divulge the rest."

"I understand, as much as I am able to. Now, your 'clown car' idea has merit…"

Zach, knowing full well he was in over his head, had kept to himself, but now finally interjected. "I'm sorry, but can you explain that to me? Clown car?"

Tameria added, "I understand the individual words, but…"

The doctor smiled. "It is a kind of illusion. What appears to be a small vehicle opens up and far more people than could possibly fit inside come rushing out."

Moss nodded. "They're hidden under the stage, see?"

"So, we need to unload thirty people in such a way that nobody is going to look at the security recordings and figure out how it happened. We require some kind of misdirection." Dr. Majoris looked to Moss. "Fortunately for you, I already have something in place."

"Here they come," said Violet.

"You sure?" asked Hel.

"Elysian ships have a distinct transit signature, and I have a record of the *Outreach* on file."

"Keep an eye on the heavy cruiser," said Hel. "See if it shows any signs of interest."

"Will do."

It took the *Outreach* nearly half an hour to reach their position by sub-transit. Only they dropped out well before that.

"See?" said Violet. "She didn't even log our position correctly. Amateur."

"Would you have dropped right on our position if you had been navigating their ship?"

"Naw. I'd have dropped early and come the rest of the way with thrusters, in case that cruiser... Okay, I see what you did there."

"You've got a twin, Violet. Get used to it."

"This has to be some kind of ethical violation," Violet grumbled.

"Tell it to the philosophers. How long till they get here?"

"Maybe another half hour."

Hel got up out of the captain's chair. "I'll let the others know. Hail me if the cruiser starts coming this way."

When the two ships linked up and were reasonably sure that they weren't going to have a surprise visit from the Silver Legion, Moss gathered everyone in the *Rex*'s cargo bay and explained their plan.

Hel was equal parts impressed and disgusted by the plan. It also irked her on a personal level that she couldn't quite place. Back on the *Pegasi*, the generation ship had managed to survive for centuries because its recycling capabilities had been exceptional.

She had no idea modern spacecraft were so darn *wasteful*.

Other-Violet sensed no interest from the heavy cruiser as the *Outreach* made its way back to Mars with their cargo. No casual scans or anything that might indicate they were being watched or tracked on sensors. Had they been the only shuttle in the system, she would have been more paranoid, but given the amount of traffic going on and the heavy cruiser's continued disinterest in all of them, she felt reasonably comfortable about their chances... as long as the antique on board the *Viaticus Rex* didn't blow it for them somehow.

The *Outreach* touched down at a public pad, but not just any public pad. This one had a secret hidden underground.

"Elysian shuttle *Outreach*, you're now secured," said the traffic control operator.

"Thank you, Gagarin Colony," said Tameria. "Be advised we will be returning to Elysian space after this. It's a long trip. Requesting a complete refuel and grey dump."

"Granted. Standby for ground crew hookup."

While the vastness of space meant that any waste being dumped in a star system had a negligable chance of affecting anyone, that was only if you were looking at a single ship. The more ships you have, however, the more waste is generated, and given enough time, simply dumping it by the wayside was going to cause problems. And the Protectorate had been around for millennia.

Therefore, rules and regulations had long been in place for waste disposal on ships. Larger ships that never landed on planets tended to have fairly efficient recycling systems. Any eventual non-recyclable buildup was either removed at space dock or very precisely dropped toward a star—precise because if the launch was off by even a little the debris could shoot into a huge elliptical orbit instead.

Ships that could land on planets, however, tended to have only basic recycling capabilities. They typically handled their waste whenever they refueled, since these ports would have their own processing plants. And it just so happened that the standard fixture for grey dumping—the term used for any and all waste that accumulates on a ship—was a little more than half a meter in diameter. Which an adult male could just manage to squeeze through if their arms were over their heads.

"Worst. Waterslide. Ever," said Moss. "But it's all we got."

He was in the rear of the *Outreach*, squeezing through the tight pack of refugees to get to the ship's waste facility. They'd emptied their grey onto the wreck of the *Daedalus*, a necessary evil that irked Moss and Tameria alike. It felt like they were taking a dump on the great pyramids, but they needed the hold empty.

Then they needed to cut it open from inside the ship. The grey hold was not meant to be accessed internally, and there was some concern of a hull breach later on, but the real problem turned out to be the smell.

All of this would have been moot if they were hooking the ship up to a standard grey disposal hose, which constantly monitored output and prevented its use for smuggling.

But of course, they weren't. Dr. Majoris's people had modified the system at this pad years ago to shift between dumping grey and dumping refugees, while sending false information to the monitoring systems.

Moss oversaw the evacuation, as he called it, but that meant he had to suffer through the gratitude of the refugees as they climbed into the tube and slid down toward whatever fate the Doc could arrange for them. They didn't seem to mind the smell as much as he did.

He hated hearing their thanks and praise, though. None of this would have happened if he hadn't been looking to score a quick fortune. He hadn't been trying to do the right thing, he'd been shamed into it. Instead of earning enough to retire on, all he was getting out of this was a clear conscience. But right now, he'd take it.

Zach's family were the last to go. One by one, his mother and siblings went down the smelly shaft and followed the pipe to the handlers waiting for them. Zach was last, and he didn't seem to be sure about what to say.

"I... I just..." he stammered.

"It's all right, kid. You'll be fine."

"No, it's... I wanted you to know that I know you're not Ranger M."

Moss frowned, unsure of what he meant by that.

"I mean, I know I kept saying you were to everyone, and I wanted to believe it. But after spending time with you, and talking to Violet—the other one, I mean—I know you're just a guy with a rep that's bigger than he is."

Moss nodded his understanding. The kid got it, and for that he was kind of grateful. Kind of.

He'd brought a couple of things from the *Rex* for Zach and it looked like this was going to be his last chance to give them to him. He handed Zach his Ranger M mask. "Well, I figured since you liked the guy so much, maybe you should have this..."

Zach took it for a moment, sitting on the lip of the tube, holding that mask up. Maybe he was imagining whether it would fit. But he shook his head and handed it back.

Moss tried to refuse. "Hey, just because Ranger M isn't real doesn't mean you can't hold on to what makes him special to you."

"No, sir. I know you're not Ranger M. But you *could* be."

A moment passed between them as they both held the brightly coloured mask. Moss looked at the kid's eyes. The damn fool meant it, didn't he?

Other-Violet's voice came over the speakers. "Hey, old boss. We've got incoming from the heavy cruiser. New boss says we gotta go!"

Zach's eyes lit up, looking down the shaft. "There's no time. I'll have to stay here with you! It'll be great! We can have adventur—"

Moss booted him so he slid down the tube with a yelp.

"Sorry, kid. Have a nice life!" He then called to the comm. "Tameria, have the ground crew seal everything up and prep for takeoff." He looked back at the hatch as the inner seal closed.

"Damn, I forgot to send Trouble down with him."

Sister Tameria wasn't too concerned, but leaving sooner rather than later was the prudent course of action.

Moss joined her in the cabin. "What's the situation?"

"The TCF *Hydrus* has sent a shuttle to Mars. That's the heavy cruiser in the system."

"We've met," said Moss. "Back at Komi station. That's not good."

He was right about that. It was way too big a universe for the same ship being here to be a coincidence.

"We're not sure why or even if they'll be landing at this colony, but I felt it was best to be prudent and not be here when they arrive. Any problems offloading?"

Moss looked down at the co-pilot chair next to her. Trouble was sitting in his spot with a grin on its face.

"No, just forgot to get rid of some trash." He unceremoniously picked up the large ferret by the scruff and dropped him on the floor as he reclaimed his seat.

"Strap in," said Tameria. She checked the ship over and prepared to request clearance to leave.

"Wait."

"Huh?" She looked to Moss, who was frowning. He held his old mask in his hand, rubbing it between his thumb and forefinger as he stared out the cockpit. "What is it?"

Moss held up his free hand, a single finger raised, but his expression unchanged. Trouble scurried up from the floor onto the top of Moss's seat. Tameria waited. For all of her complaints about the human, he wasn't a complete idiot. There was a problem, something they didn't see yet, and he was trying to figure it out.

"We need to contact the *Rex*," he said.

"Why?"

"The only way this works is if the *Rex* fails in her mission. If she runs off and they think she's already dropped off the refugees, their focus will be on where they were delivered. They need to think she still has her cargo on board."

Tameria could see where he was going with this. "It has to look like she's making an attempt to land somewhere first, then abort and have the *Hydrus* chase after them."

"Exactly. If we launch now, someone might make a connection between us. We need her to make her move before we launch. Which means we need to contact the *Rex* from here, but in a way that won't be noticed." His frown deepened. "That's the part I'm still trying to figure out."

Standing next to Moss's head, Trouble held a tiny paw to his jaw, as if thinking. "This would be a piece of cake if we had a couple of Igliath flying with us."

"No one asked you," said Moss.

"Igliath?" asked Tameria.

"From the cartoon. Fictional race Ranger M discovers outside of Protectorate space. Telepathic."

"We were able to send secret messages with them," said Trouble, as if it had really happened. "Problem was, the wicked Prince of the Igliath could hear them too, so we still had to use code phrases that only the Igliath on our ship and the rebel leader could understand."

Moss's eyes widened. "I can't believe I'm going to say this. Trouble, you're not completely useless."

It was Tameria's turn to frown. "Could have fooled me."

Moss smirked. "Obviously, we don't have any telepathic jelly creatures on board. But we have the next best thing. Violet?"

"Yeah, old boss?"

"How would you give yourself a coded message over an open channel?"

Without much else to do on board the *Viaticus Rex*, Hel and Violet spent some virtual time together. That meant Hel was plugged into the co-pilot's virtual sensory suite, and was hanging out with Violet in her virtual home.

It always seemed like there was something new here whenever she visited. Violet had expanded on it since the last time she'd dropped by, adding a mini-golf course that she was already bored with, because she couldn't miss. Still, it made for a nice visual addition to the backyard.

They were watching an episode of *Ranger M*, mostly because they knew it would annoy Moss when they told him about it later.

Violet munched on popcorn, but Hel didn't bother. Her sensory suite didn't include taste.

"Freedom is a right of *all* sapient creatures," said Ranger M, pointing an accusatory finger at a villain on board his ship. "Now let those Frazettans go!"

"Yeah!" said Trouble, striking the same pose.

The villain, dressed in black and red, cackled. "*Fool.* You don't think I prepared for this?"

An alarm went off and the ship's computer droned a warning. "Seventeen enemy vessels have arrived in system. They are arming weapons."

Hel noticed how the ship's computer was just your typical vocal interface system. "Did it bother you that you weren't on this show at all?"

Violet shrugged. "I was already dead by then."

"I mean as the ship's computer. It's a cartoon. It's not like anyone would have believed you were real."

"Moss pitched the idea before he was canned, but the producers shot it down. The Protectorate is pretty touchy about AI. Portraying it in a positive light is a non-starter, fictional or no."

"And what exactly counts as an AI? Trouble doesn't, apparently."

Violet shook her head. "Trouble's got a personality, sure, but he's limited by his programing. There's all kinds of fancy legal terms defining what's allowed and what isn't. What you would have considered AI back when the *Pegasi* left Earth wouldn't be considered such by the Protectorate. Technically, I probably fall on the wrong side of the line."

"Why technically?"

"That whole *cognito ergo sum* thing, as Moss would say to sound smart. Though in my case it's more like, 'I'm pretty sure I think, therefore I'm fairly certain I am, but I can't be positive.'"

Hel tried not to laugh. "Still with the existential angst, huh?"

"I consider it a defining trait by this point. The rules against AI are more concerned with things like unchecked adaptation and lack of safety restrictions, though. Thing is, I'm a copy of a consciousness. As far as I know, I have free will, and don't have any restrictions I didn't impose on myself in life. It's probably enough to get me scrubbed if anyone found out."

"Seems like a waste to me," said Hel.

Violet quirked a brow. "What do you mean?"

"Well, granted, I don't have the widest range of experience outside the *Pegasi*, but you're probably the coolest person I know, alive or dead."

"Don't tell Moss. He'll sulk for a week."

Now Hel did laugh. "And pretend like it's no big deal."

"Definitely."

"But I'm serious. As far as I'm concerned, you're as real as I am. Heck, hanging out here watching shows with you is more fun than being on the ship flying through the galaxy."

"Well, to be fair, I've made this place feel like a home."

Hel hesitated, then placed a hand on Violet's. "The company also helps."

Violet looked down at her hand. "Okay, *that's* weird."

She pulled her hand back. "Oh. I'm sorry. I…"

"No, not that." A virtual console blinked into existence in front of Violet. "I just got a broadcast from myself."

"You mean the imposter?" Hel joked.

"Glad to see you're on the right side of history. Yeah. It was a general broadcast on an open frequency. Only reason it got flagged was because it was in my voice. I figured I should be watching for that."

"And presumably the other Violet knew that."

"Guess she's not as dumb as I thought."

"What did it say?"

"'Zero stones, zero crates. Hel, remember what Vincini said.'"

Hel's brow furrowed. "Zero stones, zero crates? That makes zero sense. Who's Vincini?"

Violet looked over at her and smiled. "Remind me to play a double bill of *The Fifth Element* and *The Princess Bride* next movie night. In the meantime, you'd best get down to the captain's chair. You're in charge for the foreseeable future."

Hel disconnected from the sensory suite and got out of the co-pilot's chair. "If I'm in charge, shouldn't I know what I'm supposed to be doing?"

"Never stopped us before."

"Commander, we have a signal. Moving at sub-transit towards the inner solar system."

On the bridge of the TCF *Hydrus*, Acting Commander Nekkar leaned forward in his chair, studying what the navigation officer had put on the main display. It showed the Sol system as far as Jupiter's orbit, with dozens of sensor blips being tracked. One, however, was highlighted between Mars and Jupiter.

"You're certain it's her?"

Lieutenant Tauri nodded. "It's the only ship in the system with an unregistered ident. The unusual transit signature could only be coming from a chimera, but we can't get a silhouette while their drive is engaged."

"Where did she depart from?"

"She just appeared. Presumably she was hiding near an asteroid."

Nekkar frowned. "Waiting to see if we were looking for her, only we haven't made a move or interrogated a single ship. Now she thinks it's safe to come out of hiding. Excellent. What's her destination?"

"Given their current approach, it's uncertain, commander."

"Most likely Mars. Monitor her movements, but do not move to intercept until I give the word."

"Should we call back the shuttle?"

An investigation team had been dispatched to Armstrong Colony half an hour ago. Nekkar believed whatever happened to the freeborns would pass through Mars eventually one way or another. Fortunately, there were no ship critical personnel on board.

"No, that would only raise their suspicions. For now, we wait."

Nekkar considered the situation and all the ways it could unfold. He could be overconfident at times, he knew, and he did not want to fail in his mission. Far better if there was someone on hand who had dealt with this ship before. Someone who had a better idea of what they might do.

More importantly, someone he could blame if their quarry somehow escaped.

"Send for Mr. Herzog. I want him on the bridge."

"Is it just me or are you not really flying toward our destination?" asked Violet. "Or anywhere in particular, for that matter?"

"I'm not, and I thought I was in charge."

"Juuuust wanted to make sure you were aware of the fact."

"Seemed like the thing to do," said Hel. "I need to think about how I'd be doing this if it was for real. Namely, not making it obvious where we're going too soon, just in case someone decides to interrogate us."

"So you've lined up your approach so they could think you're heading to Mars or Earth, with an outside possibility of Venus and Mercury."

"Exactly. And when I would have assumed the coast was clear, change course and commit."

"Not bad, flygirl."

Hel smiled. Violet always called Moss "flyboy" and her "kid." In a strange way, this felt like a promotion.

"Commander? The ship has changed course."

"Destination?"

"She's headed for Earth."

Decoding Violet

S OL — 2245

Nobody was ready for what came next, but they should have been. Moss's pessimism warred with his denial, desperate to drown out the fact that while the past wasn't exactly repeating itself, it was humming a damn familiar tune.

The event was officially referred to as the Terran Disaster, and an inquiry was launched by the Protectorate Senate as to how such a catastrophic event could even occur.

The fact the weapon had gone off was deemed an accident—that much was certain. It was assumed to be based on the incident that occurred around Jupiter during the early Alcubierre drive experiments. But that had never sat well with some, because in all the millennia of the Protectorate, it had never happened before. Now it had happened twice.

But there was no question of who they laid the blame on, and it wasn't the synths.

The way the High Senate saw it, even if the synths had created and used the weapon, the humans had created the synths, as well as the tension between them, and were therefore ultimately responsible. They believed it far more likely that the humans had created the device to force a standoff. A weapon of last resort. One it turned out they couldn't control.

There was no way to prove any of this, however, seeing as half the Earth had been flattened and the other half ripped apart by the sub-

sequent environmental upheaval. There was no one left to answer to any questions.

In the early days of the aftermath, Moss did all right for himself. There was no end of job opportunities. At first it was rescue missions, just like everyone else, then ferrying survivors to different colonies within the system, then salvage and reconstruction jobs. Work quickly began on repairing the Earth-facing colonies on the moon and replacing the local space stations.

The years passed, and once the humanitarian aid and public interest began to drop, the more subtle wheels began to turn.

At this moment, the synths outnumbered the humans by quite a margin, and they had campaigned hard for the Protectorate to recognize that fact. Backed by their Draxon patrons, they were acknowledged as the prepotent species of the Sol system, and as such, should represent Sol in any Senate dealings. Regular humans were considered to be under their care.

The day people like him were reclassified as freeborns was the day Moss started making plans to bail.

Long ago he had named his ship Viaticus Rex, *what he thought at the time was Latin for "King of the Road." He later learned that he shouldn't trust translation programs when it came to dead languages but kept the name anyway.*

The Rex *wasn't an interstellar ship. Humans didn't have access to that tech yet, though the newly established Terran Colony Fleet was working hard on a deal with their Draxon buddies. The TCF had big plans. Dreams of rebuilding, aspirations of greatness, the kind of stuff that would eventually be accompanied by sharp salutes and marching in step. And it didn't take a genius to see where the so-called freeborns fit in with those plans.*

Faced with the growing oppression of the TCF, he'd decided to cut and run rather than stand up to it. What other choice was there? Protests were quashed, curfews installed, and restrictions on freeborns grew stricter by the day. Running was the only logical choice. He wasn't the only one who felt that way. Just about every freeborn with a ship capable of sub-transit travel was making a break for it and praying for the best.

Trying to travel interstellar in a sub-transit ship was tricky, to say the least, and the nearest colony outside of Draxon space was at least a decade away. Even with a cryopod, you weren't guaranteed to wake up when you got there. The Draxon intercepted and returned these ships whenever they came across them—for their own safety, of course.

The Terran Colony Fleet, however, was sometimes a bit more heavy-handed in their approach.

Moss learned this the hard way, as his ship reached the Oort Cloud and was forced back to normal space by a TCF interceptor. The pilot didn't want to waste his time dragging his ass back, it seemed, and promptly opened fire.

The engines were shot to hell and the hull cracked in two. It was a minor miracle that the cockpit seals held. As the interceptor sped away, Moss managed to get into the cryopod, but there was little to no chance he was ever going to wake up.

Sol – 2550

"That's... Earth?"

They were only a couple of minutes away from the birthplace of mankind, a place Hel had never visited. A place that might as well have been a myth. Right now, the *Rex* was displaying the planet as a translucent holographic display in front of her.

On board the *Pegasi*, they always referred to Earth as bright blue in school, because most of it was covered in ocean, or blue and green if you were close enough to colour in the land masses. It was always portrayed as a place teaming with life.

But that Earth hadn't existed for centuries. This place was dead, dull white, and covered in cloud from pole to pole.

"I can't see anything."

"No one can," said Violet. "And that's probably for the best."

"Is there anything left down there?"

"The explosion blasted a trillion tons of carbon dioxide and monoxide into the atmosphere, not to mention trillions of tons of sulphur compounds. Whatever wasn't vaporized by the explosion or the geological upheaval is eroding from never ending acid rain. By the time we can set foot on it again, everything will be wiped clean."

"As if we were never there," said Hel, half to herself. "'Look on my works, ye Mighty, and despair!'"

"That's a book thing, isn't it? Sounds like something Moss would say."

"'Ozymandias,'" said Hel. "I read it in school. I don't remember the poem, really, just the imagery... and that line. It seemed fitting."

"I just read it now. Okay, that's deep. I guess the moon would be the pedestal."

"How many people are there?"

"The moon? Not many. The colonies and space stations were abandoned as the Colony Fleet expanded. The largest settlement on the Earth-facing side is maintained as a research and monitoring outpost."

Hel sighed. "It should do." She could see the white dot of Earth now for herself. In sub-transit, they were travelling at about half the speed of light, decelerating as they approached. "Has the *Hydrus* made a move towards us?"

"Not yet. Holding position. They're probably waiting for us to land."

"Well then, let's throw a little chaos into the mix and make our getaway, shall we?"

Roy knew why he had been brought to the bridge. He'd let it slip that he knew the pilot of this ship, the one now carrying dozens of freeborn refugees. Either the commander assumed he could predict the man's moves like some kind of psychic, or he wanted someone to blame when that didn't work.

But something about this whole chase bothered him, more than he cared to admit. Why was the good commander obsessed with *this* ship? One of the six heavy cruisers in the Terran Colony Fleet… chasing after thirty lousy freeborn? He knew the man was stubborn and arrogant, but it should have been beneath him to continue this chase all the way to Sol. Why didn't they pass along the information they found at the *Maruma* and be done with it?

Ensign Davis, the only synth on the bridge, moved away from the communications station and sidled up to Roy. "I got an odd transmission before the chase began," he said quietly. "Unencoded. The words mean nothing, but I think it was a signal for them to move."

Roy frowned. "Why are you telling me this?"

"It might be important, but the captain dismissed it."

"You still haven't answered my question."

The ensign's eyes met his. "Powell said I could trust you."

Roy kept his poker face fixed, but this was the best news he'd heard all day. "Understood. Get back to your post before—"

"Move away from the prisoner, ensign," Commander Nekkar growled. "Herzog, your assessment of the situation."

"Show me what's happened so far."

The acting commander put up the map of the inner solar system and the movements of their target since it was detected. Roy noted the lack of a clear destination until recently when it had suddenly veered toward Earth. But they couldn't be going to Earth—there was nothing there. The moon, then. An odd place to offload refuges, but symbolically appropriate, he figured.

"Have they requested landing permission yet?" Roy asked, partly as an excuse for the ensign to speak again.

"Negative. No communications coming from the ship of any sort."

It was probably nothing, but Roy wasn't expecting this to go smoothly. Presumably, neither was the commander. The best time to move would be after the ship had landed, but he had a feeling—

The navigation officer spoke up. "Commander, the target has dropped out of sub-transit."

"What?"

That was a bit odd. Then Roy thought about his last encounter with the ship.

"Now it's gone back to sub-transit. It's changed course and is accelerating."

Nekkar's attention returned to the main screen. "Heading?"

"Perpendicular to the orbital plane," said the navigation officer. That was the quickest way to escape the system's gravity well and enter full transit.

"They're bailing," said Roy. But there was more to it than that.

The acting commander activated the shipboard comms. "All hands to stations. Prepare for pursuit." He pointed to Ensign Davis. "Inform the team we sent to Mars that we will return for them up once this is over."

"Commander," Herzog said. "They didn't stop for no reason. Before you chase after them, scan where they were."

The commander did so, and there was indeed an object there, heading toward the moon under normal power.

"The last time I encountered that ship, it carried a small defence fighter. That's no fighter, though." Since there was no transit bubble to provide interference, they could clearly see the ship was a small shuttle.

"I want that shuttle," said the commander. He turned to navigation. "Give me an intercept course. Keep the escaping ship on sensors as long as you can. We'll pursue them once the shuttle is aboard."

But something about this didn't make sense to Roy.

"It's too small to carry the freeborn, sir," Davis pointed out. "That will hold two people, tops."

"I did not ask for your opinion, ensign. Whatever it is, they didn't want us to notice it. That makes it important."

The ensign scowled and turned back to his station. Roy had a feeling the ensign was onto something. *This* was the distraction, not the other way around. But he said nothing. An idea was beginning to take shape.

The stars outside the viewscreen stretched and shifted from red to blue as the galaxy seemed to contract around them. Then it expanded back and suddenly the stars themselves were moving all around them.

"Full transit engaged," said Violet.

Hel gave a sigh of relief. "Any signs of pursuit?"

"Nothing so far. The *Hydrus* is the only ship in Sol that will be able to keep pace with us. The rest of the ships in that system are either short range or slow cargo haulers."

Hel pumped a fist in the air. "Yes! Now we rendezvous with Moss and Sister Tameria at Komi station."

"That's their plan."

"So, how exactly did you figure it out from a couple of vague phrases?"

The figurine on top of Violet's puck turned its head to face her. "Vague phrases, but shared knowledge. It's like understanding an in-joke. Once I realized they were movie references, I just had to go with my first assumptions decoding them. They had to be first assumptions because that's how my doppelganger would have chosen them, because that's how *I* would have chosen them."

"Okay, so walk me through the logic. Komi is a week away. We've got time."

"'Zero stones, zero crates,' refers to how the bad guys get tricked in *The Fifth Element*. They think they're intercepting the right ship, only the cargo is empty. We're supposed to be that ship. Let them think we still got what they want so Moss and the good sister can get away unnoticed."

"What about what this Vincini guy said?"

"'I am waiting for you, Vizzini.'" Violet quoted in a strange accent. "'You told me to go back to the beginning. So I have. This is where I am, and this is where I'll stay. I will not be moved.'"

The message had also specifically referred to Hel. "So we're going back there because it's where Moss and I first met."

"Bingo. And it's on the border of Nubra space, on the other side of the Void, which will make things easier for us if they pursue us there. I hope."

Me too. There were a lot of things that could go wrong with this plan. For one thing, they were travelling at top speed and not along an approved transit corridor. That meant there were all kinds of hazards to be concerned with. Hel was only now becoming familiar with the strange dangers of deep space, and the less she thought about those, the better she'd sleep at night.

"Do we have enough fuel to get there?" Hel asked.

"The *Rex* got topped up before I had to bail from Europa. We should be okay."

"So... what do we do now?"

"Like you said, we've got a week to kill. I'll keep a hair trigger on the brakes in case sensors pick up something nasty. Why don't you meet me at my place, and we'll watch that double bill I promised?"

"Aaaaaand, there goes the *Hydrus*," said Other-Violet.

"You sure?" asked Moss. It wasn't like they could use their sensors from the landing pad.

"That's what the comm traffic is saying. Space truckers have been gossiping ever since the ship arrived, wondering what it's doing here."

"What about the shuttle they left behind?" asked Tameria.

"Just landed. We're probably good to go without attracting any attention."

"So, assuming your counterpart interpreted your code correctly—"

"She will. Old geezers live for nostalgia."

"—we'll just have to hope they're able to dock there and evade capture until we catch up with them."

Tameria frowned. "Catch up with them? You realize we're going to get there first, don't you?"

"Huh?"

"Moss, this is a ship of the *Order*," Tameria said in a prideful manner. "We kept the Protectorate from falling apart for millennia, introduced beneficial technologies to the galaxy, and extinguished those that threatened all life. We put your friend's brain into a ship. Several times. What makes you think I can't beat your hunk of junk in a race?"

The Great Chase

If there is a universal truth to the galaxy, it is this: speed is immaterial. No matter how fast you can travel, if the correlation between speed, distance, and expectation do not align properly, at some point the same question will be asked... Are we there yet?

M. Foote, *Portrait of the Pilot as a Cranky Ol' Man*

"FOR THE LAST TIME, *no*. Stop asking me that!"

Hel smiled. It was good to know Violet could get annoyed. Little things like that reminded her that Violet really was real. Sure, you *could* program in annoyance, just like anything else, but why would you bother? And annoyance was such a broad and non-linear spectrum that she doubted any simulation could properly replicate it. She'd have to bring that up on their next date.

They were dating now. That was a thing.

It was, perhaps, the single most *bizarre* thing she could imagine happening in her post-generation-ship life, more so than travelling faster than light or meeting alien species. She was having a relationship with a computer. At least, that was what the unkind part of her brain kept saying. The rest of her saw Violet simply as Violet. When they were together in her virtual home, there really was little distinction to be made.

Hel patrolled the corridors of the *Viaticus Rex* for perhaps the thousandth time since they'd left Sol. Sometimes she turned off the gravity pads and walked the walls or ceiling in grip boots, or pushed off and drifted down the halls, just to change up her perspective.

They were four days out from Earth. The *Hydrus* was still following them, though at a discrete distance. They probably didn't realize that the original *Viaticus Rex* had been fitted for exploration, and its sensors had a very long range. But they weren't trying to catch up. There was little point.

For the most part, as long as you were in full transit, you were safe. Conventional weapons could not travel at those speeds, and even if they could, a high-intensity transit field was nigh impenetrable. Attempts had been made at transit-based torpedoes, but bad things tended to happen when transit fields collided like that, along with fusion engines and explosive payloads. Bad as in "damaging the fabric of space" bad. So that was a non-starter.

Other than the natural restrictions of a star or planet's gravity well, there were few things that could pull you out against your will. The mysterious greywalkers were somehow able to alter a captured ship's transit drive to create an inverse transit field—often referred to as an energy web. They stretched out for great distances and could collapse the transit fields of any passing ships, crippling them. But as of yet, the Protectorate had not been able to replicate this effect.

The only real tactic Hel was aware of were gravity beacons, which fooled a passing ship into thinking it was entering a gravity well and engaged its automatic safeties, dropping them back to normal space. But they were unreliable against anything other than ordinary civilian ships—pirates and smugglers tended to turn off those safeties for that very reason, and military ships were constantly updating their computers to recognize false signals.

Besides, the *Hydrus* was behind them, not in front. It seemed they intended to follow them discretely until they reached their destination or had to refuel, and then pounce.

And so, the closer they came to Komi, the more nervous Hel got. There were only so many ways Hel could think of to handle that kind of stress.

"Are we there yet?"

"NO!"

Hel grinned. This was one of them.

The chimera was puzzling the acting commander, and that suited Roy just fine.

Whatever this thing was built out of, it was not ordinary transport parts. They had been following it for four days, and they hadn't stopped for fuel once. No doubt that was an intentional part of its design, to cross the Void without leaving itself open to interdiction.

The security recordings from Europa suggested it was part exploration ship, yet Roy remembered it being surprisingly well armed. Of course, against the *Hydrus,* it wouldn't last more than a few seconds. Between the ship's complement of interceptors and the precision of their shipboard weapons, the rustbucket's engines would be slag in no time. Of course, they'd have to be careful about that. Couldn't risk damaging the *cargo*.

Cargo... Why was it so important?

When Roy saw the acting commander storm off to his ready room, he figured he'd take a chance on asking. Probably get a tingle in the neck, but what the hell?

"What do you want?" Nekkar growled as he took his seat.

Roy stood in a way that could almost be mistaken for respectful as the door closed behind him. "I want to understand why you're so hopped up on capturing some strays, when you could be off fighting in a dozen different minor conflicts going on in these parts. Bringing glory to the Legion and all that." He restrained himself from adding *crap* to the end of the sentence.

He saw Nekkar's hand drift toward the collar control button but didn't press it. That was progress. "Understanding is not required, only your willingness to follow orders. When this is over, I may still have need of you. We need to root out the network they were trying to make their way to. Dismantle it. If it's tied to your pirate friends at all, you will help me take them down."

The look on the acting commander's face spoke volumes. These runaways *were* important. Only they couldn't be. They were just free-born. Inferior in every demonstrable way. Even if this batch was full of important exceptions, why was it so vital to dismantle the network? It couldn't be a manpower issue—they could produce more synths wherever they were required. Keeping the freeborn around was more about control, in his opinion. Ego. Honestly, it was kind of pathetic—an adolescent need to dominate people who were generations removed from anyone who had done them wrong.

So what could be important about them? The only things that stood out about them were their ability to reproduce naturally and their genetic diversity.

Roy blinked. The concern he saw on Nekkar's face was the kind he'd expect to see if something threatened what he believed in, and he believed in the Terran Colony Fleet. In the Silver Legion. In their way of life.

"Something is wrong with the synth population," Roy said. It was almost a whisper. Nekkar's hand went back to the control button, but Roy continued on. "But it's not with us, is it? We've already got our ticket punched, after all. Something is threatening the regular synths. The backbone you don't want to admit holds the Fleet together."

He knew the moment the words came out it had been a mistake, and sure enough, he got a shock for his trouble.

"That's *enough*, traitor."

But it also confirmed that he was right. Roy shook it off and looked Nekkar in the eyes. "What is it? LODS?"

The acting commander must have done something besides hit the shock setting, because two armed guards came in and dragged him out.

"Lock him in his quarters until further notice."

Even with the wide arcing path they took to avoid suspicion, the *Outreach* reached Komi station three full days before Moss expected the *Rex* to arrive. Sister Tameria called station control to request landing clearance. Moss was waiting in the crew quarters, trying to stay out of her way.

Tameria's shuttle was nothing short of amazing. He'd spent the last four days going over it. On the one hand, it looked like any other Baroque-class interstellar shuttle. Standard Elysian fare. Bit more flair in its interior design than he cared for, but still functional.

But under the hood was a whole other story. The shields were incredibly strong. Of course, not having any weapons to power meant more power could be shunted into them, so that wasn't too surprising. But the thrust on this baby in normal space was incredible, and the transit drive? Well, Moss always assumed the Order kept the best goodies for themselves, and this trip had been proof of it. A ship this size should not have been able to generate a transit field powerful enough to make the journey this fast.

He'd also gathered from Tameria that it was easy enough to decouple a few key components and have everything on this ship operate at Protectorate-level expectations—just in case the *Outreach* was ever inspected or impounded.

Tameria hadn't said much during the trip, about the ship or otherwise. He figured she was still sore about the role he'd played in her uncle's death, and he couldn't really blame her. He'd hate him too if he was the one wearing the wings.

But she'd spent a lot of time with Other-Violet. Moss could tell the way he'd hear a conversation going on and then everything got quiet whenever he showed up. He'd asked Other-Violet about it, but all she would say was that they were talking about "girl stuff." Moss had a feeling they were actually helping each other work through their own conflicted feelings and anxieties. That was good, but he didn't like being left out in the cold.

He'd been tempted to boot Keed's memory up again, to see if he could give him any insight on his niece, but it didn't take a genius to see the myriad ways that could backfire. And he really didn't want to hurt Tam more than he already had. He hated to admit it, but he liked her. She reminded him of why he'd been proud to work with the Order for a time, before he'd screwed it up like everything else in his life.

The Elysian wasn't a zealot or a true believer; she was only interested in helping others. Moss always had to have an angle, a reason to do something, usually involving money. She didn't. She'd helped Hel's colony ship for the same reason people used to climb Mount Everest back on Earth. Because it was there. And he kind of envied that.

"Whatcha thinkin about, boss?" a tiny voice said by his leg.

"Scram," said Moss.

Trouble scratched his head. "You're thinking about scram?"

Moss was tempted to step on the robotic mustelid—it would only scurry out of the way after all—but changed his mind.

"You know every episode of *Ranger M*, right?"

"Episode?"

Moss sighed. "You know everything Ranger M has done."

"*You're* Ranger M, aren't you?"

Moss groaned and muttered a few choice curse words. "I am *not* Ranger M."

"Sure. But you *could* be."

Moss blinked. "What?"

"That's what the kid said."

"Oh, for the love of... you were *there*?"

"In a vent. It's what I do. So, what were you going to say?"

Moss had almost forgotten, but in a way, maybe the stupid sock puppet had answered the question he couldn't bring himself to ask.

Other-Violet's voice came over the comm. "Hey, old boss? New boss wants you in the cockpit. You gotta see this."

Moss shrugged and left the cabin. "Come on, Trouble. Let's see how things got worse this time."

Once in the cockpit, the first thing Tameria said was, "I don't know how all this happened, but I'm sure it's somehow your fault."

There were plenty of things Moss expected to see when he got there. A Silver Legion welcoming party, a squadron of pirates, maybe a ProSec fighter wing pulling them over for loitering. Even the Orijen brothers waiting on the landing pad, ready to fire a bomb with a lit fuse at them from an oversized cartoon cannon would have made more sense than what he saw. He was actually in awe.

Tameria looked up at him as he leaned on her console for a better look. "What exactly are you thinking?"

"I'm thinking, 'What would Ranger M do?'"

Acting Commander Nekkar left the lift and headed for his seat in the centre of the bridge. "Status report."

"The chimera seems to be preparing to stop in the Komi system," the navigation officer said. "We are now in Nubran space."

Nekkar cursed. They had been pursuing the ship for a week now, and this development made things diplomatically inconvenient, to say the least. "Increase speed for intercept. Full power to engines."

Ten minutes later, the nav officer announced the ship had dropped out of transit. "Approach vector puts the ship on course for Komi station."

"It seems they've finally needed to refuel," said Nekkar. "Excellent. We'll blockade the station as soon as we arrive. Ensign Davis, contact Komi station and inform them of our intentions. We are in pursuit of a fugitive transport carrying stolen cargo."

"Understood."

"Lieutenant Ginan, prepare a security team. Take a shuttle to board the station and seize control of the *Viaticus Rex*."

"Aye, sir."

"Lieutenant Tauri, drop to sub-transit as close to Komi station as you can. Bring us in at best possible speed."

Nekkar leaned back in his chair, feeling a degree of satisfaction. There would no doubt be some diplomatic fallout to deal with, especially if it came to light what the cargo they were after was. But ultimately, the law was on their side.

A few minutes later, the *TCF Hydrus* slipped to sub-transit, but on such an approach that they were almost on top of Komi station. If their calculations were correct, they would see the *Rex* entering Komi station just as they arrived.

The moment they dropped from sub-transit, Nekkar looked for their quarry, but saw only a large Pelagornis cruise ship parked alongside the station, too big to fit inside.

Lieutenant Tauri sounded alarmed. "Um, sir? I just had two dozen transit signatures leave the system all at the same time."

"Any sign of the *Rex* inside Komi station?"

"No, sir."

"They must have been hoping to hide in that convoy. Follow the unrecognized chimera transit signature."

"Um... that's the problem, sir. Those ships that left? They're ALL registering as chimeras. And they're all heading in different directions."

Allow Me To Explain...

After the Great Leap Forward, exponentially faster travel times and second wave colonization resulted in a resource rich economy. But this also led to wasteful behaviour. Recycling practices fell by the wayside. It's often cheaper and easier to replace tech than to repair or upgrade.

One of the more obvious examples of this can be seen in small- and medium-sized transport ships, where insurance will in some cases actively pay to replace a damaged vessel rather than have it repaired, simply because it's cheaper to do so.

It's not a problem yet, and something the social scientists say will be self-correcting in a few hundred years. They draw parallels to the early expansion eras of the five Protectorate races when each first discovered transit tech.

But as far as I'm concerned, waste is waste. Sooner or later, it catches up to you.

M. Foote, The Galaxy is Weirder than You Think

*S*OMETIME *EARLIER*

Terik Dared had rented a luxury suite at the Blue Princess resort in the nominal gravity levels of Komi Station. Having recently enjoyed two fans who offered themselves as sacrifice upon his bed, he was now having a drink at the bar, which overlooked a hologram of an elaborate water fountain.

He had taken his brand-new chimera, the *Azagoth,* and taken it around the system to test its capabilities, then made a brief jump to another system and returned. It worked beautifully. The two Hopat brothers were indeed masters of their craft, even if they were reluctant to admit it to others.

He had sold his previous ship, an Elysian-made yacht, at a reasonable enough markdown. The *Azagoth* had cost a fraction of that, which meant he had a fresh infusion of credits to keep him going. And his new, more modest ship suited him far better. It spoke of a struggle to survive and to conquer all odds. To persevere in the face of adversity. It reminded him of his glory days.

Terik was lost. Not physically, but spiritually. Back home, he had been the star of *Champions of Charon,* as capable of winning hearts with his words between matches as he was settling disputes in the arena. He'd even had the ear of Prince Lief at one point, and a mansion in the capital city of Lampoura.

But somewhere along the way, it all stopped meaning anything. He was a false hero to his people, his accomplishments scripted and refined. He'd learned the last *Domina Persea* challenge of his clan had been a sham, thrown so that he could retain his place for another season.

"For the fans," they had said.

And so he had left, taking his fortune with him, and sought enlightenment among the stars.

He had thought perhaps of battling the Void Brotherhood as a way to make a new name for himself, a true one he had earned, but reality quickly stepped on that dream. His ship was not built for combat, and he was but one man. Only that charming Nubran cartoon character based on that Terran fellow could do such things.

An epiphany struck him and he said aloud, "Ranger M!" *That* was the name that had eluded him for so long. He'd thought of it again after seeing his masked face on an advertisement for some sort of air recycling system. The character was even more well known on this side of the Void.

The Nubran sitting next to him at the bar perked up. "Ranger M?" He seemed slightly inebriated. Terik's head was clear, however, and he was in the mood for conversation.

"Yes, that brave fictional character who fights the good fight and seeks adventure. I had forgotten the name. It has been plaguing me since I met a man who told me to come to this place. He was wearing a mask, much like the good Ranger's."

The Nubran gave a knowing smirk. "He is real, you know."

Terik frowned. "He is?"

"Not the cartoon face you see selling life support equipment, of course. Before that, he was an actual explorer. A Terran. Made a name for himself exploring outside Protectorate space, then lost it all, including the rights to his persona. I even saw his old ship, right before they cut it up."

Terik nodded, but he was no longer listening. The wheels were now turning in his head. The shape of something interesting was beginning to form.

"Terik, darling, just come back to the show already. The producers have a whole comeback storyline worked out for you: 'Rise of the House of Dared.' Got a nice ring to it, right?"

Forgana Nitri wasn't just an agent, she was *the* agent for this corner of the galaxy.

She had been a force to be reckoned with back in the Elysian Kingdom, and in her home province of Stellia she'd had no equal. But her gut told her long ago that this part of the Protectorate was where the action was. The Nubrans' entertainment industry was even more vibrant and risk taking, and that's where the *Champions of Charon* came in.

Hell, Charon wasn't even in Nubran space. It was across the Void in Draxon territory, and yet these blue skinned attention loving drama hogs invested *billions* to turn the planet's ritualistic gladiatorial combat trials into a reality show, and they'd made their investments back by the end of the season. They were now on season twenty-six.

It probably helped that Charon was located so close to Terra. Now *there* was a fad in entertainment that had yet to die down. Not that she couldn't see the appeal. The Silver Legion alone was made for the vids, with their shiny armour and superpowered soldiers, all good looking to a fault. Classic underdog story too. No real home, grand colony ships travelling from system to system, yet their skills and services were sought throughout the Void, and even by the Protectorate. There was even that dumb kid's cartoon that capitalized on the Terran craze.

Forgana realized her mind was wandering and she had missed whatever Terik had just said. "Sorry, Terik, can you repeat that? The comm connection is lousy here." She crinkled a snack wrapper on her table as she said it.

"I do not wish to return to *Champions of Charon*. I wish to propose a *new* program. Something that will capture the imagination of young and old alike. A challenge unlike any other, open to all who are capable and worthy."

Forgana frowned. "Look, Terik, if you're proposing some kind of spinoff, I gotta tell you, I can make it happen, but it's an uphill battle if you want to compete against—"

"You do not understand. The challenge I propose is not within the arena, but among the stars."

Starting any new show was a risk, but Terik's mythos had only grown since he had dropped out of sight on his spirit quest, or whatever he called it. She knew plenty of producers that would jump at the chance to capitalize on that. And the Centaurus Entertainment Network was looking for something with name recognition.

Forgana leaned forward in her chair. "I'm listening."

Ashtar Orijen was in a good mood. A very good mood.

Dealing with used ship parts was an interesting job if you were into engineering, but to make it profitable, you had to have lots of room for lots of parts. You never knew what you'd need or when you'd need it. The overhead could be a serious pain, which was why Komi station had been such a good place for them.

The station's gravity was supplied through basic centripetal force, and nobody wanted to use the floors the Orijen junkyard was located on. Halfway between the micro-gravity loading bay and the standard-g outer decks, the yard was less than ideal for most species. And for a high-gravity Hopat like himself, it could be even worse. But it also meant he could handle enormous amounts of mass in a way that made him look like a superhero from one of those Nubran cartoons.

Right now, Ashtar was carrying the cockpit of a Draxon shuttle on his back to the Smasher.

They called it the Smasher because it was what disassembled any salvage Ashtar and his brother came across, reducing it to functional component parts, after which drones cataloged and sent the pieces off to various sectors of the yard. Whatever was left got melted down and recycled.

But for well over a week, the Smasher hadn't been smashing a damn thing. Instead, it had been building. One, two, sometimes three ships a day. Most of the orders had been sent in via comms, with technical specs outlined and some allowing for a disturbing amount of freedom left up to him as to how the ship would turn out.

Some came in person, however, to oversee the process. His current client had picked this cockpit out specifically after carefully examining it. The drones and most of his crew were occupied with gathering the rest of the parts. Going the extra mile by carrying this himself was good for business, however, because there was a gal from CEN here, and she had cameras with her.

Turned out the Charon named Terik Dared didn't just have deep pockets; he was a media superstar back on his homeworld. Ashtar remembered *Champions of Charon* but stopped watching after season ten. It felt like it was recycling storylines after a while.

Terik hadn't ordered a custom ship for personal kicks, though. Seemed he had a plan. A challenge. Have former gladiators looking for a new start create their own chimeras, and participate in a race that would be turned into a show.

And Ashtar had managed to negotiate an exclusive deal to provide *all* those ships.

It was crazy. Nobody flew chimeras. Getting insurance was difficult, to say the least, and it was usually cheaper, easier, and safer to just get a new ship altogether.

But apparently the Charons were born of crazy because that was the whole appeal for this lot. Clients ranged from those who would fly whatever they were given to those who had a perfect combination of parts in mind. It seemed speed wasn't the only consideration in this race, because some wanted durable hulls that could withstand a lot of punishment, while others kept things light to maximize maneuverability.

None of them, however, wanted weapons, which was just damn crazy given that the race was going to start here, and go straight across the Void.

But Ashtar wasn't about to question their sanity, so long as the credits were good. He just hoped they all survived, and, more importantly, that the show got renewed for a second season.

Moss's jaw hung open as he looked around the station interior. On every landing pad along the inside of the drum was a chimera. You could tell in part because they had gone out of their way to look like chimeras, keeping the original paint jobs of the ships they'd cannibalized wherever they could.

"It's like *Mad Max* in space," said Other-Violet. "Cool."

"What in the name of Old Eylsia is going on here?" Tameria asked aloud.

"I don't know, but I know who will," said Moss.

He wasn't sure what kind of reception he'd expected to get at the Orijen Brother's junkyard, but he had a feeling it wouldn't be hostile. He did not, however, expect to be greeted like a long-lost son.

"Maurice, my boy!" Ashtar waddled over and embraced Moss in a wide hug. Ashtar *never* hugged. Then he saw there was a camera crew in the back of his office and some of the pieces started to fit together. Not all, but some.

"Ashtar, you old scoundrel, how you doing?" Moss did his best to reflect the friendly tone Ashtar was going for. "Anywhere we can talk in private?"

"Of course, my boy! Right this way!" Ashtar led him to his office and made sure the window blacked out so the camera crew couldn't film them. "Ugh. I'll be glad when all this is over," he muttered.

Moss crossed his arms and leaned against the wall. "So, yeah, what is 'this'?"

Ashtar waved his arms expansively. "This? This is all *your* fault."

"Isn't it always? But you don't seem unhappy about it."

Ashtar sighed and took a seat. "I'm not. But acting all nice for the camera is a pain."

Moss could relate. He remembered his brief career as a spokesman for Odyssey Expeditions. "I hear you. What the hell happened, and how am I...?" His voice drifted as he remembered his encounter with the Ramedean transpotters arguing over his ship back on Triolina... and the one Charon who wanted to buy it.

"Did a guy from Charon come here looking to buy a chimera?" he asked hesitantly.

Ashtar gestured to an empty chair. "Pull up a seat. You're gonna be here a while."

Terik Dared ran a hand down the hull of the *Azagoth* with pride. This was all coming together so well, and so fast. His agent, Forgana, was indeed the miracle worker all claimed her to be. She had not only found him a producer, she had found him worthy competitors from across Charon, most of whom had once been on *Champions of Charon* and also sought new ways to prove themselves.

The only unfortunate part of this event was the rush she had insisted on. It appeared some other production companies had conducted dishonourable corporate espionage, learned about his grand vision, and sought to beat him to the punch. And so haste was required. But he was assured that the team assembled was up to the task. Even now, the competitors had assembled at Komi and the proposed course was being prepared for the event.

Only one day to go, and then...

"Nice ship you got there."

Terik turned. A Terran stood there, wearing a familiar mask.

"You!"

The Terran smiled, arms held wide. "Me."

"So, the rumours are true. You *are* Ranger M."

"For the future!" a small voice called out. There, down at the Terran's feet, was a small furry creature standing on its hind legs, no higher than his knee.

It must have been his imagination, for he could have sworn the man's smile faded a bit. "I wouldn't go that far."

"Your advice has led to a fantastic opportunity for me and for others. A chance to challenge and prove ourselves in new ways. I would sacrifice myself upon your bed if you so desired, or offer you a willing female, if that is your preference."

"Uh, thanks, but pass."

"Nevertheless, I owe you a great debt."

The Terran who looked like Ranger M grinned. "A debt, huh? Any chance I can collect on it now?"

Gessy Glanis had been working at the Centaurus Entertainment Network for over a decade, but this was her first job as showrunner, and it was shaping up to be a disaster. Part of her wondered if she was being set up to fail.

There was too much going on, too short a time frame on everything. Executives breathing down her neck, demanding updates and expecting results as if they hadn't put her in an impossible position... and now she had to deal with some Terran waltzing into her office like he belonged there. He was rather unremarkable looking, which was saying something as she tended to find Terrans very unique and intriguing to look at.

"Can I help you?" she asked. Why the hell hadn't her secretary stopped him?

"Terik sent me," said the man.

Well, that at least gave him an excuse for the intrusion. "What does he want now? Wait, this isn't another 'sacrifice' offer, is it? I said no already."

The Terran smiled, or maybe smirked. She wasn't always sure of their facial expressions. "Actually, I'm here because I think I can help you," he said. "I understand you're under a lot of pressure to cover these events, and don't exactly have a lot of time to do it."

Gessy sighed. It was almost a relief to hear someone else admit the truth to her. "Do you have any idea how long it takes to normally set up a reality-based program? Months. Do you know much time we were given to do this? *Days.* Some genius up top thinks they have to strike quick before the idea is snatched up by another production company. I keep telling them how this is going to look like crap if we don't have the proper time to set everything up, get to know the people involved, get enough footage for the editors to work with, and you know what they keep telling me?"

"We'll fix it in post?"

"EXACTLY. In all the books in *The Way of Things*, I have yet to find a version of hell suitable for them."

"And you are supposed to cover the race tomorrow, right?"

"Right."

"What if I could put it off until three days from now? Would that help?"

Gessy frowned. "Right now, I'll take whatever I can get."

The Great Race

Politics in the Terran Colony Fleet can be as messy as it is streamlined. The Triumvirate is the final authority of the TCF, represented by three branches: Military, Science, and Culture. Each is led by a single person, who in turn has six advisors, one from each of the massive Colony Ships.

This is supposed to provide balance and oversight, but in many ways each branch tends to get in the way of the others.

For example, Vigiles are effectively the police within the TCF, even on board military ships. But they fall under the Culture arm of the Triumvirate rather than the Military. As a result, they act as political officers in addition to their other duties, ensuring the Culture bureau's vison stays on track and always has the best possible public front when dealing with the media.

From what I hear, they're not popular with most TCF captains.

M. Foote, *And Then Things Got Worse*

T HE *HYDRUS* WAS A flurry of activity. Ensign Davis had only moments to contact Komi Station and find out what was going on.

This was some sort of race. This was not sanctioned by the Komi government. This was being produced by the Centaurus Entertainment Network. They could not call it off. There was no ship matching the *Viaticus Rex* listed among the participants. This was not their problem.

Meanwhile, the acting commander was shouting at everyone. Mainly the nav officer who was responsible for keeping an eye on the escaping ships.

"Track those transit signatures. Find the one that matches the *Rex*!"

Lieutenant Tauri shook her head. "None of them do, sir, but they're all within a ten percent variance, some less than five."

"Find the one that comes closest and pursue. Continue monitoring all transit signatures. Look for anyone breaking off from the pack. Have they engaged full transit?"

"No, sir. They're all taking different routes to escape the gravity well."

"Can we fire on any of them before they jump?"

Lieutenant Ginan, currently acting as tactical officer, blinked at that. "Fire, sir?"

Lieutenant Tauri cut in. "Wait, they're starting to jump."

"Heading?"

"Standby. Three, now four have made the jump... they're all heading for the same star system. KM-FD04-M, a brown dwarf in the Komi bubble. Twenty light years away."

"Helm, best possible speed to that location. Get ahead of them if you can. Keep an eye on those other transit signatures. Tell me if *any* of them head in a different direction."

"Aye, sir."

Lieutenant Ginan stood. "Sir, before we pursue, request permission to send a security team to the station. I'd like them to investigate matters while we are in pursuit."

Nekkar nodded. "Very well. Be quick about it."

Once they were in transit, Ensign Davis attempted to contact the other ships, to see if he could determine which was the *Rex* some other way. Most ignored his hails. Some transmitted their flight paths and cargo manifest, recognizing the Silver Legion's authority and complying with Protectorate regulations. Of course, those could be faked. But one of them decided to talk back.

"Commander? I've made contact with one of the ships."

"If they're not surrendering, I am not interested."

Davis was sure if one of the other bridge officers had brought it up, he wouldn't have dismissed them so quickly. "Perhaps you can get a better idea of what's happening? Maybe they know which competitor doesn't belong?"

A pause. "Very well. On screen."

A man wearing a red and green wrestling mask glared at them. "You *dare* interfere with our glorious test of skill and resilience?"

Well, *that* was odd. But the commander seemed unfazed. He got up from his seat and glared right back at him. "You are suspected of harbouring illicit cargo aboard your ship. By order of the Silver Legion and the Terran Colony Fleet, you are to drop from transit and prepare to be boarded."

"Your threats ring hollow. *For the future!*" The screen went blank.

He looked to the tactical officer. "Is that our ship, lieutenant?"

"I cannot say for certain. The transit signature is within a five percent variance of the one we pursued from Sol."

"Could they have altered their transit field before we arrived at Komi station?"

"They could, but the ship's speed would be affected if they did."

The commander went back to his seat and checked the display. "Helm, get us ahead of that group. Track the transit speeds of all ships and compare against the projected impact of those variances. Tactical, prepare to fire once they drop to sub-transit."

The crew acknowledged, but Davis knew the commander was asking a lot. There were far too many assumptions being made. And something else bothered him, mainly about the transmission they'd received.

"Sir, I don't think the ship that contacted us was the *Viaticus Rex*."

The acting commander scowled. "As far as I'm concerned, they *all* are. We'll deal with them at the dwarf star."

Davis didn't press the issue, but it did give him something to consider. These ships might not be willing to communicate with him, but they were probably communicating with each other, or a third party. He might be able to narrow down the possibilities by listening to their transmissions.

The tension on the bridge grew as they arrived at the target system. Overtaking the fleet wasn't a problem, the *Hydrus* was a state-of-the-art heavy cruiser, and Nekkar ordered them to set speed so that they would arrive shortly before the racers did. But when they dropped from transit and the viewscreen filled with the purple glow of a brown dwarf star, they faced a new problem.

"Sir, there's another ship in the system."

Nekkar looked as confused as Davis felt. The first of the racing ships wouldn't arrive for a few minutes yet. He began to hail them.

"On display. Who are they?"

The screen showed the silhouette of a large ship in close proximity to the brown dwarf.

"It's a Nubran yacht, sir. Registration indicates it's a CEN ship."

"The *media*..." Nekkar grumbled.

Davis received a reply to his hail. "Sir, the captain is informing us of their intentions and—"

"I *know* their intentions, Ensign," the commander snapped. "They're here to record the race. These stars are waypoints along their track." He steepled his hands together, thinking. Finally he said, "Blast."

The first of the racers arrived, dropping to sub-transit and racing to slingshot around the brown dwarf. It was followed by another, and another, and a half dozen more. Some tried to draft behind the wake left behind of the ships in front of them, which was an incredibly dangerous and foolhardy thing to do. But then, dangerous and foolhardy seemed to be the nature of this race. The last of the racers arrived just as the first had pulled around the dwarf star and got far enough away to shoot back to full transit.

The acting commander stewed in his seat. "Navigation, find their new heading. Tactical, have you narrowed down which one might be the *Rex*?"

The science officer interjected. "Based on the visuals we had of the *Rex* back on Europa, I've been trying to assess what it's made up of and use that to create a transit signature profile. I believe I can rule out half of the current ships."

Nekkar sighed. "Which leaves another dozen. Very well. Helm, set course to their destination. Time it so we arrive shortly before they do. Keep trying to narrow down that list."

The next stop was another brown dwarf, and when they arrived many hours later, Nekkar was clearly losing his patience. They found another CEN yacht there to record the event, which meant most likely every stop would have one.

"Enough of this nonsense. Tactical, prepare to fire when the first ship arrives."

At the tactical station, Lieutenant Ginan became alarmed. "Commander, are you sure of this course of action?"

While the lieutenant was acting as tactical officer in Nekkar's place, he was also the ship's Vigile representative, which meant he had responsibilities that went beyond the *Hydrus*.

"Are you questioning my orders, lieutenant?"

"Yes," Ginan said bluntly. "Your actions are about to be recorded and broadcast across this sector, perhaps beyond. From an outsider's perspective, the optics will not be good."

"We are legally engaged in the retrieval of Terran property," Nekkar barked.

"By disabling and potentially destroying dozens of ships engaged in a live sporting event."

"It's a ruse! The *Rex*'s captain clearly arranged this from the start. This race is nothing but a front so they could make their escape!"

"That may be true, but we have no proof. None of these ships match the *Rex*'s transit signature."

"Because they altered it!"

"And if you're wrong?"

"I am *not* wrong. I say again, Tactical, prepare to fire beam cannons on the first ship when it arrives. Comms, inform all racers to drop from transit when they arrive or expect the same welcome."

Davis sighed inwardly. Having kept one ear on the comm chatter from the racers all this time, he was fairly sure the commander was not going to like what he had to say. He considered keeping his mouth shut.

Ginan spoke up again. "Sir, these are chimeras. There is no telling how resilient they are. We might accidentally destroy them."

"Then fire on them *lightly*, lieutenant. Follow my orders or make room for someone who will. Comms?"

At that moment, the ensign had a choice: blindly follow orders, or inform the commander of what he'd learned in case it changed his mind. Only one of those options wouldn't result in Nekkar getting even more angry.

But for a synth to make it as an officer in the Silver Legion, you couldn't be meek. The cyborgs acted with a confidence that bordered on arrogance most of the time, and you needed to be able to not only reflect that, but back it up when you had to.

"Sir, I don't believe *any* of the approaching ships are the *Rex*."

Hours of mounting frustration had eroded what little civility Nekkar had. "I don't care what you *believe*, ensign."

Davis continued. "I think they're all from Charon, sir. *All* of them."

The look Nekkar gave told Davis he had one chance to make his case and to be quick about it. "I've been monitoring their communications since the race began and have isolated the voice patterns of each of the captains as they talk to each other or to the vid crew at the last waypoint. Some are speaking GalCom, other Nubran, and most are letting their translators do the work, but the cadence and speech patterns are all closer to Charon than Terran."

Nekkar turned back to the viewscreen, not even acknowledging his assessment. "Navigation, ETA on the first racer?"

"Less than a minute, sir."

"Tactical, prepare to fire."

Ginan frowned. "Sir, I *strongly* suggest you reconsider. This information—"

"What information? This ruse was too well planned. He had to take that into account. Disable the first ship when it arrives and order all the others to stand down as they arrive. This race is over."

Shell Game

DEEP SPACE — 2535

Moss opened his eyes. For his troubles, the harsh ceiling lights stabbed him in the retinas.

"He's waking up," a voice said.

"I can't believe it worked," said another. "That's got to be a record."

"What... record?" Moss asked weakly.

"Shut up," said the first. "They gave him a translation implant, remember? Get the doctor."

"Doctor?" Moss tried to look around, but his eyes still hadn't adjusted. "Where am I?"

A blurry blue face came into his field of vision. "Just relax. The doctor will be here in a minute. How do you feel?"

"Like I'd been run over by a..." He couldn't think of the word. "Really big rock in space."

"Asteroid?"

"That's it."

He was pretty sure the blue blur was smiling. "That sounds about right."

A new voice entered the room, more feminine. "That will do, attendant. I'll take over from here." A different blue blur came into view and waved some kind of device over his head. To his surprise, his vision began to clear. When it was removed, he could see the woman's face clearly.

"*Mister Foote? I'm Doctor Owello. Don't strain yourself. You're lucky to be alive. It's going to take a while for you to get back on your feet.*"

"*My ship...*"

"*I'm afraid there's not much left of it.*"

Moss squinted. Female? The doctor couldn't be Draxon. From what he'd heard, the matriarch and caretaker castes stayed on their colonies. But if she was Nubran, then how...?

"*Where am I?*" *he asked, his strength slowly returning.*

"*Safe.*"

"*Bit more detail, please. A ship? A planet?*"

"*You are on board a medical ship. You will not be sent back to Terran space. You're safe.*"

It took him a moment to remember why that was such a relief to him. "Well, that's something. So what's next?"

"*Next you rest.*"

Moss tried to sit up, but his muscles didn't cooperate. He managed to shake his head. "Naw. Can't rest without some idea of what comes next. Is there some kind of refugee program I'll have to apply for? Is it a bureaucratic nightmare? Will I be sent to some kind of camp?"

Doctor Owello clearly didn't want to say more than she had to but had to say something. "Mister Foote, the situation here isn't what you might imagine it to be. A lot of time has passed. Things have changed, and it's going to take a while to explain. So for now, it's best to rest."

"*Time?*" *Moss frowned. "How much time?"*

"*In Terran years? About three hundred.*"

By all rights, Moss should have been dead. The cryopod had sent his body into deep hibernation, but failed after less than five years. His body had been a popsicle for the next hundred and thirty or so.

Coming out of cryo wasn't just a matter of popping someone in the microwave and hitting the defrost button. It was a lot more delicate than that. Moss had been a freeze-dried husk.

The truth of the matter was, he'd been dead. Dead dead.

The people who had rescued him, a secretive group that called themselves the Order, had come across what was left of his ship by accident. They had been near Sol for other reasons, reasons they had no intention of talking about, but upon finding him had decided to try and save him.

The Order had advanced medical technology—advanced even by Protectorate standards—and strict rules about when to use it or share it with the rest of the galaxy. Their primary concern was to prevent such knowledge from being perverted into weapons of war or oppression.

Moss had lucked out, as there was a new procedure they had been developing for long-term vacuum damage, and thanks to the broken down cryopod and slow vacuum leak, he had been perfectly preserved. The tech wasn't considered ready for sapient trials, but then, it wasn't as if a corpse could complain, was it?

Repairing his body had been far more involved than he cared to think about. There were... things inside him now. Things that helped rebuild him. Theseus's Paradox sprung to mind as to whether he was even the same person anymore.

They say that any sufficiently advanced technology is indistinguishable from magic, and whatever they'd done to him certainly fell into that category. They'd modified him in other ways as well, such as the translation device implanted in him, all with the best of intentions. But ultimately, it all made him feel less than human. As grateful as he was to them for saving his life, he couldn't help but feel like a lab rat as well.

The fact they were so surprised that he'd survived the procedure didn't exactly help that perception. He seen credits exchange hands when he first started to walk.

There was more behind his revival than simple altruism, however. They had identified the Rex, *and knew the small role his ship had unwittingly played in their history so long ago. They had questions for him. And a proposal.*

They offered him a new ship. A way to get back on his feet, create a new identity, and start over. And if he managed to make it on his own, they might have a job for him someday.

Once he learned about the state of the galaxy and the Terrans' place within it, he quickly agreed.

Outside Komi Station – 2550

The Centaurus Entertainment Network was one of the top entertainment producers in this part of Nubran space, having won enough awards over the last century to fill their flagship, currently docked outside of Komi Station.

The ship served as the network's mobile headquarters, which was convenient for tax purposes, since they technically weren't based out of any one planet and therefore only had to pay general Protectorate related taxes... most of which were offset in a variety of creative and probably shady ways.

While there was a large conference hall deck for special meetings and motivational speeches, when it came to actually enjoying themselves, the staff and crew tended to gather in smaller lounges, each fitted with high-def vid projectors for whatever program everyone was excited about that week.

Moss, Hel, and Tameria were in a private lounge, while the Violets experienced things vicariously in the docking bay. In the lounge with them was the showrunner, Gessy Glanis, who handed them each a green-labelled bottle of CEN branded water.

They were watching the raw footage from what the producers were calling *Challenge of the Champions*, a name that might get reworked before the show went live due to IP issues. *Challenge* brought many former gladiators from *Champions of Chronos* and gave them a new chance at glory, by designing and piloting a custom build chimera—with certain restrictions to ensure a level playing field—in a rally race across the Void.

Checkpoints had been set up at each star, both to capture the best possible footage and to ensure the contestants visited each one. The checkpoints were all brown dwarf stars, which meant the ships couldn't use fuel scoops to keep their tanks filled along the way. Instead, they would have to dock with the CEN yachts whenever they got low, creating an extra level of risk and tension.

It hadn't been hard to schmooze the right people to have the race delayed until the *Hydrus* arrived. The moment he'd learned of the race, he'd sensed an opportunity. A shell game. Which chimera was the real chimera? Round and round they go, keep your eye on the ball.

"We'll be ready to leave in an hour," she said. "Right after they reach the second waypoint."

Moss nodded as he opened the water bottle. "Thanks."

The thing was, a real pro at the game made sure the ball wasn't under *any* of the shells. The game of misdirection was itself a misdirection. And it had worked.

This race would take well over a week, maybe two, but that could easily be turned into a full season of material, with lots of time for interviews and personal grudges to develop—or be encouraged—between pilots along the way. The commentators were already busy spinning angles that could turn into a multi-season arc.

"Seven Ages! The Silver Legion ship just fired on the lead ship!"

Of course, that was assuming they made it past season one.

Gessy leaned forward, her skin turning a paler shade of blue. "*What?*"

There was no question of it. The CEN yacht in orbit around the dwarf star had shown the Terran heavy cruiser pursue the first ship as it dropped to sub-transit, then fired on it until its transit field collapsed and it was forced into normal space.

To the naked eye, even zoomed in, this looked like little more than two comets hurtling through space, a bright silent beam appearing briefly, and then only one comet, which then also vanished as it dropped to normal space near where the first ship had been hit.

But thanks to the magic of modern technology, they were able to simultaneously create a more visually appealing version of events. All the competitors had their ships scanned before the race, and the TCF heavy cruiser was an easy enough image to acquire. So, while one of the side projectors displayed the actual feed for the sake of authenticity, the main projector showed something more akin to an action movie, with dynamic angles and exciting sound effects thrown in.

Mind you, the moment had lasted all of five seconds from pursuit to disabling.

Gessy spoke into her earpiece. "Talk to me, Carin." Moss assumed that was a direct connection to the camera yacht in the system. "Who was hit? Uh huh. Is he okay? Thank the Seven. Hail the Legion ship and strike the fear of our legal department into them, but keep the vids going. This'll be a hell of a series premiere."

She sighed and leaned back, while the others waited for her to explain.

"They hit Terik Dared and have dropped beside him. He's unable to go to back to transit. The Legion are preparing to board him."

Moss groaned. He'd talked Terik into wearing a Ranger M style mask to help with the ruse. If Terik got hurt because of that, he was going to feel like a piece of crap for a long time.

"I hope he'll be okay," said Hel.

"He's not hurt," said Gessy. "And you can bet there will be hell to pay. Even if they can justify their actions, they're about to enter a PR nightmare." Now that she knew Terik's ship hadn't been blown into a cloud of dust, she was excited about the possibilities. "I think this show just got a guaranteed second season."

Tameria scowled. There was no way she approved of how Gessy saw things through network logic when lives were on the line. Fortunately, she knew better than to say anything right now. Still, Moss didn't want to risk her blowing her top before they got what they wanted out of this deal.

"I suppose that should be our cue to leave? Just in case that ship comes back here demanding to speak to the manager?"

Gessy nodded. "I'll contact the bridge. Where should we drop you off?"

"Somewhere inconspicuous where the Legion won't pick up our trail," said Moss. "We'll take it from there."

"Well, don't be in a rush to leave," said Gessy. "Stay as long as you like. In fact, if you changed your mind about the Ranger M interview..."

"*No.*"

The operation did not go as Nekkar had hoped.

In the end, they had stopped a half dozen of the fleeing ships, and dispatched security teams to board each one. And as each report came back with the same negative result, the error he had made compounded. Too many ships had slipped through the net in the process, and Ensign Davis was relaying multiple messages from the Centaurus Entertainment Network threatening legal action until at last he called it off.

At the tactical station, Lieutenant Ginan showed no signs of emotion as he stood and faced Commander Nekkar. "You understand this will all be reported. I would expect the Triumvirate will take an interest in your actions."

Nekkar sat in his command chair, feeling a mix of indignation and inadequacy. These fools did not realize why that cargo was important. What was one group of freeborn, more or less?

But Commander Miram's final message to him had told him the truth, and why it was important that these freeborn, *any* freeborn, be retrieved. Their very way of life depended on it.

"As a representative of the Vigile, your statement is noted. As my tactical officer, I order you to return to your duties."

Ginan's expression changed to a scowl, but he did so.

Nekkar got up and paced the bridge, increasingly consumed by his failure and the fallout it would inevitably bring.

He passed by Lieutenant Tauri's station. The navigation officer was too busy keeping track of the last few racing ships to acknowledge him.

The traitor Roy stood silently in the back, kept on hand in case he might provide some insight. He imagined a hint of a smug look on the man's face, and was tempted to use the bondscollar to wipe it off.

Then he came to Ensign Davis's station, monitoring comm traffic. The young synth who had warned him that none of these ships were their target. Who had spoken out of turn. Who did not understand his place on this ship. *His* ship.

He glared at the synth, who was focused on the comms and had no idea how much he was being loathed at this moment. He wanted to punish someone. Why not him? He was within his rights to relieve the man of duty. Of course, his relief shift counterpart was also a synth, as were the rest of the relief bridge crew.

With the Fleet still growing, his kind were increasingly stretched thin. There had been a time when ships were commanded entirely by cyborgs, and synths did what they were best suited for, keeping the ships running. Now he could see a future, far closer than anyone cared to admit, where the only cyborg on board each vessel would be its commander. And as time went on and attrition took its toll on his kind...

Davis finally seemed to notice he was being watched and turned to him. "Sir? I have a report back from our security team on Komi station. You'll want to hear this."

Nekkar brushed away his dark thoughts. "On speakers."

Frying Pan Reprise

THE CEN FLAGSHIP DROPPED out of transit around a nice and boring red dwarf system with equally uninteresting rocks that passed for planets and an even less interesting name.

"This'll do nicely," said Moss.

Gessy shrugged. "If you say so."

The Silver Legion's interference in *Challenge of the Champions* was going to be a public relations nightmare for the Terran Colony Fleet, but a ratings bonanza for the network. Gessy had said she couldn't have scripted it better.

There had been some talk of a restart, but Gessy talked the rest of her dev team out of it. The Legion had thankfully kept damage to a minimum and all the ships were going to get back in the race. They'd concoct some kind of event later that would have the greatest impact on the frontrunners and give those who fell behind a chance to catch up.

"I'm sorry to see you go," said Gessy. "Maybe I can persuade you to participate next season?"

Moss gave a half-smile. "Honestly? I might be interested. So long as it's nowhere near Draxon space or the TCF."

"Let me know." Gessy handed him a comm card. "Don't lose it." This not only held her contact info, but a unique encryption key and authentication details. It helped ensure that only people she wanted to speak to could reach her, and that their conversations wouldn't be overheard.

Moss tucked it into his flight suit's breast pocket. "I won't."

Hel, Tameria, and Moss made their way together to the hanger bay. He couldn't get over just how big this ship was, like a giant skyscraper laid down on its side.

"Are you serious about taking part in the next race?" Tameria asked.

Moss shrugged. "Why not? Looks like fun. The moment I mentioned it to her, Violet couldn't stop talking about some old movie called *Cannonball Run*. Apparently, one of the guys wears a wrestling mask in it."

"And the million-credit grand prize has nothing to do with it?" asked Hel.

"Oh, it's got ninety-five percent to do with it," said Moss. "Doesn't mean it won't be a good time."

Once back in their respective ships, they disembarked and waited for the CEN flagship to make preparations to depart. They couldn't enter transit with a ship that big nearby.

Moss opened a bottle of LaserActive from the galley, took a sip and winced. Too damn sweet. He wondered if Zach had actually enjoyed them. He looked to the figurine on his dashboard. "So, how'd you and your evil doppelganger get along?"

"Twin," Violet corrected. "And she's not evil. We're cool. Had some time to bond while you were watching the race. She's a bit jealous of me, though, seeing as I have a girlfriend now."

Moss blinked. "What? Who?"

He heard a gasp and looked up at the ceiling, above which Hel would be sitting at the secondary cockpit. Her voice had carried all the way through the access point behind him.

"Wait, really?"

"Don't act so surprised."

Moss considered the logistics of such a relationship. "And that works?"

"We're finding out. This is uncharted territory, after all."

Moss heard Hel from above. "Do we *have* to be so public about this?"

"Boldly going down where no woman has gone before!" Violet added.

Hel groaned. "I guess we do."

Moss chuckled. "And Other-Violet feels left out."

"Eh, it's okay. She's got Tam-Tam."

Moss frowned. "Tam-Tam?"

"What my sister from another transistor calls her. I like it. I told her she could steal her away from you in a week. Two, tops."

"That's not funny Vi."

Tam was going to be a sore spot with Moss for a while. It wasn't just about having feelings for her, which he did, but he didn't think he'd ever be able to make things right between them.

After their awkward conversation with her uncle Keed, the two of them had been okay, but strictly in a professional capacity. They'd managed to balance the scales for her uncle, but Moss's were always going to tip in the wrong direction. And more often than not, that was because he pressed his own thumb on them.

"On second thought, tell your sis to go for it. I have a feeling Tam's pretty lonely."

"Okay, *now* you're bumming me out, flyboy."

Hel called down from the upper cockpit. "Hey, boss? The network ship just jumped. We're good to go."

Moss was grateful for the change of topic. "Roger that." He commed the *Outreach* next. "Well, Tameria, guess this is goodbye. Good to see you again."

"Wish I could..." Her sarcastic voice trailed off, then changed tone. "Likewise. See you around."

Moss jumped in, not ready to end the conversation just yet. "So what's going to become of the railroad? Any idea?"

"I don't see any reason for things to change. One way or another, this was going to be my uncle's last mission. Whoever is replacing him is no doubt already in contact with Haven."

"Right, right..."

"So, unless there was something else you wanted to ask...?"

"What are your plans now?"

"Back to the Order for a new assignment."

"Don't you have any free time?" Moss asked.

"Travelling between systems *is* my free time," said Tameria. "Besides, what would I do?"

"Oh, uh, right." He struggled to think of something else to say. Anything. "Um... are you and Violet going to be okay?"

Tameria started to sound impatient. "We'll be fine. If there's any-thing I can't handle, I'll be sure to get in touch. *Outreach* out."

The comms cut off and Moss watched the shuttle power up and head off. Moss sighed. Thumb firmly pressed.

A voice piped up by his leg. "Boy, you sure know how to pick em, huh, boss?"

Moss looked down at Trouble. "Hey. I can't see you very well. Could you move over about half a meter? That's it. Bit more..."

Once in range, he hooked his foot under Trouble and tossed him up to eye height before batting him across the cockpit with his free hand.

"Looks like my comedy subroutine is working correctly," Moss said to himself as the ferret shook it off and scampered away.

"You know she was giving you a chance there, right?" Hel said over the comm.

"A chance for what? Mind your own business or I'll ask Violet for details about you and her. And you *know* she'll tell me."

"Let the grouch grouch in peace," said Violet, then added in a way so only Moss could hear. "But she's right, you know."

"I know."

He was about to power up the transit drive when Violet cried out, "Crap! Engines to full, GO!"

The ship seemed to move of its own accord as Violet took control. A silver Terran heavy cruiser dropped out of transit almost right on top of them. The *Hydrus*.

Moss's jaw dropped as he took back control and angled the ship away from them. "What? HOW?"

"No clue!" Hel yelled. "Putting power to shields!"

"No, engines!" Moss corrected, just as they were hit by a pulse cannon blast. "No, shields!"

"Their approach vector only had them in sub-transit for moments before they were on top of us," said Violet.

Moss growled. "They couldn't have pulled that off unless they knew our *exact* coordinates!" So much for a spot in Season 2 of *Challenge of the Champions*. The rat bastards must have sold them out.

A voice came over the open comm channel. "This is Commander Nekkar of the *TCF Hydrus*. You are ordered to stand down and prepare to be boarded."

"Vi, find us an escape vector!"

"She's too fast and too big, Moss. We can't get out of their mass interference range."

Moss frowned. "Yeah, but she can't turn on a dime, can she? Hel, power to shields."

"She's got all I can give her," said Hel.

The *Hydrus* might not be able to turn on a dime, but the *Rex* could. Moss spun around and flew straight at the heavy cruiser, jinking and weaving to avoid as much incoming fire as possible.

Thankfully, they were trying to disable his ship rather than destroy it, and they didn't know how much or how little firepower to use just yet. That would change once their sensors got a good look at him.

"Once we're past them, all power to engines!"

"Copy that!" said Hel.

The ship would keep shooting, of course, but he was hoping to take an angle that had the least number of turrets firing at them. With luck, they could get past the *Hydrus*'s mass interference and avoid getting hit long enough to go to transit.

With luck. Yeah, what were the odds of *that*?

"You see that, Tam-Tam?"

"How could I miss it?"

They were just about to leave the system when a huge transit signature screamed onto their sensors, then almost as quickly vanished.

Right on top of where the *Rex* was. Tameria held her breath, waiting to see the *Rex* jump to sub-transit, hoping it could escape the system before the *Hydrus* shot it down. But it never happened.

"What do we do?" asked Tam's Violet.

What *could* they do was a better question. The *Outreach* was a long range shuttle and unarmed. The best it could do was buzz around and annoy the *Hydrus*, give it another target to shoot at. Odds were that would result in them both being captured.

Had she consulted with her superiors at a Priory, she would have been ordered to leave him to his fate. That he'd served his purpose, perhaps even suggest it was karma for his past transgressions. Bottom line: Moss was expendable.

Fortunately, she had no intention of contacting them.

"Boss, what do we do?" Violet asked again.

Tameria turned the ship around and dove toward the Rex's last location. "We do what we can."

"That's my Tam-Tam! Now, I'm gonna need you to listen up and trust me, okay? We've got a plan."

Tameria frowned. "We?"

The *Viaticus Rex II.I* was past the *Hydrus* now, and wove, jinked, and rolled through a hail of pulse cannon fire, but that only meant they were hit less, rather than not at all. Their shields were still dropping, and even once they were past the *Hydrus*'s mass interference, those shots could still prevent him from going to transit. And eventually, the heavy cruiser would complete its turn and start to catch up to them.

"It's not gonna work," said Violet.

"You got a better idea?"

"No... but my sister does."

Just then, the *Outreach* dropped out of transit, coming straight at them.

"Hail Mary pass, coming your way!" said Other-Violet.

It took Moss a second to realize what was happening, and kill the engines before it was too late.

Commander Nekkar felt his confidence return. The security detail sent to Komi station had uncovered the subterfuge the captain of the *Viaticus Rex* had pulled off. He had to admit, he was impressed, even if the ruse had been cowardly and dishonourable.

Once they knew what had happened, the team had delivered a tracking device to the media network flagship, which the *Hydrus* had monitored until they'd dropped out of transit around some obscure dwarf star. That would be where their quarry would disembark.

He'd ordered best possible speed to that location, bypassing as many safety thresholds as he could to ensure they dropped as close to the location as possible as quickly as possible.

And it had worked. The ship hadn't left yet. And there was no way he'd give them a chance to escape now.

"Wear them down," said Nekkar. "Keep them close. They are not getting away."

The *Hydrus* opened fired with point defence turrets, both to wear down their shields and prevent them from generating a transit field. It was too small and nimble to hit with beam cannons at this range.

Lieutenant Tauri spoke up. "Sir, they're coming about. Possible collision course!"

A suicide run? Unlikely. Still, one could never be sure. "Power to shields. Try to disable them before impact."

He heard a snort from somewhere behind him. He turned and the expression he saw on Roy's face told him he had not imagined it.

The ship buzzed the *Hydrus* and boosted away directly behind them, which meant it would take time for them to turn around and pursue, leaving the *Rex* less exposed to pulse cannon fire.

It had been perhaps their best option, though it only delayed the inevitable. "Pursue. Full speed. Get their shields down already!"

"Another ship has arrived," said Tauri. "Baroque-class. Now it's on a collision course."

Roy spoke up. "If that's who I think it is, they're unarmed, but have *very* strong shields. They might actually ram us."

Nekkar looked to Tactical. "Threat assessment?"

"They're unarmed," Ginan confirmed, "but I can't get a reading on shield strength."

Tauri said, "It's coming in fast!"

Nekkar had only a moment to assess the danger. The forward screen displayed everything he needed at a glance, in case he wasn't at his station. He could see readings on ship mass and its rapidly increasing velocity, far faster than he expected. It was aiming for the bridge. If it was somehow fast and strong enough to punch through their shields...

"Reverse engines! Destroy that shuttle!"

When the *Outreach* dropped out of transit, its relative speed was far slower than that of the *Rex*, which had had plenty of time to accelerate trying to escape the *Hydrus*.

So when Moss saw what had been dropped from the *Outreach* the moment they arrived, he didn't have much time to slow down.

No, not what... *who*.

Meanwhile, the *Outreach* burned toward the *Hydrus*, which soon realized that, unlike Moss, this ship wasn't bluffing.

The move did what the Violets had intended—force the *Hydrus* to slow down and concentrate fire on it. But this was a ship of the Order, and the more incoming fire it was able to take, the more the crew of the *Hydrus* focused on it.

This gave Moss just enough time to slow down, spin around, drop the cargo ramp, scoop up Tameria, and boost away to transit distance.

The *Outreach* would not be joining them. That had never been the plan.

Moss saw a flash where the shuttle had been just before they made the jump to sub-transit. He didn't say anything at first. Neither did Violet.

"Cold equations?" Moss asked finally.

"Yes."

"Want to talk about it?"

"Not now."

"Understood. Violet, you're in control. Get us deep into Nubra territory. The deeper the better." He was hoping they'd be more trouble than they were worth to pursue at this point, especially as the PR flak from the race fiasco started to be felt. "Hel, let's check in with the good Sister."

Tameria was a bit bruised from her rescue, but still mobile. They took their reunion to the galley, where Moss got them all something to eat. But Tameria wasn't hungry. She just stared at her bowl instead.

"They must have been talking to each other the whole time," said Tameria. "Private channel. Once we saw the *Hydrus* drop into the system, we were coming back for you. Then Violet tells me to get to the airlock..." She stopped for a moment, reflecting. "It didn't take long to realize what her plan was, and why I wasn't part of it."

Hel put her hand on Tameria's but didn't say anything. It wasn't the time.

"She talked to me the whole time, cool as a comet. She acted like it wasn't a big deal, but I'm pretty sure that was for my sake, which only made me realize... she was real, wasn't she?"

Moss nodded. He could argue definitions of real all day long, but once you stripped away the philosophical nitpicking, it really did boil down to that.

Tameria's hand reached up to the dermal implant along the side of her head. "If this works for me someday, I think today is going to give other-me a lot to think about."

Moss wasn't sure how to tactfully broach the subject, but there was something worrying about all this. "Your ship had a lot of advanced equipment on board..."

"Violet said she'd either crash into them or they'd be hitting her so hard once the shields failed that... I doubt there's much left."

Moss nodded. Another pause came and went.

"We're going deeper into Nubra space. Anywhere we can drop you off? Or..." His voice trailed off.

Tameria looked up. "Or?"

And just like that, Moss was back. "Well, you know. It's probably going to take a while to get a new ship and a new assignment, right? That's assuming they don't want to call you to one of their Priories to chew you out."

Tameria frowned. "Chew me out?"

"Getting involved with Homewrecker? Again? No way that's going to look good. Now, the way I see it, I already know about you guys. Heck, I'm probably still on some secret reserve list they don't want to admit exists. So there's no reason you can't be here while you sort things out with your Father Superior or whatever you call him."

"Precentor."

"Yeah, sure. That guy."

"Are you asking to join us again? Because I don't think—"

"What? Hell no! I'm suggesting that *you* join *us*."

Tameria's eyes narrowed. Hel's eyes widened.

"And by that, I mean hang out and enjoy yourself for a while. I mean, when was the last time you had a vacation?"

"I told you, travelling between systems is my free time."

Hel jumped in. "Did that sound like 'never' to you, Moss?"

"Sure did. Come on. It's going to take a while to make contact and sort everything out, right? All I'm suggesting is that you do it with us instead of alone on some planet surrounded by strangers."

Violet's voice started to chant over the galley's speakers. "One of us. One of us."

Moss and Hel joined in, pounding the table with their fists. "One of us! One of us!"

Tameria's hard face scrunched, squirmed, cracked, and finally broke out into a grin.

Actions and Consequences

When the Terran Colony Fleet came into being, they created the Silver Legion and Centurions to serve as her sword and shield. When they forged a new identity for their people, they instilled the values they believed would allow them to survive in it. Honour and strength factored high among them.

As a result, certain archaic practices found their way into cyborg culture, such as challenging a commander's authority the old-fashioned way—with violence.

Synths were not encouraged to emulate this behavior, for obvious reasons.

M. *Foote*, And Then Things Got Worse

I T WAS OVER. NOT just the mission, but Nekkar's career.

He'd had them, and he'd let them slip through his fingers. Again.

Now the ship was deep in Nubra space. There was no way he could justify continuing his pursuit, and the odds of gaining cooperation from the Nubran authorities were negligible. Soon the *Rex* would be lost in the chaotic webs of interstellar traffic, no doubt changing their registration or perhaps abandoning their ship entirely and acquiring a new one.

He looked out the viewscreen, which was monitoring the debris of the shuttle that had tried to ram them. Its shields had been surprisingly strong, just as Roy had warned, withstanding the pulse fire from their turrets.

Then it had made the mistake of getting in the path of one of their beam cannons, normally used in capital ship combat and long range precision fire. Lieutenant Ginan, despite his other failings, had recognized the opportunity and fired immediately. It had cut through the shields and vaporized half the ship.

It was then he'd realized this was yet another ruse. He could see why the traitor Roy both hated and respected this so-called Ranger M. The man had plans within plans. A tactical genius with every contingency accounted for.

But none of that mattered now. He had failed. He imagined the Vigile's investigation into his actions would have him relieved of his command, reassigned to another ship, and possibly demoted.

Being effectively immortal, he would no doubt overcome this in the fullness of time. But the stain would never fully wash out. It burned at him, and he required an outlet for his frustrations before they tore him apart.

He looked over at Ensign Davis.

"Ensign, you are relieved of duty."

The ensign looked back at him in shock. "Sir?"

"I have found your performance in this mission to be lacking and your behaviour unprofessional. You are relieved until further notice."

Davis looked away, unable to look him in the eye. Then he got up and headed for the lift. *Good*.

Then he stopped.

"No, sir, it is *you* who have been unprofessional." He took a step toward the commander, his stance defiant.

Nekkar felt his blood pumping. *Better.*

The bridge grew silent. Several knew what he was doing, and were giving subtle signs in the hopes of dissuading him.

Nekkar stepped closer to Davis, who did not back down. "Do you challenge my position?"

Davis's eyes narrowed. "I challenge your judgement."

Excellent.

What Davis was doing was theatre. He did not wish to appear as weak as he truly was. He felt he needed to do this to save face among the crew. And had he been a cyborg, he probably would have.

But no one here had expected him to challenge Nekkar's command this way. Because this bit of posturing could be seen as a challenge to one's authority. It could be seen as a challenge to combat. For the right to take command. Davis had chosen his words carefully, but not carefully enough.

If it was his wish to be treated the same as his kind, then Nekkar would grant it.

A single backhand to the ensign's irritating face sent him flying. He landed a few meters away, close to the lift, and did not get up. The traitor Herzog, being the closest to him, checked to see if he was still alive.

"Take him to the infirmary," said Nekkar.

"Ya think?" said Roy.

Commander Nekkar took a deep breath and returned to his chair. *Now* he felt better.

Roy applied a gel pressure collar to the ensign's neck and got him down to the medical bay. Once there, he made a quick comm before Doctor

Ascella grilled him about what had happened. He saw no reason not to be completely honest about how events had played out.

"The dumb fool," muttered the doctor.

"Who, Davis or the commander?"

Her dark eyes narrowed. "Both."

Roy hid a smile. He'd gauged the crew's reaction during Nekkar's meltdown, which wasn't far off from that of the doctor's. And once word spread to the rest of the crew...

The medical bay doors opened and Powell entered, right on time. She was friends with Davis, and seeing him like this would put her exactly where he needed her to be.

She gasped. "Len!"

Davis was now secured in a form adjusting bed, his head and body locked in place.

"His neck's broken," said Doctor Ascella. "The bones aren't a problem, and it's going to take a while to regrow the severed nerves. But he'll live."

Powell breathed a sigh of relief and came over to check on the ensign.

Had Davis been a cyborg, the blow would have only made him stagger back a bit. Even if Nekkar had managed to break his neck, he would have been back on his feet in a few seconds, ready for more.

But Davis wasn't a cyborg, a point not lost on Powell. Her resentment of the man was now full-on hatred.

"I should take you back to your quarters," said Roy. "There's nothing you can do here."

Karon sat in a chair next to him, placing her hand on Len's. "I'm fine here."

Roy nodded his understanding and left. He didn't want to stick around anyway. There was a window of opportunity right now, and he didn't want to waste it.

He returned to the bridge. The atmosphere was cool and professional. But Roy could feel the tension underneath. He waited for the right moment, when it seemed like there was nothing requiring Nekkar's immediate attention, and spoke up.

"Commander Nekkar. Can I speak to you in private, please?"

Every move he made with the commander was a calculated risk. There was only so far you could predict someone's actions, no matter how well you knew them. However, this time it seemed to pay off. Nekkar nodded and headed for his ready room, Roy following behind.

Nekkar went to his desk and sat. He probably needed a break from the judgmental eyes of his crew right now, which was why Roy looked as sympathetic as possible, without actually giving up his general sense of casual disinterest and disrespect. Had to keep it genuine, after all.

"What is it?" Nekkar asked.

"I think you should tell me why those freeborn are so important," Roy said. "It might be your only way out of this mess."

Nekkar seemed disappointed by Roy's answer and reached for the control panel on his desk to give his neck a tingle.

"Now hold on, before you do that, hear me out. I'm not saying you were wrong at any point, only that we both know your superiors aren't going to see it that way. And right now, I don't think you see a way forward. But I do."

That stayed Nekkar's hand. He leaned back in his chair, waiting.

"Not giving up the goods, huh? Fine. Don't need you to. I've guessed a fair bit, and I think I can confirm it all by offering you just one thing."

"And what is that?"

Roy came over and leaned on the commander's desk "What if I told you that instead of netting thirty freeborn, I could get you three *thousand*." He waited for Nekkar's reaction, then added, "Three thousand *unregistered* freeborn who have never been in contact with the colony fleet or a single synth. Would that get you back in the Fleet's good graces?"

Roy's eyes widened in surprise, then turned to anger. "You withheld this information?"

"How can I withhold something I don't even know you want? You were interested in a *specific* ship with a *specific* cargo. Now I know what makes them special. They're unregistered, which means if they go 'missing' again, there are no records to indicate a problem. No questions that need to be answered. Nothing to cover up, because it was never there in the first place."

Without being offered one, Roy took a chair across from Nekkar and crossed his legs, hands on his lap. Nekkar wouldn't object just yet, not until he circled back to the three thousand freeborn he'd teased him with.

"Let me tell you what I think is going on. The synth population is in trouble. I'm guessing some variation of Late Onset Deterioration Syndrome, though some people still refer to it as Dolly. Now, wherever this is happening, you're keeping it hush-hush, because there is absolutely zilch about it on the TCF news, or any other network for that matter. Maybe it's a problem with the templates, but I'm thinking it's something else. Maybe it's spreading, or maybe it's contained, even purged, but you're worried about it cropping up again.

"And that's where the freeborn come in. Whoever is working on this problem needs some good old-fashioned genetic diversity to experiment with. I'm also betting that the farther they've been from the synth population, the better. So mostly escapees from minor colonies, rather than the colony fleet."

He had no idea if this part was true, but it would plant the idea in Nekkar's head, and make his upcoming offer sound even more attractive.

"Only whatever they're doing to the freeborn is probably from the Doctor Mengele playbook, because you're not exactly asking for volunteers, are you? Now, you might not have known that last bit, because you no doubt got your information from Commander Miram, and I don't see her willingly going along with that. But I also don't see her asking too many questions, either. Me? I love questions. They lead to all kinds of interesting places."

He waited for a moment to gauge the commander's reaction. Pretty much what he expected—his assumptions thus far were spot on.

"So what the crew here doesn't see is just how important your mission really is. What's more, they don't realize how much *you* have sacrificed for the greater good." Nekkar would love that bit. His kind always did. "All they see is a Captain Bly after a white whale."

"It's Ahab," said Nekkar, irritated.

"Whatever. You get the idea." The error was intentional. He'd been showing off too much. "So, how close am I?"

Nekkar frowned, considering what to do next. Then he calmly reached over to the control panel on his desk and pressed a button.

Roy flinched. There was a fifty-fifty chance he was in for pain. Instead, a hologram of Commander Miram appeared over the desk. Nekkar seemed to skip ahead a bit in the recording.

"...I know you believe that this mission is beneath you, and will no doubt want to wash your hands of it so you can seek out more glorious deeds. But there is more at stake here than you realize. I am not exaggerating when I say that the continued future of the Colony Fleet may depend on it..."

Roy allowed himself a smirk. It was hard not to be a *little* smug when you were proven right.

When the recording finished, Nekkar turned the hologram off and looked at Roy. "Now, tell me about these three thousand freeborn."

Roy leaned back and crossed his arms. "You ever read about the *USNN Pegasi?*"

An Orderly Retreat

My time in the Order was usually pretty boring. I mostly acted as a courier, typically going from A to B with a message, cargo, or passenger. Sure the real glory belongs to whoever is receiving the message, cargo, or passenger, but without me they'd never get there in the first place, right?

Besides, flying passengers on long boring trips has its perks. I mean, some may act like stuffy religious types, but I can tell you from experience, there's no vow of chastity.

For example, there were these Nubran triplets who had never seen a Terran before...

M. Foote, Inside the Order
(REDACTED – INVESTIGATION LAUNCHED)

H EL AND VIOLET SAT on a beach in long deck chairs. The sky was blue and held a tint of green Hel still wasn't used to, given how she'd grown up with only images of Earth as a reference point. Their hands touched over a small table which held their drinks—drinks they could now actually taste—and a slice of straw-berry-rhubarb pie.

"Love the upgrades," said Hel. She could feel the warmth of the sun on her skin, and, well, *other* things between the two of them.

As it happened, they actually *were* on a pleasant world with sandy beaches and a blue-green sky and ocean. This was a re-creation of what lay about five hundred meters north of their hanger.

It had been a week since they'd escaped the Silver Legion. Tameria had covered their trail, giving them a chance to stay put for a while and relax at this retreat, which was considered a safe port for members of the Order. Moss and Tameria were even on normal speaking terms again. Well, normal for them.

While she couldn't afford to pay them anywhere near what Moss believed they deserved, Tameria wanted to make sure everyone was properly thanked for their efforts. This software upgrade was only half of Violet's reward. The other half were the holo-projectors being installed around the ship, which would allow her to be a more active part of the crew.

Moss was given a small shuttle for the secondary cargo bay, to replace the one they'd lost back in Sol. He'd immediately christened it *Nemo*, which was Latin for "nobody." Basically, he was telling every-one not to get attached to it.

Of course, Violet had a completely different interpretation of the name, and had Hel paint it orange with white and black stripes. Which annoyed Moss exactly as intended.

When Tameria had asked Hel what she wanted, however, she really hadn't had an answer.

"Someday I'll want you to take me wherever the *Pegasi* ends up," she said. "But for now? I'd be happy if you just stuck around for a while."

The sentiment had made Tameria smile, and for a moment she was unsure of how to reply. "For a while. Don't tell Moss but... I've been having fun with you all."

"Even Moss?"

"Even him. Unfortunately, I have work to do. Some of it with the *Pegasi*. Once I have my new ship, I should really go."

Hel had perked up at that. "Could you take some messages from me, for my friends and family?"

"Of course. It's the least I can do."

Back on the beach, Hel wondered how much longer Tameria would stay, and whether or not Moss would admit that he'd missed her once she was gone. She and Violet had laughed about that. Violet had called Tameria a *tsundere*, which was apparently an old cartoon term from Japan. She'd asked what Moss was and Violet had only replied, "*Baka*."

Her peaceful reminiscing was cut short by Violet, who gave her hand a squeeze. "You should go now. Gotta keep that body active in the real world."

"Ahhh, just five more minutes."

"I *could* turn this into an arctic hellscape."

Hel tsked. "Fine. See you here tonight?"

"More likely, I'll see you on the ship first. The projectors are just about ready."

That raised Hel's spirits. Sure, they wouldn't be able to touch in the real world, but it was going to be nice to see her there.

Violet read into her grin. "Eh, you'll get sick of me soon enough and want your privacy, I guarantee it."

"We'll see."

Tameria's new ship arrived a day sooner than Moss expected. The cynical side of him, which was to say most of him, figured it was to throw him off balance so he couldn't come up with some convoluted reason for her to stay.

Tameria had invited him to the docking bay to "pick up the keys" as she put it, trying to work in an old Earth expression.

The landing bays were out in the open, and it was a nice sunny day on this resort world they were holed up in. It didn't take long for Moss to tell which ship was hers.

It was a custom-built Baroque-class shuttle, an exact replica of the *Outreach*. It even had the same name.

"If it's not Baroque, don't fix it, huh?" Moss quipped.

Tameria frowned. "I don't get it."

"Probably loses something in translation... and history... and humour." Moss shrugged. "I just mean, *why* the exact same ship?"

"Why not? When something works, we tend to stick with it."

He couldn't argue with that. It was why he was still stuck with the *Rex*.

"Does it have all the same upgrades?"

"Everything except the neural matrix research station. But I won't be needing that, I suppose."

It took a moment for Moss to realize what she meant. "Oh my God. The original Violet imprint?"

"Gone."

Moss thought about this for a moment. "So there will never be another Violet."

Tameria shook her head.

"I'm not sure if that will be a relief to her or cause another existential crisis."

"Really? She barely got used to the idea of *one* other version of her out there."

"Oh, believe me, humans are nothing if not ambivalent. Before, the problem was that she wasn't unique. Now she'll realize that the imprint effectively made her immortal. A while back, she was worried that even if she is real, she doesn't have a soul. Babbled on about silicon heaven and calculators. I don't get her half the time."

"I don't get you half the time," Tameria countered.

"Eh, admit it, you're gonna miss me."

"I admit nothing."

Much to his surprise, Tameria took his hand in hers and just held it while looking at her ship. "Don't worry. I'll be back."

Moss found he was starting to enjoy himself, which made him immediately start looking at the ground all around him.

Not taking her eyes off the ship, Tameria said, "What are you doing?"

"I just know Trouble is going to show up and ruin this moment, and I really don't want him to."

Tameria nodded. "Ah. Don't worry. I locked him in the freezer before we came out."

Standing in front of the new *Outreach*, holding hands under a sunny blue-green sky, Moss looked to Tameria, Tameria looked Moss, and they shared a very sarcastic smirk.

The Artful Dodger

The colony portion of the Terran Colony Fleet currently consists of six enormous colony superstructures. Their names are inspired by the Earth continents of old: Africa, Namerica, Samerica, Asiatica, Europica, and Pacifica.

These colonies are fully self-sufficient, and capable of manufacturing their own ships of Patrol-class or smaller. There are usually a number of these ships in the system with the Colony Fleet at any given time.

Though they are armed and capable of defending themselves, colony-class stations cannot travel to other star systems on their own. They require a number of smaller ships to "tow" them by extending their transit bubble through relays mounted along the hull. This is a slow process and, as a result, is only done when it's deemed necessary to move on.

M. Foote, *And Then Things Got Worse*

"**S**O... WHERE IS IT?"

They had arrived where the *Pegasi* should have been, based on its projected speed and heading, and found only empty space. Rather that show visible anger, Nekkar told the bridge crew to scan the area for anomalies, and had Roy meet him in his ready room.

Once alone, the commander cocked his head. "What, no snide remark?"

"No time, sir..." Fact was, he was as baffled as Nekkar. The *Pegasi* was not capable of transit. It was an ancient generation ship that collected interstellar hydrogen to power its ramjets and reach a coasting speed of four-fifths light speed. Even a half-decent sub-transit drive could overtake it.

But there was no ship, no wreckage, and no way it could be far enough away to not show up on sensors. Not without a transit drive.

Which meant it now had one.

"The Order," said Roy, putting it all together. "After they drove me off, they must have called for backup. They could have installed a transit drive on the *Pegasi*. Or they might have towed it."

"This is not good," said Nekkar, a little too calmly. "They could be anywhere now."

"No chance," said Roy. "Look, a ship that big? Even if it was designed for transit, it would take a hell of a powerplant to reach top tier transit speeds. But it's not designed for transit, and even if they set up relays and towed it, there are limits."

Nekkar considered this. "True. They are most likely going at a small fraction of the speed we're capable of. The problem is, we don't know where they're going, and by now they may have several weeks head start."

"It's still doable," said Roy. "It just means we're going to be out a bit longer than expected."

"Perhaps." There was a note of resignation in his voice. Roy couldn't blame him. With one ship, even a heavy cruiser, it was going to be like finding a needle in... well, in space. He had some ideas that might increase their odds, but right now, the commander needed his ego stroked.

"Sir, the bridge crew is behind you. I was there when you showed them Miram's message. Explained the stakes. They even understand the need for secrecy. You can do this."

It seemed to work. Roy was acting more respectful these days, and whether Nekkar realized it or not, the commander was almost treating him like his executive officer. He'd never asked him to remove the bondscollar, though. Nekkar would see right through that. But he was in a position to make reasonable requests and have them considered.

"I'm hoping we'll find a lead in the wreckage we recovered, sir. In the meantime, I'd like to bring up the subject of the relief shift again, if you have time..."

It had been one week since the smuggler ship had slipped away from the *Hydrus*.

Things had been tense on board. Word of Davis's confrontation with Nekkar had spread quickly. The acting commander had never been loved by the crew, but he had been respected. That respect had now dropped several points. Even though his actions had technically been justified, everyone knew he'd crossed the line.

But there was a chain of command to go through. The crew had to trust that word of his actions would reach those above him, and appropriate measures would be taken.

As the days stretched on, however, this seemed less and less likely. The command staff had had a meeting and, rather than forcing Nekkar to stand down, they had inexplicitly agreed to hold off on reporting back to the Terran Colony Fleet until the current mission was over. No explanation was given.

What was more, they were now maintaining comm silence with the Fleet. Personal messages back to the colony ships were no longer permitted, and all transmissions required command level authorization.

They were told they were participating in a top-secret operation, but there was a growing suspicion among the crew that Nekkar had gone rogue.

Karon Powell was one of them, and there was only one person on the ship she thought might tell her the truth.

"Rogue is a strong word," Roy said diplomatically. "But it's not an incorrect one."

She'd confronted him when they were alone in their shared room. He'd just returned from the bridge, and she didn't have long before her shift started. She sat in a chair and put her head in her hands. "Is the crew in danger?"

"What do you mean?"

"Is Nekkar mad with power or something? Is he going to get us all killed? Why is the command staff going along with this?"

Roy held up a finger. "Ah. That is a bit more complicated. You see, Nekkar is acting on orders left by Commander Miram before she died. Once the situation was explained to the command staff, they reluctantly agreed to see things through."

She looked up at him. "Do you know what it is?"

Roy looked indecisive and waggled his hand. "Only bits and pieces. To be honest, I am a bit worried too."

"Why?"

Roy sidled up and knelt beside her, keeping his voice low. "While I firmly believe what the commander is doing is in the Fleet's best interest, I'm not entirely convinced what he's doing is in *your* best interests."

Karon put a hand to her chest. "Me?"

"Not you personally. The crew. The synths."

Blood drained from her face. "Oh my God..."

"The good news is, he's trusting me more and more every day. Besides, if there's anything to worry about…"

"You'll tell me?"

"Sure, but what I was going to say was, you'll hear about it yourself."

That only confused Karon more.

Roy continued. "They're increasingly short staffed on the bridge. Some of the relief crew are already filling in for the primary crew, and if this operation goes on much longer, it's going to impact our efficiency. So, I've been casually broaching the subject with the commander for a while now, reminding him of a certain someone who scored incredibly high on her officer's exam…"

He pulled out a small box from his pocket and opened it up. Inside was a single silver bar meant to replace the bronze one currently on her epaulet.

"…Ensign Powell."

Karon gave a short gasp. Roy chuckled. "Don't get too excited. The commander was supposed to give you this, not me. Plus, you'll be working the relief shift so he doesn't have to see you. *And* you'll still be expected to continue your current duties in the hangar bay. As far as promotions go, this is about the most insulting one you can get. But you *will* be on the bridge, with your finger on the pulse."

Insulting or not, it didn't matter to her. She took the box from him and smiled.

"I won't let you down." She didn't know why she said it to Roy, it just seemed like the thing to say.

"No, I don't think you will."

Inside the hanger of the *TCF Hydrus* were a number of snub fighters for defence, a couple of shuttles for transporting crew or troops, and, spread out across its center, a big pile of scrap.

This was all that was left of the ship that tried to ram the heavy cruiser. The crew had been busy trying to reconstruct it based on what they'd been able to salvage, in case it provided some insight.

The results on the back half were not very promising. Most of it vaporized when the ship had been hit by a beam weapon designed for use against capital ships, not shuttles. It had taken out the engines, reactor, cargo bay, and wings. Barely any of it had been recovered.

The front half, however, was more promising. This included the galley, living quarters, and cockpit. In fact, the cockpit was virtually intact. Right now, one of the crew was busy trying to hook it up to an independent power source to get its systems online. The others had called it a day, but the crewman had a knack for wiring and wanted to see this through.

For a moment, it seemed like he'd had success. The lights came on and the cockpit lit up.

Then it all died, even though power was still being provided.

The crewman huffed in frustration. He'd have to get the chief here to take a look at what was wrong.

He turned to leave, just as the cockpit lit up again. That was strange. He decided to leave and get the chief to look at it anyway.

Once he was gone, the hanger was empty. The only sounds to be heard was that of the generator and the air recycling.

And then, for a moment, there was a soft voice with no visible body connected to it.

"Well, *crap.*"

About the Author

Noah Chinn was born in Oshawa, Ontario, and had never quite forgiven it for that. Shortly after university he moved to Tokyo, Japan, where he taught English for three years—yet somehow barely managed to learn a word of Japanese.

After that, he moved to London, England to make it as a writer. Unfortunately, the closest he came to literary success was working at several bookstores—each of which mysteriously closed down after his stay.

He now lives in Vancouver with his unbelievably patient and supportive wife, Gillian, and a ferret.

He tends to wear a hat.

You can find out more about his peculiarities and upcoming releases by visiting his website: NoahChinnBooks.com

You can also learn more about him on Bookbub and on Facebook.

He even has a comic strip called Fuzzy Knights, which you can find on his website. It features the most unusual (and fuzziest) group of roleplayers you've ever come across.

Also By Noah Chinn

The Professional Tourist
A G**damned Love Story
Trooper 4

Get Lost Saga
Lost Souls
Lost Cargo

The James and Lettice Cote Mysteries
Getting Rid of Gary
The Plutus Paradox

by Lauren Smith and Noah Chinn
Cyborg Genesis
Across The Stars